Other Thrillers by Chuck Barrett

THE JAKE PENDLETON SERIES

The Savannah Project—Book One, An Overview

The truth can be a dangerous thing.
Terrorism, duty, and personal safety collide when Jake Pendleton, an investigator for the NTSB, is called to investigate an aircraft accident in Savannah, Georgia during the St. Patrick's Day celebration. The accident, which at first appears to be quite run-of-the-mill, turns out to be anything but. Since Jake is not willing to pretend there are no suspicious circumstances and more than the usual share of rather unlikely "coincidences," he sets off a veritable avalanche of secrets, violence and treachery. Aided by an unlikely partner, Gregg Kaplan, the air traffic controller who was the last person in contact with the airplane that crashed, Jake sets out to untangle the webs of deceit and to find a vicious killer.
Nothing is as it seems, nobody is who you thought them to be.
Nothing is sacred.
Nobody is safe.

The Toymaker—Book Two, An Overview

He's been in the business for 50 years—he makes 'toys' for spies.
Former NTSB Investigator Jake Pendleton faces a dilemma as the line blurs between right and wrong. After his judgment comes into question, Jake is entrusted to his new mentor, an eccentric old man who sees beyond Jake's flaws.
A man who makes 'toys for spies.'
A man known as The Toymaker.
Jake's first assignment reunites him with Gregg Kaplan in a daredevil mission to rescue a fellow agent held captive in Yemen. He risks his life to stop the first attack of an al Qaeda mastermind. But now, with no one to trust but himself, can Jake stop the terrorist from destroying what is most precious to the free world?
Unfortunately, more trouble comes his way as a killer from his past threatens something more important to Jake than his own life, leaving him to make the hardest decision any man ever has to make—
Who to sacrifice.

Breach of Power—Book Three, An Overview

Deep inside a glacier, a hiker finds a journal that was lost during World War II. On its frozen pages are etched the secret locations of treasures lost since the 1940s. But something more ominous is scribed in the journal, something that threatens the Presidency of the United States.

Jake Pendleton and his new partner, Francesca Catanzaro, work for an "off the books" intelligence firm and are summoned to the White House where they are instructed to locate and acquire the book. Jake soon realizes there are others on a quest to find it as well.

Others who will kill to get to it first.

THE GREGG KAPLAN SERIES

BLOWN—Book One, An Overview

Gregg Kaplan is not an ordinary man, but a man with special skills, courtesy of the United States Government.

His assignment is to stay off the grid when he innocently stumbles into a blown witness protection detail in Little Rock, Arkansas. He simply could not walk away from the impending mayhem.

After the dust settles, a mortally wounded Deputy U.S. Marshal makes him promise to personally deliver the witness to a U.S. Marshals Service safe site.

Not just a promise, an oath. A pledge between ex-Army Delta Force comrades. A trust that could not be broken—Once in, never out.

Kaplan soon suspects the witness he vowed to protect has secrets of his own; secrets that go beyond his testimony for the U.S. government. When he discovers the witness is being tracked, Kaplan teams with a WitSec Deputy U.S. Marshal assigned to recover the witness, but soon realizes some merciless people are dead set on preventing the witness from reaching the safe site.

But the witness has a hidden agenda of his own—One that could cost Kaplan his life.

DISRUPTION

Also by Chuck Barrett

The Savannah Project
The Toymaker
Breach of Power
BLOWN
Dead Ringer (eBook only)

Non-Fiction:

*Publishing Unchained: An Off-Beat Guide to
Independent Publishing*

DISRUPTION

Chuck Barrett

SWITCHBACK PRESS

DISRUPTION is a work of fiction. Names, characters, places, and incidents are products of the author's imagination or are used fictitiously. Any resemblance to actual events, locales, or persons, living or dead, is coincidental.

Edited by Debi Barrett

Cover by Mary Fisher Design, LLC. www.maryfisherdesign.com

FIRST EDITION
_____

ISBN: 978-0-9885061-8-3 (Print)
ISBN: 978-0-9885061-9-0 (Digital eBook)
Library of Congress Control Number: 2016908488
Barrett, Chuck.
        DISRUPTION / Chuck Barrett
        FICTION: Thriller/Suspense/Mystery

Published by Switchback Press

www.switchbackpress.com

For Debi

Because there are little to no consequences for conducting cyberattacks, criminals and nation-states are becoming bolder in their threats and behavior. Russia, China, North Korea and Iran are increasingly hacking into U.S. companies and government networks for espionage purposes or financial gain.

—Michael McCaul
—Chairman of the House Committee on Homeland Security

He who does not punish evil, commands it to be done.

—Leonardo DaVinci

PROLOGUE

With the cold barrel of a pistol firmly pressed against his temple, he did not dare tempt fate.

Hakeem Ahmad Khan froze at the command of the man holding the weapon, First Officer Faruq Abdul Nassir, a man he'd met for the first time a mere hour and a half ago in the ready room of the Malaysian-based Air Malacca Airlines in Kuala Lumpur.

This flight had started with the same routine as all his others. With one big exception. This was his first flight in the Captain's seat of the Boeing 777. After the pre-takeoff checklist was complete and the cabin crew had loaded the last passengers in their assigned seats, the cabin was readied for the flight to Japan.

After he coordinated the pushback from the terminal, Khan fired up the jet engines, one at a time, while Nassir requested clearance from air traffic control.

"Roger, tower," Nassir said into his headset. "Malaccan niner-one-zero cleared to taxi, runway two-one."

When Khan heard Nassir read back the clearance to Air Traffic Control, he advanced the power levers and set the jumbo jet in motion. His first flight had officially begun.

Khan had started his preparation for the flight early, perhaps earlier than he needed to; but, the excitement of his new promotion had given him renewed enthusiasm for the job.

Weather conditions were forecast to be favorable for this flight. What else really mattered? If truth were told, a smooth flight and a soft landing were how passengers judged a pilot's skill.

Khan was promoted to Captain on the B-777 only yesterday. Tonight's flight was his first flight in the coveted left seat, the culmination of his career's ultimate ambition.

After his first three years with the Malaysian-based Air Malacca Airlines, he was promoted to First Officer in the Boeing 777 jetliner where he spent six long months waiting for the left seat job to open up with the airline. His hard work and training had paid off. All the hours logged in the early years, flying anything he could get his hands on, all for the sake of building flight time, was the means to an end. This end. The endless hours spent on his desktop flight simulator, all for the sake of getting and staying proficient with B-777 procedures proved invaluable when he took his qualification check ride yesterday.

Tonight, that sacrifice felt worth it.

At almost exactly midnight, Air Malacca 910 broke ground on Khan's first flight as Captain of the Boeing 777.

After being cleared for a turn to a northeasterly heading, Khan and Nassir continued with the after-departure checklist items while the aircraft, already on autopilot, intercepted its course to Tokyo and climbed toward its cruising altitude.

So far, so good. Khan's first flight started off with an uneventful beginning. He pulled out his chart and scanned his route across the South China Sea and into the western Pacific.

Fifty minutes later, when the aircraft reached its last reporting point, Khan keyed his microphone and reported the aircraft's position to ATC. His voice calm and relaxed as he ended his transmission. "Malaccan niner-one-zero. Have a nice night."

No air traffic control facility would expect to hear from his flight until it reached the next reporting point. This far offshore, nothing worked. No cell phone coverage. Aircraft radios were marginal at best, even on the lower frequency ranges.

From the crew's standpoint, this was the boring part of any long flight. Nothing to do but sit back and monitor the aircraft's numerous systems.

By now, he knew, the cabin crew had dimmed the lights and raised the temperature slightly to help induce passengers into slumber. Sometime before daybreak, the cabin crew would lower the cabin temperature and turn the lights back on to wake everyone for a quick breakfast before they arrived in Tokyo.

A sharp rap on the cockpit door caused Khan's body to stiffen in his seat. The crew knew the protocol—communicate via the intercom prior to the door being unlocked and opened.

He cocked his head and peered over his reading glasses. Nassir shrugged his shoulders. "See what they want," Khan said to Nassir.

Khan raised his arm to flip a switch on the overhead panel. What he saw in his peripheral vision caused the blood to drain from his face.

"What the hell are you d—?" Everything around Khan faded into the recesses of his mind as he focused on the one thing he felt. The only thing he felt.

The gun barrel pressed against his head.

It was then Khan understood his fate.

CHAPTER 1

30 Months Later—October
Washington DC

Jake Pendleton heard the chimes signaling the Metro subway doors were closing. A few commuters dared leap through at the last second. High cost of parking and bad traffic in downtown Washington D.C. kept the Metro system crowded. He scanned the mass of commuters inside his car for potential threats, something that had now become second nature. The only threat in his car were frustrated commuters short on patience. His target was sitting near the middle of the subway car, two cars forward. A cyber-terrorist known only as Boris, although he doubted the man was Russian.

He had followed his target onto the Red Line at the Medical Center station headed toward Metro Center and the heart of Washington DC.

Boris' destination was unknown, yet with the Metro's closed-circuit cameras installed in every car and his handler's voice in his ear, Jake would know when Boris exited the Metro car.

Boris was suspected to be the lead hacker behind the recent cyber-attacks of thirty-five major European hospitals. In addition to the theft of the entire hospital digital databases, Boris left a Ransomware virus that corrupted and destroyed all connected networked information systems when hospital administrators refused to pay the ransom. Every doctor, clinic, and laboratory had their systems virtually wiped clean.

After exhaustive briefings with Homeland Security, the FBI, and the CIA, the President of the United States now believed that the expanding Islamic State was behind the cyber theft. The hackers had gained access to tens of thousands of patient names, Social Security numbers, physical addresses, and birth dates. The large breach could allow the criminals to create false identities, thus paving the way for terrorists to infiltrate the United States under assumed identities. Based on chatter and the increased exchanges on Twitter and other social media, the threat level had been raised and a probable 9-11 type event was believed to loom in the not so distant future. That was the reason the Metro Transit Police used K9 sweeps back and forth on the platforms.

Jake worked as an emissary for a Fairfax, Virginia intelligence company called Commonwealth Consultants. A company the President of the United States had used frequently over the past two years for her *off-the-books* assignments. And with each assignment, he and his partner answered the call. But this time his partner, Francesca Catanzaro, wasn't with him. He was operating solo for the first time in over a year while she was in Southern Italy attending her father's funeral.

Commuters elbowed in and out of the subway car at each Metro stop. Jake checked his watch, wondering how much longer he would be crammed into this tin can before he heard from his handler.

George Fontaine was a retired senior CIA analyst now working for Commonwealth Consultants. A double dipper some called him, collecting a good government pension while pulling down a lucrative salary from Commonwealth Consultants. Fontaine, a brainy analyst, had a talent for searching through an avalanche of data and pulling the pieces of the puzzle together. He was the one who had figured out Boris' involvement in the hospital data breach scheme and pinpointed the hacker's location in the United States.

As the train pulled away from the Farragut North stop, Jake tapped his com system with his finger, "George, you still there?"

"What? Not enjoying the noisy, crowded, body odor smell of the Metro?"

"Funny. The woman across from me is chewing on a burrito with her mouth open. The guy next to her is listening to rap. And some bastard two seats down from him is clipping his damn toe nails. I'm dying in here. Please, tell me you got something?"

"Nada," Fontaine replied. "Target is reading the *Post* and hasn't moved since he sat down. You know, Jake, you really should give patience a try. I hear it's a virtue."

"Not one of mine. I'm moving to the next car."

"No." Fontaine said emphatically. "Those doors are for emergency use only and an alarm will sound in the driver's booth when they are opened. Besides, I'll let you know when he gets up to exit."

"Listen George, if I stay in this car any longer, I'm going to shoot somebody. Besides, this way I'll be closer to Boris when he gets off the train. These commuters are like rats on the platform. I don't want to take a chance he could get away."

"You don't want to get made, either."

"You worry too much, George. I won't blow my cover. Can you disable the alarm so the driver won't know when I open the doors?"

"Of course I can, but that's not the point. You're taking an unwarranted risk."

"Just do it, George."

A few seconds passed and Fontaine said, "Done. I hope you know what the hell you're doing,"

"George, you're getting riled up for nothing. I know how to do surveillance."

The train slowed and braked for the Metro Center stop. Passengers began to shove toward the doors, while Jake edged into the next car using the emergency doors, conscious about not attracting attention. He peered through the glass door and spotted Boris sitting in a seat facing him, his head down still reading the *Post*.

"Dammit Jake, that's close enough," Fontaine said.

The train slowed to a stop. Passengers departed the train and even more got on. An elderly woman with a cane boarded last, but all the seats were taken. Boris folded his paper, stood, and offered his seat to the elderly woman. Jake smiled at the irony of the situation. *A gentleman terrorist.*

The hacker appeared younger than he did in the picture on Jake's cell phone. Jake didn't need the photo to remember what the man looked like, thick dark brown hair, olive skin and thick rim glasses. His angular jaw was outlined with a chin strap beard. What he didn't see in the picture were the distinctive dimples when Boris grinned. A detail Fontaine failed to mention or was unable to detect from the mug shot style photo. Boris was dressed business casual, very clean cut. A white cotton shirt neatly tucked into his slim dark navy pants. Not the image of a computer geek. The subway doors closed, the train surged ahead causing Boris to lose his balance. He grasped the metal pole, straightened, and glanced in Jake's direction.

Jake's stomach knotted, was he made? Probably not, but just in case, he bowed his head using his hands to cover his face, and faked a sneeze. Then he swiveled to face the opposite direction.

"Dumbass," Fontaine said breaking through Jake's introspection.

A little girl and her mother in a seat beside where Jake was standing leaned back to avoid any spray from his sneeze.

"God bless you," she said.

Jake thanked her while he listened to Fontaine in his ear piece. "Damn you, Jake, don't blow your cover."

"He doesn't know me from Adam. He stared right past me."

"Guess you're right," Fontaine conceded. "He's busy talking to the old woman and pointing toward the overhead map showing the stops along the different Metro lines. If I were a betting man, I'd say the old woman got on the wrong train. Her face is scrunched up, like she's about to burst into tears any second. Looks like Boris is trying to calm her down. I'm not good at reading lips but I think he's telling her he'll help her get on the right train. You'd think the guy has a heart."

"Oh, he has a heart. A black heart."

The Metro slowed. Jake peeked through the window at Boris. The guy was actually helping the elderly woman to her feet. When the automated audio announced the stop, Jake muscled his way to the side of the exit door. "Let me know if Boris does not get off."

"I think it's a safe bet they're getting off at the Chinatown transfer station," Fontaine said.

"Do you have eyes in the station?"

"You didn't seriously ask me that, did you?" Fontaine's

sarcasm bellowed through his earpiece. "Jake, I have eyes everywhere."

"Roger that," Jake said. "Keep those eyes open."

"No problem."

The Metro pulled into the station, came to a stop and the doors parted. The flow of commuters on the platform began shoving their way into the car before the passengers on the train could exit. Jake pushed through the oncoming passengers, exiting onto the platform. He stopped and stared at the overhead signs. Not reading, waiting.

"It appears my logic was right, Jake, they're heading for the Green Line southbound."

"Why the Green Line?"

"Probably because it arrives before the southbound Yellow Line," Fontaine said. "I'd bet he'll take her off the Green Line at the L'Enfant Plaza transfer station and put her on Silver, Orange, or Blue."

"Now you have eyes in Boris' head?"

"Not exactly. It's the only plausible scenario," Fontaine explained. "She got on the Red Line by mistake at Metro Center and the common denominator is the Silver, Orange, and Blue Lines. The question is eastbound or westbound."

Jake skulked on the edges of the crowd to the Green Line boarding platform and spotted Boris with the silvered haired woman about fifty feet down the platform. He waited.

When the doors to the Green Line opened, Jake climbed in. "Boris onboard?"

"Boris and grandma are onboard. You're good to go."

The Green Line pulled away from the Chinatown station making a brief stop at the Archives station before departing again. Boris was still standing next to the feeble woman. The next stop, L'Enfant Plaza was where, if Fontaine were correct, Boris would direct the elderly woman to her train and then he would proceed back on his original route, which he should be able to accomplish at the L'Enfant Plaza transfer station… unless he needed to be on the Red Line. Either way, he should be easy enough to follow.

"Jake?" Fontaine's voice interrupted his calculations.

"What you got?"

"Just got word from the boss, he wants you to go ahead and put the finger on Boris and bring him in."

"You made my day. I'm tired of this cat and mouse bullshit."

"And Jake?"

"Yeah?"

"He was adamant about this, there is to be no public spectacle. No witnesses. We don't want your pretty boy face plastered on the Washington Post."

"Not a problem."

"Just follow orders this time, Jake."

CHAPTER 2

The fog in Daniel Luzato's head lifted as he struggled to regain consciousness.

Drugged.

He could feel it. His head pounded like he had been hit with a sledge hammer.

No matter how hard he tried to open them, his eyelids were glued shut. The room was cold and damp. Stale air. He wrinkled his nose at the pungent smell of mildew.

No sound.

His labored breathing was all he heard in the silent room. He tried to move, but his arms and legs resisted, seemingly paralyzed. But he wasn't. He could feel the painful pins and needles in his nerve endings firing to his toes and fingertips. He opened his mouth to yell for help.

Nothing.

His throat was dry; like he had swallowed a bucket of sand.

Then he felt the sharp pressure on his neck. Piercing barbs against his skin, like a studded dog collar turned inside out.

The last thing he remembered was sitting at the dining table in his Trastevere flat. He was alone, eating the meal he had prepared, and feeling good. He remembered nothing after that. Now he was here, with no recollection of anything in between.

Left sprawled on what must be an earthen floor.

Naked.

Shivering from the cold air.

He managed to open his eyes and saw nothing but darkness. He detected a faint and distant sound of trickling water somewhere above him. It activated his senses and he shuddered with a dire need to urinate.

A peaceful man by nature, he was educated in the ways of the world, especially the underground world of evil. A sordid place of betrayal and murder. He'd seen the lust for power and violence and vowed never to return. Not willingly, anyhow. And now, he knew he had been dragged back down to the depths of hell.

As the effects of the drug began to taper off, mobility returned to his limbs. Although he still felt sluggish, he managed to bring his hands toward his face and feel the collar clamped snug around his neck. It was metal, the inside lined with sharp prongs that pressed against his flesh. His fingertips caressed the exterior of the collar, feeling for anything that might release its grip. But found nothing, except a single hole in the back. A keyhole he surmised, but he had no key.

He rolled to his hands and knees and crawled forward with an outstretched arm until he found a wall. It was stone. Actually, stones, and he could feel the curvature in the wall. With one hand, he found a tiny gap in the stones and used it to pull himself to his feet while he used the other hand to feel for anything above his head. He slowly stood with his back against the stone. With up-stretched arms, he felt for a ceiling, but found none.

One hand used the wall like a blind man's cane while he held his other hand outstretched for protection. He walked slow and cautious, desperate to find an exit of any kind. The floor, rough on his bare feet, felt like hard packed dirt filled with tiny pebbles. After a few seconds, he realized he was walking in circles.

The curvature of the wall.

Is this a pit or the bottom of a well?

He laid on his stomach, feet touching the wall, and moved himself forward using his hands and feet until he reached the other side of the pit. Three meters, maybe a little more.

He dug his fingertips into the creases between the stones and made a futile attempt to climb, but the stones were too flush and he slipped back to the dirt floor with each effort. Finally, when his arms ached and were too weak to try again, his body crumpled to the hard earth of the pit and he wept.

What was happening?

But, deep down he knew.

His fingertips once again explored the metal collar around his neck. The prongs kept digging into his tender flesh and he wanted if off...or at least loosened. He dug his fingers between his neck and the collar and gave a slight tug. Nothing.

Grabbing the collar from each side, he grunted and pulled harder. His pulse pounded against the sharp prongs with every beat. The metal prongs pressed against the bone of his spine causing a sharp, intense pain.

The collar had to come off.

He pulled harder. Red lights inside the collar flashed, a tone blared. The collar clamped tighter around his neck, pinching his fingers inside. His body twisted, wrenching in agony as the collar came alive delivering a wave of electrocution into his body.

His chest constricted, his bladder emptied, his body convulsed involuntarily until the pain overwhelmed him.

And then—nothing.

CHAPTER 3

Capture Boris.

That was the last order he received from Fontaine. And a welcome one at that. He didn't like tailing suspects, even with the high technology and expertise Fontaine brought to the table. Jake's partner, Francesca, was a different story. She always reminded him she loved the clandestine missions. Espionage was in her blood. And she was good at it. Damned good. He wished she were with him on this assignment. They were a good team. As a matter of fact, they had instinctively worked well together from the beginning. So much so, they seemed to be able to just know what the other was thinking without verbal cues. And in most cases, without body language cues either. She always had his back and he had hers. In a job without moral or legal constraints, a good partner could be the difference between life and death. Literally. Francesca had never blown her cover in all the time she'd been with Commonwealth. He, on the other hand, had. On more than one occasion. He didn't realize how much he depended on her until she wasn't with him.

The Green Line was only one of the five Metro lines that stopped at the L'Enfant Plaza transfer station making it the busiest station of the Washington D.C. Metro system. The Green Line and the Yellow Line crossed on north-south routes while the Silver, Blue, and Orange Lines crossed on east-west routes. Fives lines in one transfer station. According to Fontaine, Boris was three rail cars behind him. Three very crowded cars.

So crowded he might not be able to get any closer to his target than he was now. But, he tried anyway. Traversing one car at a time until he managed to reach the car next to where Boris and the old woman were sitting. This time, though, Boris was sitting and facing in the opposite direction. Eyes on the target was better, especially at this busy station.

He didn't know why his orders had changed, but Jake was glad they had. The hardest part would be fingering Boris without witnesses. Experience had taught him there was always a way. And he usually found it.

This wasn't the first time his boss had changed his orders at the eleventh hour. It seemed Elmore Wiley had an uncanny knack of throwing a wrench into an assignment in progress. The boss didn't share all the information about the missions with his emissaries. It was always need to know. So, there was never any point in asking. When the boss was ready to tell more, he would, and the old man's instincts were pretty damn accurate.

Elmore Wiley recruited Jake several years ago from his quite brief employment with the CIA, a job he only secured because of his long-term working relationship with the CIA director and his former boss in the Navy, Admiral Scott Bentley. It seemed, unbeknownst to Jake, Wiley had been watching him for quite a while, ever since the disastrous St. Patrick's Day festival in Savannah, Georgia. That day still remained the bloodiest day in Savannah's modern history.

The Green Line slowed as it approached L'Enfant Plaza. The platform was packed with commuters eager to board.

When the doors opened, a mass of people flooded into the Metro cars, creating a barrier for passengers trying to exit onto the platform.

"Hold up, Jake," Fontaine instructed. "Boris and grandma are having trouble getting to the exit door. They might not make it off in time."

Jake stepped back and waited inside the door. The hoard of people hustled in, refused to move to the center of the car, bumping and shoving him away from the door. He squeezed past commuters who gave him dirty stares. At the same time, he heard the chime signal the door was closing, he was knocked back again.

"Dammit, Jake, get off the train. Boris and the old woman are pushing through now."

"I'm trying, I'm trying."

"Move it, Jake. If you don't get off now, Boris gets away."

The doors started closing.

Jake manhandled two people out of the way, knocking one to the floor. As he reached the closing door, a large man snatched his arm. The doors were only three feet apart and closing. He spun, landed his elbow on the man's chin freeing himself from the grip. The doors were now only a foot apart as he sprinted to jam through. Rubber linings on the doors smashed against his chest and back. He pushed the door as hard as he could to widen the gap and squeezed through.

He heard Fontaine shouting in his ear when his unsteady foot tripped on the edge of the platform causing him to fall face down. But, he made it out of the car. The doors to the Metro closed behind him. He pushed himself to his feet and rubbernecked down the platform. Throngs of commuters scurried for the exits leaving only Boris and the old woman staring at him from twenty feet away.

The recognition in Boris' eyes was clear—an epiphany that he was being followed.

Jake had been made. His cover blown.

The Green Line pulled away from the platform leaving the tracks empty.

Their eyes bored into each other as Jake advanced toward them. Boris moved behind the old woman.

"Step away," Jake called out. "It's over."

Boris suddenly shoved the old woman off the platform and onto the tracks below.

Jake drew his gun. "Stop, Boris."

The few remaining commuters ran for the exits. Some were screaming. Some, already on their phones trying to call 9-1-1.

"Or what? You'll shoot?" Boris taunted.

"Help," the old woman cried out from below. "Help me." She was straddled across the tracks.

Jake raised his gun and took aim. "I will shoot."

Boris raised his hand to his ear. "Hear that?" He pointed at the old woman on the tracks. "In thirty seconds. Maybe less, she's dead." He turned and walked toward the exit.

Jake ran to the edge of the platform where the woman was thrown to the tracks. He yelled at Boris, "Stop."

Boris threw up his hands. "Go ahead and shoot."

Jake heard the distant whine of the oncoming train barreling down the tunnel. His eyes darted at the woman and Boris. He aimed at Boris and fired. The cyber-terrorist fell to the platform.

Jake looked up the track and saw a light growing brighter. He bounded down onto the tracks, scooped up the frail woman, and rushed her to the edge of the platform. He heard the blast from the approaching train but, was afraid to look. The sound of the Metro was deafening at track level and growing louder with each passing second. Several bystanders reached down and lifted the woman from his arms.

Another blast from the approaching train.

A man's hand reached down, clasped his arm and helped pull him onto the platform. The lead car whizzed past, horn blaring in the tunnel. Jake sagged against a pole, while the man praised him for risking his own life to save the elderly woman. The train slowed to a stop in front of him.

"Son of a bitch," Fontaine sounded like he was out of breath. "I thought you were a goner."

"So did I."

Jake, shaky on his feet, stared down the platform. A few people stood back with horrified looks on their faces. He ran to where the cyber-terrorist had fallen. A small puddle of blood marked the spot. He searched the crowd. Several people pointed to the stairs leading to the street.

Boris was gone.

CHAPTER 4

The collar, now silent, had loosened its stranglehold around his neck. The electrifying pain from the sharp prongs was gone. Luzato's head was awkwardly pressed against the rocky wall of the pit and it hurt like hell. He felt a lump on his head and figured he must have hit it when he fell. The taste of blood filled his mouth where he bit his tongue during the convulsions.

He rolled onto his back, completely disoriented in the darkness of the pit, and wondered how long he'd been unconscious.

Above him, he heard the sound of footsteps. Each one growing louder than the one before. He stared into the void of darkness above him. "Hello?"

No reply.

The footsteps stopped. A blinding light hurt his eyes. He rolled to his stomach, shielded his face with his hands, and shouted, "What do you want from me?"

Another course of electricity jolted into his neck—not nearly as strong as the first, but still painful.

"It is sensitive to sound." The calm voice above him said in his native Italian tongue. "Speak softly and it will not bring you pain."

"Dove Sono?" Luzato asked. *Where am I?*

"Do as you're told," the voice said, "and it will not hurt you. Disobey and you will be punished."

Luzato spread his fingers to let his eyes adapt to the light. The walls of the pit gradually came into focus. He removed his hands from his face, and squinted toward the light using one hand to shade his eyes. As his eyes adjusted, he saw the light was a single bare bulb hanging from a metal grate about five meters above him.

A hatch in the middle of the grate opened and a bucket lowered into the pit, a u-shaped hook under the handle. When the bucket landed on the dirt floor, the shadow above dipped the line, freeing the hook from the handle, and withdrew the line.

Luzato peeked in the bucket—it was empty except for a roll of toilet tissue.

When he looked up, he saw a tray being lowered. It stopped half way down.

"Step away or the collar will force you."

Luzato stepped back, not wanting another shock from the metal ring secured around his neck.

The tray lowered to the floor. Again, the line dipped and the hook swung free from the handle on the tray and was hoisted above him and out of sight.

An arm appeared through the hatch. Inside the gloved hand was a rolled up cloth with a matching belt lashed around it. The hand tossed the cloth toward Luzato.

He caught it. It was a long cotton robe.

"Do your business. Cover yourself. Eat," the voice said. "He will come to talk to you later."

Who *he* was, Luzato wondered, although he already had a good idea. Not the individual so much as what he represented. Or *whom* he represented.

And that was what frightened him the most.

CHAPTER 5

Chiesa di San Pietro
Squillace, Italy

Dressed in black, Francesca held her mother's hand while the widow leaned over and kissed her husband on his forehead as he lay in a casket.

It had been three years since Francesca Catanzaro had seen her father and when they last spoke, it had been one of those awkward, unpleasant conversations. He demanded she give up her job with Commonwealth Consultants in the United States and return to Italy where she belonged. With her family. Her roots were in Italy, not America, working for a man with a sordid past in the intelligence industry.

The conversation was heated and they both said hurtful things. Things that, according to her mother, brought much despair to her aging father.

Now he was gone. She would never be able to mend those fences.

Her father, born and raised in Squillace, moved north to Cosenza at age twenty where he met her mother. There, they courted, married, and eventually had one child—a daughter. Her parents later moved to Naples for the sole purpose of providing Francesca with the finest education. As soon as she graduated from the University, her parents returned to

Cosenza.

Francesca clutched her weeping mother's hand while the widow said her final goodbyes. Her mother buried her head into her father's chest and muttered words Francesca couldn't hear. When her mother withdrew, she wiped her eyes with the crumpled tissue still in her hand.

The two women turned and walked to the front pew where they sat alone until the casket closed for the final time.

Her mother sobbed as the lid was sealed shut. Francesca, who hadn't shed a tear, wrapped her arm around her mother in an attempt to comfort her. The priest stepped forward and knelt in front of her mother and offered a final prayer. He stood, and signaled for the casket to be removed from the church. The casket was to be placed inside a chamber in the mausoleum beside the Church of St. Peter. As her mother calmed, Francesca stood and turned toward the sound of voices behind her. In the doorway of the church stood two shadowy silhouettes, both unmistakably men. The bright sun behind the open church doors made it nearly impossible to recognize them until one of them spoke.

"Francesca, I am sorry for your loss," a voice said in Italian.

The voice belonged to Marco Serreti. It was a voice she could never forget. He was her former partner while she was employed with the *Agenzia Informazioni e Sicurezza Esterna*, Italy's External Intelligence and Security Agency. He had been more than just her partner; he was also her ex-lover. Her mind flashed with memories. Many were good. The most vivid ones, painful. His voice rekindled the scar in her heart, which was more prominent than the one on her cheek.

"Marco?" She left her mother's side and edged closer until she recognized the man standing next to Serreti. It was the

Director of AISE, Lorenzo Barzetti, the man who had hired her many years ago. She stared at Marco and then focused her eyes on Barzetti. "Director, thank you for coming." He leaned over and kissed Francesca on each cheek. "I, too, mourn the loss of your father. If it were not for him, I never would have had the honor of your employ." Barzetti said in English.

She lowered her head. It was a fluke her father had even met Barzetti. To think her short-lived career with AISE was a result of a bar brawl where her father stepped in to help out a stranger who was attacked by two young tourists in Naples. That stranger turned out to be Lorenzo Barzetti, who showed up at their home the next day bearing gifts of gratitude. That was when she first met him. Years later, after he was appointed Director of AISE, he recruited her.

She returned the customary affection and turned to Marco. "What are you doing here?"

Barzetti interrupted, "Deputy Director Serreti—"

"Deputy Director? My, you have moved up the food chain."

"As I was saying," the director continued. "Marco informed me of your father's passing. It was his idea to come here."

"I'll bet it was," she replied. Her eyes narrowed to crinkled slits at Marco. "What do you want?"

"To merely comfort you in your time of grief," Marco replied.

She feigned a laugh. "Yeah…I doubt that." She flashed a look at Marco and then the director. "What is this really about, Director? Neither of you would have traveled here merely to pay your respects. If I know Marco, he's up to something. He always has a hidden agenda."

Barzetti laughed. "That is what I like about you, Francesca.

No one can get anything past you and you are always the first to cut to the chase." He paused and took a long breath. "Let's take a walk up to Castello di Squillace, where we might have some privacy."

"Just the two of us." More a statement than a question.

"I'm afraid you will have to indulge me as Deputy Director Serreti must accompany us," the director stated emphatically. "This, I'm afraid, is not open for negotiation."

A few minutes later, the three of them entered the gates of Castello di Squillace. There were a dozen upset travelers who had been denied entrance to the castle by Barzetti's men who had cleared out and sealed off the castle.

"This must be important," she said. "You have gone to a lot of trouble simply to talk to me."

Barzetti lit a cigarette, took a long draw, tilted his head, and blew a pillar of smoke into the air above his head. "That is because what I have to say is of grave importance. Not only to Italy, but also to most of the world. It is a matter of life and death...on a global scale."

CHAPTER 6

**Commonwealth Consultants
Fairfax, Virginia**

Jake closed the door to the taxi, tipped the driver in cash through the window, and watched him maneuver into traffic. He glanced up at the building's facade, still amazed at how deceptive the exterior truly was. The seven-story glass building with the words *Commonwealth Consultants* discreetly stenciled on the entrance door was, in reality, a high-security technological fortress. Behind the exterior glass veneer were two steel-reinforced solid concrete walls. Between each wall a two-inch lead and copper lining, all of which was grounded deep beneath the building. No signals got in. No signals got out. Even Elmore Wiley's penthouse had lead and copper-lined walls as well as copper-infused windows.

He entered his 24-character password into the keypad followed by a thumbprint scan. When the door clicked, he entered the lobby through an enhanced body-scanning unit. The unit didn't screen for weapons, since weapons weren't unusual at Commonwealth. The unit sniffed for explosives, and most importantly, it scanned for electronic eavesdropping devices.

The security checkpoint lobby was a small fifteen-foot square room with three linebacker-sized armed guards, none of whom smiled or greeted him as he walked through the door. Their demeanor was dictated by Wiley—strictly business. He walked to a steel door where, next to it, a retina scanner was mounted on the wall. After passing the retina scan, Wiley's uniquely designed facial recognition software confirmed his identity and allowed him passage through the steel door and into the building. He couldn't help but wonder if all Wiley's security precautions were overkill; then again, in Wiley's line of business there was no such thing as being too careful.

He took the elevator to the fourth floor where many of the same security measures were also in place. Prior to entering the operations center, the same 24-digit password and thumbprint recognition was required, except with one minor difference. Instead of the right thumbprint scan used at every other security checkpoint, this one required the left thumbprint. Another precaution Wiley put in place prior to anyone entering the heartbeat of his off-the-books operations center—an added layer of security for this most sensitive area of Wiley's business. Only Wiley and his elite cadre of emissaries were allowed inside. For now, Jake, Francesca, and Fontaine were the extent of that elite team.

Jake walked in and found Fontaine where he always seemed to be, monitoring live video feeds from assorted trouble spots around the globe. Today, the feeds came from Iran, Russia, Israel, and an unlikely country—Italy. That was where Francesca had been for the past several days and Fontaine's apparent interest in Italy troubled Jake. *Was Francesca in some sort of danger?*

As usual, Fontaine seemed to be in his happy place. Never a grumpy moment, even when an operation turned dicey or went awry, Fontaine seemed upbeat, always a can-do attitude.

He was overweight, probably from sitting day in and day out in front of computer screens eating pizza, and he had a full head of silver hair. His nose shifted slightly to one side and he had a prominent jaw. Jake called it a Jay Leno chin. Fontaine despised the reference.

"Rough day at the office?" Fontaine quipped making light of Jake's failed attempt to capture Boris.

"Not one of my better days, that's for certain." Jake pointed at one of Fontaine's monitors. "Francesca?"

"No. Europol has issued a cyber alert in Italy based on some intercepted chatter by Homeland. They think it's aimed at the banking system, but I can't find anything to support their theory."

"I might have some more information on that soon," the voice came from behind Jake.

Elmore Wiley. Boss Man.

Jake and Fontaine turned to face the man. He hobbled toward them with a cane in his hand; still limping from the car wreck last year near his home in El Paso. He was driving his Mercedes when he was t-boned by a young woman who ran a red light in a hurry to pick up her child from school.

He had thinning gray hair and wire rim glasses, both of which he adjusted every few minutes. Wiley had recently turned seventy-three and Jake was impressed at how well the man could move. Like a man in his late forties or early fifties—up until the traffic accident. Now he moved a little slower, more cautious with each step and without the same pep as when they first met.

"How much longer before Francesca comes online?" Wiley tapped his cane on the floor.

Fontaine faced his monitor. "Five or six minutes. 8:00 p.m.

Italy time."

"George, you and Jake go upstairs to the penthouse conference room and setup for her call. I'll be right up."

"Yes sir," Fontaine replied.

Jake nodded. He and George took the stairs, since Wiley went down in the elevator. "What information do you think the old man has?" Jake asked.

"No clue. But, you can bet it will be classified."

Five minutes later, Fontaine brought Francesca's secure video feed online and her face appeared on one of the many giant monitors hanging from the conference room wall.

She looked tired. More than tired—exhausted. And tense.

"Hello Francesca," Fontaine said.

"Hi George." A wary smile surfaced on her lips. "Jake."

"Hey partner," Jake said. "Sorry to hear about your father. Wish I could've been there for you."

"You were on assignment, Jake, what could you do?"

"Everything okay?" Jake assumed she had a wearisome few days dealing with her father's funeral, but he'd never seen her look quite like this—almost haggard. He was concerned she might be taking her father's death too hard since they hadn't been on good terms when he died. Or maybe her mother was causing her elevated anxiety level. He knew firsthand how that could be when his own father died two years ago. His mother was a wreck and acted out in ways he'd never seen her behave before. To say she was difficult to deal with was an understatement. It was six months before she finally started accepting and dealing with his death. Even Jake did not have time to truly mourn the loss of his father, because he'd been so busy with his mother. In retrospect, dealing with his mother kept his mind off the loss, something he wasn't consciously aware of until she passed the following year. He attributed her death to a broken heart.

"Everything is fine," she said. "Why do ask?"

"You look tired is all."

"It's been a hectic few days. Where's Wiley?"

"He'll be up in a minute or so," Fontaine answered.

"Jake," she said. "Heard you let Boris slip through your fingers."

"Bad news travels fast. It was either go after Boris or let an old woman get run over by the Metro."

"I would have shot him."

"I did shoot him, Francesca, in the leg. But he got away while I was saving grandma."

"I meant, I would have killed him."

"That would have been my first choice," Jake answered. "But, my orders were alive…not dead."

"That is correct," Wiley's voice bellowed from the back of the room. "We want him alive. We will have another opportunity to capture Boris. Jake did the right thing."

"We?" Jake saw Francesca's expression change as she straightened in her seat. Then he heard the familiar voice behind him.

"Mr. Wiley was speaking for me. We need Boris alive," the voice said. "But I have a more pressing matter that needs attention first."

Jake craned his neck in the direction of the voice.

It was Rebecca K Rudd, President of the United States.

CHAPTER 7

Alex, Alexei as his parents called him, was late for his first class of the new semester.

His final semester of classes.

It had been a long road to his PhD, and now it was so close he could taste it. The incident on the Metro earlier in the day left him stranded inside the Beltway while the entire Metro system was temporarily shut down by Homeland Security in search of a man who threw a woman onto the tracks. She survived due to the heroic efforts of an armed man who allowed the assailant to get away in order to save the woman from an approaching train. Alex had seen the man pull the woman from the tracks. In reality, he didn't pull her off the tracks, instead, he jumped onto the tracks, picked her up, and boosted her onto the platform with the help of bystanders. The man had barely made it onto the platform himself before the fast-moving train reached the spot where he rescued the old woman. Alex was sure the man was a goner, but the man somehow managed to get clear with only a few feet to spare.

The assailant was injured, shot in the leg, but fled the scene before authorities could arrive. Alex saw the small puddle of blood left by the gunshot wound. The manhunt spread fast as Homeland Security locked down several blocks surrounding the Metro stop. But to no avail, the man still escaped the dragnet.

Alex was forced to find alternative transportation from downtown to the George Washington University campus where his class met.

At this level of education, it was never a good idea to be late for a class, much less on the first day. And he wasn't just a little late, like five minutes or so, something that might be forgiven and forgotten by the instructor. No, he was forty minutes late.

Hesitantly, he pulled the door open and slid into the closest seat he could find at the back of the room, which still wasn't far from the front. Actually, as small as the classroom was, even the back row of seats was only seven rows from the podium.

The instructor stopped speaking when he came in, and Alex could feel his eyes following him to the seat.

"Mr. Nikahd, nice of you to join us," the instructor's voice full of sarcasm.

"I'm sorry," Alex said. "I got caught in the Metro shutdown."

The instructor put his hands on his hips. "That was three hours ago. You're not the only one who was delayed by the shutdown. And yet, everyone else made it to this class on time." The instructor turned around and walked back behind the podium. "Perhaps from now on you can see fit to be more punctual."

Alex nodded.

It was best not to draw any more attention to himself than he already had. Over the past few years, he had had numerous classes with this instructor, and had done well in all of them. He hoped the instructor would overlook this, his only transgression.

Class lasted a mere fifteen minutes more and was then dismissed. He gathered his belongings and stuffed them into his backpack.

One of his friends approached. "What the hell, man? Never be late to old man Sizemore's class. Ever."

"I know, I know," Alex responded. "I couldn't help it. I got here as fast as I could. You think I should go talk to him?"

"Hell, no. He'll eat you alive. Of all the instructors to bang in late on, Sizemore. Geez, are you out of your freaking mind? Shit, man, I wouldn't have come in at all and said I was sick or something. What were you thinking?"

Alex pushed himself out of his chair and stood. A twinge of pain rushed through his body, but he shook it off. He grabbed his backpack and slung it over his shoulder. When he looked up, his friend had a spooked look on his face.

The young man pointed to the floor next to Alex's right shoe. "Dude," he exclaimed. "Are you bleeding?"

CHAPTER 8

Jake was caught off guard by her unannounced presence, although he shouldn't have been. It had become quite routine for the President to visit Commonwealth Consultants. According to President Rudd, it was better for her to come to Fairfax than have Jake and Francesca continually showing up at the White House where the multitude of media hounds might become suspicious.

"I'll get right to the point," Rudd moved to the front of the conference table. Her Secret Service body guards stood by the door with their hands down and crossed in front of them. "We have been following an escalating threat to national security in the cyber warfare arena. To the point where, if you'll pardon the expression," she paused, "all hell is about to break loose."

Jake had seen this president at her best and at her worst. On those rare occasions when the worst reared its ugly head, Elmore Wiley was always there to make her problems disappear. And that's where Jake and Francesca came in; they basically took their orders from the president. Always with Wiley's approval, of course, but nonetheless when President Rudd called, the two emissaries leapt into action. Most of the times the missions were preemptory in nature. Fix a problem before it became a problem.

Rudd was dressed in her standard public eye attire. The public expected a certain dress code from their Commander in Chief, especially a female. Pants were acceptable if worn with a blazer. Collars buttoned up tight around her neck. The clothes made her appear older and concealed her trim figure by the attire's loose fit. Occasionally, she would step out in front of the cameras in a slim figure flattering dress, but the public, and certainly the press, didn't seem ready for a president with too much sex appeal. Therefore, she kept her attire *Presidential* most days.

"The Department of Defense has only two IT monitoring companies on the Unified Capability Approved Products List," Rudd explained. "Yesterday, the Chief Operating Officer of one of those firms had his Annapolis mansion burned to the ground, killing everyone inside including the COO, his wife, and their three children."

"I saw that on the news," Jake said.

"So did I," Fontaine added.

Rudd motioned with her arms. "Please, gentlemen, sit down." She turned toward the monitor. "Francesca, I'll keep this as brief as possible so you may return to your mother's side.

"Thank you, Madam President." Francesca nodded.

Jake sat down between Fontaine and Wiley.

Rudd continued, "This morning a suspicious suitcase was found outside the main entrance of the second company. Inside were remains so mutilated the authorities had to call in the medical examiner to determine if they were animal or human. They were human. Although recognition is impossible at this point, DNA samples were taken. All attempts to locate the Chief Executive Officer of the company have turned up empty, so we strongly believe the remains might be hers."

"Sounds like someone is sending a message," Francesca

weighed in.

"It does," Jake agreed. "But to whom?"

"Do you think Boris is involved?" Fontaine asked.

"Boris might have some knowledge that this happened," Rudd continued. "But we don't think he's directly involved, no. We're reasonably sure he didn't kill these two company executives."

"How can you be certain?" Francesca asked.

"According to the Cyber Threat Intelligence Integration Center and the FBI's National Cyber Investigative Joint Task Force, Boris is only a cyber-threat and not a physical threat. He hires out his services for money. Period. So, they think it's a good bet he's working for someone. We just don't know exactly who yet."

"Any ideas who did kill them, then?" Jake asked.

"We have a lead," Wiley broke his silence as he pushed his glasses up with his finger, "but at this moment, it is more a hunch than a solid lead."

Rudd delivered the answer. "Ever heard of Tarh Andishan?"

"Iranian hacking team," Fontaine stated. "Tarh Andishan is a Farsi term meaning thinkers or innovators. They've wreaked all kinds of hacking havoc around the globe lately. But, violence isn't their M-O…at least not in the past."

"Maybe they hired someone to do their dirty work for them," Francesca said.

"That's one possibility we're exploring," Rudd said.

Jake tapped his fingers on the table and added, "The news claimed the fire in Annapolis was a tragic accident."

"Tragic no doubt, Jake," injected Rudd. "But, hardly an accident. We know in both instances these executives had intimate knowledge of the functional and operational specifics of their clients, in particular the Department of Defense, their major client. The products and services of these two companies are contractually bound to stay domestic. Our enemies would kill to gain access to both companies' technologies."

"Literally, it seems." Jake's forehead creased and his brow furrowed.

"We know for a fact the mutilated body was not a random act of violence," Wiley sounded emphatic. "The positioning of the suitcase at the main entrance was intended to look suspicious and get the authorities involved. When that happens, it becomes public knowledge. All over the news media outlets nationwide…worldwide, for that matter."

"Granted, the suitcase is pretty much in your face, but what about the fire?" Jake questioned.

"Here's what we know about the fire," Rudd explained. "Accelerants were used. Very volatile accelerants and a lot of them. The fire burned fast and it burned hot. The entire structure collapsed into the basement. And there has been a larger than normal Alcohol, Tobacco, and Firearms presence at the mansion since the fire…fifteen, perhaps as many as twenty agents."

"And we know," Jake inserted, "the CIA, NSA, and DIA have been known to embed agents inside ATF."

"That's right," Rudd agreed. "And I'll concede a couple of the ATF agents at the mansion right now are embedded by one or more of those agencies you just mentioned. It is this administration's belief these company executives likely discovered something they shouldn't have and were silenced before they could report what they knew to anyone at the Department of Defense."

Rudd leaned over, picked up a bottle of water, and took a

sip.

Wiley pushed his chair back, leaned on his cane and grunted as he pushed himself to his feet. "We believe these two murdered executives located the exact source of signals from Tarh Andishan cyber-attacks against the United States and were eliminated," he said. "Tarh Andishan carries out its attacks through a sophisticated infrastructure and target systems, control networks, and espionage, among other things. We know these attacks originated from Tehran, the Netherlands, UK, and Canada. Most targets thus far have been concentrated in the U.S. with some attacks against targets in Israel and Pakistan. There have been some strategic attacks in South Korea which might indicate—"

"North Korea has allied with Iran," Fontaine interrupted.

CHAPTER 9

Luzato had eaten, taken care of his physiological needs, and clothed himself with the robe provided. The chill in his body had dissipated. He studied his new environment and ruled out the possibility he was in a dried up well. There were hundreds, no, thousands of places like this in Italy. Underground pits were used for grain storage in ancient times. Not decades ago or even centuries ago, no, this pit was much older, perhaps one or two thousand years old.

That knowledge did nothing, though, to help him determine his location. Not in Italy. Nearly everything was ancient here. Even before the Roman Republic in the 4th century BCE, there was the Etruscan civilization as early as 700 BCE. Earthen floors were predominant in most houses until the mid-14th century in Europe.

Through the metal grate, he could barely make out the expanse above him. Another room, subterranean, like a basement, or perhaps a sub-basement. What he could see was a slightly arched ceiling made of a combination of stone and brick, indicating vastly different time periods of construction. No walls were visible, only the glow of lights reflecting on the ceiling.

A door in the room above him opened and two sets of footsteps entered. He closed his eyes and traced the steps in his mind until they stopped. Above him, he saw the shadowy figure from earlier raise the hatch on the metal grate and flip it over. A long wooden ladder lowered down into the pit, its legs pushed against the pit wall for stability. One shadow retreated and the footsteps grew faint and disappeared. The other remained, hovering over the opening to the pit.

"You are allowed to climb out," the soft spoken voice said. It was the same voice from earlier, still with an unthreatening tone. "You may rest here. There are water and a bathing bucket. Please leave your waste bucket in the pit and do your business down there as well. Forget not what I have instructed you about the collar. The jolt is more painful at this level. Obey the rules and you will not suffer."

The shadowy figure disappeared.

Luzato stepped to the ladder, placed his hands on the rails, and shook it checking for sturdiness. It was an older ladder and crudely made, but it seemed sturdy and heavy, which explained why it took two people to lower it into the pit.

He placed his feet gingerly on the first rung and gave a slight bounce. Convinced the ladder wouldn't collapse under his weight, he began to climb. Half way up he froze, his hands began to shake and his body trembled. He examined the ground below and then above, praying his capturers would not kill him, or worse, torture him. After a few seconds, he continued to climb, being careful not to make a sound that would unleash a jolt from the collar.

It didn't.

The room above the pit was large and sectioned off into smaller rooms. The first thing he noticed in the room above the pit was an old olive press mounted inside a stone arch. The ancient relic was at least a thousand years old.

A room in the back, more like a long corridor which dead-ended in both directions, had two wooden olive oil barrels and several empty olive oil bottles lying on the floor. One green bottle was resting inside a wooden bucket similar to the one the stranger lowered into the pit, except this bucket had two smaller rope handles on each side instead of the one longer rope attached to both sides. Stacked against a wall at one end of the narrow corridor were several ancient pottery olive oil containers, some of them broken, and he guessed they also dated back over a thousand years.

Many of the ancient buildings in Italy, had new buildings and even roads built on top of the old structures. It was a European phenomenon to build on sites where someone had been living before. Sometimes it was a deliberate attempt to erase the physical reminders of what came before, sometimes it was simply easier. When you descended below street level, you stepped back in time, hundreds of years in many places and thousands in other, older areas. This clearly was one of the older structures, which could put him near his home in the Trastevere section of Rome near Ponte Garibaldi. The problem with the ancient areas surrounding Rome were that most dated back anywhere from the first century BC to the sixth or seventh century BC. And those areas stretched long distances from Rome. From the ancient Etruscans in the north to the Umbrians, Sabines, Aequians, Marsians, Hernicans, and Volscians in the east and south of Rome. In retrospect, he could be anywhere. And he had no idea where.

The main room was crude with walls of stone and brick arched ceiling. At one end of the room, a ventilation shaft had been chipped out of the stone wall and a metal air duct installed. Three bare light bulbs were strung across the room and hung a foot below the brick ceiling. At the opposite end of the cavernous room was a large wooden door. Solid. And undoubtedly locked.

In the middle of the room was a rough-cut wooden table with two heavy chairs at each end. In the corner, a cot. As promised, on a table near the pit was a tin pale filled with water and a wash bucket along with two towels and a wash rag.

As old as the building was though, it was not without signs of modern technology. Closed circuit video cameras were strategically mounted to eliminate all blind spots. There would never be any privacy in this dungeon. No way to escape. Someone would always be watching. And no doubt someone controlled the device fastened around his neck.

He scanned every inch of the chamber, searching for anything that could help him escape, when the sound of a thud drew his attention toward the thick wooden door. A man walked in carrying another tray of food and drink in his gloved hands.

A man wearing a mask.

He walked into the room and placed the tray on the table. The tall, lanky man wore a robe similar to the one provided Luzato, except this man's robe was black.

"I see you are a man of wisdom," the masked man said as he pointed toward a camera, "so you must have realized by now that we are in control. Please, do not make a futile attempt to escape, as the consequences will be swift and severe. Your only chance to stay alive is to cooperate fully. Do so and you will be treated well."

The man held up one finger.

Luzato felt a slight trickle of electricity vibrate into his neck, not painful, but enough to let him know the collar still controlled him. The man closed his fist and the trickle charge stopped.

"As I said," the man reiterated. "Resistance is futile."

CHAPTER 10

Fontaine's revelation caught Jake off guard.

If he were correct, a cyber warfare alliance between North Korea and Iran would not only be a threat to the national security of the United States, but to the rest of the West as well.

"Why the sudden move of aggression by Tarh Andishan?" Jake asked. "Until tonight, I'd never even heard of them."

"In 2009," Rudd began, "we—and by we, I mean the United States with the aid of Israel—inserted the Stuxnet worm and Botnet malware into nuclear installations in Iran. It affected, or perhaps I should say *infected*, a thousand of the five thousand centrifuges. In part it was an attempt to curb Iran's advances toward building nuclear weapons. If we could disrupt their centrifuges, then they couldn't reach weapons grade material. In response, Tarh Andishan has sworn revenge against Israel and the United States."

"That's been quite a few years," Francesca said from the overhead monitor. "Are they only now seeking revenge?"

"Not at all, Francesca," Rudd answered. "T-A has been involved or believed to have been involved in numerous cyber events over the past few years. In several instances, other hacking groups have taken responsibility, but the signature and signal indicate T-A. Numerous incidents of phishing, SQL injection, web attacks, other worm-type viruses, and keystroke logging have been documented and attributed to T-A. Also, credit card theft attacks on major corporations like Ebay, Home Depot, Target, several banks, airlines, and court systems. And now with T-A's suspected involvement with North Korea, we strongly suspect this group of hackers is responsible, or at least partly responsible, for the recent cyber-attack on Sony Pictures that forced the company to postpone the release of *The Interview* over the holidays because of an explicit terror threat against movie-goers."

Francesca gave a sharp nod.

Jake noticed Francesca's face was rigid with tension. Totally uncharacteristic for her personality. Perhaps Rudd was right; maybe the death of her father and the stress of her mother were taking its toll.

"I don't know much about hacking," Jake injected into the conversation. "But it seems to me these are more like cyber-crimes than all out cyber warfare."

Rudd had a sly grin and looked at Fontaine. "George, you want to field Jake's observation?"

"Certainly, Madam President," Fontaine said. He inhaled sharply and slowly let his breath escape. Jake could tell he was nervous. Fontaine clasped and unclasped his fingers as his legs bounced up and down. "We live in a world where we can't trust the technology we depend on. There are two types of people, those who have been hacked and know it, and those who have been hacked and don't. Hacking a phone, for instance, is pretty trivial. The greatest weakness in mobile security is human nature. That being said, cyber-crimes range from nothing more than nuisances to major destructive attacks on IT systems. Simple things like telemarketing and internet fraud, identity theft, credit card account theft, hate crimes, stalking, social media fraud, and phishing. Your major cyber-crimes range from corporate data breaches, to bank fraud and cyber intrusions where mass volumes of data are corrupted, lost, or destroyed."

Fontaine, took a few gulps of water and then continued, "Cyber warfare, on the other hand, is two-fold—strategic and tactical. Tactical, meaning the methods used directly in combat, much like on the battlefield. Strategic is what it takes to win the war, not single engagements. As in all warfare, tactics are part of the overall strategic plan. The tactics used in strategic cyber warfare are espionage, sabotage, hacking, and attacking. Espionage is how we obtain information to gain the advantage. Sabotage is the use of inserted source codes to thwart or stall the enemy. Hacking is where we take a look inside our enemies' systems and find flaws we can use to our advantage or to acquire information from their servers. Attacking is simply exploiting those flaws and bringing our enemies to a halt. The biggest problem with strategic cyber warfare is, much like nuclear warfare, it does not distinguish between military and civilian targets. There are many flaws in the system. In many cases, deliberate flaws. Flaws our intelligence agencies don't want fixed. It's in their best interest to exploit those flaws in the name of national security. It's how they catch bad guys... it's how we catch bad guys."

"Before Boris went off the grid, we discovered he had hacked both of our dead IT executives private email accounts," Rudd's voice was tense. "This might be the reason they both ended up dead. As it turns out, both executives had been communicating with the same source overseas. A source who had warned them repeatedly about how their own corporate cyber security networks had been breached and sensitive information stolen. The two companies were the gatekeepers of some very sensitive information. Mr. Fontaine hacked into their accounts, and determined the source only identified himself...or herself, as *The Jew*. After an exhaustive search through thousands of protocols, George back-traced the IP address to a flat in the Trastevere section of Rome, Italy. The flat is registered under a false identity and has been dark for the past few days. Jake, I need you and Francesca to find and secure this person who goes by the hacker code name *The Jew*."

Wiley said, "Jake, the Citation is fueled and ready to go. You'll be stopping in Belgium first to drop off Kyli, then you can fly to Rome and meet Francesca." He turned toward the monitor. "Francesca, I need you to wrap things up and meet Jake in Rome tomorrow. Is that possible?"

"Yes," she replied. "Tell me when and where and I'll be there."

Francesca was more than ready to get away from Squillace and Southern Italy. And her mother. As much as she loved the woman, the past couple of days had been unbearable.

The conference call with Commonwealth Consultants and POTUS concluded. She signed out of the secure video conferencing app that Elmore Wiley had created specifically for meetings like this with encryption algorithms well beyond her knowledge base. With her right hand she closed the cover to her laptop computer.

"You see, Francesca," AISE Deputy Director Marco Serreti quipped from the other side of the room. "That wasn't so hard after all, was it?"

She had a problem, a really big problem, and one she didn't quite know how to handle.

Yet.

CHAPTER 11

Somewhere over the Atlantic Ocean

Jake closed his briefing packet and slipped it into his backpack. The sick feeling in his stomach had tightened its grip and made concentration almost impossible. He knew that feeling all too well. The gut-wrenching emotional stress that manifested itself in the stomach when he knew things weren't right. And this time, as most times, it had to do with a woman.

Jake had not seen Kyli since he boarded Wiley's Citation 750.

He stared at the door to the bedroom located in the aft of the aircraft. Kyli Wullenweber had been in there with the door closed ever since he boarded at the Washington D.C. airport. They were already four hours into the flight and she still hadn't come out.

Jake first met Kyli several years ago when Elmore Wiley recruited him from his short-lived employment with the CIA. Jake liked his new boss's granddaughter right away. It wasn't long before their friendship evolved into a whole lot more. Jake experienced a passion with her he had never felt with anyone before. In his mind, Kyli was *the one*.

Then again, his past was filled with women he thought were *the ones* as well. Jake always fell hard and fast in love. This time, though, it was different. Kyli was different. Although a scientist with impeccable credentials, she was a free spirit with an inviting smile and intoxicating eyes. Amber eyes he found himself lost in time after time.

The past few months had been tough on their relationship and he understood her trepidation. He was gone on one mission after another, chasing bad guys for Wiley. When Kyli and Jake managed to have some time together, it never lasted long. His phone would ring at the wrong time with orders from her grandfather for another mission. Kyli made it clear she didn't like *flying solo* as she called it, and she especially didn't like worrying about getting that dreaded phone call.

He knew it was driving a wedge between Kyli and her grandfather, but worse, it had already driven a wedge between Kyli and him. She didn't want to hear another promise that he would not accept an assignment when they had plans. And now, he was about to do it again. Drive that wedge a little deeper between them. This time, though, at the direction of the President of the United States.

According to the briefing packet Fontaine handed him prior to leaving for the airport, the intercepted intelligence pointed toward an imminent cyber-attack on a major target or targets in the West or with Western allied countries. As vague as it seemed, Fontaine's hint of an Iran/North Korea alliance was extremely unsettling.

If it were true.

A physical attack couldn't be ruled out either. Not with the loose-cannon ruler in North Korea involved in any way. He was unpredictable in every sense of the word.

Jake gazed out the window. Below him, some 37,000 feet, was the North Atlantic Ocean. Night had fallen fast after he left D.C. and by the time he reached Brussels, it would be morning.

Convinced Kyli wasn't coming out, he reclined the plush

leather seat, turned down the cabin lights, and closed his eyes.

†††

He awoke to the gentle shaking of a hand on his shoulder. "Jake, you need to wake up now."

He opened his eyes. The cabin lights were on and his groggy mind could only make out a blur. A woman with shoulder length hair. "Kyli?"

"No. Kyli is still in the back. She left strict instructions not to be disturbed until we arrived in Brussels."

Jake's eyes adjusted to the light and he focused on the woman, her hand still on his shoulder. "Thank you, Jimi." He patted her hand with his. "Any chance for some coffee?"

"Better than that," she replied. "I've got a hot breakfast all ready for you. Your favorite, French toast with lots of cinnamon and molasses."

"That sounds perfect. Jimi, you're awesome."

"I have to take a tray back to Kyli first, then I'll bring yours right out."

"That'll be fine."

Moments later, she walked by with a silver tray and carafe and stopped at the bedroom door. She lightly rapped three times. The door opened. Jake strained his neck, but still couldn't catch a glimpse of Kyli. Jimi carried the tray in and he heard voices, clearly recognizing Kyli's. Then Jimi returned and walked back toward the galley.

As she walked by, she poked him on the shoulder, "Yours is coming right up."

He barely got his table secured in front of him when she put a breakfast tray on it. She placed a coffee carafe in front of him and removed the lid from the tray. "As advertised," he said, rubbing his hands together. "Looks great."

"If you need anything else, give me a shout."

"I think I'm all set. Thanks."

He scarfed down the last piece of French toast and took a long pull from his coffee cup to wash it down. The moving map on the screen mounted in front of him indicated forty-five minutes to Brussels. He checked his phone for messages. Nothing of interest except one message from Fontaine. It was marked URGENT in the subject line. He opened the message and read it.

Shocked, he read it again to make sure he did not miss anything. Fontaine indicated Wiley's El Paso factory had been broken into and trashed by someone who was obviously looking for something. However, on first inspection, nothing seemed to be missing. This caused his usually calm boss to raise the caution level for Commonwealth Consultants as well as all his holdings. Jake's new instructions were to personally escort Kyli to her new flat in Leuven and ensure it was all clear, prior to flying on to Rome. He was also instructed to make a security sweep at Wiley's complex outside of Leuven as a precaution, and report back when he completed the inspection. His last instruction was to keep Kyli out of the loop. *Out of the loop* was bolded and underlined. He did not like holding back this information. He was already having relationship issues with Kyli and leaving her out of the loop could only make it worse in the long run. Once again, he was faced with a personal dilemma when it came to his relationship with Kyli or his allegiance to Elmore Wiley.

CHAPTER 12

"I don't understand why you have to escort me to my flat," Kyli complained as they both climbed into the back seat of the limo.

"Your grandfather asked me too," he said. "In reality, he ordered me to. You know how he gets sometimes. You're all he has left. He's an overprotective grandfather who loves his only granddaughter very much." *So far, so good. No lies, yet.*

"Why can't Max do it?" She pointed to the limo driver. "Wiley has had him do it before...more than once."

"You'll have to ask Wiley," Jake said. He saw Kyli roll her eyes skyward. She clearly didn't want Jake involved, but why? "What's going on with you, Kyli? This is the most you've spoken to me in five days. You haven't returned my calls. You didn't come out of the bedroom the entire flight. Not to say hello, or kiss my ass, or anything."

Kyli's eyes raked him with freezing contempt.

"Have I done something to piss you off? Whatever it is, I'm sorry."

"Jake," she hesitated. "You're just doing your job, I get that. I know it can't be easy trying to juggle your job and duty to Wiley and our relationship. I don't think I signed up for this. You know how I feel...and yet, I don't think you get it."

"Kyli, believe me, after this mission, you and I will go somewhere, the two of us, and work this out."

She patted his hand with hers. "Another promise. You forgot to say promise, Jake."

The eleven miles from the airport to her flat passed in edgy silence. Jake knew anything he said at this point would only make matters worse. The limo pulled to the curb in front of her flat. He escorted her up two flights of stairs, while the limo driver retrieved the luggage. One medium sized bag was all she ever used when she traveled, regardless of the length of the trip.

While she waited outside, Jake inspected every room, every closet, inside and out. Everything seemed normal. Or as normal as he could expect with Kyli's eclectic design tastes.

"I should only be gone a couple of days." He wanted to kiss her, but he was sure now was not the right time. "And then we can talk, okay?"

"Sure, Jake." She gave him a quick kiss on the cheek and patted him on the chest with her hand. "You need to get moving. MEtech Labs is waiting for you…as is Rome and Francesca."

The barbs in her words stung like a mad hornet. He was in a time crunch so he let it go.

MEtech Labs was a few miles north of downtown Leuven. He usually took the train, but today he had the limo, which shortened his travel time considerably. No train schedules, less headaches. The drive took less than ten minutes. From flat to factory. Door to door.

Inside the secure facility, they were expecting Jake's arrival. He went through all the usual security procedures to gain access. First, the key card and next, the thumbprint. Lastly, the newly installed 24-digit access code.

This was the place where he first met Kyli. Elmore Wiley

brought him here several years ago and Kyli gave him the orientation while the old man sped off in his Mercedes on some unknown afternoon adventure. She was flirtatious on the very first day and he was uncomfortable with the attention, especially when he found out she was Wiley's granddaughter. He remembered blushing several times at her brashness. It wasn't long before she made her wants and desires known. By that time, he had already fallen for her.

It took a year and half to get a key card that granted him access to the entire facility, especially Wiley's living quarters on the top floor, which was where he started his security sweep. It took a hurried hour to run through the entire complex. His last stop was the security office where he found all the monitors in good working order and all security personnel mindfully doing their duty.

Satisfied everything was as it should be at MEtech, Jake got back in the limo and instructed the driver to take him to the airport where Wiley's Citation was waiting to take him to Rome.

†††

Germano Caminiti stared at the monitor and felt sympathy for his captive.

The man had been drugged, abducted from his apartment in Rome, then placed in a grain cellar deep underground beneath the ancient building in this small Tuscan village. He was stripped of all his clothes and *the collar* was locked around his neck.

The Collar, a devious invention of the man Germano answered to and the man he feared most. It was an electronic marvel with sinister capabilities and a unique way of controlling its host. Once the collar was locked, it was active, meaning it was completely tamper-proof. It had a ring of prongs capable of delivering an electric shock to the host. The shock could range from a painless trickle to a paralyzing electrocution, much like being debilitated by a Taser gun. It also had a failsafe mechanism. Inside the metal collar was an explosive compound, similar to C-4, with enough power to decapitate the host if the collar was removed without the key or if it was transported beyond a certain distance from the cellar. Only the key could disable the collar.

The man was an easy capture. Germano broke in while he wasn't home and put a heavy tranquilizer in his food. Strong enough to knock him out for many hours, yet mild enough not to kill him. A delicate balance of chemicals that took several attempts to perfect. Now it was a concoction he'd used many times without failure. The prisoner was moved to the larger room above the grain cellar and given everything he needed—food, water, and clothing. A bucket with toilet paper was left in the grain cellar where he was to take care of his business. The bucket was removed daily and replaced by a clean bucket.

The captive would be treated well provided he followed instructions. If he didn't, then Germano Caminiti's boss would make the prisoner's life a living hell.

Until he broke.

And they all broke sooner or later.

Or died.

CHAPTER 13

Eastern Colorado

Watching the sunrise from atop the tower was his favorite way to spend each morning. Until the weather turned cold, which had already happened a couple of times. Out here on the plains this late in October, cold snaps could happen with little warning. When the strong cold wind blew, there was no way in hell he would make the long climb to the top of the abandoned transmission tower.

As soon as the sun broke the horizon to his east, he only had a few moments to look west before the bright sunlight splashed across the eastern face of the Rocky Mountains.

Although slightly over 120 miles to the west-northwest of the tower, on this clear morning he could see the fading lights of Colorado Springs through his high-powered binoculars. From his perch, he watched dawn slowly sweep across the plains on its never-ending journey.

Most mornings since he started the assigned project, he counted the seconds from when the sun hit the tower until it lit up the mountains in the distance. It was never the same. As a matter of fact, it was never even close to the same.

He studied the barren rolling landscape until a gust of wind washed across his face. The air was cool and dry and the wind stung his skin. He grew up in a dry climate and thought he would be used to it, or as a minimum, would have acclimated to it quickly. But, after spending the past three years on the humid Southeast Coast, being relocated to this dry climate had wreaked havoc on his nasal cavities.

Ethan Wogahn had been working long hours on the tower project for the past four months, many days with his small cadre of handpicked workers from the nearest town, Lamar, Colorado—population less than 8,000. The tower project demanded utmost secrecy and he paid his workers well for their silence. All were of Mexican descent. And all were illegal aliens. Another way to ensure their silence.

Most days, however, he worked alone. It was safer that way. Today, he would continue with the tedious and most critical aspect of his project, aligning the arrays. There was no margin for error. He had already put in a lot of man hours on the arrays and would put in many more before this, the fourth tower was activated. When that blessed day came, mankind would see things in a different light. A new power would rise from obscurity and the world would be incapable of stopping it. It would occur without warning.

Not some damn bloody war.

Put simply, it was a takeover.

A hostile, yet non-violent, transfer of power.

Domination.

As quoted from religion, *Blessed are the meek, for they shall inherit the earth.* Now, was that time. And the meek would rise to power.

It had taken the better part of two years to put all the pieces together, to get the right people in strategic locations, and to obtain the required information to make the project a success. That had all been done.

There were nine other locations like his, all strategically

located around the globe, and all getting ready to be activated in a synchronous manner. The Colorado tower renovation was ahead of schedule and under budget, something that had already earned Wogahn plenty of accolades from his superior. Especially the ahead of schedule part.

Tomorrow, Wogahn would start running diagnostics on the equipment to make sure every component was operational and met the high quality standards to make this takeover possible. If any of the variances were off by the tiniest of margins, his tower would fail. This tower was one of four local sites designed around his entire project. This tower would be the arrow that pierced the heart of the infidel. The death knell that would make the transfer of power possible worldwide. From this most critical array atop the tower, he had line of sight to Cheyenne Mountain. And deep inside Cheyenne Mountain, in his opinion, was the greatest of all targets. A military facility with the utmost capability of detecting and thwarting his leader's plans. A facility that, for years, had remained a secret to the masses. Now, its location was known worldwide. It was easy to find with a simple search on Google Earth. Simple to study from the outside with just the use of a computer. Knowledge he'd gained from an insider, though, revealed a chink in its armor. A chink Wogahn had already exploited and stood ready and waiting to render this great facility defenseless. The Cheyenne Mountain facility was one of the most revered and one of the most feared. Soon, North American Aerospace Defense Command—NORAD— would be rendered inert.

A failure, however, of any one of his four local sites meant failure of his project.

And failure of his project meant only one thing for Wogahn. Death.

CHAPTER 14

Rome Fiumicino Airport
Rome, Italy

A fire in one of the terminal buildings delayed Jake's arrival by nearly two hours. After landing, the Citation taxied to a general aviation designated terminal where Jake would be escorted to Customs. He slung his backpack over one shoulder and snatched his overnight bag from the bin next to the air stair door.

This was his first time in Italy, except for a brief fuel stop at Naval Air Station Sigonella a few years ago on his way from Yemen to France in pursuit of a terrorist. NAS Sigonella was actually located in Sicily, technically not Italy, although many people considered Sicily to be part of Italy.

At the bottom of the air stair door was a younger man in uniform with a sidearm mounted on his hip. His hat was white with a shiny black brim and his uniform obviously pressed with heavy starch. Hard creases in his pant legs and sleeves coupled with his rigid posture made him look uncomfortable on the hot tarmac. Jake noticed a bead of sweat trickle down the man's cheek.

When Jake reached the bottom of the air stair the man said, "Follow me, per favore." The uniformed officer escorted him through the terminal without speaking. He stopped at a door with a large *Customs* sign above it, opened it, waved Jake through, and closed the door behind him.

Customs was packed with travelers. People of all nationalities shuffled from line to line toward the two entry checkpoints that were staffed. Or, at least what should have been lines but seemed to have morphed into some sort of free-for-all. There were couples and families and tour groups, all pressed tightly together like ants swarming to a bread crumb.

Jake let loose a sigh and joined the crowd. There was no need to hurry since nothing seemed so important to Italians that they felt a need to hurry.

It took thirty minutes to get clear of Customs. When he passed through the final door that opened into a lobby, lined up in front of him was a column of Italian men dressed in suits and ties holding signs for arriving passengers. The air inside the terminal was warm and had the smell of stale cigarettes. Italians were yelling and pointing and motioning with their hands. At times, it caused the noise level to become a deafening roar. Behind the row of men holding signs was a long bank of windows and doors. Beyond that, a street where a procession of cars and vans were parked, waiting for their next fare.

Jake shoved his way through the masses toward the exit sign when he heard her familiar voice.

"Welcome to the chaos that is Italy."

He swung around and saw Francesca.

She looked much better now than she had on the video conference yesterday, but still weary. Now, her creased forehead made her look troubled. She had removed all of the red from her hair and dyed it closer to what he suspected was its natural dark brown color. Her already dark eyes were darker, the circles underneath even more pronounced. He attributed it to the stress of her father's funeral and dealing with her distraught mother.

The bags under her eyes were gone or covered up with make-up. He could rarely tell if a woman wore make-up, unless it was overdone. She was wearing black leggings, a gray tunic top, a rich brown cropped leather jacket and gray ankle boots. She looked European to him.

"Chaos is an understatement." He hugged and kissed her on the cheek just above her three-inch scar. He motioned at her with his hand. "Is this how all the Italian women look? Because if it is, I'm in big trouble."

She smiled weakly and said, "The women, not so much. It is the men here who are vain. I've never met an Italian man who could pass by a shoe store and not stop to admire the merchandise."

Jake glanced at his clothes. "I might not fit in here. Maybe you can take me shopping."

Francesca laughed and her face brightened. He liked hearing her laugh. The other day he was upset to see his partner look so unhappy.

She pointed toward the window. "Come on, I have a car waiting. It's a long drive into town, thirty-one kilometers, but it will still take the better part of an hour to reach Trastevere."

The car Francesca had waiting was actually a small van and the driver, a man named Mario, must have thought because of his name he had to drive like the famous Italian race car driver, Mario Andretti. The only vehicles on the road faster than their van, were the preponderance of scooters zipping from lane to lane, between cars, down the medians, and around the sides. Sometimes the scooters used the curbs and sidewalks to maneuver their way through traffic. Based on what he was witnessing, he figured there were no traffic laws in Italy. At least none he could detect.

Tailgating was common on the streets of Rome and Mario would get too close to other vehicles…even at highway speeds. He observed Francesca's face and was surprised she appeared unfazed by the traffic. "This doesn't bother you?"

"Does what bother me?"

Jake pointed with his finger toward the cars. "I don't know. Maybe the fact that people are driving like they want to kill somebody." He swallowed hard and gestured at Mario. "His driving."

"He's a good driver. This is normal for Rome." She chuckled. "I guess I should have warned you. It might seem like mayhem to you, but this is normal for Italians."

"Accidents? Pedestrians being run down?"

"Not many big ones. Lots of dings and scratches, but typically nothing more than that. Fender benders are part of life here. That's why you don't see many new cars on the road. At least not during the day. Nighttime in Italy is quite different, especially in Rome. Not only is it the difference in night and day by clock time, but culturally as well. Rome at night transforms into a magical city, full of romance and charm."

"I find that hard to believe."

"You'll see." He noticed a gleam of devilry in her eyes.

As they neared the city, traffic slowed. At least to a speed that didn't seem quite as perilous, although still more than his comfort level wanted to tolerate.

"Are we getting close?"

Mario spoke in Italian and pointed out the left side of the van. Francesca replied in Italian. "Look this way, Jake," her voice excited. "There's Vatican City. During the medieval decline and after many barbarian invasions, Pope Leo IV began building these walls. They date back to the mid 800s."

"*This* is the Vatican? I expected a little more pomp."

"These are the exterior walls. Technically, on the other side of the walls is another country," she explained.

"I do remember that from history."

"The *pomp*, as you put it, is inside. I'll take you to St. Peter's Square and you'll understand. But first, we have to check out this apartment." She reached inside a duffle bag and handed Jake several items. The first was a burn phone, which Jake tucked away in his backpack. Second, a pocket knife similar to the one he carried while in the States. Third, were three boxes of ammunition and a handgun.

"Holy crap, what the hell is this? A freaking cannon?"

"It's a .45 cal. I know how partial you are to Glocks and it's the only one I could acquire on such short order. Don't get caught with it in Italy or we'll both be up the proverbial creek."

He took the weapon and checked the magazine. Fully loaded. He ensured there was a round in the chamber and tucked the Glock inside his belt in the small of his back, letting his sports jacket conceal it. He tossed the remaining ammo inside his backpack.

Less than three minutes later, the van pulled to a stop in front of an old building. Then again, all the buildings in this part of Rome were old. It was simply a matter of which century.

Jake and Francesca got out of the van from opposite sides. Francesca walked to the driver's window and handed something to Mario. Without another word, Mario drove off leaving Francesca standing in the middle of the street.

She walked up to Jake while securing her cross-body bag. "Trastevere is the thirteenth rione of Rome. It dates back as far as 750 BC." She directed his attention to a bridge. "Tiber

River." Then she pointed to the ground. "West bank. In ancient times, the hostile Etruscans were across the river."

"I'll bite. What's a *rione?*"

"It's an administrative division or district of the city. Or regions…which is where the word actually originates."

"And this is relevant, how?"

"You did poorly in history class, I'll bet."

"I did okay, but it wasn't my favorite subject. Too many dates to memorize."

"History is important," Francesca said. "And before we leave here, I going to make it my purpose to give you a new appreciation for history. Especially Italian history."

"Well, I'm not opposed to learning more about the romance and charm of night time in Rome."

"You are hopeless. Right now, we need to get to work."

She retrieved a slip of paper from her bag.

She pointed to the building in front of them. "According to Fontaine, this is where *The Jew* lives."

"What are we waiting for? Let's check it out."

The street level door was open. Technically, it was locked but the lock had been busted and rendered inoperable. No telling how long it had been that way, either. Perhaps years or months. Or even four days. Which was how long *The Jew* had been dark.

Francesca followed Jake up the stairs to the third floor, where he located the apartment door. He pounded with his fist several times without getting a response. Then he remembered, Francesca was a whiz at picking locks, a trait she learned from her now deceased father, a locksmith by trade. He said, "Can you do your thing—"

She was standing there with her lock pick in her hand.

"Out of my way, Jake. I'll take it from here."

In a few short seconds the door was unlocked. Holding the knob, she pushed it open and that's when the smell hit them. Decay. Rotten flesh. He recognized the smell. Unfortunately, from more than one assignment.

It could only mean one thing.

They were too late.

The Jew was already dead.

CHAPTER 15

Jake was wrong about the origin of the smell. It came from the dead mouse in the kitchen that had been eating food left on the table, not from the dead man lying on the floor with the bullet hole in his forehead. That had just occurred. Within minutes, in fact, as the blood pooled around the man's head had not had a chance to congeal.

The flat was not much more than one large room and a bathroom. No separate bedroom. An efficiency apartment that reminded him of his old college dorm room. At least size-wise, anyway. A long desk was shoved against one wall and was lined with several computers, all wired into the same internet portal. Everything had been shut down. No blinking lights. No cooling fans humming. Only dark monitor screens and silence.

To the left was a bed where the man slept. A Murphy-style bed was bolted to the wall and extended. Linens stripped from the mattress and piled on the floor.

To the right, a small kitchen area. Refrigerator, stove, sink, and a two chair dining table. Nothing fancy. Very basic. And cheap. On the table, the dead mouse lay next to an unfinished meal. Flies buzzed around both the food and the smelly dead creature.

Disturbing as that was, the dead man on the floor was even more so. He was not Italian, but Middle Eastern in appearance. He wore black pants, a black shirt, and boots. On his head, a black *kufi*. How it stayed on after the man took a bullet to the forehead was strange. Blood ran from underneath and onto the floor forming a red halo around the dead man's head.

"You think this is *The Jew?*" Jake asked.

"Don't be absurd. This man is Muslim, not Jewish. No Muslim would ever refer to himself as a Jew in any fashion... and the other way around as well. They're sworn enemies."

"Then what the hell is he doing here? You think *The Jew* killed him?"

"I don't know, but—"

At the sound of the door opening behind them, Jake and Francesca spun with their guns drawn only to be staring at the rifle barrels of three officers of the Italian Carabinieri.

Jake could hear his pulse pounding in his ears as the three officers aimed their rifles at them, center chest. Two red laser dots pointed at his chest, one on Francesca's.

One man shouted something in Italian.

Jake raised his hands before Francesca could translate.

She said in an excited tone, "Jake, don't move. These guys are Carabinieri. Italian paramilitary police. They will shoot us, so let them take our weapons."

His eyes scrutinized the floating laser beams on his chest. "Not a problem."

While two men kept the rifles trained on Jake and Francesca, the other removed the guns from their hands. First Francesca, then Jake. He felt the gun leave his grip and immediately the officer knocked him to his knees and pushed him face-down on the floor. The officer's bony knee jammed into Jake's spine. The officer grabbed one arm and yanked it behind Jake's back, then the other, and secured both hands with flex cuffs. He watched the same officer repeat the maneuver on Francesca.

He remembered what she had said to him ten minutes ago when she handed him the Glock. *Don't get caught with it in Italy or we'll both be up the proverbial creek.* Well, what now? He figured he'd find out soon enough.

†††

They were thrown in the back of a van, blindfolded, and driven to a location that was about ten minutes from *The Jew's* apartment. Or at least, they were in the back of the van about ten minutes. Since he knew nothing about Rome, they could be anywhere. Blindfolded, they were led inside a building and separated. His blindfold was removed and he was left alone in an obvious interrogation room. A large mirror covered one wall. In opposing corners were video cameras, both with glowing red lights. It could have been any room from a hundred different TV cop shows where suspects were taken for interrogation. It so happened this one was in Rome and struck him as being the same as those in the United States, and smelled just as bad.

He had visions of some badass Italian Carabinieri coming in and giving him the roughed up treatment, but that never happened. As a matter of fact, he never saw another Carabinieri. After at least an hour alone in the room, the door finally opened and a man dressed in a suit and tie walked in and sat down across from him at the table.

"My name is Marco Serreti," the man said. His Italian accent somewhat pronounced. "I am the deputy director of the Agenzia Informazioni e Sicurezza Esterna, Italy's External Intelligence and Security Agency. Like your CIA in many ways." The man reached into his coat pocket and pulled out

Jake's Glock and pocketknife and placed them on the table. He patted his hand on the Glock. "Mr. Pendleton, you have broken many Italian laws having this in your possession. Most carry stiff prison sentences, especially for non-Italians."

"So I've been told."

A smile crept across Serreti's face. "Yes, of course. Francesca Catanzaro, your partner."

"Francesca told me she used to work for Italy's External Intelligence and Security Agency," Jake said. "If you are deputy director, then you must know her."

Serreti had a deadpan expression. "I know everything there is to know about Francesca, Mr. Pendleton. She was my partner long before she was yours. We have shared…many secrets together."

It was the expression on Serreti's face that spoke more than his words. Jake knew the implied meaning. And it pissed him off. Not that Serreti could have had sex with his partner, after all, Francesca was a beautiful and desirable woman, but that he would try to use it as leverage.

Jake leaned forward in his chair. "What is it you want from me, Deputy Director?" This time he hoped Serreti would understand his implied meaning.

Serreti folded his arms across his chest and looked hard at him for several seconds without speaking. Suddenly, he unfolded his arms letting them rest on the table and said, "I like you, Mr. Pendleton, you are much like me. Direct and to the point. Determination with a touch of crass, the director calls it." Serreti pushed the Glock and pocketknife across the table. "My apologies, Mr. Pendleton, I was having fun at your expense. I have come to rescue both of you from the Carabinieri."

"Where is Francesca?" Jake narrowed his eyes, he did not like this asshole and was ready to wipe that smug look off his Italian face.

Serreti motioned with his head. "On the other side of the glass, watching."

Jake glowered at the two-way mirror. He couldn't believe Francesca would have allowed Serreti to use his former relationship with her in any attempt to leverage him. Then again, who said she had a choice?

He could understand why Francesca might have found Serreti attractive. He could see it. Serreti had the look. Tall for an Italian man, maybe six feet, bronzed skin, perfectly coifed dark hair and a three-day-old stubble beard. He wore a slim custom-tailored suit. Jake couldn't see his feet, but imagined he was wearing some expensive fancy-assed shoes since, Francesca told him Italian men liked shoes. A handsome man by anyone's standards.

Serreti continued, "My agency and yours have agreed to collaborate in locating the whereabouts of this man you call *The Jew*. Francesca has your backpack. All the contents have been returned." He placed a hand over his chest. "You have my guarantee nothing will be missing and nothing has been tampered with. You and Francesca are to escort me to our secure Rome office." Serreti eyed his phone. "Where we are due to be on a video conference call with your Commonwealth Consultants in less than an hour."

Jake pushed up his sleeve and looked at his watch. "How long will it take to get there?"

"If we walk?" Serreti said. "About four minutes."

CHAPTER 16

**External Intelligence and Security Agency
Secret Location
Rome, Italy**

The AISE's *secure Rome office,* as Serreti called it was nothing more than an old warehouse two blocks from where he had been detained by the Carabinieri. And it certainly didn't look secure, not from the outside anyway. Jake knew outside appearances had nothing to do with interior security. Commonwealth Consultants was the perfect example. What appeared like a simple glass facade office building, was truly an impenetrable fortress with lead and copper-lined concrete walls, copper-infused penthouse windows, and a dozen former Special Forces soldiers guarding every point of entry.

The inside of this AISE warehouse compound was relatively secure, perhaps by Italian standards of security, but certainly not by Elmore Wiley's. The one thing they did have, which was likely their biggest defense, was fifty armed military soldiers standing guard. A tremendous deterrent in and of itself.

Jake and Francesca were escorted by Marco Serreti to a conference room on the second floor where the AISE Director, Lorenzo Barzetti, was sitting behind a desk, an unlit cigarette hung immobile from his mouth. An older and distinguished man. He dressed the part of a director. Conservative, off the rack suit, gray hair with a matching gray mustache. He stood when he saw Francesca.

"Francesca, how nice to see you again, my dear," the director said. It was easy to tell he genuinely liked Francesca and he let the cigarette fall from his lips. He caught it in his open palm without looking down, something he'd apparently practiced many times.

She made a slight bow of the head. "And you as well, director."

"Mr. Pendleton, I presume? I am sorry about your run in earlier with the Carabinieri, I hope Marco rescued you in time." He motioned to a chair. "Please have a seat."

"Thank you, sir."

"Please don't let this incident taint your view of Rome. I think you'll find the remainder of your time in Italy a little more enjoyable. As a courtesy to Mr. Wiley, I have taken the liberty of authorizing you and Francesca to carry your weapons. The credentials will be ready before this meeting is over."

"Thank you, director," Francesca interrupted. "But that wasn't necessary. Jake and I can take care of ourselves."

"Like you did earlier today?" Serreti laughed.

"Marco is right, Francesca. There is no need to chance another incident like today. Please carry the credentials. As you know, they will open doors that otherwise would remained closed."

"On behalf of both of us," Jake glanced at Francesca, "I thank you for your thoughtfulness. We gladly accept your offer."

"At least one of you has a level head," Serreti said. "Right, Francesca?"

Jake listened to Francesca, Barzetti, and Serreti reminisce for the next few minutes. He kept quiet, absorbing every detail.

It seemed Barzetti, who answered directly to the President of Council of Ministers, was in his last year of a four-year appointment as director. Serreti was the favored next in line. If he received the appointment, Serreti would become the youngest ever appointed to the coveted position.

Jake prided himself on being a good judge of character, which rarely failed him. Something between these three seemed off, but he couldn't quite pinpoint exactly where. They were hiding something, his partner Francesca included. And that troubled him. The missions often required placing their lives in their partner's hands. Could he still trust Francesca? Serreti, he didn't trust. The young heir-apparent to the job of AISE director had secrets. And it wasn't just because he had insinuated an intimate affair with Francesca, which Jake resented; no, it was much more than that. Barzetti, on the other hand, knew something but still came across as a straight shooter. It was like he was covering for a friend. Perhaps he was. Or perhaps he knew Serreti was involved in something, but didn't want to expose him. Not what Jake would have expected from a man in such a position of power.

Jake wondered what the odds were he was right about the unsettled feeling in his gut. If he was 99% wrong that something sinister was going on, then it was the 1% he was right about that would keep him alive. Perhaps sinister was too harsh a word, certainly not above-board. Neither of the men worried Jake. He could handle them. What concerned him the most was Francesca.

A familiar voice came through the speaker. "Italy, is everyone present?" George Fontaine.

Serreti responded, "All here as requested. Let me turn on the video feed."

The large monitor on the wall blinked once then the image on the screen became clear. It was the conference room at Commonwealth Consultants. At the large table were Elmore Wiley and George Fontaine.

"Gentlemen, if you please, we are ready to proceed," said Barzetti.

"Good," Wiley said. "Let's get crackin'. George, tell them what we know about the body they found in the flat."

"The dead man in the flat is obviously not *The Jew.* We traced his identity to this man." A photo popped up on the screen. "He is not Iranian, but he has suspected ties to Tarh Andishan. He was educated in the United States with a doctorate in computer science. He was arrested on charges of suspicion of hacking three of New York's hospitals admission and birth records. Nothing was proven and the charges were dropped, but he was deported back to his home country."

"Which is where, George?" Francesca asked.

"Actually, he was a citizen of Austria. He has a Vienna address. Travel records indicate he flew from Vienna to Venice two weeks ago. Day before yesterday, he traveled by train to Rome."

"And now he is dead," Serreti said.

"That is correct." Fontaine adjusted his stack of papers.

"How can we be of assistance?" Barzetti asked.

Elmore Wiley stood, holding his cane for support, and faced the camera. "Jake, I want you and Francesca to go to Vienna and check out this man's home. Then go to Venice and see if you can find out what he was doing there. George will text you a couple of locations to check out. Director Barzetti, George will send you the files of two men, we would appreciate any assistance you could provide on obtaining their identities."

"We will be more than happy to assist any way we can," Serreti interjected. "But don't you think I should accompany Mr. Pendleton and Francesca?"

"That is Director Barzetti's call to make, not mine," replied Wiley. "But, I certainly have no objection."

Jake already didn't like the idea of Marco Serreti accompanying Francesca and him. It would be too dangerous. Serreti would be a distraction and could very well make their objective even more dangerous than it already was. Jake saw Francesca's face didn't look surprised. She did a one shoulder shrug.

Marco Serreti was watching him.

A smirk on his face.

Jake needed Francesca to speak up and protest that it would be unwise for Marco Serreti to accompany them. She put up a fuss when the Director offered the concealed weapon documentation, yet now she remained silent. She didn't appear to care. That 1% he was correct something was not above-board with Francesca, Serreti, and the Director just got a lot bigger. His partner was not herself. They needed to talk, but not now. Wiley's instructions were unambiguous, leave now, his jet would be ready and waiting for them at the Rome airport.

CHAPTER 17

Luzato feared the meeting with the *main man* must be coming soon. In his mind, it had to. He'd been down here long enough for whomever was in charge to arrive. And then he would know with certainty the real reason he was here. He would know his own fate. For now, though, all he could do was wait.

And pray.

He'd been doing a lot of that over the last…, he had no idea how long he'd been down here. He had lost complete track of time. Was it a day? Two days? Three? Surely, not more than three. He tried to gauge the days by the prolonged lengths of time between the door to his chamber being opened. But the gaps were too hard to track. He expected three meals a day, perhaps he shouldn't have. It seemed like all the meals came at the regular time intervals, but it was difficult to discern breakfast from lunch from dinner. It all seemed to be the same food with very little variation.

Other than the door to the chamber opening and closing and the man bringing him food, clothes, or changing his toilet bucket, there was no other noise of any kind except the occasional sound of water running through pipes. No street noise. No voices. No banging.

Silence.

Lonely silence.

He tried to recall when this all started. It was an ordinary day spent running errands in Trastevere. When he returned home, he saw he had not received replies from the two CEOs he'd tried to warn. He planned to send follow up emails to them. They needed to be warned. Sensitive information from their company servers had been compromised. Luzato had thwarted some of Boris' hack attempts, but knew he would attack again. The CEOs needed to increase security on their servers. He wanted confirmation they were aware of the attacks, and had taken measures to stop the inevitable future attempts. He had to make contact with both of them.

As usual, he prepared his evening meal and let his pet mouse out of its cage. He always fed the mouse morsels and crumbs off his plate while he ate. During supper, he had realized it had been several hours since he was online, and he planned to do more coding after he finished his meal. But, he never got the chance.

That was it, it had to be the food. Someone had tainted his food. He had a slight recollection of his pet mouse falling asleep at the table, something that had never happened before.

Then he woke up in this place. Wherever this place was.

His stomach growled and almost on cue, the bolt on the chamber door unlocked. This time both men walked in, one with a food tray and the other with a clean bucket. The second disappeared into the grain cellar with the bucket and reappeared moments later with the used one. The second man left the chamber and locked the heavy door behind him.

"I brought you something different this time."

"How long have I been down here?" Luzato asked.

The man, still wearing his black hood, walked over to the table and placed the tray at one end. He pulled out a large meal and place setting and placed them on the table. Then he opened two carafes, a 500 ml one and a smaller 250 ml one.

He held up the smaller one. "I thought a little wine might be nice with your meal. And I have a special treat. White truffles, dogs sniffed them out this morning."

"Is it evening?"

The man didn't answer.

"How long have I been here?"

"Come, eat, then we'll talk."

Luzato walked to the table and sat. The food smelled good. "What is it?"

"Wild boar smothered in mushrooms and gravy."

"Who are you?"

The man didn't answer at first, his two dark eyes stared from beneath his hood. "You can call me Germano."

He raised his right hand and placed it on his head. Next, he did something Luzato never expected, he removed his hood.

Germano was almost bald with a long face and pointed chin and his captor's stature wasn't much bigger than his own. His features were not harsh, nor kind, just amicable. And clearly Italian. Certainly not what he would have expected.

"Why did you let me see your face?" his voice quivered.

Germano replied, "I grow tired of the hood. And it matters not if you see me."

"What does that mean? Are you going to kill me?" His hand began to tremble.

"You control your fate, not I. If you want to die, he will accommodate you. You will be offered a choice. And your decision will be honored." Germano pointed to the plate. "You should eat. Do not worry about things that make no difference."

Luzato took a few bites. The food was delicious. "When will he come?"

"When the time is right," Germano said. "You alone will make that determination."

"How will I know?"

Germano pointed to Luzato's neck. "First, you must understand and respect the collar. Accept the fact it is in control, and this will be much easier. And faster."

"How long have I been here?"

"Four days. You were out for the first two." He pushed back from the table, stood and moved toward the door. "Enjoy your meal and try to get some sleep. Tomorrow might be a long day."

Germano left the chamber.

What did he mean by *tomorrow might be a long day?*

He looked down at his plate and wondered if he'd been drugged again.

CHAPTER 18

Ethan Wogahn laid the schematics across a large drafting table and double-checked the alignment of all four towers.

The first tower was located outside a small town in Western Kansas at what was left of a local cell phone company. Acquired a year ago at a bargain price, the building and accompanying tower had been substantially damaged by a tornado and since the owners had not insured it, they opted to close the doors and the business instead of attempting to fund the repairs. It took a crew of ten working around the clock for eight weeks to make the structural repairs necessary to get the building to meet minimum specifications.

Next came the covert installation of the electronic equipment. All exterior improvements and installations had to ensure the building had the outward appearance of a startup cell phone company taking over for the now defunct one. The interior equipment, though, was substantially different. Its primary purpose was two-fold, receive satellite data and transmit that data to the two relay towers and, at the appropriate moment, transmit data back to the satellites.

The idea for the two relay towers was his brilliant idea. Since the area of West Kansas and extreme Eastern Colorado was already littered with wind farms, Wogahn approached two different farm owners, at geographically strategic locations, and bought from each a wind turbine tower. After repurposing the two towers, Wogahn finally had his relay towers linked to the two main complexes, each with its own power supply.

Four towers, one project.

Each a separate stage of his project.

Each location's primary function to serve the ultimate goal of bringing down the Infidel.

And the countdown to that glorious day had already begun.

All ten worldwide locations were slated for completion within the next two days with final diagnostic testing in three days.

If all sites passed testing, activation would occur on schedule in six days.

Halloween.

A night never to be forgotten.

The only item remaining on his checklist after he double-checked the array alignments was to ready the software, yet to be given to him by Boris, for upload to one satellite. Not really a virus, so much as a temporary malfunction. One that would render the United States, and many other nations, incapable of striking back with military force.

On Halloween day, the project would be implemented in a series of installments until the final installment at midnight Zulu or Universal Coordinated Time. He would upload the software at 6:00 a.m. per Boris' instructions so his software program could propagate itself throughout many of the satellites surrounding the globe. A process Boris claimed would take only minutes. Then at noon, he would initiate the software, and the program would go active. The software's effect on the world would be exactly the name Boris had given his program.

Disruption.

CHAPTER 19

Vienna, Austria
8:00 P. M. Local Time

The flight from Rome to Vienna was quiet. Too quiet. It seemed neither of Jake's travel companions had a single word to say. Francesca kept her nose in her laptop the entire flight and Marco Serreti slept.

Fontaine had arranged for a driver to pick them up at the airport and drive them into town. As they approached the city, Francesca finally broke her silence.

"Ready for your first history lesson?"

"On Vienna? I thought Rome would be my history lesson."

"Rome later. Wein now."

"*Veen?*"

"Spelled W-E-I-N. Pronounced *Veen* in German."

"You speak German too?"

"Some. Only enough for basic communication." She pointed at Serreti. "Marco is fluent."

"Figures."

"Vienna is a laid back city," she continued. "For most of its 2500-year history, Vienna was considered the frontier of civilized Europe. It's home to great music composers like Beethoven, Mozart, Brahms, and Strauss."

"And scientists like Doppler and Boltzmann," Serreti added.

"Anyway," she continued, "Vienna sits on the Danube River and is divided into twenty-three districts. Each district has a number. District one is old town Vienna. Old town is surrounded by two rings. Inner ring, or Ringstrasse and outer ring, or the Gürtel. Everything in district one is much more expensive than outside. We are going to 7 Lindengasse, which is Linden Street in the seventh district. I can't begin to tell you all the history that is in this city. You have to experience it for yourself. This is one of my favorites, if not my favorite, city of all time. It is so easy to get around too. The transportation system can't be beat."

He doubted that. It seemed like a never-ending flow of bumper-to-bumper traffic. As they turned on the Gürtel, there were cars and buses and an overabundance of pedestrian traffic.

"I thought you said Vienna was laid back. It's after eight already, it's almost dark outside, and look at the mobs of people."

Francesca and Serreti laughed. Francesca said, "That's because this is the height of tourist season. September and October are the busiest times of the year. It'll die down in a couple of weeks."

The car made several turns when he noticed a street sign that said Lindengasse. The street was almost barren except for a crowd of people standing in front of an open door. Within seconds the driver pulled to the curb. He said, "We are here. The apartment you want is this side of those people."

Jake, Francesca, and Serreti stepped out of the car.

Serreti leaned over the driver's window, "Wait here. We shouldn't be too long."

The driver nodded.

The three of them walked a couple blocks down the sidewalk toward a crowd of people gathered under a black and red sign flashing the image of a naked woman. The sign read

Monaco Bar. The type of bar was obvious. Two women pushed their way out of the door, both yelling something in German.

Within seconds, a police car with its siren blaring rounded the corner behind them. A drunk across the street tried to run, then gave up and stashed his bottle in a garbage can. The two women jumped in a car paralleled parked on the street, but were blocked when the police car screeched to a halt thwarting their escape. Two police officers jumped out, a woman and a man, both drawing their firearms. The officers barked commands and aimed their weapons at the two women who were frozen with their hands in the air.

Jake and Serreti were watching the fracas when Francesca got their attention. "Jake. Marco." Both men craned their necks toward Francesco and bumped into each other. "This is the place. Let's go."

Francesca pulled her small lock-pick kit from her jacket and within seconds had the green door open. Inside, the landing was dark, illuminated only by a glow from a street light which exposed an old wooden staircase. Not enough light to see beyond the first three steps. Jake took the lead and felt his way as he slowly climbed toward the top of the stairs. A light illuminated behind him along with a bump on his shoulder.

"This might help," Serreti said. He handed the mini flashlight to Jake.

"Thanks."

The top of the stairs opened to a long dark hallway. Jake shined the light down the hallway. Ten doors, each with a number. Odd numbers on the right, even on the left.

Francesca opened up a folded piece of paper and held it in front of the flashlight. "Number seven."

When they reached the room, Francesca, still with her lock

picking set in her hand, stooped to her knees and unlocked the door while Jake held the light for her. Jake used his foot to swing the door open and shined the light inside. Unsure of what or who was inside the room, he swept the light in front of them. Suddenly, the overhead light illuminated the room. Surprised, he turned. Serreti had a stupid grin plastered on his face.

"No sense stumbling around in the dark. Right, Jake?"

It wasn't what they found that surprised them, but what they didn't find. Barely any evidence the man lived in the apartment at all. Everything in the apartment was too neat. Too perfect. His clothes were meticulously organized in his closet on color coded hangers. All hangers were the same distance apart. About half an inch to be exact. The towels in his bathroom were hung perfect. Not one thing out of place in the whole house. Bedroom. Kitchen. Pantry. All of it with the same degree of OCD. There was no clutter to be found. Anywhere. Even his dirty clothes were folded and placed in a dirty clothes hamper. Jake was sure this guy was a neat freak.

On a small desk sat a laptop computer. Next to it, a large manila envelope. Inside the envelope were several pictures, a roster of names, and an investigative file. Jake laid the papers and pictures across the dining table while Serreti took something from his pocket and inserted it in a USB port and booted the laptop.

Francesca picked up the pictures and flipped through them. She placed one on the table and tapped on it. "I've been there before." It was a photo of a large courtyard surrounded by several buildings, including one next to a wall containing several black plaques. She sighed and placed another photo on the table. "I know this place. It is in Venetia…Venice."

It was the photo of the front facade of an old building with the words *Casa Israelitica Di Riposo* above the doorway. There was a man walking out of the building. He was a man of around fifty with long gray hair and a gray goatee. The same man as in all the other pictures. He was wearing traditional Jewish garments and a black hat. He wore frameless spectacles low on his nose.

"These were taken in the Jewish ghetto," she said.

"What do these words mean?"

"Basically, Jewish House of Rest."

"Okay, what is a Jewish House of Rest?"

"It is an old age home," Serreti interjected.

Serreti was leaning back in a chair in front of the laptop holding the investigative file. The deputy director held up a photo. "Is this the man in those pictures?"

Jake carried the photos over and held them next to the one Serreti pulled from the file. "Same guy, don't you think?"

"The file says his name is Daniel Luzato. The only address given is Casa Israelitica Di Riposo."

"Any mention of Rome?"

"No, sorry Francesca. That is the only thing in this file. Several pictures of the same man and the address."

"You think because he happens to be Jewish, that makes him The Jew?" Jake concluded she had made that assumption. In reality, so had he. At least, he hoped it was the case.

"If we can put the two of them together and can tie Luzato to the flat in Rome, then yes."

"You two look at this," Serreti insisted. "I think we have bigger problems."

"How did you get into the computer?" Jake asked. "Wasn't it password protected?"

Serreti showed Jake the USB thumb drive. "Password decoder from our AISE cyber department. I take it with me everywhere. I never know when I might need it."

Jake and Francesca stood behind Marco Serreti while he scrolled through several files on the laptop. He doubled-clicked one file and a list of names popped up on the screen. A click on each name brought up a photo, presumably of the person listed. Only one name stood out. All three of them recognized it. Serreti clicked on the name and the photo opened.

"No doubt that's him," Francesca said.

The man in the photo had cold dark eyes sunk deep into his face with dark circles around each. His hair and full beard were mostly gray, unlike his black thick bushy eyebrows. They recognized him as the former head of the Iranian Revolutionary Guard. The feared and ruthless, Qasem Kazemi. A sworn enemy of the United States, Israel, and all of the West.

Serreti clicked on several other names. Neither the name nor the picture were recognizable to any of them. Serreti clicked fast and minimized, but not before Jake saw something interesting.

"Wait," he protested. "Go back."

Serreti reopened the photo file. Jake leaned closer to the screen to study the young man in the photo. Olive complexion. Thick black hair slicked back with some sort of hair gel. Green sweater with a large open collar. And dimples.

Jake read the name out loud. "Alexei Nikahd. Son of a bitch."

"Who is it, Jake?" Francesca asked. "Who is Alexei Nikahd?"

Jake's eyes lit up.

"Boris."

CHAPTER 20

Jake called it in to Fontaine.

At his request, the contents of the dead man's laptop hard drive were uploaded to a quarantined section of one of Commonwealth's protected servers. Fontaine walked Serreti through the procedure which allowed Fontaine to take control of the computer and initiate the file transfer.

While Jake was still on the video chat line with Fontaine, Wiley entered the command center and stood behind Fontaine so Jake could see him. Jake brought the old man up to speed. Due to the late hour in Vienna, and the fact the Casa Israelitica Di Riposo in Venice would not open their doors until morning, Wiley instructed Jake, Francesca, and Serreti to remain in Vienna for the night and make a thorough search of the apartment before leaving.

"Photos," Fontaine interjected. "Take lots of photos and email them to me."

"Mr. Wiley?" Francesca walked over and stood next to Jake. He adjusted his iPad so Wiley could see her on his screen. "Tourist season is in full force here in Vienna. Vienna's version of Oktoberfest, Wiener Wiesn, ended a couple of weeks ago so I imagine every room within a kilometer of downtown is booked. Except a few penthouse suites, but they'll be outrageously priced."

Wiley ran his hand through his hair and pushed his glasses

up with his finger. "I'll authorize up to five thousand Euro total for the three of you."

Serreti interrupted, "AISE can pay its own way."

Jake thought his tone sounded too harsh, especially since Wiley was offering to cover the deputy director's expenses, too. He could see Francesca's furious eyes tell Serreti she wasn't happy with the way the deputy director spoke to Wiley.

"Very well, Deputy Director, my offer still stands in case you need it."

"As soon as we disconnect," Fontaine added. "I'll see what I can find."

"I have my people on it now," Serreti said while typing on his smart phone.

"Suit yourself," Wiley said. Then he gave Fontaine the cutoff signal and the video chat went dead.

"You know, Marco," Francesca said as she strutted over to him waving her finger in his face. "Why do you have to be such an asshole? My boss made a kind gesture and you had to be a jerk about it. You once asked me why I left AISE. I'll tell you why. I was sick and tired of putting up with your bloated ego, so when Wiley offered me a job, I was freaking ecstatic. I couldn't wait to get away from your pompous ass."

Serreti leaned back in the chair. Jake couldn't tell if it was anger in his eyes or fear. Francesca could definitely be a force to be reckoned with, so it was never a good idea to get on her bad side. Nonetheless, Serreti had it coming.

Best of all, the old Francesca was back.

Francesca tossed her hair over her shoulder, and wrapped her arm under his. "Jake, why don't you and I walk around downtown, while George finds us a room? Marco is on his own. He can meet us at the airport in the morning."

Jake enjoyed seeing the color drain from Serreti's face. "I like the way you're thinking, partner."

✝✝✝

Jake and Francesca left the dead man's apartment, strolled down the dimly lit cobblestone street to Lindengasse and turned on Stiftgasse. The streets were full of nocturnal dwellers wandering in and out of taverns, cafes, coffee shops and listening to live music in clubs. Most of the establishments kept their doors open to entice passersby to come inside. Which was hard to resist at times, with the intoxicating aroma spilling into the streets.

The faint wind had a chill in the air making Francesca snuggle closer to him while they continued to explore the city. They almost passed by a shop with people lined up outside to get in when Francesca stopped him with a hard tug on his arm. The sign painted on the window, *Gelateria La Romana*. "Ice cream. Good thinking, Francesca."

"Not ice cream," she replied. "Gelato. Better than ice cream."

Once they were able to get inside, Jake was amazed at the vast assortment of flavors. Francesca spoke something in German to the young woman behind the counter and said, "Chocolate, as usual?"

"As dark as it gets."

She gave him a double take. "All right," she said. "That will be quite a caffeine buzz. Don't blame me if you can't get to sleep tonight."

"That strong?"

"Oh yeah."

The young woman handed him a cone scooped high with dark chocolate gelato. Her unrelenting stare puzzled him. She said something to Francesca who shook her head and exchanged a few more German words. All he understood was nein, nein. *No, no.*

"What?" he asked.

Francesca motioned toward the exit. "She thinks you're cute."

"I am cute." Jake glanced over his shoulder and saw the young woman waving at him. He turned back to Francesca. "She's not so bad herself."

"She asked if we were a couple."

"What did you tell her?"

"I told her we were not, but you were not on the market, either."

Jake licked the rapidly melting gelato. "After today," he said. "That might not be true."

"What the hell, Jake? Did you do something to piss off Kyli?"

They rounded the corner and walked past a store full of old American LP records displayed in the window. "I think it's the same thing that's been going on with her. My job. Wiley. Being gone all the time. It has been a source of conflict for a while now. It seemed worse this morning when I dropped her off at MEtech."

"If you'll remember, I warned you this might happen. As wild and fun-loving as Kyli is, she still has a need for stability and security. You being gone all the time and always in danger creates anxiety and loneliness. Perhaps you two should cool it for a while."

"What? Why should we do that? Kyli and I—"

"Yeah, yeah, Jake. I've heard it all before. You and Kyli think you're in love…and perhaps you are, but neither of you has truly made a commitment to your relationship. You two have been through a lot together. Right out of the gate, too. From the moment you two met, you've been hot and heavy lovers. You saved her life. Twice. I think that's part of the attraction… and maybe part of the problem. Neither of you have slowed down enough to get to know each other."

They rounded another street corner and the view opened up. Jake saw the beauty and vastness of downtown Vienna unfolded in front of him. Dotted along the night time horizon were spires and steeples and lush green lawns bracketed with sidewalks and trolley tracks and pavement. They ambled past the Volkstheater and the Museum of Natural History. His thoughts were not on the historical wonder his eyes saw, so much as fixated on what Francesca had said to him.

"Has Kyli talked to you about it?" Jake asked.

"No. And I don't want her to, either. I don't want to be stuck in the middle. You, I'll listen to. I like Kyli a lot. She's sweet. I'm not sure she is right for you. Your job and her grandfather will *always* come between you two. And that's a fact you can never change, partner."

Jake was silent for a couple of minutes while he finished his gelato. Francesca identified more historical buildings, the Hofburg Palace and a short history lesson on Maria Theresa. He didn't pay attention to what she was saying, instead, he noticed beer tents in the street, along with pretzel and bratwurst stands. In the square, he heard a band playing American rock-n-roll music.

"Speaking of partners," he said. "Why did you let Serreti say that shit to me in the interrogation room?"

He was surprised how quick she snapped her head toward him. "Do you think for a second I would have gone along with it if I'd known what he was going to say? I was with Barzetti and had just walked in when he said that to you. I let the director have a piece of my mind. He said he would have a talk with Marco. You can understand why we parted ways."

"What point was he trying to make? Did he think you and I were lovers too?"

"No. He had asked me earlier while he and the director were talking to me in another interrogation room. I made one thing clear to both of them, we are partners, never lovers, nor would we ever be. And it was none of their damn business even if we were." She paused. "I thought you handled Marco well. And he kind of apologized…in the only way he knows how."

As they continued walking, she identified the Spanish Riding School and the Jewish Museum of Vienna. His partner was a walking encyclopedia. His thoughts drifted back to the dead man found in the apartment in Rome, and the information they found in the apartment here in Vienna. Francesca said something in the dead man's apartment that still resonated in his mind. Could the Jewish man in the photos in Venice be the same man they were looking for? Could he be *The Jew?*

She elbowed him in the ribs. "Jake, are you listening?"

"What?"

She put her hands on her hips and motioned with her head.

He craned his neck straight up to see a sixty-foot column of clouds sprouting angels and cherubs. At the top of the lighted statue, the Trinity. The column was wrapped in an anti-pigeon net as was most of Vienna's prized outdoor monuments. He looked around and saw throngs of people.

"It's a big statue of something."

"This is interesting stuff. Try to pay attention for five minutes. Is that too long for your attention span?"

"Sorry, blast away."

"In 1679," she said. "Vienna was hit by a massive epidemic of bubonic plague. Killed around 75,000 people. Emperor Leopold I," she pointed up at the statue, "knelt in public, which was unheard of back then, and prayed for God to save Vienna. Afterwards, he vowed to erect this monument."

"Will there be a quiz on this later?"

She pursed her lips. "This way, smart ass." Thirty yards down the cobble street and they came to an abrupt halt. "St. Peter's church. Leopold ordered it built as thanks for surviving the 1679 plague." In front of them was a large church covered with a green dome.

"What is this place?" Jake waved his hand up and down the large street filled with people.

"This is the Graben pedestrian area. Basically, this is *the* center of Vienna." She pointed back in the direction of the plague monument. "And back that way is St. Stephen's Cathedral and Stephans-Platz."

"And beyond that," a voice said behind them. "Is the Mozart Museum."

They both turned.

Marco Serreti.

CHAPTER 21

"Marco?" His unannounced presence annoyed Francesca. "How did you…?"

"Pardon my bluntness, but I'm not sure why you would ask, Francesca," Serreti said with a cocky look on his face. "Where else would you bring our young friend?"

"You can wipe that grin off your face or I will. I know your lying ass followed us."

"No. I—"

"What do you want, Deputy Director?" Jake interrupted.

"As I was about to say, our respective companies have located lodging. Luck has it, we will be staying at the same hotel. The only vacancies in District One." Gesturing with his hands he continued, "How do you Americans say it, ah yes, the hotel is very elegant." He glanced back at her then faced Jake. "Your Mr. Fontaine has been unable to reach you."

She checked her phone. "Oh crap, I turned my ringer off."

Jake pulled his phone out of its case. "Yeah, so did I. Right before we went inside the apartment. I have three missed calls from Commonwealth."

Jake walked out of ear shot of Serreti with his phone against his ear.

Serreti leaned too close causing her to take a step back. "Our rooms are at the Ritz." He winked and his gaze dipped to her décolletage. "Remember our night at the Ritz. I think of it often. Neither one of us slept. Wine and chocolate covered strawberries."

"Shut up, Marco."

Jake walked up, holding his phone in his hand. "We're staying at the Ritz-Carlton Vienna. George says it's not too far from here. The only room left was the Presidential Suite. A little more than Wiley originally allowed, but George said he ran it by the old man first and got his approval."

She asked, "The Ritz is pretty pricey, how much?"

"5500 Euro per night. George said the Presidential Suite has Club level access, whatever that means."

"It is a restricted access level," Marco explained. "You need a special key to get the elevator to stop at Club level."

"You sound like you're a regular."

Marco eyes darted toward her then back to Jake. "I have stayed at this Ritz-Carlton in the past. I am familiar with the routine."

"George sent me a map." Jake passed his phone to her.

Although she already knew where the Ritz-Carlton Vienna was located, she feigned a look at Jake's phone for appearance sake. "The Ritz is on the inner ring, perhaps a ten-minute walk from where we are now." She handed the phone back to Jake. "We should go, partner," she said coaxing Jake with her arm looped around his arm.

Ten minutes later, the three of them crossed Schubertring and entered the lobby of the Ritz-Carlton through the revolving door in the center. She and Jake walked up to one of the two front desks and checked in. They were given their room key and instructions for Club level access. Marco, it seemed, had already checked in and waited for them to complete the process. A fireplace in the lobby was filled with several large candles glowing, their flames flickering with each draft of air.

Marco parted ways with them at the Club level. He stated he was going to the bar while she and Jake checked out their room. The Presidential Suite was spacious by anyone's standards. Throughout the suite, handcrafted rugs and unique artwork coexisted alongside stunning artifacts and furnishings, all tied together by a chocolate-brown color scheme accented with luminous brushed gold and deep red accessories. The master bedroom featured upholstered silk walls and a spacious walk-in closet paneled with sycamore. Equally stunning was the adjoining bathroom, outfitted with honey onyx walls and featured an over-sized tub and glass-enclosed steam shower for two. Furnished with custom-designed pieces, the large living and dining area were serviced by a gourmet kitchen, while the wood-paneled study provided an elegant working environment for business travelers.

"You take the bed, I'll take the sofa," she said.

"How about I take the couch and you take the bed," Jake countered. "I sleep on the couch all the time."

"Not this time, I insist." She knew he wouldn't put up much of a fight.

"Okay," he said. "Since you insisted." Jake jumped on the middle of the bed. "Comfy. You're going to be sorry."

"You're probably right." She headed to the door. "I'm going to get a nightcap, care to join me?" She knew Jake would refuse. He almost always did.

"I'll pass." He got off the bed. "Think I'll take a shower while you're gone."

"Okay. If you change your mind, you know where to find me."

She hesitated a few minutes by the door, heard the shower

come on in the bathroom, and saw the bedroom door was shut. A minute later, she left the suite.

Down the hall she stopped, checked in both directions and lightly rapped on a door. The door opened without any words exchanged.

She stood in front of him, as handsome as ever.

He put one hand around the back of her neck gently pulling her close to him. He leaned in toward her up-stretched face. Francesca's heart raced, her breathing unsteady. Their eyes locked on each other. The warmth of his lips made her feel limp. She kissed back. While his other hand was on her back, he pulled her in. She did not resist.

When their lips parted, he slid the jacket from her shoulders and let it drop to the floor. He unbuttoned her shirt, slowly, one button at a time. She touched his face and brought his gaze to hers. She was overcome with desire as she pulled his shirt up and ran her hands underneath, sliding them up and down his smooth bare back, then, moving them around toward his chest.

He slid her unbuttoned shirt from her shoulders, letting it fall to the floor.

They kissed harder and deeper while he began to walk her backwards toward the bed. Her knees felt weak, but his strong arms kept her steady. She grabbed his belt and pulled it loose. With the snap of his fingers, her bra was unlatched. She lowered her arms momentarily and let it slip off between them. She grabbed his shirt, pulled it over his head, and threw it across the room. Her pants came loose and he slid his hands down her backside. Her pants went with them.

They fell embraced onto the bed.

"That was a nice deflection during the video chat with your

company. I almost believed you were angry."

"Marco, I meant every word I said." She ran her hands down his chest. "Now shut-up."

†††

Jake waited thirty seconds after Francesca left, before coming out of the bedroom. He was still dressed. His gut told him she was up to something. His partner, who he trusted with his life, wasn't the same as on their last mission. Not the sad Francesca from two days ago, either. Different somehow. It wasn't what she said, it was her behavior. And he didn't like it. When she walked close to him earlier, arm in arm, the old Francesca would never have done that. In the past, she had always been forthcoming about everything. And honest. Sometimes brutally honest. There was something going on she didn't want him to know about and he was determined to find out what it was.

He eased into the hallway, checked both directions and walked with long strides in the opposite direction from the bar. He thought he saw a door close a few doors down from his room. He padded to the room and placed his ear against the door.

The sounds were unmistakable. The throes of passion. He heard sighs and moans. And voices. Familiar voices.

He had heard enough so he headed back in the direction he came.

His suspicions had been confirmed.

†††

When Francesca returned to the suite, it was empty.

Jake was gone.

She went to the bar and saw him sitting at a table drinking a beer, still in the same clothes as earlier.

"There you are," she said. "I went for a walk and when I came back, you were gone." She hated lying, but it was necessary this time. Besides, it was a harmless lie, in her opinion. Jake didn't need to know where she had been or what she had been doing.

Jake narrowed his eyes, glanced sideways and tightened his lips.

"What is it, Jake? Has something happened?"

"Sit down, Francesca," he said. "It's time we had a talk."

CHAPTER 22

It had been a trying two days at school. Yesterday, he was late for class because of the incident in the subway station. Fortunately, the bullet wound to his leg was nothing more serious than a deep gash. The bullet only grazed his leg but it bled a lot and for a long time. Yesterday, he had to limp a little. Today, none at all. Being young and on the college track team had paid off in his recovery time. When his friend questioned him yesterday about the blood coming from his leg, he downplayed it as nothing more than a cut from climbing a fence to retrieve a neighbor kid's baseball. His friend bought it, and that was all that mattered.

As Alexei Nikahd rounded the corner to the Georgetown neighborhood, he spied two people getting out of a black Lincoln Town Car in front of his parent's house.

He ducked behind some shrubs, using them as a screen while he watched the man and woman approach his front door. They rang the doorbell and when someone answered, he saw them flash their badges. *How did they get onto me this fast?*

But, he knew.

The man who had chased him in the subway wore a tiny earpiece. He saw it when the man jumped onto the tracks to save the old woman. Someone was communicating with him, through an earpiece, which meant they had probably accessed the Metro's closed circuit cameras. And that meant someone higher up the law enforcement food chain other than the Washington Police Department. Perhaps FBI or Homeland Security. Doubtful it was CIA, not in D.C. But, the guy chasing him didn't look like a LEO of any kind. Law enforcement officers were typically easy for him to spot, even in a crowd.

This guy he didn't spot. Not until the man fell onto the platform after squeezing through the Metro car's closing doors. Then he saw it in the man's eyes.

His mother stepped onto the front step. She was shaking her head, so he knew they must have asked her to go inside and she was refusing. His parents came from drastically different backgrounds, but they had one thing in common, they learned early in life not to trust their respective governments, nor their new one. His mother was Russian and his father Iranian. An odd pairing, however they had been married for over thirty years, so something worked.

He heard sirens, but saw nothing. He turned back toward his mother and saw her eyes squint in his direction. She quickly stepped on the other side of the officers drawing their attention away from the corner where he stood. He understood her warning and left in the opposite direction.

He had another problem now, though. If law enforcement, or whoever was at his front doorstep, knew his name, then his anonymous identity as Boris was no longer anonymous. He'd long since known they had his picture. Now they had his real name to go with it. And the only way that could have happened was if his contact in Austria had been compromised. If his identity had been compromised, so had several other assets in T-A. Another thought occurred to him, it was now extremely likely the leader of Tarh Andishan had been exposed as well.

He needed to mitigate the damage. And to do that, he needed

his laptop. Not the one in his backpack, it was clean. School and social media use only. He needed his hacking computer. It was well hidden and not in jeopardy of being found, of that he was sure. But the computer was in his house and that was the last place he could go right now. If the authorities knew his identity, it was only a matter of time before they showed up with a search warrant. When that happened, he would never be able to retrieve his computer. He had to figure out a way to get it … and get it tonight.

He had an idea, but it would require asking a favor. The last thing he wanted was to be indebted to someone who would expect reciprocity.

Not expect, demand.

But at this juncture, he had little choice.

†††

Lueven, Belgium

The Korean looked at his GPS receiver as the small skiff glided without a sound down the canal. The screen marked the lab's location behind the abandoned flour plant. Planning the mission to the last detail, he knew his team would have to breach several layers of security, each demanding different access requirements. Fortunately, he had acquired the floor plans, the location of the security cameras, the alarm deactivation codes, and the exact spots he was to plant the devices.

He signaled toward the small dark pier and instructed the helmsman to steer the cramped vessel to the designated spot.

His research had allowed him to predetermine the darkest spot to tie up the black skiff. Reeds from the shoreline had been cut earlier in the day and adhered to the sides of the skiff leaving it nearly impossible to detect from the opposite shore of the canal.

The outboard motor wouldn't be used within a half-mile of the lab's location. Attention of any kind could jeopardize his plan. The electric trolling motor was slow but quiet.

MEtech Laboratories was housed in a building originally designed as office space, now renovated into a laboratory. Located on Remylaan, or Remy Lane, in Wijgmaal on the outskirts of Lueven, the laboratory was surrounded by an office complex, a railroad, a canal, and an abandoned manufacturing plant. The owner of the laboratory was an American who owned several top-secret contracts with IMEC, also located in Lueven. IMEC was a world leader in research in nano-electronics and nano-technology. The research was used to improve healthcare, smart electronics, sustainable energy, and safer transportation.

MEtech's public mission was research in radio frequency and microwave emission technology, but its private interest went much deeper. It produced prototype equipment far more advanced than public knowledge. Its prototypes were tested by many western nations' military and intelligence agencies including NSA, CIA, MI6, and Mossad.

The Korean trained his team of four well for this assignment. In and out in ten minutes was the plan. Expediency was critical. So was secrecy. That's why he had sent his smallest man, a man of boyish size and shape, earlier that night with a pellet rifle to take out the critical lights surrounding their ingress and egress route. The man plinked every light the Korean had identified, creating a large unlit area along the canal as well as the parking area between the buildings. Authorities would likely chalk it up to juvenile vandalism, put on a superficial search, and then forget it ever happened.

The approach to the abandoned plant was dark and the teams' movements unseen. The old structure had suffered with time. Moldy walls covered by intertwining vines climbing up the sides, coupled with broken windows panes, a result of age, made the structure look haunted. The deserted plant was situated in front of the lab making undetected access easier. Its canal-side approach provided extra cover with a ten-foot tall hedge that led to within fifteen feet of the backside of the lab.

The Korean's biggest obstacle was there was no rear access door on ground level, only a fire escape balcony from the third floor by a retractable ladder. Access to the lab was available only from the front of the building, the vulnerable spot. He instructed his team to use their climbing gear, as planned, to scale the rear of the building and wait for him to open the third floor door.

The Korean rounded the corner of the building, checking for anyone who might notice his approach. In the darkness, he sidestepped the broken glass beneath each street lamp. He used his penlight to illuminate the keycard slot, pressed the timer on his watch, inserted the key-card, and entered the lab.

The clock had started.

Within ten minutes, the team must be back in the boat and making their escape up the canal.

After disabling the alarm, he whisked his way to the third floor where he deactivated the rear fire escape door alarm allowing his team to enter the building.

Six minutes and twenty-seven seconds after the Korean

entered the lab, the entire team had exited the building and rappelled from the fire escape balcony, leaving no trace of their break-in. One minute later the five men were in the boat heading northward along their prearranged escape route.

He checked his watch, phase one of his employer's plan had been set into motion.

†††

Georgetown
Washington D. C.

Boris looked at his watch from his neighbor's backyard.

10:30 p.m.

He should get the signal any time now. All he was told was he would know it when it happened. He would have less than two minutes to get in the back door, retrieve his equipment, and get back out. If it took him longer than that, he was on his own.

He knew this day might come and had prepared for it. Hidden away in a secret compartment in the crawl space under his parent's home, were two backpacks, one with his computer and the other with his setup hardware. All he needed was a secure access point and he was on the deep web.

His contact was right. When he heard it, he knew it was time. The explosion was loud and it shook the ground. He didn't know what blew up, but by the feel of the shockwave, there couldn't be much left.

He scrambled to his feet, climbed the fence, and jumped into his backyard. He ran across the tiny yard and opened the exterior access to the crawl space. Underneath the house was a hatch into the secret compartment. He had installed an exterior access panel to his bedroom in the event of such an incident as this. Tonight his forward-thinking preparedness had paid off. He dropped to his knees and crawled to the compartment. He opened the door and reached in. Within seconds, he had both backpacks. Out on the street, sirens grew louder. Voices yelled. He pushed the distraction away and used a mini flashlight to check the contents. Everything was exactly as he had left it. He crawled back to the exit and pushed the access door open.

He crawled out into the back yard and stood. He turned to run when a voice called out.

"Don't move, Boris."

He held up his hands, a backpack in each one.

He turned around to see a man pointing a gun at him.

"Slowly lower the backpacks," the man instructed.

Suddenly a shot rang out from behind him and the man fell to the ground.

"Get out of here, Alexei," the voice said. "And never come back."

CHAPTER 23

Venice, Italy
9:00 a.m.

Jake stood next to the helm as the driver of the water taxi steered the vessel across Venice Lagoon. The cabin was warm and comfortable and he stared out the windows in a locked gaze as the driver followed the channel markers from the Marco Polo airport toward the historic old water town. Francesca and Serreti sat across from each other in the passenger compartment below deck. This was his first trip to Venice and the romantic hype he'd seen on TV and the movies seemed misleading as the city grew closer. Venice was old, its buildings crumbling and moldy. And dirty. The canals were littered with trash. And it smelled. It was anything but romantic. A city in great need of repair.

The water taxi dropped them off at the bridge on Calle Ghetto Vecchio along a canal named Rio di San Girolamo in what was the Jewish Ghetto section of Venice. The cloudy coastline of Venice was colder than it was in Austria just two hours ago when they left Vienna. The flight had taken barely thirty minutes to travel the 455 kilometers from Vienna to Venice. It was clear in Vienna and cloudy in Venice. The pilot said the forecast called for rain, so Jake grabbed his jacket as he left the aircraft.

From the airport, they basically had three options: boat,

auto, or train. Auto and train would only get them to the edge of the island where they would then have to travel on foot. Venice was wholly a pedestrian or boat city. As Francesca explained, there were many options for water travel. From water taxis to water buses to Vaporetti. And, of course, gondolas, although not from the airport to town. Venice was an island, and being a tourist mecca, it was crowded, usually overcrowded, and the best way to get around on the island was on foot. Unless coming from the airport. Since the airport was located on the water, a hired water taxi that could drop them off at their destination was their best and fastest option.

Jake held out some Euros to pay the water taxi driver his fare plus a small tip. Francesca and Marco Serreti waited on the dock for him to join them. Last night, he doubted she liked what he had to say, but she raised no objection nor did she seem upset after they returned to their suite. She didn't speak much, but she did speak, and they spent several minutes discussing the mission, before he retreated to the bedroom and she settled in on the sofa.

Perhaps their talk last night had helped her understand it was not wise to mix business and pleasure. He hoped so. She hadn't spoken ten words to Serreti since they arrived at the airport in Vienna. They didn't speak during the flight to Venice, either. It was an uncomfortable situation he found himself in with Francesca. She could sleep with whomever she wanted, but not at the cost of jeopardizing their mission. And it was *their* mission. Not Serreti's. Not AISE. Jake wasn't sure how far he could trust Deputy Director Marco Serreti. Or if he even wanted to trust the man at all. Serreti was a last minute tagalong. Why? Was it simply an opportunity to pursue Francesca or was it motivated by some AISE initiative?

He was glad the pilot suggested he take his jacket with him since the gray clouds had become threatening. "Looks like we might get wet," he said. Francesca and Serreti glanced up at the sky and did not respond. He was beginning to wish he was solo on this mission.

"Okay, which way?" He gestured in both directions, glancing at the bridge and then at the street.

Francesca moved toward the street. "This way, into Campo di Ghetto Nuovo, or Square of the New Ghetto, and then around the corner to the right."

Indeed, it was just around the corner. The street ended fifty feet later as it opened into a large square surrounded by four, five, and six story buildings. The ground level floors were typical; restaurants, art galleries, tourist shops, a Jewish bookstore, kosher groceries, and a sundry mix of assorted businesses. Above them were structures that appeared to be apartments. Linens and clothes hung from lines strung across balconies. In the center of the square was a public water fountain. A young blonde was filling a bottle. A dozen pigeons pecked at the ground in search of morsels. In front of a cafe, a man was setting tables under umbrellas in preparation for today's lunch crowd.

Mounted on a brick wall across the square between two doors were seven plaques. In front of the plaques was a green gazebo-shaped shelter with two men wearing camo fatigues, green berets, and packing side arms. Jake asked, "What's up over there?"

"Holocaust monument," Serreti said. "The soldiers' presence keeps the peace here."

Two men walked out of a building to his left. Both men wore black jackets, pants, shoes and white shirts, with no tie, something Jake recognized as traditional Jewish attire. They had full beards and covered their heads with black hats. The two men walked diagonally across Campo di Ghetto Nuovo and exited down a street in the far corner.

"Jake, Casa Israelitica Di Riposo is here." Francesca was facing a building perpendicular to and adjoining the Holocaust memorial wall.

Casa Israelitica Di Riposo had a weathered white marble facade with two large green doors and arched windows flanking each side. All the windows on the ground level were barred. Jake stepped to the door and tried to open it. Locked.

One of the armed men approached them and said something in Italian. Serreti responded then reached into his jacket and pulled out a leather wallet and handed it to the man. The armed man snapped to attention and his once foreboding tone changed.

Maybe Serreti was good for something after all.

Francesca joined the conversation, still in Italian, and then all three stared at him. He heard the word *inglese* and knew they were talking about him.

The man handed the wallet back to Serreti. "Use the knocker and someone will come to the door," he said with a heavy Italian accent. "Enjoy your stay in Venezia and good luck."

Serreti banged the heavy metal knocker on the door several times. No one came to the door so Serreti reached for the knocker a second time when the door swung open. A woman in her late sixties spoke to Serreti. Her tone made it obvious she was perturbed about the disturbance. The short blonde haired lady had a stern eyeful of disapproval on her face. Serreti showed her his AISE credentials, but her unyielding expression did not soften. Her face scrunched even more. She waved her arms saying something in Italian.

Jake leaned close to Francesca, "What did she say?"

"She scolded him for rapping so loudly. She said some of her guests are still sleeping."

Serreti pointed at his watch and shrugged.

The woman and Serreti were still arguing in Italian, when Francesca approached the woman in the doorway. "Parla inglese, per favore?" She turned her head toward Jake.

The woman raised her eyebrows and squinted at Jake "Si, Si, of course, signore. How may I help you?"

"Could we please come inside and ask you a few questions?" Jake clasped the old woman's hands.

"Si, you are pleasant man. Not like him." She nodded with her head at Serreti.

Jake smirked at Serreti. "I like her."

"If you keep your voices low, we can use the sitting room." She motioned with her arm. "There on the left."

The warped floor creaked beneath their feet and there was an unpleasant smell, a combination of stale air, mildew, and urine. They sat down on chairs that might be as old as some of the buildings in Venice. The dingy, cracked plaster walls were in dire need of repair and a fresh coat of paint. Some color might be nice, too. Anything to spice up the sterile institutional feel.

Jake began by introducing himself and then Francesca and Serreti. The woman's face was pleasant until he introduced Serreti, then the smile evaporated from her eyes.

She wore a name tag that read, Mariella. "My name is Marie Rizzo. I am…what you would call the administrator of Casa Israelitica Di Riposo."

She pronounced her name RIT-zo. "Ms. Rizzo," Jake attempted her pronunciation.

"Per favore, you may call me Marie," she interrupted.

"Thank you, Marie." Jake decided the best approach was the direct approach. "Would you happen to have a guest here by the name of Luzato?"

Marie rubbed her chin. "There is no one here by that name, no."

Francesca frowned at Jake and then asked Marie, "Perhaps a visitor? Or a next of kin?"

"No," Marie said. "I am not familiar with anyone with the name Luzato."

"Would it be possible," Serreti asked, "to see a register of your guests?"

"That is not possible," Marie said. "At Casa Israelitica Di Riposo, the privacy of our guests is of utmost importance."

Once again, Serreti reached into his jacket and pulled out his AISE credentials. "Signora Rizzo, this is a sensitive matter of national security, I was being polite when I asked. Let us see your register of guests, per favore. Adesso." *Now.*

Marie glared at Serreti for several seconds not moving. Then she left the sitting room. She returned less than a minute later and handed Serreti a piece of paper.

"You only have eight guests?" Serreti said. "I find that hard to believe."

"Believe what you want," Marie replied hotly. "We have had no more than ten registered guests for several years. We are not accepting any new residents. When these guests die, this facility will be converted into a bed and breakfast type hotel. We already offer meals to paying patrons in the cafe next door."

"That's it, then." Serreti stood and handed the paper back

to Marie. He rolled his eyes at Francesca and Jake. "You have wasted my time chasing these ridiculous leads. I insist we return to Rome immediately." He stormed out of the room.

Francesca put out her hand toward the paper in Marie's hand. "Per favore."

Francesca examined it, shook her head, and passed it to Jake. He scanned the names. Eight men. No Luzato. A dead end.

He handed the paper to Marie. "Thank you for your time. I'm sorry we bothered you."

"Is okay," Marie said.

Serreti and Francesca were already waiting in Campo del Ghetto Nuovo when Jake was about to leave the building. Walking across the square in front of him was a man dressed in the Jewish religious attire. *Shit.* A thought occurred to him and he didn't know why he hadn't thought of it earlier. He pulled out his phone and thumbed through the pictures he'd taken from the dead man's apartment in Vienna. He opened the picture of the man who had visited Casa Israelitica Di Riposo. Using his thumb and forefinger, he zoomed in on the face and held it up for Marie to see. "Do you recognize this man?"

Marie's face took on a sad look. "Si. This is Daniel."

"Daniel Luzato?"

"No. Daniel Manzone. Ricardo Manzone, his grandfather has been here many years."

"Really?" Jake felt energized he was right all along. "Please, Marie, it is urgent I speak with Ricardo Manzone immediately. This concerns his grandson."

Marie momentarily lowered her head then looked him in the eyes. "I'm sorry, signore. Ricardo Manzone died two nights ago."

CHAPTER 24

When he awoke, he knew his food last night had been tainted. He had slept too soundly and for too long for there to be any other explanation. So, why would Germano do that? He wasn't a threat, the collar ensured that would not happen. When Germano returned to the chamber, he would ask.

Then he felt it.

During the night, a metal cuff had been secured around his ankle. His eyes followed the four-foot chain to the floor where it was secured to a ring.

The lock clanked and the heavy rustic door swung open. Germano brought in a tray of food and juice and set it on the table. The leg chain was barely long enough to allow Luzato to sit in the chair at the table, even then it was awkward as he had to sit sideways with his foot pulled behind him.

"Is this drugged too?"

Germano stared at him and said, "Last night, it was necessary. I am sorry. This food is safe."

Luzato was about to speak, but never got a chance as a man walked in the chamber and toward the table. He recognized the man immediately. He had salt and pepper hair and a full beard that matched. All well-groomed. Thick black eyebrows exaggerated his deep-set brown eyes. Now, he fully understood his fate.

The man walked to the opposite side of the table. He

grabbed a chair and turned it backward. He sat sideways in the chair and propped his left arm on the seat back. He was dressed casual, a long-sleeved gray shirt beneath a lightweight khaki jacket. On his left hand, he wore a gold ring with a large red stone. In his other hand, he held a string of beads. The man gave him a blank look and moved the beads between his thumb and forefinger. He said nothing.

"Go ahead and eat," Germano said impatiently. "You will talk afterwards."

Luzato pushed the tray away. "I am not hungry."

The man's eyes narrowed becoming cold and hard. His piercing stare felt lethal. He turned to Germano and said in Italian, "When he is hungry, he will eat."

Germano nodded. Actually, it was more like a slight bow than a nod. A sign of respect or, more likely, fear.

Without changing his expression, the man spoke to Luzato in English. "Do you know who I am?"

"I do. Qasem Kazemi. Former general of the Iranian Revolutionary Guard."

"Very good," the man replied. "But now, I am called Omar. Does that name mean anything to you?"

Luzato knew the name from the dark web. "I am familiar with an Omar who is leader of Tarh Andishan. A man sworn to destroy Israel and the West."

"And you are the hacker known as *The Jew.*" Omar stopped threading the beads through his fingers and leaned forward. "Do you know what I want from you?"

"Yes."

"And you know I will go to whatever measures necessary to acquire this information."

"I am aware of your reputation."

"And this frightens you, yes?"

Luzato thought about the question for a few seconds and then answered, "I have accepted my destiny and what I must do. Believe it or not, Omar, no, I am not afraid of you."

"Perhaps you should be persuaded to reconsider your position." Omar began threading the beads between his fingers again. "We both know I will get those decryption codes. It is up to you to choose how much pain you will endure before you hand them over."

Omar raised his finger and Luzato felt a slight trickle of electricity tingle his skin under the collar.

"How do you like my invention?" Omar tapped his neck to indicate the collar. "An ingenious apparatus for control, don't you think?"

"Is that why you built it, control?"

Omar made a small circle in the air with his finger and the collar sent a stronger jolt to his neck.

"Or punishment," Omar said. "Again, it is up to you which one it shall be."

Omar lowered his hand and the collar stopped. "Germano said you were a compliant Jew. Perhaps he misjudged you."

"Compliant? Or smart enough to postpone my inevitable death? You should know, I have warned the American CEOs. By now, they have taken precautions to thwart any attempts to regain control of their servers."

Omar stood. "And you should know, because of your emails, I have had both Americans executed and their bodies served up as a statement to the United States government. Because of you, my insider's identity has been compromised and he is on the run from the authorities."

Omar raised two fingers and the collar delivered a painful

course of electricity. Luzato's body began to twitch. His blood pressure rose and he felt like his eyes were going to bulge from their sockets. His leg jerked against the restraining chain. Omar raised three fingers. Luzato bounced in uncontrollable spasms in his chair until he tumbled to the floor.

Omar stood over him and spit on his face. "You have caused me a lot of trouble, Jew. A man can only stand so much pain before he breaks. You, too, have a breaking point. Let me warn you now, I am not a patient man. You *will* give me the decryption codes." Omar lowered his hand and the collar stopped.

Luzato lay still on the floor. He felt the pain in his leg where the shackles ripped his skin during the convulsions. His neck seared. The after effects from the uncontrollable spasms sent sharp stabbing pains down his back to his legs. He searched Omar's face. The ruthless former general of the Iranian Revolutionary Guard hovered over him with a smile dangled on the corner of his lips. He had read the accounts of the sadistic manner in which he maimed and killed. And how he laughed at their pain and suffering.

He knew his suffering was only beginning, because he had to take some of his secrets to his grave. The Western world could not be held captive by this monster.

He mustered enough strength to speak three words.

"Kiss my ass."

Omar's eyes turned darker and he raised his fist.

Everything went black.

CHAPTER 25

"What?" Jake did not want to accept what the woman just told him.

Marie repeated herself, "Ricardo Manzone passed away two nights ago."

"No. How did—" A second ago he felt vindicated and excited that he was on the verge of a breakthrough in the mission. Now, his hopes had evaporated. He could see Francesca and Serreti as they walked toward the middle of the square. They appeared to be whispering. He turned back to Marie. "I'm sorry. It's just…"

"It is okay, signore. He died peacefully in his sleep. He had not been well for years."

"How old was he?"

"Ricardo turned ninety-three last week. That was the last time Daniel was here. We have tried to contact him about his grandfather, but have been unsuccessful. Maybe you know how, si?"

"I'm afraid not," he replied. "In fact, I was hoping Mr. Manzone could help me find Daniel." And now he might never know how or where to find Luzato. "Is there any chance I could see Mr. Manzone's room?"

"It has already been cleaned and all of Ricardo's belongings have been stored away in boxes. Daniel can get the boxes next time he comes to Venezia. Ricardo's wish was to be returned to his birthplace where he would be buried next to his parents."

"And where would that be?"

"Hallstatt, Austria."

"Austria? That is a little surprising."

"In the early 1900s, Austria, as with Germany, was not a good place for a Jewish family to live," she explained, "so when Ricardo was a child, his parents fled Hallstatt to Venice. He lived outside this square for many decades before moving into Casa Israelitica Di Riposo. Both of his parents died the same year, just one month apart, and their bones were the last ones placed in the Hallstatt Charnel House."

"Their bones?"

"Si. Their bodies were buried for fifteen years. Next, their skulls and large bones were removed, cleaned, and bleached by the sun and moon and then placed in the Charnel House. Ricardo had roses painted on their skulls, the symbol of love, a tradition started in the early 1700s. At the time of his parents' deaths, Ricardo made a personal testament to be placed next to them in the Charnel House. There is a picture in Ricardo's belongings of his parents' final resting place. Would you care to see it?"

"Yes, I would. Thank you for asking."

Jake glanced back into the square and saw Francesca and Serreti sitting on a bench in front of the Holocaust memorial wall. That troubling feeling returned.

Marie tapped him on the shoulder. "This way, signore."

He followed Marie into a storeroom behind the office. There were several boxes labeled with last names. "I guess you don't throw any of these away?"

"The policy of Casa Israelitica Di Riposo is to keep personal belongings for two years. If they have not been claimed by that time, we donate what we can and discard the rest." She bent down and picked up a large box from the floor. "This is what is left of Ricardo Manzone's belongings."

"What to do mean *what's left*"

"Some items were to be buried with him. They have been placed with his body."

"What types of items?"

She seemed reluctant to tell him.

Finally, she said, "Mostly religious items specific to the Jewish faith. And a necklace Daniel gave him last week for his birthday. Ricardo loved his grandson and the necklace meant a great deal to him. It was the only gift Daniel had ever given him."

"What type of necklace would a grandson give his aged grandfather?"

"It was a sterling silver and gold Star of David on a long gold chain. Daniel brought it back with him from a recent trip to Israel. It was, uh, what is the word, bulky, but Ricardo treasured it. He was clutching it when he died."

She opened the box and pulled out a photo of Hallstatt Charnel House. It was as she described, only a little more morbid. She pointed to two skulls in the foreground of a sea of skulls and bones. These two belong to his parents.

Jake scrutinized the box and pointed. "May I?"

"It is against our policy, but, this once I guess it will be okay."

"Grazie." Jake rifled through the box containing Manzone's belongings. The usual things were inside, he guessed. A watch, wallet, lots of pill bottles, toiletries, shoes, clothes, and a few books. It seemed Ricardo Manzone was quite the fan of thriller novels. Although the titles were in Italian, the authors' names were quite familiar, including some of his favorite authors.

"I figured I might find something to lead me to Daniel, but I see nothing at all. No address book or anything." He studied her as he held his charming smile. "Do you have Daniel's address on file?"

"I'm sorry, signore. All I have is his email address and phone number."

"Do you mind if I get those from you before I leave?"

"Not at all. I'll write them down for you now." She walked over to a large black file cabinet and opened the top drawer. She pulled out a folder and wrote down the information on an index card.

He put his hand on the small woman's shoulder. "What about Mr. Manzone's body? Is it still here?"

"No, signore, he is already on the way to Austria. The, uh," she fumbled with her hands and with a frustrated expression said, "the becchino took him away yesterday."

"Becchino?"

"Undertaker." The voice behind him belonged to Marco Serreti.

And standing next to him, Francesca.

"Who died, Jake?" Francesca gave him a disapproving look. "Did you find something and not tell us?"

Her attitude, coupled with his increasing wariness concerning her loyalty, pushed the limits of his patience. "First of all, you two are the ones who wandered off while I was still talking with Ms. Rizzo. If you weren't so eager to call this a dead end, you could have gotten this information first hand."

Jake gave Francesca and Serreti a censored version of what he had learned using a little selective omission due to his ever increasing distrust for Marco Serreti. And in a sense, Francesca.

"So, it is a dead end after all," Serreti said with an air of sarcasm.

"We don't know that yet. I'll have Fontaine do a search on Daniel Manzone as well as Ricardo Manzone." Jake paused, "Perhaps, Marco, you should have AISE do the same. Unless you think that would be too much trouble." It was his chance to return the sarcasm.

"Enough," Francesca commanded. "This is embarrassing." Marie's shocked face told him why Francesca had interrupted their banter.

"Marie, thank you for your time," Jake said apologetically. "I hope we didn't disrupt your routine too much."

"Non c'é problema." She patted him on the shoulder.

This time, Jake didn't need a translation.

††††

"What the hell is wrong with you two?" Francesca barked as the three of them walked out of earshot of Casa Israelitica Di Riposo. "Marco, enough of this pissing contest to see who was the better partner? I left AISE years ago and I have no intention of ever returning. So get over it."

They stopped in the middle of Campo del Ghetto Nuovo. Marco looked like he was about to reply to her when his cell phone dinged.

Marco glanced at the text message. "I must return to Roma at once," he said. "There has been a catastrophic computer failure at the main office of one of Italy's largest banking institutions. It shut down their main bank as well as their entire chain of branches." Marco paused as he looked at this watch. "Are we finished in Venezia?"

"You are," she said. "Jake and I will remain here for a few hours. Have our jet drop you in Rome and return for us. We'll be ready by then."

"That will not be necessary," he said. "AISE has sent a jet for me. It will be here in less than an hour. He looked in the direction of Calle Ghetto Vecchio where the water taxi had dropped them off earlier. "I must go now."

He left and headed toward the water taxi without saying another word.

She took Jake's arm. "Come on, partner. I want to show you Venezia."

"Don't you think we should go back to Rome, too? We still haven't had an opportunity to search Luzato's apartment for clues."

"There are no clues left to find, Jake. AISE will have stripped it clean by now. It will be a waste of our time, I'm sure."

"I thought Director Barzetti agreed this would be a joint effort."

"He did."

"And?"

"And it is the nature of Italians to take credit for any arrests without the help of outsiders. *We* are outsiders."

"What if there was a clue that could lead us to Luzato?"

"Then Marco promised he would read us in," she said. "In the meantime, let me show you some sights in Venice."

"Deputy director or not, I don't trust Marco Serreti. And neither should you." He spun her around by the arm. "He's a jackass. What's the deal between you and him anyway? You two have been whispering and keeping secrets. I'm not sure I can trust you, Francesca. Time to come clean or I'm going to recommend Wiley remove you from this mission."

Jake's tone startled her more than his words. Like a parent chastising an insolent child. He had never spoken to her like that before. She had been a little abrupt with him when they first met in San Sebastian, Spain, but that was several years ago—before they were partners. That was also Jake's test run for Wiley. His first mission, from which he came through with flying colors. He saved Elmore Wiley from an explosion and his granddaughter, Kyli Wullenweber, from the hands of an Irish madman. He actually had saved Kyli twice during his test run, which was probably why the old man hired him. The first time was in France as she and a friend were in the wrong place at the wrong time while terrorists detonated simultaneous bombs at the Louvre and the Eiffel Tower. The second time was on the Greek island of Ios.

"Francesca," Jake growled. "Are you listening?" He held up his phone. "Talk to me now or I'm calling it in."

"All right, all right. But, I'm ashamed and embarrassed."

"Ashamed and embarrassed? You?"

"Yes, me." She led him to a bench in the middle of the square. "Let's sit down and I'll explain, under one condition."

"What's that?"

"This stays between you and me and you never bring it up again."

He reeled back. "I guess it depends on what this big secret is. If it will interfere with you doing your job, no, I can't make that promise."

She hated talking about it, but it was only fair to Jake, so he might understand. She had always been able to share personal feelings with Jake in the past. But, this was different. This was where she felt most vulnerable.

"It has nothing to do with doing my job or not doing my

job. It's personal."

He was silent for several uncomfortable seconds, as if he was processing what she had said, or more than likely, knowing Jake as she did, trying to figure out what it was without her saying anything.

"You're in love with him," he finally said. "With Marco."

She lowered her head and took a deep breath. "Not in love, Jake. This might be hard for you to understand since you're a man." She blew out a breath. "Marco is my weak spot, my Achilles heel. He always has been. He's arrogant and a jerk, but when he comes on to me, I cannot resist. I'm weak. I've tried resisting my urges to be with him...at his beck and call, but I cannot. It's not just a physical attraction. It is more how he makes me feel when he is making love to me."

"So, it's more than his handsome Italian body?" Jake grinned.

"I knew you wouldn't get it, Jake. It's more than that, much more. I don't love him, and I would never sell you or Wiley out, certainly not for him. American women would call him a bad boy. Most Italian men are. But Marco knows he can have me anytime, at a moment's notice. He calls, I run to him. And afterwards, I hate him for it." She paused and said, "Until the next time."

"Lust," he said.

"Typical male. Not lust, much, much more. It's like wanting something you know is bad for you. The only way I found to stop it, stop me, was to leave Italy. When he showed up at my father's funeral of all places, I knew what was going to happen. It was inevitable. Even my father's death and my mother's constant grieving couldn't stop me. That's why I feel ashamed and embarrassed. It's worse than an addiction...or maybe that's what it really is, an addiction. But, to a person rather than a chemical."

"Then it's not really about sex, is it?"

"Oh my God." She stood and threw up her hands. "I knew I shouldn't have said anything to you. You'll never get it. Your single-minded male brain will never get it. Yes, Jake. It is very much about sex and so much more."

CHAPTER 26

Single-minded male brain?

What the hell was wrong with her? Or perhaps that was it. Perhaps males don't get it. Finally, she did open up. And what she said helped alleviate a lot of his concerns about her loyalty. Loyalty to Wiley. Loyalty to the mission. Loyalty to him. Then again, the deputy director was a distraction she did not need. One he didn't need her to have either. Not during this mission. He needed her to stay focused and that meant keeping her away from Marco Serreti.

How he was going to do that, he had no idea. At least not at the moment.

"Come on," she said as she waved him to follow. "Let me show you some of Venice."

The wind picked up and there was a slight chill in the air. The pilot was right; it did feel like rain. He zipped up his jacket and hurried to catch up to his partner who was already halfway out of the square.

She explained to him that Venice had main walking streets and numerous side streets. She said if someone unfamiliar needed to get anywhere in Venice, it was best not to use a map, but rather follow the signs to the area you wanted to go. They started walking toward St. Mark's so they followed the San Marco signs. It didn't matter, he was lost and confused from the get-go.

"The best way to learn your way around Venezia," she said, "is to walk and get lost. Sooner or later, you'll get where you are going."

"Glad I have a guide, because I'm lost."

"People either hate it or love it. There doesn't seem to be an in-between. There is a lot of history here. And a lot of tourists and romance. There is also a lot of crime."

"Crime, what kind of crime?"

"Nothing violent to speak of, petty thefts, pick pockets, that sort of thing. Especially where there are big crowds like St. Mark's Square and the train station. Gypsies, we call them. There are quite a few in Rome, too."

"Again, glad I have you with me."

"You know, Jake, there is someone who has the same problem with you that I have with Marco. With a few exceptions, of course."

"If you're talking about Kyli, you're wrong. Yesterday she made it abundantly clear that was not the case."

"You know I'm referring to Kyli. Why do you think she stayed in the bedroom on the flight over the Atlantic? She knew if she let you in, or even saw you for that matter, she would go weak in the knees, so to speak, and give in. One big difference between Kyli and me is that she is in love with you. And not a little bit, either. Madly in love."

"She told you this? I thought you said you two didn't talk about it. Last night in Vienna, you said you hadn't talked to her. You said you didn't want to be stuck in the middle. Was that all a lie?"

"Not really."

"Not really? Either it is or it isn't."

"Kyli knows my first allegiance is to my partner. That's you,

Jake. But we still talked. Or rather, she talked, I listened."

"That's not what you said last night, Francesca."

"Okay, I whitewashed it a little. The truth is I love you both. A lot. With Kyli, it was nothing but girl talk anyway. And you... you're like the quirky brother I never had. You are my family."

"Quirky?"

"Maybe quirky isn't the right word. More like goofy."

"Thanks. Goofy makes me sound so much cooler. Does Kyli know about Marco?"

"I told her about him, yes."

"You tell her about all the stuff you told me?"

"Not with the same amount of detail or intimacy, no. But she knows I have a hard time saying no to him. Just like she has a hard time saying no to you."

"It's not the same."

"No, it isn't. There are big differences. Like I said, I don't love Marco. She loves you. Marco is a jerk who knows he can have any woman he wants any time he wants. When it comes to women, Jake, you're the epitome of the good guy. Don't get me wrong, you can be ruthless as hell in the field, downright scary at times, but inside," she patted him on the chest, "you are faithful to the woman you love."

"Does Wiley think that?"

"If he thought any different, he wouldn't allow you and Kyli to ever see each other. He'd fire you before he'd let you hurt his granddaughter."

Earlier she had pointed out the famous Rialto bridge and took him to the top so he could recognize the main canal from the movies. Now, where ever they were, he had no clue.

"Could we change the subject for a while?" He took a deep breath and smelled the sweet aroma of Italian food. "Let's eat,

I'm starving."

"You're always starving, Jake. As much as you eat, you should be fifty pounds heavier."

"It's my high metabolism, I'm telling you."

She pointed toward the corner ahead. "Turn left and there is a great place to eat down the side street."

He followed her to the ristorante where she spoke to the waiter in Italian. After a brief exchange, the waiter walked off and returned with a bottle of wine and two glasses of water.

"After we eat," she said, "we'll walk to Hotel dell'Opera. A friend of mine works there, he will order us a water taxi to take us to the airport." She glanced at her phone. "It's 1:00 now so how about we have the taxi pick us up at San Marco at, say, 4:00? That gives us time to eat and stroll through St. Mark's Square."

"You're the tour guide, I'm at your disposal."

†††

At the Hotel dell'Opera, her friend was working, and ecstatic to see her again. After a few minutes of visiting, she asked him to make arrangements for the water taxi at St. Mark's Square. It took less than five minutes to make the stroll and she watched Jake's face as the square opened up in front of him.

"Piazza San Marco," she said. "And over there, is Basilica di San Marco. St. Mark's Basilica. It's named after the Mark who authored one of the four gospels in the Bible. The original church burned down in the year 976 AD. Construction on this structure started in 1063 AD. Would you like to go ins—?"

Her question was interrupted by a woman screaming beneath the Campanile at a man running away, a purse, presumable hers, clutched under his arm.

Without a word, she and Jake bolted in different directions. She ran after the man with the purse while Jake angled across Piazza San Marco. The man was wearing men's capri-length jeans, a black jacket, and athletic shoes. Dark locks of hair protruded beneath his black baseball cap. He was fast, but not as fast as her and she slowly reduced their distance. He ran across the Piazzetta toward Grand Canal and St. Mark's Basin. She knew she could cut the distance between them when the man turned at the waterfront, allowing her to angle across the Piazzetta. He turned right and ran west on Riva degli Schiavoni, which paralleled the Grand Canal. She ran by vendors at stations, some with umbrellas, selling trinkets and other worthless tourist junk. Most of the vendors appeared to be the dark-skinned gypsies she had warned Jake about earlier.

Tied to the docks on the left were boats of every size and shape. She slowly closed the distance. The man crossed a footbridge and turned right on Calle Vallaresso. She closed the margin even more when the man slowed to make the turn. She rounded the turn at full speed and nearly wiped out two pedestrians. The man was no more than thirty feet in front of her and she knew he had to turn left at the t-road ahead. Left or right, but right put him headed back toward Piazza San Marco. He didn't dare return to the square. The store front facade and the end of the street said *Omega*.

But the man never made it that far.

As he reached the corner, another man stepped out and planted a fist in the thief's face, knocking him to the ground. It was Jake. Her partner had somehow cut the thief off.

Jake rolled the man to his stomach and got on top of him, burying his knee in the thief's back. As he did, both his and her cell phones beeped signaling an incoming text messages.

"Get that for me, would you?" he said. "I have my hands full at the moment."

She pulled out her phone and read the message. Her heart sank.

"No. Oh God, no. Shit." She let her hands fall to her side. "Jake, let him go."

"What? No way. We'll take him to the cops in St. Mark's Square."

"Jake," she repeated adding more urgency in her voice. "Release him. We have to leave immediately."

He raised his head and gave her a dumbfounded look. "What the hell are you talking about?"

"The lab in Leuven just blew up." She hated to read the rest of the message.

"What? What is it?"

"Jake, I'm sorry. Kyli was inside."

CHAPTER 27

Milan, Italy

The Korean was escorted through several layers of security before he was allowed access to the office of the deputy director. At each checkpoint, he was subjected to a full body scan and a hand pat. His briefcase, although never opened, received an even more exhaustive examination—x-rays, sniffers, scanners—all to ensure the safety and protection of the deputy director.

He'd never been in Italy before today, but the safe transport of the items stolen from the Belgium lab, MEtech, required his personal handling. His employer had been specific about his instructions, making transportation readily available once the Korean reached Amsterdam. Getting to Amsterdam was his problem. Arrive at the Hotel Seven Bridges in Amsterdam, his only instructions. No time. No date. No contact.

The break-in at MEtech was successful; every detail of the mission went as planned. He had been instructed with precise details and was certain the deputy director would be pleased.

The Korean gazed at the skyline of Milan and the midday view was breathtaking. The peaceful city below deceived his naked eye. It was an epicenter of turmoil.

The door behind him opened, interrupting his thoughts, and the deputy director entered the room with two armed bodyguards. He motioned for the Korean to sit on the leather sofa.

The deputy director asked, "May I offer you something to drink?"

The Korean nodded.

"I trust you encountered no difficulties."

"No problems." The Korean's leg bounced. He wanted to get his money and get out of there. This man made him nervous. "Everything went exactly as planned. The entire operation took less than ten minutes."

"I am most pleased." The deputy director nodded and one of the bodyguards placed a small leather briefcase on the coffee table in front of the Korean and opened it. He waved his hand over the neatly stacked and wrapped hundred Euro bills. "Two million Euro. As agreed."

The deputy director pointed to the case in the Korean's lap. "May I?"

"Certainly." The Korean handed the case to the man. "It belongs to you now, anyway."

He placed the case on his desk, then dug into his front pocket and pulled out a small key. After unlocking the case he raised the lid. He removed the lone folder and reviewed its contents.

"Very good." He motioned toward the money case. "You may count it if you'd like."

"I trust you." The Korean closed the briefcase, a bead of sweat rolled down his forehead.

"It is not wise to be so trusting in our line of work."

The deputy director continued reading. "Everything appears in order here. I have a car downstairs that will take us to the airport."

"Us?" the Korean said as he stood. "You're going with me?"

"Yes," he said, "I want to ensure you leave this country safely. But most of all, I want to make sure you leave. Your presence here poses a threat to me."

"I understand." The Korean cradled the briefcase of money in his arms. "I am ready."

The deputy director led them to a private elevator inside his office. "This will take us to my secure parking garage." The four men entered the elevator with them.

Moments later he knew something was wrong. The elevator stopped and the door opened. It was not a parking garage. The Korean's stomach churned. "What's going on?"

One of the bodyguards grabbed the briefcase filled with money. "You won't be needing this."

The other bodyguard drew a gun and waved the barrel, "Move."

Another man behind, shoved him out of the elevator.

He stumbled into a strange room. All concrete with a drain in the middle. Meat hooks hung from the ceiling. It resembled a slaughterhouse.

Finally, he understood.

"But we had a deal," the Korean begged. "I did my part. You have the package. I planted the devices exactly as you requested."

Deputy Director Marco Serreti edged closer. "Like I said, it is unwise to be so trusting in our line of work."

CHAPTER 28

Jake could not comprehend the words he had just heard. He didn't understand, he felt sluggish and dazed.

"What are you saying, Francesca?" It was sinking in too fast. "Is … is Kyli de …is Kyli dead?"

"They don't know, Jake. All the message says is Kyli was inside the lab at the time of the explosion and they haven't located her yet."

Jake slowly got up off of the thief. The man stood to his feet talking in Italian.

"Silenzio," she yelled. And proceeded to kick him in the groin. The man doubled over and fell to the ground. "That'll keep him until the polizia arrive. Now, let's go."

Onlookers swarmed around to gawk and many were already on their phones. The voices sounded distant to Jake. He struggled to focus.

He followed Francesca to the waterfront, which was back down Calle Vallaresso to Riva degli Schiavoni where there was a public transportation depot.

"Wait here and I'll go get us a boat."

He pointed to a garbage can next to a light pole. "I'll be right there by the rail."

She disappeared in the crowd surrounding the depot. His stomach was in knots and he felt his pulse pound against his temples.

Ten minutes later, as he was getting restless at how long she had been gone, she returned. "I secured us a fast ride." She clutched his arm. "This way, he's waiting."

The ride was indeed fast. The boat barely cleared the docks when the driver slammed the throttle to the max and the boat surged forward. Several gondola drivers yelled in Italian and shook their angry fists as their passengers were rocked by the boat's wake. "He said he could get in a lot of trouble for going this fast. Big fines. I gave him enough to cover it."

"Good thinking, Francesca. I called George while you were getting the boat, he didn't know anything new."

"Of course not, Jake. It had only been fifteen minutes since he sent the text."

"He did say the old man was on his way to the airport. Yesterday, his El Paso factory was vandalized and today his Belgium lab blows up. Something is going on and we need to find out what it is."

"Jake?"

"Yeah."

"Aren't you worried about Kyli? Because if you are, you have a funny way of showing it."

"Francesca, of course I'm worried. All my mind can do is playback the explosion in France. There were bodies and body parts everywhere. I wasn't sure I'd find her in all the chaos. And when I finally did, she was a bloody mess. I wasn't sure if she would live or die. There was so much blood. Normally it wouldn't bother me, but—"

"It was Kyli. That's totally understandable. That was the early days for you two, Jake. This is different now. You two have been together a long time."

"It's been a few years."

"Do you know how long, Jake? I mean exactly."

He did know exactly how long it had been since he and Kyli met. He knew how long it had been since they were first intimate. He knew how long since the explosion, since he rescued her from the Irishman. He remembered everything.

"You do know, don't you? Exactly?"

He nodded.

"It has been three and a half years since you met. Am I close?"

"Close enough. What? Are you keeping track or something?"

"I know how long I've known you, Jake. When we first met. And that time frame is almost the same."

"Three and a half years." Jake muttered.

It didn't seem that long ago to him. Now, he understood why Kyli struggled with their relationship. She knew his missions were dangerous. And never knowing if he would come back alive, mission after mission, was too much. The fear and anxiety Kyli must have felt. Right now, he was so scared he would never see her again. He should have kissed her the last time they saw each other. He might never get to kiss her again. How could he survive losing another woman he loved? If she did survive, maybe he should quit.

"Jake, where are you? You look lost in your thoughts. Are you okay?"

"Yeah." But he wasn't.

The boat pulled into the airport docks and he followed Francesca down the long walk to the airport and eventually out to the waiting Citation. Within minutes of arriving at the aircraft, they were taxiing. A few minutes later, they were in the air and on their way to Brussels, Belgium.

†††

The Brussels airport had only been reopened for a week since a three-day lockdown, due to a Level 4 terrorist alert issued by the Belgian Interior Ministry. The alert shut down all subway lines, airports, and train stations. All concerts and sporting events had been cancelled or postponed. This followed recent terrorist attacks in Paris. The intel Belgian officials based their actions upon seemed reliable to them at the time. However, it seemed Brussels wasn't the target after all, but rather MEtech, Wiley's top secret research lab in Leuven, which was a short twenty-five kilometers from downtown Brussels.

As the Citation started its descent into Brussels, one of the pilots buzzed the cabin phone. "I'm patching Mr. Wiley through to the SatCom speaker phone. He has instructions for the two of you."

Jake looked across the table at Francesca. She nodded. "Tell Mr. Wiley we're ready when he is."

"Roger that."

Moments later the speaker phone buzzed. Francesca reached down and pressed the *Connect* button. "Jake and I are on the line," she leaned toward the device.

"Good," the voice on the other end said.

It was Wiley, but his voice sounded strained. "Max will meet you at the hangar and take you directly to the lab. When you get there, I need you to assess the situation and report back to me immediately."

"Any word on Kyli?" Jake could hear the tension in his own voice.

"Still unaccounted for."

"What about the other employees? Any reports on them

yet?"

"Everyone on the first floor apparently got out unscathed. The explosions were on floors above them. The last report was three confirmed dead, five injured, and two unaccounted for... Kyli being one of them." His voice cracked.

"Kyli is a resourceful woman," Francesca said, "I'm sure she will be okay, sir."

He knew she was only trying to ease the old man's mind, but Wiley might think she was patronizing him. Never one for sugar-coating any situation, even a personal one. And usually the first to call a spade a spade.

"I'm aware of the severity of the situation, Francesca," Wiley said. "Thank you for your positive comments, but nothing is really going to help until I get word on my granddaughter... one way or another."

"We understand," Jake said. "As soon as we get to the lab, I'll check in with you."

"Thanks, Jake. You too, Francesca. I don't know what I'd do without you two."

Jake and Francesca exchanged looks, both slightly stunned by the old man's comment. It was totally unlike Wiley to ever show his vulnerable side.

The conversation ended when the cabin door opened and the pilot signaled to Jake he needed to end the conversation with Wiley by sweeping his hand across his throat.

Max and his limo were waiting at Wiley's hangar as the Citation pulled to a stop. The first officer lowered the air-stair door and Jake and Francesca moved quickly to the limo with their backpacks slung over their shoulders.

Less than thirty minutes later, the limo pulled as close to

MEtech Labs as the authorities would allow. Even with all the emergency response vehicles moving in and out of the area, Wiley's connections with local authorities still put them in a small parking lot across Remy Lane from the main Campus Remy entrance. The term *campus* always seemed confusing to him since he only associated the term with an educational institution, but in this case, it was their way of describing a business park located at the old Remy manufacturing plant where Remy made flour from grain. Several years ago, when the low-cost opportunity presented itself, Wiley built his secure laboratory in the Campus Remy business park. It was a brick building located behind the old Remy flour mill. Now it was a smoking, smoldering husk of a building.

When he and Francesca approached the hot, smoldering building, it appeared the blast blew out most of the windows of the five-level lab. Jake had learned from prior experience not to use the terms floor or story in Europe when referring to buildings' levels. In the United States, *the first floor* was the bottom level, but in most European countries, the first floor was actually the first level above the *ground floor*.

Broken glass littered the perimeter of the building. MEtech was originally built as a high-tech electronics company providing a European base servicing the aerospace sector in Europe. At that time, MEtech worked closely with IMEC, also located in Leuven. As demand for Wiley's technology grew in the United States, so did the need to expand his off-the-books black-budget operations overseas. Seeing the future need of the U. S. Government's covert warfare against threats to the Homeland, Wiley brought in his granddaughter to add a new segment to MEtech: biological warfare research and development. As Kyli once explained to him, it wasn't necessarily the need to create biological weapons, so much as to learn how to defend against them.

Several MEtech employees whom he recognized were standing or sitting in front of the statue of Edouard Remy located in the middle of Campus Remy. The statue of the seated industrialist was erected atop of a brick pedestal. Authorities used the cordoned off area surrounding the statue for personnel roundup and triage after the explosion.

He and Francesca hurried to the statue and checked on the status of the surviving employees. Some were wrapped in blankets. Others were in triage being treated by medics. Several of the women were crying. One of the uninjured security guards was swearing revenge on whoever planted the explosives.

When they saw Jake, they all went quiet for a few awkward seconds. He understood why. It was no secret at MEtech about his long-term love affair with Kyli. And they all knew Kyli well.

Finally, one woman spoke, "Jake, we're so sorry. You must be…" Then the woman broke down into tears.

While he and Francesca were talking with the MEtech employees, they were greeted by the officer in charge, Lars Peeters, who, Jake knew through prior dealings, spoke English reasonably well.

"Status update?" Jake asked, deadpan.

"The building seems still structurally sound, however the third and fourth floors are inaccessible. I have crews trying to clear the stairwells, but Mr. Wiley's security measures have hampered our efforts. Of course, the elevators are inoperable."

"Just so we're on the same page," Jake said looking for verification from Peeters, "you're saying the fourth and fifth levels of MEtech are inaccessible?"

"Correct," Peeters confirmed. "From now on we will use levels to avoid confusion."

"Good idea."

"I can open any of the locked doors," Francesca said.

"That's right," Jake said. "We know the security protocol bypasses for most of the systems and there are no locks she can't open."

"Great, we could use all the help we can get."

"I will go back to the car and grab my bag." She turned and ran off.

"What about the two unaccounted for? Any updates on them?"

Peeters' face hardened. "I'm sorry, there is only one unaccounted for now. We found a body on the second level about ten minutes ago.

"Who is unaccounted for at this time?" Jake's heart was racing as he tried to remain calm.

"Kyli is the only person we haven't located."

Jake released a big sigh of relief. "You think she's on the fourth level?"

"If she is, she is running out of time," Peeters said. "According to Mr. Wiley's specifications, that level has self-containment protocols and is sealed off in the event of such an event. Anyone still on that level is running out of oxygen fast."

CHAPTER 29

The smell of burnt flesh lingered in his nostrils. His own flesh. The scent nauseating, sweet, and putrid. Now, every sinew in his body ached from convulsing violently during the electrocution like being bludgeoned with a wooden bat. Even his toes were sore.

The distant murmur of whispers grew clearer until he could understand the words.

"I told you the setting was too high," one man argued. "We're lucky it didn't kill him."

"When can I talk to him again?" the other man commanded.

"It will be hours before he has recovered enough to answer your questions. Perhaps by morning."

"By morning?" The voice sounded angry. "I don't have that long. We don't have that long. I need those codes."

"If you try to talk to him any sooner, you'll be wasting your time."

"What about a truth serum?"

"Those don't work except on the weakest of minds. You need clarity and pain to extract the information you want."

"Very well," the angry man said. "Inform me when he regains consciousness."

Footsteps pounded across the stone floor. A heavy door slammed.

A hand grasped Luzato's wrist, feeling for a pulse.

Luzato was on his back, warmth encompassed his naked body like a cocoon. Blankets, he thought, but warmer. Electric blankets. He blinked his eyes, bright glowing lights slammed them shut. Heat lamps. He tried to focus through the cloud in his brain. Trying to let his mind run a diagnostic on his body. It wasn't easy and he barely mustered the strength to complete the process. The collar had been removed. A warm hand was rubbing some sort of ointment on his neck. It felt thick and slimy. And cool. He tried to move, but to no avail. Was he paralyzed? No. He felt his extremities. Something was holding him down. He focused on the restraints. Gradually he felt them. Ankle cuffs. Wrist cuffs. Some sort of bar across his chest and another across his thighs. In his left arm, he felt what had to be an IV.

Then he felt the warmth of a body next to his ear. "Daniel," the familiar voice whispered. "It's Germano. Do not open your eyes or try to move or he will know you are awake. You need rest." Germano paused and said, "Mi dispiace. Ho cercato di fermarlo." *I am sorry, I tried to stop him.*

"Where are my clothes?" Luzato whispered, trying not to move his lips.

Germano quietly chuckled in Luzato's ear. "The jolt was so strong, it caused your body to flush its waste. As the Americans say, you pissed yourself and shit yourself. Your clothes are being cleaned. Now, try not to talk, just rest. I will delay his return as long as possible."

"Germano," he said through clenched teeth, "don't let him put the collar back on me."

"If you give him what he wants, he will not hurt you again."

Luzato cracked open his eyes. Germano's eyes cut in his direction, then away as he inserted a hypodermic needle into his IV line.

"Daniel, it is time for you to sleep."

He watched Germano push the plunger and his world gently faded away.

†††

Even though it was early morning on the Eastern Colorado plains when Ethan Wogahn's cell phone rang, he had already been double and triple-checking the array alignment for the past two hours. In reality, his portion of the project was complete and had been for some time. All he had left to do was receive the software from Boris and prepare it for upload to the designated satellite.

But, Boris seemed to have gone dark.

Yesterday, he was supposed to receive the link to download the software from a private server, but the email never arrived. And the countdown was getting shorter.

He looked at the caller-id and his chest tightened. Omar. What could he want?

He pressed Answer. "Guardian."

"Ethan, there has been a delay," Omar used Wogahn's real name instead of the code name. Omar had been adamant about no one using anything other than coded names over unencrypted phone lines. If he broke his own rule, this couldn't be good. "We have not been able to retrieve the decryption codes or the stolen software yet."

"Those codes are only a portion of your plan."

"The software is the most important part to my plan. I need it in order to bring down my greatest enemy."

He thought about what Omar said for a moment. That was

true, taking down Omar's biggest enemy was indeed reliant on acquiring the software. Or rather, reacquiring the stolen software. His enemy's defenses depended on them.

"I understand. I am ready on my end. All I need is the package from Boris."

A short silence and then Omar spoke, "Boris should have delivered the package by now, Ethan."

"He is late. I have not heard from Boris in days."

"That is unfortunate. I know he had a couple of close calls in D.C., but I have been assured he successfully eluded his captors. For Boris' sake, I hope he has a good explanation for not delivering the package as planned."

"He has never failed to come through. I'm sure I will receive the package today."

"If you do not get it by sunset, inform me immediately."

"Yes, si—"

The line went dead.

A delay at this juncture could only mean one thing, someone would have to pay for their mistake.

And that usually meant death.

CHAPTER 30

The fourth level of MEtech contained the bio lab and was a self-contained level. Good in many respects, but bad in the event of a back-up power generator failure, which was the case now. A closet-sized room contained a bank of batteries that were supposed to power the bio lab, which might or might not be functional after an explosion. If functioning normally, Kyli would have backup power for several hours, which had been the case thus far, although now, time was of the essence. Not just for Kyli, but for the many biological agents that needed power to remain contained.

Peeters' radio filled with a voice in a language Jake didn't understand. Peeters responded to the radio and then spoke to Jake. "Looks like the stairwell is clear and we have access to the fourth level."

Francesca apparently heard the officer's radio as she returned from the car. "Great." She held up a small black bag. "Let's go unlock that door."

"Wait," Peeters said. "According to Mr. Wiley's specifications, under circumstances such as these, no access is to be attempted without biological hazard protection suits." He showed them a parked van. "We have only six suits."

Jake said, "We'll take two and have one of your men suit up with us."

"I will go with you myself," Peeters insisted.

Jake studied the man and figured it would be futile to protest. "Lars, I'm sure Mr. Wiley will be pleased you are handling this personally."

"First," Peeters said, "my men need to set up a negative pressure containment area around the door or we run the risk of contamination outside of the lab."

"How long will that take?" Jake asked. "Kyli is running out of time."

"We have all the necessary equipment on site now and are ready to install immediately. Give my men five or six minutes and we should be able to go in. It will take us a few minutes to suit up, anyway."

"Well then, what are we waiting on?" Francesca interrupted. "Let's get moving."

Peeters spoke into his radio and three of his men each picked up a black duffle bag and rushed into the building. Jake, Francesca, and Lars Peeters went to the nearby parked van and collected biological hazard suits, stepped inside them, and suited up. Next, they installed and sealed their headgear. Peeters ordered the checking and double checking of the seals to prevent the chance of accidental exposure. With oxygen tanks flowing, the three walked into the MEtech building.

When they arrived at the landing on the fourth level, Jake noticed Lars Peeters' men had erected a three meter by three-meter protective barrier around the entrance door using a thick mil plastic sheeting. Duct tape sealed the sheeting to the wall and together at the seams. Attached to one side was some sort of large fan he had never seen before. Peeters said it was used to provide negative pressure for the containment tent.

Francesca was the first to approach the door. "This is a good sign, the card reader and keypad lights are on," she said, "maybe we will get lucky." She inserted her secure access card into the slot and punched in her corresponding personalized secure access code.

The lock released and she pulled the door open. Jake heard and felt the pressure differential between the lab and the containment tent. Guess it was a good idea after all.

The door opened into another small glassed off area, roughly two meters by two meters. In front of them was another door, this one with a glass window allowing him to peer inside the expanse of roughly half of the bio lab. Kyli was nowhere in sight. A countdown clock on the far wall was counting down the time remaining before containment power was exhausted. Next to it, a flashing red light. As far as he knew, neither had ever been used before except for mock drills. With each pulse of the light, a warning buzzer sounded. Jake motioned to the timer, "Kyli only has six and half minutes of power left. Think this lock will be as easy?"

Francesca shook her head. "No. There's no power to this card reader or keypad, so I'll have to give it my magic touch." She dropped her bag on the floor in front of her and unzipped the top, reached in and laid out several tools. "Now's the time to wish me luck," she said.

She made several unsuccessful attempts. He surveyed the timer inside the lab. "Three and a half minutes, Francesca, we're running out of time."

"I know dammit, don't pressure me."

He could see beads of sweat on her forehead through the hood.

She stretched out her arms in what appeared to be an attempt to relax her hands.

He knew his partner was nervous, it was the only time he'd

ever seen her hands shake. He could think of only one way to calm her down. "It's okay, Francesca," he said. "If we don't get in there in time, Kyli dies, the containment field collapses, and Lars will have to evacuate the entire town. But, really, there's no hurry."

Her hands immediately relaxed and a few seconds later she turned toward him and glared. "Jake Pendleton." Still staring at him, she turned the lock picking tool with her wrist and opened the door. "You are a number one asshole."

He glanced at the wall, three minutes ten seconds on the timer clock.

He followed Francesca through the door. Two steps behind him was Lars Peeters.

"Let's spread out. Locating Kyli is the number one priority."

Peeters grabbed his arm. "What about the biological agents? Shouldn't we contain them first?"

Jake eyes scanned the lab. For some reason, the source of the explosion, or explosions, was not on this level. However, the lab had sustained substantial damage. Metal tables were overturned. Racks of metal shelves toppled. Broken glass littered the floor. "No. First, we need to make sure Kyli is safe. We need her to identify which agents to contain."

He peeked again at the countdown timer. Two minutes forty-five seconds.

Francesca tugged on his shoulder. "Jake," she said in a high pitched voice. She pointed to the far wall. "Over there."

He spotted Kyli limping toward them with a panicked expression. Her pant leg was blood stained.

He ran to her side, and clutched her by both shoulders. Through his hood he shouted, "Kyli, you're hurt. What happened to your leg?"

"Forget about my leg," she said with labored breathing. "We need to get power restored to the vault immediately. We're running out of time."

"What about the other agents?" Lars Peeters asked.

"After the explosion, I put everything in the vault and sealed the door."

Jake turned her head so she was facing him. "I thought Wiley was the only one who could get in the vault?"

"Jake, we're wasting time." She faced Peeters and said, "Can you get electric power up here?" She checked the timer again. "In less than two minutes?"

He snatched his radio and said something into it. Jake could hear his voice, but with the helmet on, he could not understand what the lawman said. Peeters leapt into action and disappeared out the door.

Kyli yelled at Peeters before he left, "A regular power cord plug will suffice. The containment field in the vault uses very little power."

Francesca put her hand on the arm of Kyli's lab coat. "How did you get in the vault?"

A question he wanted answered too.

"I have access to the vault," she said.

"Since when?" he asked.

"I've always had access. Wiley and I are the only ones allowed inside. He required my access be kept secret…even from you two. Safety precautions."

His heart hammered inside his chest, one minute fifteen seconds. *Shit.*

"What happens if power is lost to the vault?" Francesca bobbed up and down in her suit.

"Let's hope that doesn't happen?"

"What if, Kyli?"

"Then everything inside is lost."

"None of it can be saved?"

"What you don't know," Kyli's eyes were wild as her head went from the clock to Francesca then him and back to the clock. "What neither of you know is the vault has a self-destruct mechanism built inside. A precaution in the event of an incident such as this."

"What type of self-destruct mechanism?" he asked.

"If complete power is lost for more than sixty seconds, an incendiary device will activate, destroying everything inside. And along with it, MEtech is out of business and Wiley loses everything." She placed her hand on his suit. "One more thing, Wiley thinks the heat might destroy everything on levels three, four, and five of this building. And right now, that includes us."

He glanced again at the timer, fifty-six seconds.

Francesca spoke, "So let me get this straight, we have one minute after the timer hits zero before the incendiary device activates."

"I'm afraid so," Kyli said. "Provided the timer is accurate. It could be off by several seconds either way. When the battery power to the vault is exhausted, a different warning system will sound."

"Then you and Francesca need to get out of here now," he said. "When Lars gets here with the power cord, I'll plug it in."

"I can't leave," Kyli said.

"Why the hell not?"

"I might have been contaminated. I need one of these," Kyli pinched his hazard protection suit, "just in case."

Thirty-five seconds.

"I'm not leaving you here, Kyli," he said.

"No way I'm leaving here without both of you," Francesca said.

Twenty-eight seconds.

"Where the hell is Peeters?"

Almost as if on cue, two things happened. Lars Peeters walked through the door carrying a power cord. And a loud blaring alarm sounded from the vault.

"Batteries are dead," Kyli clicked the timer on her watch. "We have sixty seconds."

Jake snatched the power cord from Lars Peeters' hands and, as fast as he could make his legs stretch in the hazmat suit, darted toward the vault door. Two rotating red lights flashed on each side of the door.

"Keep calling out the time, Kyli," Jake said as he hurried past.

"There's a panel near the floor, opposite the hinge side of the vault door," Kyli hollered. "Open the panel door, plug in the power cord, and then flip the selector lever to *External*."

By the time he reached the panel door on the vault, he heard Kyli yell, "Thirty seconds." He opened the panel door, the inside looked exactly as Kyli had described.

An aural warning sounded, Thirty seconds to incendiary activation.

"What the hell?" he muttered.

He plugged in the power cord and flipped the switch to *External*.

Nothing happened.

"Kyli, it's not working."

"Fifteen seconds." Kyli sounded frantic. "Keep trying, Jake. Keep trying."

Jake's breathing was coming in gasps, his sweat stinging his eyes. He flipped the lever back to *Internal* and then back to *External*.

Nothing.

"Ten, nine."

All right, shut up Kyli, I can't get it to work.

His mind went into a free-fall, unable to figure out what to do.

His hand exploded in motion, flipping the lever back and forth, left and right.

"Six, five."

He slammed his fist into the panel. "Shit, shit, shit. Work, dammit."

"Four."

His hand flipped the lever from *External* to *Internal*.

"Three."

And then back to *External*.

The alarm stopped.

CHAPTER 31

Cleaning up the mess after a biological mishap was far more in-depth than Jake had expected. Kyli was immediately placed in a personal protection suit and taken to an isolation ward at a local hospital. It was several hours before Francesca, Peeters, and Jake were allowed to leave the fourth level of the MEtech building. By then, it was dark and the parking lot was lit up with several portable utility lights. As he found out, at Wiley's expense, the Belgian version of a temporary HazMat decontamination facility was set up in the parking lot. Wiley flew experts in from all over Europe to mitigate the contamination of MEtech.

When the decontamination facility was setup, the three of them were led down the stairs and taken into separate makeshift cleansing rooms. While still in his protective suit, he was placed in a small space and given a shower, which he found out later was mostly bleach water. He was stripped of his suit, next his clothes, and bathed in a special soap blend, then scrubbed by a decontamination expert from head to toe, including under his fingernails and toenails. His ears were cleaned as well as his nostrils with something that left a burn in his nose for hours.

Francesca's, Peeters', and his clothes and towels were bundled in sealed bags and taken away to be burned. He thought the whole ordeal overkill, but Wiley insisted on their compliance with the experts' requests. After blood was drawn, analyzed, and they were given a clean bill of health, he and Francesca and Peeters were given hospital scrubs to wear, and allowed to leave the containment trailer and released from the site.

Wiley instructed his HazMat teams to start with the thorough decontamination of MEtech, a procedure he anticipated might take several days to complete.

He and Francesca drove to the hospital where Kyli had been taken. She explained she had endured most of the same decontamination routine they had. The only difference was, Kyli had to stay in isolation and observation for forty-eight hours, the effective life of any biological agent in MEtech's bio lab. After that time period elapsed, the doctors would know if she was free from contaminates. If not, she would be gravely ill and could possibly die. Her blood was to be drawn and analyzed every six hours.

At his request, Francesca and the medical staff left him and Kyli alone in her ward room. Separating them was a triple-paned wall of glass. They spoke to each other privately using hand phones on each side of the glass, much like those used in prisons, which was what he thought the Belgian hospital isolation ward resembled in many ways.

"How do you feel?"

"Other than feeling violated from all the scrubbing, I am fine. My leg is still a little sore." She lowered her head. "You saved my life again, Jake."

"It has become a pastime of mine, you know?"

"I haven't heard from Wiley, how come?"

"He's been on the phone to the head physician several times checking on you. When the doctor assured him you were doing okay, he stayed at the lab to take care of what has rapidly turned into a PR nightmare. That's one reason Francesca and I were told to get out of there as soon as we could. Wiley wanted to keep us off the cameras and out of the news. He'll be by later to see you."

Her face flushed and her lips tightened. "Jake, find whoever did this."

"Oh, you can count on it." He pounded his fist on the counter. "And then I'm going to kill him."

"Be careful, Jake. These people are smart enough to know we'll come looking for them." She put her hand to the glass. "I'm sorry about what I said last time we were together. I love you…and I don't want to lose you."

"Hey you two, break it up," Francesca's voice spoke from behind him. "Jake, we need to leave. We have to get back to Rome."

Jake lined his hand up with Kyli's and pressed it against the glass. "I don't want to lose you either."

†††

Three hours later, Jake sat in the car and gazed out his window at the skyline of Rome. Francesca instructed the driver to cruise by several of the more prominent Roman landmarks. He enjoyed the ancient city more at night than he had in the daytime. It was silent and in many areas deserted as the hour approached midnight. The lack of crowds and the night sky revealed the beauty of Roman history, the chapels, fountains, cobblestone roads. The piazzas were lit up. He thought when this mission was over, maybe he could bring Kyli here.

The driver weaved through the abandoned streets until he pulled the car to the curb in front of the flat in Trastevere. The flat belonging to *The Jew*. Armed officers were guarding the entrance to the flat. At his request, Francesca had called Marco Serreti from the airport, who agreed to arrange for Francesca and him to do another walk-through of the apartment.

Francesca told the driver to wait while they were inside. "Come on, Jake," she walked toward the door to the flat. "I'm pretty sure this will be a waste of time."

Serreti had indeed made good on his promise to arrange for their arrival and continued investigation at the flat. The officer in charge escorted them to the flat.

Francesca had also been correct in her prediction AISE had picked the scene clean of any clues that might lead to the location of *The Jew*. "You weren't kidding about AISE, were you?"

She frowned. "Huh?"

He spread his arms outward to indicate they really worked the place over.

"Actually, I'm surprised it's not cleaner than this," she said.

As it turned out, AISE had gone so far as to allow a cleaning agency to enter the premises and clean up where the body had been laying, as well as where the mouse had died on the table. All the food was gone, the refrigerator emptied, clothes taken, along with anything else that could be considered a personal item.

"What happened to all of the victim's belongings?" Francesca asked the officer.

With a heavy accent he replied, "I am sorry. It was like this when I arrived."

Jake could tell the man was lying, but what difference would it make? The scene had been compromised and AISE had confiscated anything of interest that could help Francesca and him in their quest.

"Like you said, this was a waste of time," he said to Francesca. "Let's get the hell out of here."

"I've known Director Barzetti since I was a child, he owes me a favor. I'll try to collect in the morning."

"What about Serreti?"

"Don't worry about him. I know how to handle Marco Serreti."

And that worried him.

CHAPTER 32

Jake, still half asleep, threw his hand on the nightstand patting around for his buzzing cell phone. His rubbed his eyes and squinted to read the name of the incoming call.

Commonwealth Consultants.

He answered. "Do you know what time it is here?"

"Time to get up." It was Fontaine on the phone and his tone sounded serious. "Set your computer up for a video call with Wiley. Francesca is already on her way to your room."

Within seconds, there was a light rap on his door. He slipped on his pants and padded barefoot across the hotel room to open the door. Francesca pushed him out of her way and walked in. Her head resembled a rat's nest piled with knotted and tangled hair. She opened his backpack and pulled out the Atlanta Braves baseball cap he always kept inside and slipped it on her head, tucking her unkempt hair underneath.

She shot him a look. "Best I can do with no notice."

He opened his sleeping laptop and immediately got an incoming chat request on Wiley's customized, highly-encrypted app. He accepted the request and saw the bloodshot eyes of George Fontaine holding a mug of what looked like coffee.

"Wiley will be here in a sec," he said.

"What's so urgent?" Francesca still pushing hair beneath Jake's cap.

"If I were a seismologist and intel chatter were tremors,

I'd say we're about to have a massive earthquake of global proportions."

"Or the worst volcanic eruption in the Earth's history," a recognizable voice said in the background. Wiley's face appeared next to Fontaine's. "I hope you slept well. It might be several days before you get another good night's sleep."

"Why? What's happened?"

"Putting aside the recent attacks against MEtech and me personally, plenty. And none of it good." He raised a coffee cup with shaky hands and took a swig. Coffee dribbled down his chin. "Shit."

Jake saw him wipe it with his sleeve. "I'll let George fill you in while I clean up my mess."

"As you know, "Fontaine started, "Italy's banking system was shut down for several hours yesterday due to malicious hacking and the main bank's central location in Rome."

Jake looked at Francesca. "I honestly thought Serreti made that whole thing up so he could leave Venice."

"No, that was real," Fontaine confirmed. "But AISE had no involvement in the investigation. It was handled solely by the Guardia di Finanza. GdF officials are still at the bank trying to figure out what happened and who is responsible."

"Don't they primarily handle tax evasion issues?"

"That's only one of their areas of purview, Francesca. They also handle smuggling, money laundering, credit card fraud, counterfeiting, and cyber-crimes, to name a few." Fontaine rolled his neck and Jake could hear it crack through his laptop's speaker.

"Long day?"

"And it's only going to get longer." Jake could tell Fontaine feigned a smile. Then he continued, "It seems Italy was a test run. Overnight, several more banking systems were shut down at midnight local time in a dozen different countries. China and Japan fell first, then India, Saudi Arabia, and eventually most of Europe. The German Chancellor is calling for a global search to locate these hackers. It has already had an effect on economics. Asian markets tanked as soon as they opened. I don't mean they substantially fell. I mean they were almost completely wiped out. European markets are expected to follow as well as the New York Stock Exchange. POTUS is already contemplating suspending trading before the markets open."

Jake asked, "If one of these systems is debugged, do you think the same fix can be applied across all the banking systems to get them up and running?"

"It's possible, Jake, problem is the banks are locked out and have found no portal to get back in."

"Has anyone claimed responsibility?" Francesca queried.

"Islamic State has, but that's not really credible. They are nowhere near this level of sophistication."

"What about North Korea? They hacked Sony."

"Not them either," Fontaine replied. "Possibly China, but why would they shut their own systems down? I'm leaning toward someone a little closer to home."

"Like Tarh Andishan?"

"T-A does have that level of sophistication and expertise. It's the choice of targets that makes me doubt them."

"Where should we go next?"

"Oh I'm not done yet," Fontaine said in a monotone voice. "I'm afraid there is more. The system that tracks all maritime shipping has been shut down. Admittedly, that doesn't have a big impact in many respects, but it could be a test run for something much bigger. Like maybe the rail systems, or worse, the air traffic control system."

"Not good." Jake shook his head. "I know first-hand what happens when one FAA facility loses its computer, much less system wide...or world-wide."

"In Europe, two hospitals were hacked through portals open to the Internet. Both had surgeries in progress where live video feeds were being transmitted to assisting doctors in other countries. The hackers used that portal to gain control of the hospital's surgical and life-support equipment. And then the equipment was summarily shut down. In both cases, the patients died on the table, before the medical staff knew what had happened. The more connected our societies get, the more opportunity exists for this type of hostile takeover. And society today is becoming more and more dependent on connectivity for everything. And each and every connection is a vulnerable spot. A way for hackers to get in and take control. This need for connectivity has permeated nearly every aspect of our lives. The more connected we are, the more vulnerable we are."

"Now that you have succeeded to scare us half to death," Francesca injected, "dare I ask if there is anything else?"

"As a matter of fact, there is. I recognized a familiar characteristic about the digital signatures in some of the code used to hack the maritime shipping system."

"Wait," Jake interrupted. "What is a digital signature?"

"In layman's terms," Fontaine explained, "it's a way hackers—and programmers—put their personal stamp in the code. It's a way of identifying the code as their own in case someone else tries to steal it. Like a regular signature, only embedded in the code. But, in this case, it is impossible for it to belong to the persons whose signatures I recognized."

"Why do you say that?"

"Jake, do you recall Air Malacca 9-1-0?"

Jake scratched his head. "The Boeing triple seven that disappeared in the South China Sea about two and a half years ago or so?"

"One in the same."

"What does that have to do with what's going on today?"

"The digital signatures belong to two of the passengers on that aircraft."

"Are you sure, George?" Francesca asked. "Perhaps it's just really similar."

"It's not similar, it's exactly the same."

"Could someone be reusing old code?"

"I'm afraid not. This code was recently written."

"What are you saying, George?" Jake could feel the tension of Fontaine's looming answer.

"I'm saying at least two people onboard the missing aircraft are still alive."

CHAPTER 33

Still alive? Jake wrestled with a combination of overwhelming astonishment and bewilderment.

Over thirty months and not a trace of the B-777 had ever been recovered. The search for the missing aircraft was long and exhaustive and stayed in the media for months on end. Finally, the Chinese and Malaysian governments ruled out every possible explanation, except that the aircraft mysteriously nose-dived into the Gulf of Thailand, the South China Sea, or as many believed, the South Indian Ocean a few hundred miles from the west coast of Australia, killing everyone onboard and sinking to the bottom without leaving a trace on the surface. He knew, from his NTSB training many years before, if any aircraft nosedived into the sea, the aircraft would have broken up on impact and there would be at least some floating debris eventually located.

There had been a couple of false alarms. Aircraft debris washed up on a shoreline near the search area and everyone automatically assumed it belonged to Air Malacca 910. Ultimately any debris was ruled out as belonging to the ill-fated airliner.

No, the only circumstance he could envision where the aircraft went down in the Gulf of Thailand, the South China Sea, or the Indian Ocean without a trace was if the aircraft was deliberately and carefully landed on the water's surface.

And subsequently sank to the bottom of the sea. And, even given those circumstances, to vanish without a trace was still a long shot. On the other hand, throughout history, aircraft have crashed into the oceans without a debris field being located, not initially anyway. Debris had been known to wash up on isolated shorelines or get caught in the oceans' never ending current circulation.

"George, if what you're saying is true, then Air Malacca 910 didn't crash, but rather secretly landed somewhere else, meaning all those people are still alive."

"That's right, Jake. And those conspiracy theorists were right all along."

"Like yourself, George," Francesca said.

Fontaine had made it clear from the moment the aircraft disappeared thirty months ago he thought there was more to it than simply a downed aircraft. He guessed the aircraft had been hijacked.

"Everybody focused on the aircraft or pilots and forgot the clue was the passengers," Fontaine said. "Onboard the aircraft were twenty employees of a U. S. Technology company based in Malaysia called Hardwire Semiconductors, Incorporated that makes microchips for several different sectors, including the defense industry. Scuttlebutt is they were carrying highly sensitive industrial secrets with them on the flight. One source went so far as to suggest the United States government feared those secrets would fall into the hands of the Chinese, so they hijacked the plane and took it to the U. S. Base on Diego Garcia. Another suggested the Chinese took it. There are numerous hypotheses out there. Most make no sense. However, a few are very reasonable."

"What was your take, George?" Jake asked. "Something

about Iran I think you once said."

"That premise was based on the discovery of two stolen passports being used to put Iranian passengers onboard. Iran has the resources to hijack and hide that plane and all those people who were on it. HSI made semiconductors in Asia at production companies called *foundries*. Since most semiconductors are made outside the United States and if they were tooling a new product, it is possible these employees might have had the design and tooling equipment necessary to produce parts with them. The microchips they produced are used for encryption of *point of sale* applications and for maintaining cell phone towers. If you can protect data, you can also do the reverse. Think about it, what if no one were able to process any electronic payments in this country for a period of time? That would bring us to our knees in short order. Imagine the disruption to everyone's lives. The same could be true if someone could stop all wireless or cellular communications. Jake, you used to be an intelligence analyst in the Navy. How many other transfer possibilities can you think of to use that technology for other purposes?"

"I can think of a lot. None of which have pleasant outcomes. So is that what you think, George? That Iran hijacked the aircraft and stole those secrets? For what purpose?"

"Let me be clear, Jake and Francesca, I don't believe the Iranians wanted any of those so-called industrial secrets. Perhaps some of the tooling designs. Mostly, I believe Iran's interest in the Air Malacca 910 was the twenty employees themselves."

"But, I thought Iran was inching its way toward Western thinking," Francesca said.

Wiley's face reappeared in the video chat. "There are two

kinds of people never to trust," said Wiley, "Russians and Iranians."

"So, our national security is at risk?"

"Of course, our national security is at risk. Every country's national security is at risk and we all should be prepared to fend off any potential threat. Now, more so than ever. All NATO countries have elevated their threat levels. Keep in mind, all of Islam sees Israel as the enemy and they despise all Jews. Forget what they claim about eradicating Islamic State, toppling Israel is their true objective."

"When we were in Vienna," said Jake, "we found the photo of former head of the Iranian Revolutionary Guard, Qasem Kazemi, in the dead man's apartment. Do you think there is a connection with him and what is going on now?"

"Kazemi is an organizer of terror," Fontaine said. "He is one of our prime suspects as *the* mastermind behind whatever is being planned. He has the knowledge and experience, but mostly he has the resources capable of backing a cyber-attack of monumental proportion. And he is certainly in a position to have influence over T-A. There are several others, of course, but he is the only Iranian on the list. Last reports put him in Italy somewhere, exact location unknown."

There were several seconds of awkward silence. It was obvious the preponderance of information just delivered would take some digesting.

Jake was the first to speak. "So, what's our next move?" It was a certainty today would prove to be another long day.

"I need to split you two up for a while," Wiley said. "Francesca, I want you to stay in Italy and keep on the trail of *The Jew*. Something tells me he has some involvement in all this. George and I haven't figured out what yet." He leaned back in his chair and took a sip from his coffee cup. Then he pushed up his glasses and ran his fingers over his hair. "Jake, I want you to get to the airport as soon as you can and fly to D.C. I have requisitioned copies of all the data the NTSB has gathered on Air Malacca 910. I want you to take a look at it and see what you think might have happened to the airplane."

"I'm sure they've looked at all possibilities, sir."

"Perhaps…but they don't have the inside information we have, now do they? Which means they could have been looking in all the wrong places. George will have a full dossier on the tech company and all of its known technology. Maybe some of its secret technology, too. I want you to put together every scenario you can think of and you and George can lay them out and start eliminating them one by one."

"What about you?" he asked. "Don't you want to have a look as well?"

"Jake, Kyli started running a high fever last night, doctors don't know why, her blood work keeps coming back normal. Although I just arrived back in D.C., I'm returning to Belgium in a few minutes."

"Is she going to be all right?"

"Let's hope so, Jake. Let's hope so."

With that, Wiley stood and walked away. George signed off and ended the video feed. He felt Francesca's hand stroke his bare back. Then she put her arm around him and quietly spoke into his ear. "She's a tough cookie, Jake. She'll beat this thing, whatever it is."

He swiveled in his seat. She was still wearing his Atlanta Braves ball cap. "Thanks, Francesca. I'm sure Kyli will pull through. She has to. I have made a decision…and it involves her being alive."

Francesca pulled back. "What decision is that?"

"When this mission is over, I'm giving Wiley my notice... and asking Kyli to marry me."

CHAPTER 34

Boris followed his escape plan to the letter.

Last night, after his near capture when he went to retrieve his two backpacks from the secret compartment under his house, he traveled a predetermined safe route to the bus station and used a ticket purchased earlier in the day with cash and under a false identity. He boarded the 11:25 p.m. *Greyhound* to Atlanta, Georgia. Keeping his two backpacks safe by his side, he rode six and a half hours, changing buses in Richmond, Virginia, until the bus stopped in Raleigh, North Carolina. He got off under the pretense of using the restroom inside the station, but never returned to the bus. Instead, he hailed a taxi and had the cab driver drop him at the NC State University North Campus at the traffic circle of Hillsborough and Pullen. In the predawn light, he got out of the taxi, paid the driver adding a generous tip, and walked west across the North Campus.

It was much warmer in Raleigh than in Washington D.C.

Muggier, too.

Dawn was typically the most humid part of the day, or so he thought anyway. He pulled off his sweater and wrapped it over his shoulders, folding the arms across each other on his chest. Then he secured one backpack on his back, arms through each strap, and carried the other like a briefcase by the strap.

He cut across the Court of North Carolina, though the Gardner Arboretum, and walked along the edge of Governors

Scott Courtyard until he reached Dan Allen Drive. As he crossed the railroad tracks, the distant shadow of Doak Field rose from the darkness on his right. He followed Dan Allen Drive across Western Boulevard until it came to a T at Fraternity Court. He angled southwest through the middle of Greek Village until he reached Varsity Drive, where he zigzagged three more blocks until reaching his destination. His secret safe house, an apartment complex filled entirely of college kids his age. Someplace where he knew he blended in with the rest of the residents. A comfortable spot for him to run the rest of his mission.

Three months ago, he had secured the apartment as a backup in the event of a blown identity, such as the predicament he found himself in now. Fortunately, his ingrained need for failsafe planning pushed him to locate this ideal location well in advance of the mission timeline. He had all the utilities turned on, including the highest speed internet service he could find, stating he was really into streaming movies and playing high-end video games with his computer. He was no longer Alexei Nikahd, the half-Iranian, half-Russian young man from Georgetown. He was now Alex Skylar from Washington, Iowa, the son of Ukrainian immigrants and third year student majoring in Graphic Design, something about which he knew plenty.

He unlocked the door to his new digs and entered with only one thing on his mind—sleep. He placed his backpacks on the kitchenette table and walked toward the bedroom when there was a knock on his door. He glanced at his watch, 7:45. Who could possibly be knocking this early? He wasn't able to sleep on the bus, too nervous about last night's events, and too paranoid that someone might have followed him. And now, all he wanted to do was crash. A second knock on the door. He pulled the sweater from his shoulders and tossed it on the bed and went over to the apartment door. He looked through the security viewer in his door and saw a woman not much younger than he. She was rocking from foot to foot, shifting her weight in some nervous ritual.

He opened the door, "May I help you?" She was an attractive and shapely young woman, a couple of inches shorter than him. Her long dark hair braided into a single pony tail draped over her right shoulder. She was wearing purple high cut gym shorts and a white spaghetti strap workout top that plunged deeply in front highlighting her already buxom figure.

She stuck her hand out, "Hi," I'm Ashley, I live next door. I saw you come in and wanted to meet my mysterious neighbor. I saw you a few months ago, but you never seemed to come back around after that."

Fortunately for him, he'd already devised his cover story. He grabbed her hand. It was warm and soft like her brown eyes. And he noticed those eyes were scanning him from head to toe with definite interest. "I'm Alex, good to meet you." He stepped back. "Would you like to come in?"

She craned her neck, obviously scoping out the inside of his apartment. "Well," she said dragging out the word. "I can't stay long. I have a class at nine."

"You'll have to excuse my lack of amenities right now," he explained. "I had been living with my girlfriend and we had a nasty break-up. I must go to the store today and stock up." That part was true, but first he'd have to get his scooter out of the rented storage unit nearly two miles away.

"Sorry to hear about you and your girlfriend." He noticed she was still sizing him up. It happened to him frequently, he recognized the signs. "Well, Alex, do you have a last name?"

"Skylar," he replied. "Alex Skylar."

"I'm Ashley Madison."

He couldn't help but laugh. "No way."

"Yep, way. Just like the cheating website."

What she didn't know, and would never know, was that he had helped with the hacking of the *Ashley Madison* website when he did a short-term stint with the hacking group *Anonymous*.

"Well, Ashley Madison, what's your major?"

"Elementary Education. What about you?"

"Graphic Design. Third year."

"Cool," she said and her face lit up. "My roommate has the same major. Do you know her, Emma Thornton?"

"The name isn't familiar, but I'm not good with names." He paused and looked her in the eyes. "Yours I won't forget, though." He grinned and they both laughed.

"Hey, I have an idea," she said with energy and enthusiasm, "if you're free tonight, why don't you come over for supper? It will take your mind off your girlfriend. You can meet Emma. Do you like spaghetti?"

She was pushy, but pleasantly so. Pushy with a smile. And what a wonderful smile she had. A big toothy smile, like a Julia Roberts smile. Straight white teeth. Perfectly straight actually, top and bottom. The longer he gazed at her, the more desirable she became. And it had been a while since he'd been intimate. He longed for the touch of a woman. Self-gratification only goes so far and then a man needs the real thing. Ashley Madison was definitely the real thing. "I love spaghetti," he finally said.

Ashley stood and took a step toward the door. "Then it's settled. How about around 6:30?"

"6:30 sounds perfect. Can I bring something to drink? Beer? Wine?"

"Nobody drinks beer with Italian food, unless it's pizza. I have plenty of wine, though. My father owns a vineyard in California. He sends me like, a case a month. You show up and I'll take care of everything else. I hope you like garlic bread."

He nodded.

He walked her to the door and pulled it open. "See you tonight," she said.

"Looking forward to it." He watched her walk down the second floor walkway and open the door to the apartment next to his. Before she entered her apartment, she gave a slight wave with her fingers. He went back inside his apartment, closed and locked the door behind him. He grinned as he strolled into his bedroom. The clock on his nightstand read 8:15. He needed to be up and online in five hours, so he set the alarm for 12:30. That would give him plenty of time to take a shower and set up his equipment before his scheduled video chat with Omar. He undressed, pulled down the sheets and crawled in bed.

As he relaxed in the bed, trying to bring on sleep, he thought about her, Ashley Madison. She was sexually interested in him, he picked up those signals loud and clear. He imagined her naked body, young, smooth, and curvy in all the right places. She was certainly a package well put together. He was sure she was not very strong in common sense and a long conversation might prove difficult. But, it wasn't her mind he was interested in, it was her other redeeming qualities. He rolled to his side, his desire for her grew stronger.

CHAPTER 35

Ethan Wogahn checked his encrypted email for the fourth time in an hour. Yesterday, Omar had made it clear to report immediately to him if Boris didn't deliver the software package by sunset. It still hadn't arrived. Omar was not a patient man nor a forgiving man. If he informed Omar of Boris' failure to deliver the package, Boris was a dead man. Not something he wanted to see happen.

Over the course of the past few months, he had worked extensively with Boris. He could tell Boris was young, and at times a little immature, but it didn't matter, he'd grown to like the man. A lot. He was easy to talk to, and even more, he was fun. Boris excelled at what he did, and that was develop software, usually computer viruses, and hack. He could hack anything. There wasn't a firewall he couldn't break through. Wogahn knew that to be true when Boris found the chink in the armor of NORAD's cyber security software. An access portal that was still unknown to the foolish United States government. That's what happened when you hired the lowest bidder. You get what you pay for, and this time, the infidels would pay dearly.

But not if Boris didn't deliver the software.

Boris had been dark for several days and Wogahn was beginning to worry about the young hacker's safety. Was he even still alive? Omar eluded to a couple of close calls, but nothing specific. Was it possible that somehow, somewhere Boris' identity had been breached? And, if so, who else's? His own? Would authorities be showing up at one or all of his facilities?

Boris always seemed relaxed about everything, not a care in the world as far as Wogahn could tell. But, he wasn't on the front lines either. He worked in the shadows, in the darkness from wherever he chose. He could stay out of sight and move around while the rest of us had to remain stationary. Wogahn wished he was carefree like Boris, but that wasn't his nature. He was a worrier, that was why he had his portion of the project finished way ahead of schedule. It wasn't from fear of Omar, well maybe a little, so much as fear of not completing his part on time in the event something went wrong. His glass was never half-full, but always half-empty.

His thoughts were interrupted by the chime on his computer—an incoming video chat.

Boris. *Praise be to Allah.*

He clicked accept and the young man's amicable face appeared on the screen. He was wearing a two-tone green sweater with an extra wide collar. A gold chain hung from his neck with some sort of coin attached. He looked freshly showered and shaved. His jet black hair was slicked back with some sort of gel, except for one tuft dangling right above his left eye. He had olive skin and dark features which added to his good looks.

"Guardian," Boris said.

"Boris. You're overdue. Omar is anxious and angry."

"When was the last time you spoke with him?" His voice sounded worried.

"Yesterday afternoon. He said if I didn't get the software by sunset yesterday, I was to contact him immediately…regardless of the time. He was so upset and mad that he used my real name instead of my code name."

"Did you contact him as he instructed?"

"No. I had faith you would come through…also I knew what it would mean if I reported it to Omar," Wogahn explained, hoping Boris had good news. "You do have the package ready for me, don't you?"

"Relax, Guardian. I uploaded it to the server a few minutes ago. I sent you the link, go get it whenever you want." Boris held up a finger. "If Omar asks, tell him you got it yesterday, right after you and he talked. You'll do that for me, won't you?"

"What choice do I have? If I don't lie for you, he'll have you killed."

"If he finds out you lied to protect me, he'll have you killed too."

"So we have an accord, right?"

"Of course."

Boris paused for some reason and looked away from his monitor as if something was happening. "Anything wrong?" Wogahn asked.

"No. I think it's one of my neighbors outside the door. Nothing to be concerned about. Do me a favor, will you Ethan?"

"Dammit, Boris, you did it too. How did you know my name?"

"I know everyone's name, Ethan, including Omar's. I'm the one who came up with all the aliases and set all the passwords. And I can change them all, too. If it makes you feel any better, my real name is Alexei Nikahd and I grew up in the Washington D.C. area, Georgetown to be specific. I'm telling you this because I can never be that person again or go back there again. My identity was compromised and the breach had to come from our man in Vienna. He was the only one unaccounted for and, as I found out a few minutes ago, he's the only one dead."

"Did Omar kill him?"

"No. Someone else is out there. He was in Rome looking for *The Jew* and someone got to him. He was found dead in *The Jew's* apartment by two Americans. They traced him back to Vienna and searched his apartment."

"Did they find out anything?"

"They had to have found something. How else could they have identified me?"

"What about me?" Wogahn asked. "Do they know about me?"

"Ethan, I'm sure they have your real name and your face to go with it. But I left you a surprise on the server. Check the file named *FaceOff*. I set you up a new identity. When the countdown is complete and our day has come, take your new identity and disappear forever. Canada, maybe. Or the Caribbean. Go off the grid permanently. And never, under any circumstances, contact Omar again."

Alexei's words came as a shock. Like he knew something grave, but wouldn't share the details. "What about you? Are you doing the same?"

"I've already put my plan in action, Ethan. And I suggest you do the same. Get your documents as soon as possible so you'll have them when you need them. I enclosed all the instructions you'll need in the file. When you execute your part of the plan, don't hang around to see the results. Burn everything you have, pack your belongings, and get as far away from there as you can. As fast as you can. The Americans aren't stupid. They'll pounce on those facilities in the harshest manner as soon as possible."

"But the damage will be done, right?"

"It will, but you don't want to be there when they arrive. If they arrive. It's possible they'll just blow everything up in an attempt to stop the attack, but it won't work. Those towers will have already been rendered inert. By then, the satellites will be in control. And if all goes according to plan, Omar will have total control of the world and our greatest enemy will be annihilated."

"If we're in control, why should we run?"

"This time, Ethan, you'll have to trust me. It's not safe for you to ever be seen again. If you reappear, you will die."

CHAPTER 36

By the time Jake showered, gathered his belongings, and made it to the Rome Airport, he'd already burned nearly two hours of his morning. His return to Commonwealth headquarters was a top priority of Wiley's. Fortunately, he was flying west making his arrival time in D.C. late morning Eastern time. Early enough to put in a full day's work. Unfortunately, it made for a very long day, since Wiley had a package of information for Jake to read enroute. He had spent so much of the past few years of his life time zone hopping, the effects of travel weren't as draining on his body as they were in the beginning. Especially traveling west, which used to wipe him out for a couple of days. Now, he grabbed sleep when he could and adjusted his routine to whatever time zone he found himself in that day.

He found it difficult to concentrate on the Air Malacca 910 package during the flight. When he asked for an update on Kyli, her conditioned had worsened and her isolation ward room had been converted into a makeshift intensive care unit. Her body temperature had topped out at 103.5° before the medical staff was able to get it under control. It had now stabilized at a manageable 101.7°. The team of physicians had yet to identify the source of her infection, and Kyli remained incoherent to the point she couldn't provide any insight as to which agents she was exposed to during and immediately after the explosion at MEtech.

He had worked out his feelings for Kyli and, as he explained to Francesca, was ready to make a permanent change, one that included terminating his employment as an emissary for Commonwealth Consultants and the Greenbrier Fellowship.

Emissary. In its simplest definition it meant a person sent on a special mission, usually as a diplomatic representative. True, he had been sent many times on special missions—none of which were as a diplomatic representative. At times, most times, it was with orders from the Greenbrier Fellowship to stop someone from doing something contrary to what the Fellowship had deemed in the world's best interest. Usually that involved some form of lethal action be taken by the emissary, of which there were exactly two—Jake and Francesca.

During the Jimmy Carter administration, when Carter outlawed political assassinations, Elmore Wiley and several of the most influential and powerful individuals in the world formed the Greenbrier Fellowship. Typically, the Fellowship met annually at the historic Greenbrier Hotel in White Sulphur Springs, West Virginia, thus the name Greenbrier Fellowship. These individuals foresaw issues on a global scale. The world's belief there could be freedom without a price was one of the most ill-conceived ideals put forth by the world's leaders. Freedom had a price, a grave price, as could be attested by anyone who served in combat.

Wiley, who had been involved in the secret radio frequency and microwave emission technology business for well over fifty years, landed a ground floor invitation to the clandestine inaugural meeting of the Fellowship. Since the government couldn't do business directly with the Fellowship—an organization that technically didn't exist—each member formed their own company to covertly meet the goals of the Fellowship. Elmore Wiley formed Commonwealth Consultants, an off-the-books, black budget funded company located in Fairfax, Virginia.

Francesca was upset when he told her of his intentions to resign from Commonwealth. She asked him, no, she begged him to not do anything drastic, like resign, until after the two of them had the opportunity to talk about his decision. He had agreed, but in retrospect wish he hadn't. It was his decision and nothing Francesca or anybody could say would sway his decision. It wasn't like he financially ever needed to work again. Between his inheritance, his lucrative salary with Commonwealth, and the bountiful finder's fee he was given by President Rudd several years ago when he located several caches of treasure stolen by the Nazis in World War II, he had enough money to live like a high roller for two lifetimes. And he had no heirs to leave it to. No parents, they both had died within the past few years. No brothers nor sisters. And no wife and children, something he planned on changing as soon as this mission was complete. He'd let Francesca have her say, he'd thank her, then he'd do what he intended to do, settle down with Kyli and raise a family.

The Commonwealth limo picked him up from Wiley's private hangar at Dulles International Airport and dropped him in front of the Fairfax complex. He followed the standard routine security procedures to gain access to the building where he immediately tracked down Fontaine, who wasn't huddled in front of his computers as usual, but asleep on the couch in his private office.

He grabbed a dictionary from the table, held it up and dropped it. Just before it hit the floor, he yelled, "George, watch out." The book hit the floor with a loud thud.

Fontaine bounded out of a dead sleep and rolled off the couch onto the floor, bumping his arm on the coffee table.

He howled with laughter to see the silver-haired man sprawled on the floor.

"Son of a bitch, Jake." Fontaine rubbed his elbow and struggled to get up. "That shit isn't funny."

"So, why am I laughing so hard?"

"Because you never matured past the age of twelve," he said. He rubbed the crust from his eyes and looked at his watch. "Are you just getting here?"

"Just walked in. Pilot said the headwind was stronger than forecast."

"Let's go to the command center," Fontaine said as he ambled toward the door, "I dug up something I think you will find very interesting about the technology company that had twenty of its employees on Air Malacca 910."

"What is it?"

"It's better if I show you," said Fontaine, "I found a video that might explain a lot. Don't know why anyone else hadn't found it yet…oh wait, yes I do. Because no one else has hacked the company's server but me." He had an uncontrollable grin. "This way, dickhead."

He followed Fontaine to the command center, which was only a few steps from Fontaine's office and where he spent most of his time. "Pull up a chair," Fontaine said. He opened a folder on his desktop and entered a pass code, and clicked a file inside. A separate window opened on the desktop and the cursor turned into a colored pinwheel for a second before a video started loading. "Jake," Fontaine said, "if this technology was used, and I think it was, then it explains an awful lot. Wiley said to make this your top priority, because the ramifications of this technology being in the wrong hands is staggering."

"George." He was getting frustrated at Fontaine's vagueness. "What the hell are you talking about?"

"Watch."

Fontaine let the fifteen-minute video run through its entirety without saying a word. Although some of the engineering went over Jake's head, he got the gist and understood Fontaine's concern about the technology being in the wrong hands. If Air Malacca 910 actually was hijacked by a hostile country, then the technology was already in the wrong hands.

"Is this technology real? Because it sounds like science fiction."

"Wiley said it's not only possible, but probable based on his expertise and knowledge of Hardwire Semiconductor Industries. The old man said he'd caught wind of it a couple of years ago, but because the technology was never released by HSI, he figured it must have failed test trials. He knew HSI was working on radar-blocking aeronautical hardware technology that could mask or cloak the aircraft from electronic detection. This new stealth technology makes an airplane invisible to radar leaving visual confirmation as the only way of identification. This is high-tech electronic warfare weaponry. Imagine if an aircraft could fly into a war zone undetected."

"You're thinking too small, George. Air Malacca 910 disappeared at night when visually spotting an aircraft without lights is virtually impossible. An aircraft equipped with this stealth technology could fly anywhere at night undetected. Anywhere, George. Over any city, any capitol, over any military installation. And no one would be the wiser—"

"Until it was too late."

"Precisely."

"But, it's still speculation until we can prove it, right? We need to find evidence, one way or another, whether Air Malacca 910 crashed into the water or was hijacked by some foreign country and hidden away during the dead of night."

"You realize how difficult that will be, right, George?" Jake picked up the folder Wiley left for him to study on the flight across the Atlantic. "We're trying to do what all the best aircraft accident investigators in the world haven't done yet. Remember, they seemed to think the aircraft went down southwest of Australia."

"So, you're saying we'll be here a while?"

"Days, perhaps."

"Let's get to it, then," George said as he rolled his eyes. "What do we need? Satellite photos? I have digital copies of thousands. ATC records?" He slapped his hand down on a stack of folders lying on the table. "Radar tracks, I have them from takeoff until hours past fuel exhaustion time. Where do you want to start?"

"Let's start at the beginning, loss of radar contact." Jake walked over to the world map and placed his finger on a spot at the mouth of the Gulf of Thailand. "From here, let's draw an arc at fuel exhaustion time." He motioned a large circle with his arms. "Then we'll narrow our search by process of elimination."

"You know that won't be a perfect circle, right?" Fontaine asked.

"Correct, after we account for winds and curvature of the earth." He motioned an oval shape. "It will look more like this."

"I have already loaded all the data into the computer." Fontaine pulled up a map on the large overhead monitor. An

X marked the aircraft's last know position. He typed on the computer and a large oddly-shaped ring appeared. "This is fuel exhaustion range at each degree plugged in assuming the course was never subsequently changed."

"Then we know for certain Air Malacca 910 is somewhere inside this ring."

"That's a lot of area to cover, Jake."

"It is, but it's mostly water. Let's eliminate the possibility of an overwater crash and move forward under the assumption the aircraft made a normal landing somewhere. On land, that is. Land capable of safely handling a Boeing 777."

"Okay, genius, you got any idea how far that is?"

"If these pilots are top-notch and can land in the shortest distance possible, from the slowest airspeed possible on final approach, you still better allow for at least 5000 feet when you set your parameters."

Fontaine typed on his keyboard for a few seconds and the wall-mounted monitor map updated, leaving only possible geographical landing spots highlighted in green. "There you go, Jake," Fontaine said. "That eliminates 61.756% of the search grid. Still an awful lot of possibilities, though."

"Too many. George, can you take all the satellite data, taking into account the known flight path until loss of radar, and overlay visual imagery with thermal scans?"

"I see where you're going with this, Jake." Fontaine nodded. "It'll take a while, but I think I can program some algorithms that will allow us to locate and track Air Malacca 910 both visually and thermally. As long as the airplane stayed over water, we should be able to get a good contrast on thermal scans." Fontaine paused and said, "You know I'll have to tap into the Department of Defense satellites to do this, right?"

"George," he said with all sincerity, "that has never stopped us before."

CHAPTER 37

Daniel Luzato, restrained and unconscious, lay on the stretcher inside the dark, damp cellar. Germano Caminiti had deliberately kept him that way. His conscience bothered him about the abuse Omar had already inflicted on the poor man. Luzato might have what Omar wanted, but he doubted he had it all in his head. This man was smart. Too smart to have all the codes memorized. The man was only human and anything he did know could be extracted with the right degree of torture and pain.

Omar was not a reasonable man, that's the main reason Germano kept Luzato unconscious. Otherwise the man known as *The Jew* would already be dead. Omar knows no tolerance and no patience. He would have already started severing digits, a technique that had never failed him in the past. No one got past the excruciating pain of having the second finger slowly and methodically severed before cracking. Most never even made it to one before they screamed for mercy and told Omar everything he wanted to know. And in every instance, as soon as Omar got what he wanted, he killed them anyway. This was Daniel Luzato's fate as well.

Germano did not know all the details of Omar's overall plan. Yet, he knew it involved the collapse of many nations. Not the military collapse, something far worse in today's modern world. The digital collapse. As technology grew, and the dependence on this type of technology soared over the past two decades, so did the vulnerability. The computer age ushered in more than convenience, it allowed a new gateway for destruction. Soon enough, if all went according to Omar's plan, he would control most of the world's computers, of the countries that matter anyway. Then he would strike them while they were trying to figure out what happened. He would strike hard and decisive. Omar's sworn mortal enemy would be obliterated, and when that occurred, Omar swore to catapult the world to a simpler time, a time without technological advantages. It would signal the end of most country's electronic infrastructure. A jump back in time. No more high-ranking military officials stuffed away in bunkers fighting wars from thousands of miles away. No more satellites. No more drones. No more George Orwell's *1984*. Wars and battles would be fought where they should be—in the trenches. Omar would level the playing field. By the time the allied nations could confer and formulate a game plan, they would have already been defeated.

Germano's sympathy for Luzato had cost him. Every time Omar came storming into the ancient basement, Luzato remained unconscious. The last time, Omar threatened to kill him if he didn't have the man ready for interrogation by the time he returned. And that time was rapidly approaching. Germano inserted a needle in the line of the IV and slowly pressed the plunger. Within seconds, Luzato showed signs of regaining consciousness.

He gently shook the man's shoulders. "Daniel," he whispered. "Daniel, wake up."

Luzato's eyelids opened and closed several times. His lips moved, but nothing came out.

"Daniel, time is up," he whispered. "*He* will be here any

minute. If you don't give him what he wants, he will inflict more pain. Worse than the collar. Much, much worse. Do as he asks. For your sake, give him what he wants."

†††

He awoke in a cloud of desperation. The man above him was gently shaking him from his unconsciousness, urging submission. But, what was he saying? Something about pain and codes. Through the brain fog, he remembered where he was and why, and understood the man's whispering pleas.

A fleeting thought pulsed through him, had he given up any information in his drugged stupor? No. Why else would this man be making a case for compliance with Omar's demands? He had divulged nothing. "Water," he managed to squeak out through his parched throat. Within seconds, a straw was placed in the corner of his mouth.

"Small sips," the familiar yet gentle voice said.

The water cascaded over his tongue and down his throat bringing relief to the drought in his body like rainfall in the desert. He indulged again and again until the straw was removed.

"Slow down," the voice said. "Too fast and you'll get sick to your stomach."

He remembered the voice. Germano. The amicable bald man who had been looking after him during his captivity. No, imprisonment was a better definition. Germano showed him compassion until Omar arrived. Then everything changed, and for the worse.

Omar wanted the decryption codes. Codes to bypass the firewalls of Omar's enemies' defenses. Luzato had prepared for this day. The inevitability of this day was as certain as death. Ironic how death would be his fate. And at the hands of this twisted Iranian man. He would not make it easy for Omar. He tried to prepare himself for the extreme suffering he was about to experience. It would be sadistic, even more than the electrocution from the collar. Then, he would break, partially, and give Omar a morsel. Maybe two or three. Enough to temporarily slake the madman's thirst, but not enough to fell nations. Enough to alarm those nations. His only hope was that someone out there would piece together enough information and prepare their defenses in advance. Attacks were coming, he could not prevent that, but he could allow them to happen in such a manner where Omar tipped his hand to the world.

The straw returned to the corner of his lips and he took a long draw, filling his mouth and then gulping down the water like it was the elixir of life. "Grazie," he said. He peered into Germano's eyes and saw his forehead puckered like he was worried.

"Prego," the gentle man replied.

There was a thud as the door pushed open and banged against the stone wall. The expression on Germano's face turned to dread.

Luzato turned his head and watched as Omar and another man strode across the expanse of the basement. He assumed this man was the man who had helped Germano over the past few days, but the expression on Germano's face indicated otherwise.

Omar stood over him while the other man stepped behind Germano. "Soon, you will give me what I want," Omar said.

He heard a thump and Germano disappeared from his peripheral vision. He turned his head, Omar's new man had knocked Germano unconscious and was hefting him into a chair. Then he strapped Germano's legs, arms, and chest to the chair using what looked like duct tape.

"I'm going to demonstrate," Omar said, "the extent of my resolve."

Without another word, Omar splashed water in Germano's face, and the man regained wakefulness with a jerk. Omar reached behind his back and pulled out a large knife with a nefarious looking curved blade, like the type of knife used to slice open the carcasses of animals in a slaughterhouse. Germano's eyes bulged with fear. The other man grabbed Germano's left hand and pulled his little finger away from the rest. Germano jerked in the chair, pleading for mercy. Omar reached down with his knife and, with a crack of the bone and a tear of the flesh, severed the finger from Germano's hand. His protector screamed in agony. The whites of his protector's eyes turned blood red like the small fountain shooting from his hand where his little finger used to be. Omar held the finger up and then cavalierly tossed it into a tin cup. Blood smeared the rim where the digit ricocheted before landing inside.

Luzato did not expect the mad man to torture somebody who had been helping him, yet he should have expected this from a man with no conscience.

His protector's screams turned to loud sobs and prayers. Luzato remained silent.

"You do not care what becomes of him?" Omar swung the knife across the sobbing man's face.

"Stop," Luzato yelled unable to bear seeing the man tortured. "I'll give you what you want." He closed his eyes tight and then reopened them. "I'll give you whatever you want, just let him go."

"I'm afraid it's not that easy, Jew. You see, Germano betrayed my trust. He interfered with my inquisition in order to protect you. His allegiance to me was not strong, and for that, he must pay." Omar nodded and the other man lifted Germano's left pointer finger. In a swift, efficient motion, Omar severed the finger and tossed it into the tin cup as casual as a chef preparing a meal.

Germano's hand was difficult to look at. His hand was now deformed with only two fingers and two blood-soaked meaty holes where two fingers were once attached. A small river of blood flowed from Germano's hand, over the armrest, and cascaded to the floor like a thick red waterfall. The face of the man was even more difficult. Wrenched in pain, his shrill screams were garbled and pitiful.

Luzato did not want to see the suffering face any longer. *Enough, you sick bastard,* but Omar did not stop. He seemed to enjoy inflicting the pain, determined to continue the torture. Two fingers on Germano's left hand already lopped off and tossed into the cup. He wanted Omar to stop, but he couldn't speak. He tried again, but nothing came out. Like his voice was muted by some unseen force. The horror of seeing Omar torturing his own man was almost too much to bear.

"Stop, please I beg you to stop," Luzato pleaded.

Germano's expression changed. He looked directly at Omar. Surprisingly, he said but one word, "Mercy."

Omar, with no emotion on his face, simply nodded and walked behind Germano. He reached his arm around from the right side of Germano's head and placed the tip of the knife below Germano's left ear. In a whisper loud enough for Luzato to hear, Omar said, "Goodbye, old friend."

In a single fluid motion, Omar ripped the knife across

Germano's throat while holding his head back. The gash tore deep, severing the windpipe and slicing the carotid artery. Blood spurted and poured across Germano's neck and onto his chest, covering the man in blood. The man's eyes bulged with recognition of his own death rapidly approaching. He couldn't speak and his neck made wet gasping sounds as his chest heaved in and out.

Within seconds, Germano Caminiti was gone.

Omar wiped the blood from the knife with a towel and slipped the blade inside a leather sheath. "Clean this up," he said to the other man.

The man nodded and silently went to work.

Omar lumbered over to the stretcher.

Luzato readied his lips and spit in Omar's face.

With his hand, he wiped the saliva off his face and leaned very close to Luzato's face, "I won't be so gentle with you."

CHAPTER 38

Firenze, Italy

Francesca sat atop the famous 13th century tower of her hotel watching the sun set over the beautiful Italian city. The tower was erected in 1280 by the Buondelmont family. Firenze, or Florence as it was typically referred as, was her favorite city in Italy and Florentine architecture was, by far, the most interesting. In her opinion, anyway. For Italians and Europeans alike, most buildings in Florence were considered modern. As was any building less than five hundred years old. She liked it because Florence was the home of the Renaissance, birthplace of the modern world. It was home to Michelangelo's David, one of the world's most renowned sculptures, that sat minutes only a few short minutes away in the Galleria dell'Accademia. From her vantage point atop the tower, she could also see Uffizi Gallery only two blocks east and next to it, Palazzo Vecchio. However, the most prominent landmark on the horizon was the Duomo Cathedral with its massive tower and red dome, a picturesque view that epitomized what Florence was all about.

After she and Jake finished the video call with Wiley and Fontaine this morning, she saw Jake off to the airport, then took a taxi to Rome's Termini Train Station, where she boarded the next train to Florence. She had made arrangements to meet a source from her AISE days, shortly after lunch in Florence. Her source was a man who had proven reliable in the past. He seemed to be in the know about most underworld things in all of Italy. And Florence was his safe haven. Southern Italy was his danger zone, especially Sicily, where he was known as a stoolie for AISE. His life was in peril anywhere south of Rome. In Florence, he could lay low and stay alive. And he owed Francesca a favor as she was the one who, several years ago, rescued him from the clutches of a Mafioso don, whisked him from the Amalfi Coast, and set him up in Florence under a new identity. Time to collect on the favor.

With her she brought the pictures and data she and Jake had gleaned from the dead man's apartment in Vienna. Hopefully, he could shed some light on those Fontaine had been unable to identify and was now too busy to worry with since Wiley had changed his priorities. Enzo Mantova was now a *go-to* for a handful of the most covert of Italian law enforcement agencies, especially the Firenze Carabinieri.

She had taken the train from Rome to Florence since the jet was unavailable. The ride was as expected and the landscape as she remembered. It amazed her that in Italy, even as the years had passed, not a lot seemed to have changed. In many places, in fact, nothing had changed for centuries. The terraced landscapes lining the tracks with the many Tuscan vineyards, were still as lovely as ever. Being out of the hustle and bustle of the cities made her miss her homeland. Being in it, though, reminded her of why she wanted out.

When she arrived in Florence and left the Santa Maria Novella Train Station on foot, she noticed most of the shops along her route to her rendezvous point on Borgo la Noce were closed. Typical this time of day in Italy. The Spanish term for it was *siesta*, but in Italy it was called *pausa pranzo*, or lunch break—usually between 1:00 p.m. and 3:00 p.m.—when many of the shops closed for what the Italians considered a *relaxed lifestyle*. She knew, however, that her destination would not be closed. Her source's half-brother—not real half-brother, but only on paper by Enzo's new identity—owned the leather shop and rarely closed the doors during the day. *Open early, close late*—was his business model. And something about the model had worked because he was making money hand over fist.

When she had rounded the corner at the Basilica of San Lorenzo, less than a block from her destination, she saw some sort of protest in Piazza San Lorenzo, right in front of Medici-Riccardi Palace, home of Lorenzo the Magnificent. The group of young people were wearing gas masks and waving red banners. Purple smoke from gas canisters filled the piazza. A man donned a bullhorn and yelled his message to the gathering crowd. Most of the crowd were tourists only paying the demonstration minor attention, taking photos of the smoke or selfies with the protest in the background. There was a heavy presence of Italian authorities to assure a peaceful protest. She had seen many of these during her lifetime in Italy, everybody seemed to have a cause. She didn't know what this one was about nor did she care, she had a contact to meet and she was already a few minutes late, mostly due to the unreliability of the Italian train schedules.

Protesters blocked the street, which did not matter, since she turned north on Borgo la Noce. Racks of leather jackets lined the outside of the shop. The door was the metal roll-up type that retracted into a metal casing mounted above the store front entrance. In many ways like a garage door, but different. Leaning against the graffiti-laden wall across the street from the shop was Enzo Mantova, a plume of cigarette smoke swirled around his head. He must have seen her when she rounded the corner. With an imperceptible nod, he acknowledged her arrival, dropped his cigarette to the street and crushed it with the toe of his shoe. He disappeared into the leather shop.

She followed him into the store past the many customers who were too busy rummaging through racks of leather jackets to notice them. A closed curtain separated the back room from the shoppers up front. A large man with balding hair greeted her before she could enter the back room—Massimo, Enzo's backstopped brother. They greeted each other with a cheek to cheek kiss. A gesture of good will. Even men typically greeted each other in the same fashion. "Enzo said you were coming. I hope he is not in danger." His English was good.

"No," she said. "Nothing like that. I need his help to identify a couple of people, that's all."

"You know *that man* was here, look for Enzo."

"Who?"

"You know, AISE man, Serreti. He came yesterday with two of his goons. Flash credentials and ran off my customers."

"Marco was here? What did he want?"

"He want talk to Enzo…lucky my brother not here, yes? Lucky for me, too. His men search for him. He angry Enzo not here."

"Does Enzo know?"

"Yes, he hide in back, wait for you. He had just lit smoke when he run back in. I afraid AISE come back."

"I thought this would be a safe place. Dammit, we should have met somewhere else." Francesca was worried about why Marco wanted Enzo. If he showed up here and missed Enzo, he would certainly return. He might even have the place under surveillance. Not good. This could be a trap and she just walked into it. She needed to get Enzo out of there, fast. Serreti could prove as much harm to Enzo as the Mafioso.

"Problema," Massimo muttered in a low voice. "AISE return."

She twisted around and looked. Marco Serreti entered the storefront opening. "What are you doing here?"

"I might ask you the same question, Francesca," Serreti said. "But, I already know the answer. Without consulting me or AISE, you took matters in your own hands."

She grabbed a handful of the deputy director's shirt right below his chin and said, "Let's get something straight once and for all. I don't work for AISE and I damn sure don't work for you."

Two men, obviously Serreti's puppets, moved toward her. Marco waved them off with his hand and looked down at her hand, still clutching his shirt. "Do you mind?" She backed up and let loose, leaving Serreti's shirt crumpled. He smoothed his shirt with his hands and readjusted his tie. "There is no need to get so rough. That can be for another time." His cocky wink and confident smile infuriated her. "Now, please where's Enzo?"

"I have no idea. I came to see Massimo…and buy a leather jacket."

"I hardly believe you took a train all the way from Rome to buy a leather jacket in Firenze. Now, I'll ask you again, where is Enzo?"

Patrons began to leave the store when Francesca and Serreti raised their voices. It was a well-known fact in Italy any confrontation with the deputy director of AISE wouldn't end well for the person doing the arguing. "You do not listen, Marco, I have no idea. I just arrived and have only greeted my friend, Massimo."

"What business do you have in Firenze?" His authoritative and combative tone pissed her off even more.

"My damn business…is none of yours, Marco. Now leave me alone."

"Are you carrying?"

She was surprised by the abruptness of the question. Of course, she was carrying and Marco knew it. She didn't answer.

"Let me have your weapon, Francesca."

Nothing.

"Search her," Marco said to his puppets.

When the two men moved toward her, she shoved them backwards. She kept one hand up to signal not to advance again. "I'm authorized to carry," she finally said. "And you know that."

"I'm revoking your authorization."

"Not likely," she said. "Director Barzetti signed my authorization and, unless he is no longer in power, you do not have the authority to countermand his directive. So, I'll keep my weapon and you and your little body guards can get the hell out of here and leave me alone." Her words crowded together as she panted. "Or I will call the director myself."

Both men waited for Marco Serreti to respond to the insults. "She can keep her weapon for now," he said to them. "Search the building. Find Enzo and bring him to me. He could not have gone far." The men nodded and rushed through the curtains and into the back room.

After the men left, he gripped her arm and pulled her behind a rolling rack of Italian leather jackets. His grip was firm. She yanked her arm in an attempt to free it, but he only tightened his grip. And this time, it hurt. "Marco, I'm warning you to let go of me now."

His mouth so close she could feel his breath, "You will do as I say. You are coming back to Rome with me."

In a split second, she jabbed him in the neck with her knuckles sending his throat into spasms. He released her arm and she did a hard quick snap with her lower leg to the target—his groin. He doubled over, one hand holding his throat, the other his groin. He fell backward against a concrete block wall hunched over while using the wall to keep him from dropping to his knees. She whispered in his ear, "If you interfere with me again, Marco, I'll kill you." Then she lifted him by the arm and pulled him upright. His bulging eyes revealed the pain he felt. She crouched forward. "And you know damn well I won't hesitate to do it."

That was nearly six hours ago. She hadn't seen Marco Serreti or any of his stooges since. She checked the time on her watch. It was a new Apple Watch specially upgraded by Wiley with proprietary apps that would never be available on the open market. She hoped Enzo was not captured by Marco's men. If he didn't show, she could expect the worst.

Within seconds the wait was over. Enzo Mantova's face appeared as he strolled up the last few steps to the terrace on the top of the hotel's tower. "You look happy," she said when she stood to give Enzo a cheek to cheek kiss.

"Massimo told me what you did to Serreti. I'm surprised he didn't come after you."

"He knows better, Enzo. I told him if I saw him again, I'd kill him."

"Nice bluff."

She contorted her face and spit out the words like a rabid animal. "I wasn't bluffing."

He stood silent, obviously trying to determine if she was serious or not. The corner of his mouth finally turned up. She could see he knew she was serious.

"Did you walk down Via De Calzaioli?" he changed the subject.

"No. I came down Calimala by Mercato Nuovo." The market. "It never ceases to amaze me that Italian men like to shop more than women. And not a one of them can walk past a mirror without checking themselves out. Why do you ask about Calzaioli?"

"There's this new chalk artist on the street. His stuff is 3-D. He's making a fortune. Not only from tourists, but locals too. Nobody has seen anything like it. He did a chalk of David that was out of this world. I felt like I could step inside and touch him."

"I'll have to check it out in the morning. How'd you get away? The secret escape Massimo put in years ago?" She made reference to a trap door in the floor of the back room, usually covered with a large oriental area rug, that led down and underneath to tunnels beneath the Medici Chapels.

Enzo nodded. "Massimo is a smart man." His finger tapped his forehead. The bartender came up and Enzo ordered a glass of red wine. When he disappeared down the stairs, Enzo said, "So, Francesca, how may I help you?"

She pulled out a folder from her backpack. She removed several 8 x 10 photos and placed them on the table in front of Enzo. She heard footsteps coming up the stairs so she flipped the pictures over. Enzo took a glass of wine and handed the man a €10 bill. When the bartender retreated down the steps, she flipped the pictures upright.

Enzo lined them across the table. "Never seen him." He

tapped on the picture of Ethan Wogahn. He tapped on another picture. "This is Qasem Kazemi…but I think you already knew that." He picked up several more pictures and shook his head. "Never seen any of these either." He stopped at a picture and held it up at eye level and leaned back in his chair. "This guy I know. He's a hacker known as *The Jew*. Heard he got himself into a lot of trouble, but I don't know what it was. He dropped off the grid about a week ago, I think."

Francesca nodded. "Exactly a week ago," she said. "And we think he is in danger. Any idea where he might be?"

"No, but I'll ask around. See if I can dig up something for you."

She slid the last picture in front of him. "Ever seen him?"

"Oh yeah." He nodded and tapped his finger on the picture. "This guy, I remember. I could never forget him. Took me for €10,000 last year at the Secret Agent Party. He goes every year, without fail."

"Secret Agent Party? What is that?"

Enzo leaned back in his chair and once again raised the wine glass to within an inch of his lips. "It's a gambling junket at Casino Baden, B—"

Enzo's wine glass shattered in his hands covering the pictures on the table with glass and wine, and something else.

Stunned, she looked at Enzo.

His face was gone.

CHAPTER 39

Jake sat silent as George Fontaine worked his magic on the computer in the command center of Commonwealth Consultants located in Fairfax, Virginia. After Fontaine loaded all the parameters the two of them could think of, the computer's electronic brain started processing and churning out data. Slowly, possible landing sites were eliminated from the map on the large overhead monitor. This was where Fontaine excelled. By coupling data and satellite imagery from the Department of Defense's computer, any sites that were possible landing sites were excluded by visual satellite imagery confirmation.

As *Old Blue,* Fontaine's nickname for Wiley's computer complex, dropped possibilities from the map, the areas turned gray with thin red hash marks streaking across the screen. Within two hours, one by one, all of the smaller South Pacific islands within the fuel exhaustion ring were eliminated. In the upper right hand corner of the monitor was a percentage countdown of areas where a Boeing 777 landing was possible. It ticked down. When Fontaine initiated the run sequence on Old Blue, the initial percentage eliminated was 61.756% leaving an area of 38.244% for possible landing sites. It had now ticked down to 16.575%.

To Jake, 16.575% seemed like a small number and he was getting excited the search area had narrowed to something he considered manageable, but Fontaine quickly informed him the real work was just beginning as the overwhelming majority of the remaining area left no real way of detection without visual confirmation. And visual confirmation was next to impossible due to darkness.

At Jake's request, Fontaine started plugging in the data from several conspiracy theories floating around the internet. One involved a United States cover-up and that the aircraft had been hijacked by the U. S. Government and flown to a military and intelligence base in the Indian Ocean called Diego Garcia. One conspiracy theorist suggested that a text message emanated from the aircraft less than five miles from Diego Garcia and was traced using GPS coordinates from an iPhone. This proved to be a discredited claim, but nonetheless, Jake had Fontaine check it out anyway. Visual satellite confirmation proved easy and any possibility of a landing at Diego Garcia was invalid.

"Let's rule out countries where we are relatively certain the aircraft wouldn't have gone," Fontaine suggested.

"For instance?" Jake challenged.

"Okay," Fontaine explained, "take Australia, for instance. Australia is an ally and they have nothing to gain."

"Yeah, but there are a lot of possible landing sites in western Australia."

"A few years ago, weren't you involved in an op in the Australian desert? You busted up an al Qaeda training camp I believe, right?"

"Yes."

"Then you know the terrain is pretty harsh and unforgiving. I'm pretty certain if the airliner landed in Australia, our intelligence community would have uncovered it by now."

"I see where you're going with this George, and that's a good idea, but instead of eliminating them entirely, can you create a new designation?"

"You mean like this?" Fontaine typed on his keyboard and within two minutes, all of the area inside the fuel exhaustion arc in Australia turned yellow. In the upper right hand corner, a new percentage total appeared next to the elimination total. It was simply designated as *Improbable*. The percentage dropped to 12.372%.

"I like it," Jake said as he patted Fontaine on the back. "How about China and Southeast Asia?"

"I say we leave all of that area as a possibility for right now. We can come back to them later if need be. Let's talk about India."

Jake reached up and placed his finger on the monitor. "I think we can eliminate everything from the Gulf of Martaban here." Jake touched his finger to point west of Thailand and drew an arc up and to the left following the coastline. "To include all of the eastern coastline of India."

"That's a huge chunk to knock out as a possibility. What's the reason?"

"Simple. Check the locations of our U. S. Naval fleet on that night. Look what was sitting in the middle of the Bay of Bengal."

"The U. S. S. Mount Whitney." Fontaine turned to Jake and smiled. "You used to work on that ship."

"That's right, George. The U. S. S. Mount Whitney is a naval intelligence ship and has all the capabilities to detect any aircraft, day or night, regardless of altitude, and whether it has any or none of its electronics turned on. Air Malacca 910 could not have entered the mainland through the Bay of

Bengal without the United States Navy knowing about it. And by the time the aircraft could have reached the Bay of Bengal, our military had already been alerted to its disappearance. The U. S. S. Mount Whitney would have been on the lookout and certainly detected it."

"In that case, we should probably move all of India into the yellow. Given our geopolitical standing with India, it's highly unlikely they have any involvement with the airliner's disappearance."

"Good idea, George. Do it." Within seconds the map updated and the entire area turned yellow on the map.

"Should we continue right to left?"

Jake moved his hand to the southern tip of the island of Madagascar, off the South African coast. Fuel exhaustion distance had eliminated South Africa and barely covered Northern Madagascar and the tip of the northeast Africa coastline. "Let's start here and work back toward India."

"Okay," Fontaine said. "But you know you're leaving the hardest for last."

"Deliberately, I might add."

"As you know already, the United States had several Naval and Coast Guard vessels lining the Eastern Africa coastline due to all the pirate activity. Our government already ruled out Madagascar, Kenya, Ethiopia, and Somalia. By then, the airliner would be approaching its fuel exhaustion limits. Because of our heightened activity in the Middle East, we have a preponderance of vessels in the western portions of the Arabian Sea as well. Jake, I'd have to rule out Yemen and Oman too."

"Which leaves us with?" Jake asked.

"Pakistan in the west, Southeast Asia and China in the east."

"Precisely."

"Pakistan doesn't really have the resources or wherewithal to conceal that airliner," Fontaine said. "So you have to figure what, Afghanistan?"

"Nope, too risky in my opinion. We still have boots on the ground there. And personally, I think China had too much to lose if they got caught, and I don't think any of these Southeast Asian countries want to get involved in this mess in any way."

"Well," Fontaine said, "that pretty much leaves Iran."

"That's right. Pakistan won't do or say anything…provided they even knew an aircraft crossed their border from the Arabian Sea to Iran. Which I doubt seriously they did. And we're only talking a small border crossing too. Air Malacca 910 didn't have enough fuel given the route it would have to take to make it to Tehran." Jake tapped his finger on the southeastern section of Iran. "I know from my Naval Intelligence days, the Lut Desert is not only capable of landing an aircraft of this size, but concealing it as well. Iran actually has several prepped areas in the Lut that have been used for takeoff and landings. They camouflage not only aircraft, but entire villages as well, beneath giant desert colored tents. And because they keep a tight lock on their borders, these desert villages and airstrips remain basically undetected."

"Large enough for a Boeing 777? That's one hell of a big tent."

"Yes it is. And the ends of the airstrip jut out of each end of the camouflage so most of the takeoff roll is under the tent. By the time the aircraft appear, they are nearly up to takeoff speed. Same on landing, most of the roll out is under camouflage. It can make it very difficult to track. And visual confirmation doesn't help much either since most of the aircraft using these strips are painted in desert camo."

"But not Air Malacca 910," Fontaine said. "We need to find a way to search for a visual crossing of the coastline, don't we?"

"That would help, but there wasn't much light in the sky by the time the aircraft could have reached the coastline. Look on the bright side though, George. We've narrowed the search area down to what, about four hundred miles or so?"

"*Only* four hundred miles," Fontaine said and then laughed. "You make it sound like we've almost figured this whole thing out. I told you earlier our work was just beginning. *If* we are correct, and that's a pretty big if, then we have four hundred plus miles of coastline to scan for a relatively long time interval in order to capture a visual image of something that will take a fraction of a second to cross from water to land. Jake, if the sun was up, we might be able to pick out a few reflections off the airliner's skin while it was still over water, we could start a good visual track maybe, but it will be below the sun when it crosses the coast."

"Wait, what did you say?"

"I said—"

"No, I heard you. Let me check something." Jake flipped through a few weather reports for the area. "See here, George. Skies were clear over the north Arabian Sea and it was two days away from a full moon. If the sun could reflect off the aircraft's skin, what about the moon? And if we can locate it over water where the contrast will be greater, we should be able to follow it to its landing location."

"You know, Einstein, that might work. What we need to do is determine its most probable route, then program a visual scan for that area."

"Why don't we go all the way back to the point when it disappeared from radar and see if we can pick up any reflections from there?"

"That won't work, Jake. The skies weren't clear all the way from Malaysia to Iran."

"No they weren't, but I'm betting the aircraft didn't descend right away either. I'd be willing to bet the pilots knew they needed to conserve as much fuel as they could so they kept the aircraft at high altitude…and that would keep them above the clouds and with any turns at all—"

"The reflection from the moon might be visible on the enhanced satellite imagery."

CHAPTER 40

Midnight in Italy

When Omar returned, Daniel Luzato knew his fate was sealed.

After Omar's goon cleaned up the bloody remains of Germano Caminiti, he reattached the collar around Luzato's neck and removed the restraints allowing him to move freely around the cellar. In the back of his mind he thought wearing the collar was a good sign, a sign Omar wouldn't kill him, but instead torture him in order to acquire the decryption codes. In his foresight, he saw this day coming and had secreted the codes in a place where they could not easily be retrieved. Someplace safe. And far away. If his assessments had been correct, they were in a place far from Omar's reach.

The codes were too complicated to memorize them all. Some codes and software backdoors were simpler. And those were the tidbits he would feed Omar. Codes that were only slightly effective, enough to lull Omar into a false sense of victory, but only allow him access through the first line of cyber defenses…and no further. And after he used them, he would unknowingly activate a sequence of events that should be detected by the Americans allowing for Omar's plot to be uncovered. *Should be* was the key. If the Americans failed to notice, Omar would have more time to realize he had been duped. Then the angry man would return and Luzato knew he would have to die to protect the future.

The world's future.

Something he was willing to do. His heritage was at stake.

He paced around the cellar in anxious dread. He knew his immediate future was full of pain, but he couldn't give Omar what he wanted too freely or else the former Iranian Guard general would become suspicious. No, he would have to endure great pain. His performance had to be convincing. Omar had to believe he had broken *The Jew*.

He started to sit down, but stopped himself. It was the chair in which Germano had suffered and died. Although the man cleaned it feverishly, the chair was wooden and the dry porous wood had absorbed some of the blood and the arms and legs were now permanently stained. Even though the man cleaned the floor, a dark blotching pattern remained in the dirt.

He continued pacing, wondering if others had met the same fate as Germano in this ancient cellar. He studied every mark and discoloration in the floor, but nothing resembled the spot where Germano died. No marks on tables or chairs either. After a few minutes, he was convinced Germano Caminiti was the only one who had suffered and died in this basement at the hands of Qasem Kazemi, aka Omar.

After fifteen or twenty minutes, the bolt thudded on the heavy wooden door.

It was time.

He waited in dreaded anticipation for the door to open in what seemed like minutes, but was only a few seconds. And then the large figure of a man entered, but it was not Omar, it was his goon carrying a tray of food.

He stared at the man and asked, "Where is Omar?"

The man walked across the room without speaking and

placed the tray on the table. He turned to him and said, "The general is not a young man and the events of the evening have taken a toll. Germano was one of his most trusted friends so as you might expect, he is extremely upset at Germano's betrayal. The general wanted me to impress upon you this might be your last supper if you don't cooperate when he returns in the morning." Without another word, the man turned and left the cellar, bolting the door behind him.

Luzato removed the silver dome from the tray. For the first time since his imprisonment in this underground chamber he was being fed a kosher meal.

†††

Raleigh, North Carolina

After Boris learned of Germano Caminiti's betrayal from Omar during their video chat, he made the inference to the general that any betrayal could be a threat to his plan and should be handled with swift and decisive permanency. He was sure Omar understood. It was important for success of the project. Germano was the second of Omar's men who had failed his part of this mission. The first man ended up dead in *The Jew's* flat in Rome. His death led investigators to the man's apartment in Vienna where the man had kept a file on everyone working in Omar's plan.

And that led them to Boris, which was why he narrowly escaped Georgetown. Precaution and preparation for the worst case scenario was always the best plan for self-preservation.

After the video chat, Boris had electronically removed all existence of his former identity as Alexei Nikahd. His true identity no longer existed. Now, he was Alex Skylar, a third-year NC State University graphic design student.

At 6:30, he left his apartment and walked the thirty feet to the apartment next door. He raised his hand to knock when the door opened. A short blonde stood with an overnight bag slung over her shoulder. "Oh," she said with surprise in her voice. "You startled me." Alex gazed down at the young woman, she couldn't be more than 5' 2" at the most. She was wearing black tights that stopped mid-calf and a red NC State t-shirt. The below average height and her broad shoulders, thick arms and legs made her resemble a fireplug. She had soft features and a fair, almost pasty, complexion.

"I'm sorry, I didn't mean to startle you," he said.

Her startled face softened. "You must be our not-so new neighbor." A statement, but with the hint of a question mark in her tone.

He stuck out his hand. "Alex Skylar. You must be Emma?"

She shook his hand. "That's right." She craned her neck toward the back of her apartment. "Ashley, your date's here."

"Be right there," Ashley yelled back.

"She's cooking." Emma moved to the side. "Come on in."

A tantalizing distinct savory smell floated from the kitchen filling the room. He did a quick assessment of the apartment. The floor plan was the mirror opposite of his next door. The furnishings were cheap college furniture. There was an old black bean bag chair next to a large flat screen TV on top of a particle board stand painted black. A green hand me down microfiber couch with lots of oversized cushions lined a wall. Somebody had used their carpenter skills and made a coffee table from pallets. Two closed doors to his left must be bedrooms.

"Ashley tells me you are a graphic design major too," Emma said.

"That's right."

"Third year, I understand. I'm starting my fourth year. I'm supposed to be on the eight semester program, but I think it will take nine." She hesitated. "It's weird I've never seen you around, have you been here the whole time or did you transfer?"

"Been here the whole time. This is my fifth semester."

"What classes are you taking this semester?"

"Branding, Interaction, and Service. Online and Mobile Interaction Systems. Information and Publishing Systems. And—"

"Do you have Peters for Info and Pub Systems?"

He laughed. "I do. Nice guy, but that thing on his face." He let the remark hang.

"I know. What is that thing? Like, a birthmark or something? It is so gross. You'd think he'd have had it removed. I can't look at him in class because it's so distracting."

"Right. When he talks to me, I have to force myself not to turn away."

He noticed her relax a little now that they had found a common bond. She didn't know it was all a ruse. Boris had already hacked the NC State computer and obtained all of her records, including her current and past classes, instructors, and grades. Then he looked up every instructor profile and stored it all in memory. Precaution and preparation. Emma was now convinced he was a student with the same major as hers and that was all he needed for validation. As soon as he'd leased the apartment several months ago, he'd done his homework and learned the identity and majors of his neighbors. He learned their habits and patterns. He knew their family histories, including the fact Ashley's father owned a vineyard in California. The fact the vineyard was failing due to the California drought was a secret Ashley's father had apparently kept from her.

Ashley appeared in the room. "Sorry it took so long," she said. "I had to get the pasta going." She looked stunning. The simple navy dress stopped right above her knee with a neckline low enough to tease. The black heels added three inches to her height. Her warm chestnut hair hung loose on her shoulders.

He glanced down at his attire and said, "I suddenly feel under dressed." He was wearing jeans, athletic shoes, and a sweater pulled over a button-down shirt.

"Nonsense," she reassured him. "You look great."

Emma laughed. It was that *I have a secret* kind of laugh.

"Am I missing something?" Boris didn't like being made fun of regardless of which identity he had at the time.

Ashley laughed. "Relax, I had an interview at 4:30 for a part-time job and haven't had time to change."

"I cannot imagine you not getting the job. You look very beautiful."

Ashley was used to compliments, her eyes told him that. He was convinced she enjoyed the seduction of men. Woman like her needed to feel desired. Tonight, he would ensure her needs would be fulfilled. She stood a few feet away, but her mischievous eyes kept him from looking away.

"Ahem. Alex, it was a pleasure." Emma glanced at Ashley. "I'm sure I'll be seeing you again soon."

"Yes, you will."

Emma left the apartment closing the door behind her.

"Is she going to the gym or something?" Alex asked.

"Nope," Ashley said. "Now, come in here with me, I need to

check on the pasta." He followed her into the kitchen. "Emma is spending the night with her boyfriend, so we'll have the place to ourselves. How about some wine?" She held up a bottle of Cabernet Sauvignon sitting on the counter next to two glasses.

He nodded. "That would be perfect."

"Well," she said, "don't just stand there, pour."

He poured two glasses of wine. She insisted he fill the glasses all the way up instead of halfway like he originally had poured. She took her glass and they toasted to new friendships. She drank half her glass during the toast, placed it on the counter. "Keep it full while I cook." She slipped out of her heels, kicked them into the hall, and stood barefooted in front of the stove.

During dinner, Ashley polished off another full glass of wine and she began to talk louder and giggled at almost everything he said and a lot of what she said. She opened the second bottle of wine, instructed him to leave the dishes on the table, and the two of them went into the living room where she tuned the TV to an all music, no video station. They sat next to each other on the couch, and continued to drink and talk and laugh. She inched closer to him until their bodies were touching. He decided to her be the aggressor and see where it led them. He didn't have to wait long before her hand was rubbing his thigh. The tactile sensations were spine tingling, euphoric. She placed her wine glass on the coffee table and took his glass and did the same with it. Next, she leaned over and placed her hand on the side of his face and kissed him. His heart began to beat faster, as they kissed harder and her hands moved across his body. She ran her hands up and down his chest until finally she grabbed a handful of his sweater and pulled it over his head. His eyes began to droop after she had stripped him of his shirt. Then, she passionately licked and kissed his neck and chest. The woman was wild and he liked it. The apartment felt warm and soon they were both sweaty.

She stopped and moved off of him. "What the—"

She placed her finger over his lips. She unbuckled his belt and stripped him of his pants and then stood up straight. She reached behind her back and unzipped her dress in tantalizing motions while she moved in rhythm to the music. Her moves were provocative and promiscuous, like she'd rehearsed this many times.

Excitement coursed through his veins. He was entranced, like he was in some hypnotic state. She teasingly slid the straps from her shoulders and let her dress drop to the floor.

He felt the prickling on his back run down his spine.

She was stark naked.

She stepped forward and placed one knee on the couch beside his bare leg and then the other knee. As she straddled him, she lowered herself onto him. She clasped her hands behind his neck and rocked back and forth, gently circling her hips.

They made love.

Slowly at first, until she let out a soft moan. Then she pressed herself firmer against him until all gentleness was gone. Her hips rotated faster until she arched her back, dug her fingernails into his neck, threw back her head, screamed, and climaxed with a shudder. Then, covered in a sweaty sheen, she collapsed against his chest and let out a soft sigh.

CHAPTER 41

It was already after midnight as Jake drank his third cup of coffee sitting next to Fontaine while the analyst was keying in more programming data into the computer. On the overhead display, he observed the track of Air Malacca 910 disappear in the south China Sea.

"Hold up, George. We made a mistake."

"What do you mean?"

"Earlier I said we could rule out the Bay of Bengal. And why? Because the U. S. S. Mount Whitney was on patrol in the middle of the Bay of Bengal. I also said we could rule out Yemen and Oman because of preponderance of Naval vessels in the area."

"Yeah. Have you changed your mind?"

He took a gulp of coffee. "Remember the video from Hardwire Semiconductors? What if the aircraft electronically jammed the Navy's equipment?"

"Then it's feasible the airliner went on a direct route to its destination."

"That's right, George. And that means our search area just increased substantially."

George typed feverishly on his keyboard for a couple of minutes before a map on the overhead display updated. "Taking into account those factors, this is our new search area." Fontaine moved his cursor onto the display "Now, we have to account for Russia as a player."

"That sucks," Jake finally said.

There was a several second pause as both men exchanged glances and no one spoke.

"But wait," Fontaine said with a smile. "We forgot to account for something."

"What do you mean?"

"This," Fontaine answered. "I forgot to couple the thermal imagery scan to its known track? Then, when I add it, look what happens." He pressed a key and the display updated again. A small red line appeared behind the track of Air Malacca 910 and continued past where the aircraft disappeared on radar. "If I program the thermal scan for heat signatures from a Boeing 777 engines, here's what I get."

It wasn't a continuous line, there were gaps in the heat signature. In the middle of the night, especially in this part of the world, there was little jet traffic in the skies so connecting the gaps wasn't difficult at all, even without the help of *Old Blue*. After Fontaine reprogrammed the algorithms, a bright blue line traced the flight track of Air Malacca 910.

"Look at that, Jake, you were right. The pilot's played it safe and stayed over water."

Jake studied the flight path of the B-777 aircraft while rubbing the two-day stubble on his chin. After turning off all of their electronic equipment, including their transponder and Aircraft Communications Addressing and Reporting System, or ACARS, which transmitted key information on an aircraft's condition, the pilots made a long slow turn to the right barely keeping them off the northwestern coastline of Borneo. Then Air Malacca 910 flew due west, right over their departure point of Malacca and across Sumatra where it entered the Indian Ocean. It remained on a westerly track until a point four hundred kilometers east of the Maldives Islands, where it turned northwest paralleling the western coastline of India roughly three hundred kilometers offshore. It continued on the same track crossing from the Arabian Sea across southwestern Pakistan and into Iran where the heat signature track disappeared over a dried up lakebed in the southern Lut Desert.

"Yes," Fontaine shouted. "We got those bastards." He raised his hand and gave Jake a high five. Jake watched the overhead display gradually zoom in to the spot where the track disappeared. As the high-definition satellite photo became clearer and closer to ground level, he could see the lakebed wasn't entirely dried up as the southwestern corner still held water. Closer still, a slight glow from the heat signature could be seen beneath the camouflage netting covering the airstrip. Even closer, vehicles appeared in the open desert, a trail of dust giving away their direction of travel. Beneath the netting, though, nothing else could be seen. The netting completely screened out what was underneath. The netting proved better than even he had anticipated as it blended in perfectly with the landscape and it was almost impossible to tell where the netting ended and the desert began. As the time lapse ticked on, the glow from the heat signature faded.

"Remember, George, this was two and a half years ago. No telling where anything is anymore, even the aircraft. Can you get a current satellite shot of these exact coordinates and compare the two?"

"Buzz killer," Fontaine clicked on his keyboard and brought up a new image and placed it side-by-side with the old one. "How's this?"

"Looks different."

"What if," Fontaine stroked the keys and moved the image with his mouse. "I overlay one on top of the other like this."

The outline of the camouflage netting came into view. The lakebed was full of water and the surrounding landscape different. "I was afraid of that. They broke camp and moved everything. The question is, when? How long was the aircraft under the netting before they moved it…and where did they take it?"

"And where are the 239 passengers?" Fontaine added.

They sat silent for several seconds when their shared contemplations were interrupted by an aural alarm.

Fontaine spun around in his chair and faced his monitor. "Oh, shit."

"Oh, Shit? What do you mean, oh, shit? Oh, shit can't be good."

"It isn't. Someone just hacked the European rail system and shut it down."

"Which country in Europe?" he asked.

Fontaine face tensed. "All of them. Almost every rail system across Europe just ground to a halt."

"How could somebody shut them all down at once?" he asked Fontaine whose brow had furrowed so deeply that it looked painful. "Could you have hacked into them and shut them all down?"

"I've never taken a peek inside any of them before," Fontaine said as he turned back to his computer and started pecking on his keyboard, "but yeah, I probably could if I had enough time. Whoever did this is good…very good." Fontaine paused and without raising his head said, "You need to call Wiley."

Jake peeked at his new *Wiley-enhanced* Apple Watch. "It's like a quarter to seven in Belgium, can it wait?"

Another alarm sounded.

"No. No. No," Fontaine voice jumped an octave. "The Charles De Gaulle Airport in Paris just went completely offline."

"What do you mean offline?"

"I mean someone shut down everything. Power, computer systems, all support systems, environmental systems, everything, including backups. The entire airport is dead in the water, so to speak." Fontaine did not simply raise his voice, he shouted, "Call Wiley now. Tell him…it's happening now."

"Tell him what's happening now?"

"Disruption."

CHAPTER 42

It felt like every fiber and sinew in his body was on fire. Pain radiated up his arms and legs and triggered every alarm in his brain. Omar kept his promise from last night, he had not been gentle. He hadn't been merciless either. He needed information and had come to realize, as the dead Germano Caminiti had warned him, that if he inflicted too much damage, Luzato would not be capable of giving up the decryption codes. Even the ruthless Qasem Kazemi had learned something through this ordeal.

Daniel Luzato had endured much pain through Omar's information extraction. Several times the sadistic interrogation was almost unbearable, but in the back recesses of his mind he knew he had to hold out. He had to convince Omar he'd been broken. That the former Iranian Revolutionary Guard general had succeeded in exacting enough pain to squeeze out the decryption codes. Only he hadn't gotten the ones he needed, not all of them. Instead he was given activation codes to trigger a string of events that *should* raise interest from the world's intelligence agencies.

If those agencies looked deep, very deep, into his coding, they should find what they needed to stop Omar from his cyber terror. Or at least slow him down. He deliberately planted those clues for a situation like this one. Although the former general would never admit it to him, he knew Omar's plan involved a tactical and strategic misdirection. One designed to throw off the intelligence community and that misdirection needed to be exposed, but in a stealthy manner. It had to be so vague that only the best of the best in the hacking world would notice it. Problem was, Omar had one of those *best of the best* in his cadre. Omar's plan was good, at least the part of it Luzato had seen prior to his capture. He had barely finished his coding, uploaded his software, and enjoyed a celebratory dinner before he awoke here. Wherever *here* was.

When Omar and his muscle men arrived early this morning, at least they said it was morning, they stripped him naked and strapped him to a chair, the same chair in which Germano had died. Then, Omar's muscle beat him. At first, blows to his face, not too hard, just hard enough to see how tough he really was…and then, the force of the blows knocked his head with such force, his neck popped. Repeated jabs to the torso and face. His busted lips flowed blood down his chin, his nose was broken, and his left eye already swollen shut. After a short respite, he was splashed with water and Omar asked for his cooperation. He remained silent and spit on Omar's shoe, not having the strength to aim for the face. A man picked up a wooden baton, much like a police baton, and started striking him, hard enough to deepen the bruises, not hard enough to break bone or cause him to lose consciousness.

Oddly enough, through all the beatings and all his agonizing screams, the collar remained calm. No shocks due to loud noises—of which there were plenty. He could only surmise that Omar had turned off the sound activated function of his sadistic creation.

But his resolve didn't break, not yet. He had to resist. If he had given up then, Omar might have suspected something was amiss. The stakes were too high to give in without considerable resistance. He knew Omar was aware of that. To give in to the general too soon would be to raise the man's suspicion that he was being tricked. Luzato's plan was a well thought out trap that he could never reveal, regardless of the pain.

Next, the man unrolled a leather bag. Inside the bag were what looked like wooden skewers, only the color and texture were all wrong. More like the bamboo poison darts used in a blowgun. Omar's goon pulled out one dart and poked him in the left leg. A searing burn instantly shot through his leg radiating upward into his lower torso. Within seconds, his skin reddened and swelled where he was stabbed with the barb. Maybe they were poison darts. This was repeated time and time again, multiple stabs to each leg and then his arms. No pain he'd ever experienced equaled what he felt at that moment. The nerves in his limbs were on fire like he was burning from the inside out. He knew it must have been some kind of poison on the tips of the darts. The intense burning caused him to scream and his body fought to escape the restraints.

The torture stopped. Omar stood, waiting for him to speak. He couldn't give in to Omar. Not yet. He must suffer more.

Luzato did something that baffled his captures. He began to sing. Loud, as loud as he could.

Omar was not amused. He ordered his henchman to continue. The man picked up a fresh dart and poked him several times in the chest and back. A burning fire raked upward through his torso. Sweat coursed from every pore. The pain in his arms and legs were muted by this new wildfire raging through his body. He let loose a piercing scream, sobbed and begged the man to stop. "No more, stop, stop…"

With the swift movement of a hand, Omar signaled the

man to stop.

"You are now ready to tell me?" Omar had asked.

Luzato couldn't speak. His head hung low, his mouth full of blood. A weak nod was all he could manage to signal the end of the torture.

The ordeal seemed to last forever, although he knew it was likely less than an hour in duration. It had been the longest hour of his life, though. Now Omar had what he wanted, at least he thought he had what he wanted. Phase one of Luzato's backup plan was in place. The only thing remaining was to trick Omar into booting up Luzato's laptop. Deep inside the operating system of his computer, he had installed a subroutine that would seek out the strongest WIFI connection, crack the password, and automatically and invisibly log on using the most secure VPN in the world. After logging in to the virtual private network and without entering the proper sequence of characters on the keyboard, the computer would transmit his current location to the United States intelligence community. A failsafe he had installed in the likely event he was kidnapped, as he was now.

Hopefully, when Omar returned, he could convince the general to allow him access to his laptop in order to retrieve the remaining decryption codes. Or at least, that is what he would tell Omar.

CHAPTER 43

Jake placed the call and Elmore Wiley answered on the first ring.

"Hello Jake, calling to check on Kyli again?" Wiley's voice tired. Over the course of the past year or so, Jake noticed Wiley was starting to show his age more and more. Physically, anyway. Now, his voice held a slight tremble, but his mind was still sharp. The old man's physical decline seemed to start with the car accident and his associated injuries. At his age, the recovery process wasn't like the younger years. He didn't bounce back as fast this time; a slow and steady procession, but he hadn't reached full recovery yet. And perhaps would never be quite the same active man Jake remembered scurrying around with endless energy.

"That's one reason for the call. How is she?"

"Still the same as when we last talked last. Her condition is stable but the source of her infection hasn't been determined yet and, since Kyli is still in an induced coma, we can't ask her what she might have been exposed to in the lab."

"Do the doctors think they'll bring her out of it anytime soon?"

"Last thing they mentioned was they wanted to control her vitals and let this thing run its course. When she improves, which they are hoping might be today sometime, then perhaps they'll bring her out of it and she can provide some needed insight." Wiley coughed into the phone. "Why else did you call?"

"George and I found out what happened to Air Malacca 910."

"I had faith in you two. I knew you'd be able to crack that mystery. Don't keep me in suspense, Jake, where is the airplane?"

"We don't know where it is now, but we do know where it went."

"With everything that's been happening lately, my money is on China…or maybe Iran."

"Iran," Jake stated. "After it disappeared on radar, it took a long slow right turn and rolled out on a westerly heading where it stayed for a long time to a point south of the Indian Coast near the Maldives. Then, it turned northwest and flew across the Arabian Sea, the southwestern tip of Pakistan, and into Iran. It landed, or perhaps I should say disappeared, on a dry lakebed in the Lut Desert."

"And you don't know where it went?"

Fontaine gave him a dirty look and flipped his palms upward.

"Not yet," Jake hesitated, "we were interrupted. Which is the main reason I'm calling."

"What is it, son? Spit it out." Wiley seemed irritated by the delay.

"We have a situation brewing in Europe…and since you're there, George told me to tell you that it's happening now."

"Dammit Jake, I don't have time for games. For crying out loud, what's happening?"

"Disruption. That's all George said."

There was a long silence on the phone.

"Sir?"

"Shit," Wiley grumbled into the phone. "I knew this day would come, just not so soon. I'd hoped it was a long way off. This thing with MEtech and Kyli is unfortunate, I'm not in a position to handle it from here with my lab out of commission." Wiley went silent again. Jake knew he was mulling over the news. He could picture the old man pushing his wire rim glasses up on his nose and running his hands over his gray hair. "What has happened thus far?"

"As you remember, someone shut down Italy's banking system two days ago."

"Yes, you briefed me."

"A little bit ago, the European rail systems were hacked and shut down."

"How widespread is the outage?"

"That was my initial question to George. He said all of the rail systems, sir. According to George, everything's ground to a halt."

"Can he repair it?"

"We never discussed it, we didn't have time. Within seconds of the rail system outages, Charles De Gaulle Airport was taken out."

"What do you mean, taken out? Like a bomb blast?" Wiley was clearly alarmed.

"No sir, not a bomb. According to George, it was hacked and everything was shut down. The entire airport is out of commission, no backups, nothing. He said everything is cut off, both inside the airport and outside. Not only power, but all bypasses, fail safes, and backups have been disabled as well."

"Okay, Jake, I've heard enough. I'm going to have to return to the States. I'll be in the air in thirty or forty minutes."

"With all due respect, sir, do you think that's a good idea?

What if they target the airspace system next?"

"You better hope that doesn't happen, Jake, because you're coming here. I want you to get to the airport ASAP and hopefully we'll pass each other in the middle of the Atlantic."

"But, sir—"

"No buts. I can command best from Commonwealth and you can operate better in Europe."

"What about locating the missing aircraft? Air Malacca 910?"

"Let me worry about that, Jake. I want you in the air in less than thirty minutes."

"That's cutting it close."

"Give the phone to George, get your go bag, and get enroute to the airport. The Citation will be fueled and ready."

"Yes sir," he resigned. Wiley was the boss and had an insight into long range planning unmatched by anyone he knew. He handed the phone to Fontaine who started writing down Wiley's instructions on a notepad. He patted Fontaine on the back, left for the ready room. *Ready Room* was the term Wiley had tagged for what was in reality an office/lounge designed especially for Francesca and Jake. No other employees other than Wiley and Fontaine were allowed inside. Not only did it have computer terminals with instant secure access to Wiley's servers, it also had lockers and showers and a fully stocked kitchen. Best of all, when he and Francesca worked late into the night, they had separate bunk rooms. He checked his bag and replenished anything inside he felt he might need for the next few days like a few changes of clothes, ammunition, weapons…all the necessities of his job. He came back into the command center, and saw Fontaine was off the phone, but focused on typing on his keyboard.

"I'm out of here, George."

Without turning around, Fontaine raised his arm. "At least one of us will get a little sleep. Be careful out there."

"Always am," he replied to Fontaine's favorite parting line. It was a line he stole from one of those TV cop shows. Fontaine tried to lead Francesca and him to believe it was his own line, but Jake had seen the show once or twice many years ago.

He left the command center and made his way down to the secure underground parking garage. As he stepped out of the elevator, Wiley's limo pulled up and Jake crawled in the back seat.

Since it was the middle of the night, there was virtually no traffic so the ride to the airport was fast and uneventful. As promised, Wiley's Citation was ready and waiting for Jake's arrival. Within a couple of minutes of boarding, he felt the aircraft taxiing. A few minutes later, they were airborne. He had a lot on his mind, but his energy was gone. Back in the bedroom, he smacked the pillow a couple of times to fluff it like he liked it and then let his head sink into place. He collapsed on the bed, pulled the covers up to his neck and closed his eyes, knowing he would be lucky to catch a few hours of shut eye before he would be interrupted.

†††

As if he'd written the script himself, the one and only flight attendant shook him out of a deep sleep only four hours after they left D.C. Almost to the minute.

"What is it, Jimi?"

"Mr. Wiley, Ms. Catanzaro, and Mr. Fontaine will be on a conference call in ten minutes. I have some fresh coffee brewing and I'll heat up a breakfast. Mr. Wiley said it was urgent, something has come up and our destination has been changed."

"Where are we going now?"

"The pilot said Florence. That's where you'll meet up with Ms. Catanzaro." He noticed her toothy smile. "I've never been to Florence before and Mr. Wiley ordered the flight crew to remain in Florence until you and your partner were finished with your business."

"I've never been there either. Sounds like you'll have more fun than me, though."

Jimi left the bedroom and returned to the cabin. He shook to clear his head like a dog shaking after a bath, and sat up on the edge of the bed rubbing his eyes. He could use a shower but that was one amenity Wiley's Citation didn't offer. He got dressed and walked into the cabin and sat down where the secure satellite phone was located.

Jimi walked up and handed him a large mug of coffee. "Plenty more where this came from," she said. "I'll bring the food out as soon as it's ready."

"Thanks, Jimi." As he spoke the phone buzzed. He pressed the Connect button. "Jake's on."

"Very good, Jake." Wiley's voice crackled as it came through the speaker. "George is already up and we're waiting for Francesca to come online. George, I'll let you brief Jake on your latest discovery from the Lut Desert."

"Roger. I ran a comparison on the desert landscape where Air Malacca 910 landed. Turns out the camouflage netting was installed nearly six months prior to the airliner going missing."

"So they had been planning the hijack for a while. Just waiting for the right time…or right payload."

"Looks that way."

"Did you find out when the net was removed?"

"Yep. Three months and four days after 910 landed, the camouflage netting came down."

"I'm on," Francesca broke in. "Sorry about the delay. Rough night last night."

"Hi Francesca," Fontaine said. "We'll bring you up to speed in a minute or so. As I was saying, Jake, two days before the netting came down, it seems they broke camp. Tons of vehicles of all sizes left and went in many different directions. Nothing big enough to haul airliner pieces, though. When the netting came down, 910 was gone."

"Wait," Francesca interrupted, "you guys found Air Malacca 910?"

"That's right," Fontaine said. "In the southeastern Iranian desert. It was Jake's hunch that had us looking there in the first place."

"So, it didn't crash? It was hijacked?"

"No other explanation."

"Nice detective work, Jake. Looks like your employment with the NTSB has paid off." She made reference to the few years he worked as an aircraft accident investigator with the NTSB. His first job out of the Navy was with the National Transportation Safety Board and one he had tried for so long to put out of his mind. Most of the time successfully, but on occasion, the memory of how tragically it all ended floods back with painful memories.

"When did the aircraft fly out?" he asked.

"Still working on that," Fontaine said. "I'm using our trick, Jake, I programmed in heat signatures from a Boeing 777, and using the thermal satellite scans, searching for anything that matches leaving the desert. So far, nothing. But I've only been able to run a few days."

"So, why the destination change to Florence?"

It was Wiley's turn to speak up. "George found something imbedded in the hacking code. Some sort of identification code."

"That's right," Fontaine said. "Just like you leave a signature when you write a check or sign a document, hackers leave a hacking signature as well. It tells the hacking world who did it. Sometimes it's as blatant as a name. Most times it's a trademark. Kind of a bragging tool. They almost all have some identifying feature. When I looked at the hacking code used to take out the rail systems and De Gaulle, I noticed some similarities. Actually not a similarity, it was exactly the same. These two hacks were written by the same hacker but altered by a different hacker. The hacks were altered by a hacker who left his trademark and that trademark belongs to *The Jew*."

"You sure about that, George?" Jake asked.

"I compared it to some other hacker code we know positively came from him, and it's an exact match."

"So *The Jew* is our bad guy hiding away somewhere creating havoc around the world." Francesca sounded resentful at the thought they might have been trying to rescue the bad guy all along.

"Not so fast," Wiley interrupted. "George seems to think otherwise and has some pretty convincing evidence to back it up. Go ahead, George, explain it to them."

"In layman's terms please," Francesca urged.

George continued, "Thanks to the dead man in Vienna, we now know *The Jew* is Daniel Luzato. Inside the two hacks were messages. Distress messages is my bet. Luzato put those messages in his codes in the event something happened to him, which is what we thought all along. Until the hacks on Europe's rail systems and De Gaulle, Luzato had never done anything destructive, actually his prior hacking had helped law enforcement break up mafia rings, drug cartels, child porn websites, and a lot more. He's a white hat hacker. Like the Good Samaritan of the hacking world, so it goes against his norm to actually produce a vicious hacking attack. Keeping that in mind is what helped me see his other messages. Imbedded deep in the hacking code was an encrypted message. He had already foreseen Disruption coming."

"Excuse me, but, what is *Disruption?*" Francesca asked.

"Remember the conversation with President Rudd?"

"Sure, I do," she said. "Shit. You mean it is happening now?"

"I'm afraid it has started," Wiley said.

"Having said all that, Luzato named future events and the man behind it all."

"Qasem Kazemi," Jake said.

"That's right. And guess who is Kazemi's top hacker and the man who wrote the original hacking code?" No one attempted to answer Fontaine's not so rhetorical question. "Boris."

"Dammit, Jake," Francesca said crossly. "I told you, you should have killed that bastard in the subway."

"Why is Kazemi targeting Europe?" she asked. "Why not attack the U. S.?"

"And how did Luzato get Boris' hacks?" Jake added.

"This is how I believe Luzato did it." Jake could hear the boasting in Fontaine's voice for figuring out this mystery. "Remember I said Luzato was the Good Samaritan of the hacking world, well it seems he hacked Boris and altered the code rendering it inert without entering a decryption code."

"You mean like a Ransomware virus?"

"In a sense. I believe Luzato was kidnapped so someone could get those decryption codes. But, also inside Luzato's altered code were random letters and symbols that made no sense. After I extracted those letters and symbols and ran them through a decipher program, I found the message. Europe's rail systems and De Gaulle aren't even a preamble of things to come."

"You make it sound rather foreboding," Jake said.

"If Qasem Kazemi isn't stopped," Fontaine warned. "Technologically, *Disruption* could set us back decades."

CHAPTER 44

6:30 A. M.
Raleigh, North Carolina

Boris lay satisfied, yet exhausted, in her bed reflecting on last night's adventures. As it turned out, his neighbor Ashley Madison was quite the energetic lover. So much so, he was hoping for a repeat performance this morning as soon as she woke up. But, since she was still sound asleep, it might have to wait unless she woke up pretty soon, which didn't seem likely. He was an early riser and had already been awake for an hour laying there thinking...and listening.

In her slumber next to him in the bed, listening to her deep breathing helped him relax after a very trying forty-eight hours. He had successfully escaped Georgetown and Washington D. C. without being followed or traced. Of that, he was certain. Last night, during a brief respite from their sex-capades, he ensured his *black hat* hacker programs had been executed. A brief check of the news outlets confirmed they had worked flawlessly. Perfect. That should keep Omar off his back for a while. Or at least until he gets more decryption codes from Daniel Luzato.

Boris was very proud of his legacy as one of the top *black hat* hackers. They engaged in malicious hacking for personal gain, sometimes for notoriety, but usually, and certainly in his case, for financial gain. On the opposite end of the hacker spectrum were the *white hat* hackers. And like the cowboys in the old westerns, white hats symbolized the good guys and black hats the bad guys. The white hat hackers used their skills for ethical purposes, usually to thwart the black hats and secure the integrity of computer systems. And then there was Daniel Luzato, aka *The Jew,* who fell mostly in the white hat category but had been known to exhibit traits of a *gray hat* hacker. He would sometimes break the law in pursuit of a hack, but not for malicious reasons or for personal gain. Instead, Luzato vowed to crush as many black hat hackers as he could. And that was Luzato's motivation when he hacked Boris' computer and installed an encrypted subroutine virtually locking Boris out of his own computer. In doing so, though, The Jew unintentionally revealed his identity thus allowing Boris to warn Omar who, in turn, went on a manhunt for Luzato in order to obtain the decryption codes.

The Jew's damage was much worse than initially thought. He had planted *logic bombs* in all of Boris' programs. Fortunately, he discovered the intrusion and avoided the trigger that would have activated the malicious attack. These programs were the impetus of Omar's overall plan. Without them, his attack was doomed to fail. Boris quarantined the programs until Omar could get Luzato to reveal the crack. The world of hacking and hackers was a world Omar didn't understand, he just used it to further his cause—the cyber destruction of the West. Omar's big scheme was to cripple the western countries and then launch a physical attack against his enemies. An attack his enemies would be incapable of defending. In reality, it would be an attack they would be unable to even see coming. They would be so busy trying to pick up the pieces of the cyber attack, they wouldn't see Omar's true plan until it was too late.

But, Daniel Luzato had foreseen Omar's plan from the beginning and that troubled Boris. He could see from his vantage point thousands of miles away that Luzato was stringing Omar along, giving him tiny morsels to satiate his yearning a little at a time. What Omar could not see, what Omar's arrogance would never allow him to see, was Daniel Luzato would rather die than give up the codes allowing Omar's ultimate plan to work. And as much as Boris tried, he was unable to undo the damage Luzato had already caused. Without Luzato's codes, Omar's ultimate plan was dead in the water. In reality, it was actually software instead of decryption codes that the success of Omar's plan hinged on. Software stolen from Boris' computer by Luzato. Removed without a trace of its prior existence. Luzato was no idiot, he wouldn't leave that software on his computer. No, he probably had it stored on a USB drive or portable hard drive hidden away for safe keeping. Where that drive was, was Omar's problem. Boris had done his part.

He looked at Ashley as she rolled over, now facing him, she put her hand on his chest and rubbed in a circular motion, slowly working her hand lower on his body. Instantly, the arousal clouded his impending troubles with Omar and Luzato.

"Do you want me to fix us some breakfast first?"

"No. You are all I want right now."

†††

Waiting for Omar to return seemed endless.

The fire that had raked through Luzato's body from the tips of the wooden darts had since subsided. In fact, his brain couldn't register any residual after effects. Whatever the poison was, it had dissipated quickly, leaving him with only a feeling of enervation. Then again, he had that feeling ever since he was kidnapped and brought to this God-forsaken dungeon. At least it was better than the oubliette where he had originally been detained. The deep dark chamber where he had first awakened, wearing the metal necklace of death. A sadistic man's torture tool.

By now, some of the European countries must be experiencing the mildest of the cyber-attacks Omar had initiated. The former Iranian general's plan had been spelled out in intricate detail in Boris' computer, information he stole and encrypted inside the coding for the first wave of cyber-attacks, Omar's warning to the world. They were attacks he certainly could have prevented, but if he did, he would be dead and Omar and his cadre would be free to start all over again. And there would be no one to stop him. That was his mission now.

Although he couldn't do it alone, he had to rely on someone at the other end detecting his message, deciphering it, and taking the next steps to stop Omar. That message should have been received by now, and somewhere in the dark recesses of the CIA, NSA, and the rest of the intelligence community, other white hats should be hard at work unraveling his code. If the white hats at the other end weren't good enough, the world would pay for their incompetence. If the world powers still existed after the dust settled, then heads would roll. Fall guys were a way of life in these oversized bureaucracies. Those who didn't get jail time would end up on the unemployment lines.

His reflections were interrupted by the clank of the lock on the large wooden door.

Omar returned, and he didn't look happy.

†††

Although steamy, the encore performance this morning paled in comparison to last night's raucous escapades with Ashley Madison. It seemed she had another 9:00 a.m. class. One she couldn't, or wouldn't, miss.

It worked out for the best because as soon as she got up to take a shower, he got a message more decryption codes were available on the secure site. When he returned to his apartment, he wasted no time in downloading the decryption codes, hacking into the next sites, and uploading the viruses. Accomplishment was a great feeling. He fixed and ate breakfast, put his computer to sleep, and went to take a shower. The hot water cascading over him would feel good after so much exercise at Ashley's apartment.

While he was in the shower, though, a disturbing thought occurred to him, one that might cause him to become expendable to Omar. He hadn't double-checked the code before he uploaded the *time bombs* to take out the European rail systems and the Paris airport. Perhaps expendable wasn't the right word. It could be Omar would see him as a liability and take action to have that liability eliminated.

Most of Omar's plans revolved around his use of the *time bomb* hack. It was what it sounded like, a virus whose payload was deployed at a certain time. The only way Boris would do business with Omar. It allowed him to upload the time bomb and then relocate, allowing him to stay at least one step ahead of authorities, and hell and far away from Omar.

Jumping out of the shower, he did not bother to dry off or dress. In his living room, he woke up his computer and logged into the secure VPN where he checked the code, everything seemed normal. A feeling of satisfaction crept in until he decided to think like the white hat Daniel Luzato. If he had been in Luzato's shoes, he would certainly have altered the coding with more than just a temporary encryption. Even though the encryption was top-notch, it didn't kill the program. *He* didn't kill the program. Which meant only one thing, Luzato wanted the viruses to be uploaded. He wanted someone to examine the hack coding that was used to take down the rail systems and the Charles De Gaulle Airport. He wanted someone to look deep and find something.

But what?

He shivered as the water on his body evaporated.

CHAPTER 45

He met Francesca at Ponte Vecchio. Together, they walked along the cobble street to her hotel where her source had his head blown off on the terrace last night. The deck at the top of the tower was still considered a crime scene by the Italian authorities and no one without the proper credentials, was allowed to enter. Fortunately, AISE director Lorenzo Barzetti had given Francesca and him credentials when he wrote them their letters of authorization to carry their firearms inside Italy.

Ballistics experts were trying to recreate the crime and determine from where the shot might have been fired. After arriving on the top deck, Jake understood the complexity of that task. The shot could have come from so many different angles, getting that determination correct might end up falling into the blind luck category.

When Francesca initially reported the incident to Elmore Wiley, he redirected Jake to Florence as extra protection for Francesca, something she argued defiantly against. Her argument was simple; she didn't need protection from anyone since she was perfectly capable of taking care of herself. In reality, Francesca was more correct than Wiley gave her credit for, and was perfectly capable of handling anything that came her way. But, the old man's demands were not to be denied and here he was, in Florence, Italy with a pissed off partner.

Fontaine had finished his briefing while Jake was still a thousand miles from Italy. What he had to say was troubling and Wiley had enlisted as much help as he could find to help locate Qasem Kazemi, Alexei Nikahd, Ethan Wogahn, and Daniel Luzato and nine other persons of interest. Apparently the old man was calling in favors from the entire intelligence community, including the United States Government agencies, CIA and NSA, in order to locate these men. At Francesca's request, AISE was left out of the loop this time. She relayed her distrust in AISE and especially Marco Serreti.

By the time he and Francesca arrived, Italian authorities had allowed the hotel to hire a biological cleaning company to start with the task of cleaning the blood and brain matter from the deck and surrounding area downwind of the head shot. There were two men scrubbing the stained concrete and brick with some sort of liquid and what looked like a toothbrush on steroids. With each dousing of the liquid, bubbles foamed and the man would scrub harder. Jake assumed it must be a corrosive acid because the thickness of the protective gear the men were wearing.

"Where were you sitting when this happened?"

She pointed. "I was there, facing that way. Enzo was there, looking at me. Based on an initial trajectory theory, the bullet couldn't have missed my head by more than a few inches," she said with no emotion. "The shot had to come from somewhere over there." Her hand showing the direction. "Just a little south of due west. Definitely the other side of the river. The sun was about to set behind that hill when Enzo was shot. The sun was still in his eyes, but there was a thin overcast so it wasn't bad. He wasn't squinting."

"What's out there? I see a building and a steeple or something and hill behind it. Where could the shot have come from?" Jake opened a map of Florence he picked up from the hotel lobby. "Where are we now?"

Francesca tapped her index finger on the map. "We are here."

Jake reached in his shirt pocket, pulled out a pen, and drew a black dot over the spot marking the hotel. Then he drew a line due west and another southwest forming a conical shape on the map. "Is it safe to say the shot was fired from inside this area?"

"I would say that's accurate."

Jake called to one of the investigators on the tower. "How far is it to that hill?"

The investigator said, "Non parlo inglese."

Francesca translated to the investigator. The man pulled out a ranging scope and looked through the viewfinder and said something back to Francesca.

"1660 meters."

"So, that's over a mile. What about the steeple, how far is that?"

Francesca translated again.

"Basilica Santo Spirito, 410 meters."

Jake ran the calculations in his head. *450 yards.* "So, likely the shot was taken between here and the church, right? I see an awful lot of windows between here and there. That's a lot of possibilities."

"These guys will search every one of them, I'm sure," she said with a hint of hesitation in her voice.

"Don't you want to know who took the shot. Who killed Enzo…or who might have been trying to kill you?"

"Truthfully, Jake, what difference does it make? It's not getting us any closer to Daniel Luzato or any of the others."

"So, what's our next move?"

"We go back to where this all started."

"Rome?"

She nodded.

Jake took one last look over the beautiful old city of Florence. The most prominent feature to the skyline was the Cattedrale di Santa Maria del Fiore, or the Duomo di Firenze as Francesca called it. Its gigantic red dome muted all other nearby structures. Even the Uffizi Gallery, which was only three small blocks away. "All right," he said. "Let's go."

He didn't get far, only a few flights of stairs when his and Francesca's phones beeped.

"It's George. He wants us to call in ASAP."

He speed-dialed Fontaine and put his phone on speaker.

"Jake," Fontaine said. "Is Francesca there."

"I'm here."

"Great. You're not going to believe what just happened—"

"Another malicious hack attack?"

"Not yet. Are you ready for this?" He heard Fontaine take a deep breath and exhale. "I found *The Jew*. To be perfectly honest, Daniel Luzato found me. His computer came online and when I went to track it, it sent out a homing signal."

"A homing signal?" Francesca asked.

"You wanted layman's terms, that's about as layman as I can get. His computer reached out to us, transmitting its location including, get this, GPS coordinates. I'm sending them to your phones as we speak. It is definitely a distress signal. The coordinates are a small village not too far from Florence in the heart of Tuscany. Fifty-three kilometers…or for you Jake, thirty-two miles."

"That is close," he said. "What's the name of the village?"

"Volterra."

CHAPTER 46

Volterra, Italy

What was supposed to be a relatively short distance from Florence to Volterra turned out to be anything but. Fontaine's *as the crow flies* distance turned out to be much longer by road and obtaining transportation to the hilltop village proved even tougher with the rail system outage. It seemed the outage had caused a miniature panic among tourists who, in turn, depleted the area's rental cars. Even the taxi services were booked solid.

Finally, Jake and Francesca settled on a bus, which was supposed to take slightly over two hours. That was after an hour and a half wait at the bus terminal until they could get a bus with two vacant seats. Seventy-four kilometers was what the bus driver stated, but with the winding roads, it seemed like it was taking forever. The only saving grace was the beauty of the Tuscan landscape as the sun sank lower on the horizon and the day's light began its slow fade toward dusk. Anything to take his mind off of the bus's never-ending uphill struggle. The bus chugged through the narrow twisting roads lined with olive groves and vineyards for over an hour until there was a small explosion outside the back of the bus.

Blue smoke billowed into the air as the bus heaved engine parts onto the Tuscan highway as it gulped its last breath. After ten minutes of clanging around under the hood, the Italian driver threw up his hands and declared the bus dead.

At least until a mechanic could perform major repairs, which he claimed meant the bus had to be towed back to Florence. In the meantime, the passengers were going to have to wait for another bus, also coming from Florence, to take them the remainder of the way to their destination.

"We don't have time for this," Francesca said with some urgency in her voice.

"How far to Volterra?"

"Twenty-five, maybe thirty kilometers."

"Okay," he said, "fifteen to eighteen miles, give or take?"

"Sounds about right."

He reached down and grabbed the strap to his backpack. "Let's hoof it, then."

"Dammit, Jake. It's uphill all the way to Volterra."

"What choice do we have? I'd say we're out of options and Luzato is running out of time. So, let's go."

After they got outside the bus, he slung his backpack over one shoulder. Francesca slipped her arms through both straps and clipped the straps together.

After thirty minutes of walking uphill in total silence, breathing harder and harder with every step, a car drove toward them headed uphill. Jake and Francesca waved their arms as the car approached, but it swerved to the far side of the road and honked its horn as it whizzed past.

"I thought we were going to get lucky for a moment," he said. "Guess we keep walking."

"Not so fast, partner." She craned her neck back down the road. "I hear something else coming." In the distance, a truck was coming their way. "This time, we don't take no for an answer."

"What are going to do?"

"Watch and learn, rookie."

As the truck approached, she reached behind her back and withdrew her handgun. She jumped into the middle of the road, held up one palm, and blocked the road with her body.

Her plan worked, although it wasn't something he would have tried, and the wide-eyed driver stopped the truck in the middle of the road waving his hands in the air.

She walked around to his window, and started talking to him. Within a few seconds, the traumatized look on the man face softened and then he smiled.

She waved at him, and yelled, "Get in."

The truck was old. And rickety. The single vinyl bench seat was torn in several places and repaired with several years' worth of tape. The back of the truck was open with wooden sidewalls surrounding the bed. Inside the bed was produce. According to the young driver, who spoke relatively good English, he made the run daily to Volterra to deliver fresh produce to several restaurants and hotels, including the pizzeria owned by his mother.

"Is Italian pizza good?" Jake searched for a seatbelt.

"Compared to pizza in Italy, American pizza is shit," Antonio bragged. "And my mother's pizzeria is best in Volterra."

Jake sat on the passenger's side and Francesca sat in the middle with her feet on the hump. The driver, who introduced himself as Antonio, jammed the stick shift in gear, grinding it as he let off the clutch. With a jerk, he and Francesca were on their way to Volterra with only a forty-minute setback.

Antonio grew up in Volterra and seemed happy to have someone to talk to on the long drive up the mountain. "You know history of Volterra, yes?" he asked.

"Not really, no," Jake replied.

"Much history in Volterra." Antonio explained. "It one of oldest villages in Italy. Date back to 7th century BCE," he explained. "Walls surround village built by peasants. 5th and 3rd centuries BCE. Design and architecture very medieval. Volterra was grand Etruscan city and, in day, was key trading city for the Etruscans. Original name Velathri or Felathri in Etruscan. After absorbed by the Roman Empire around 260 BCE, Romans changed name to Volaterrae. Today, simply called Volterra. Back then over 25,000 people live within walls. Today, is only 11,000 in all and many live outside the walls."

Jake kept checking his watch. Time was ticking away and he started getting antsy. All he could think about was finding Luzato. "Can this truck go any faster?" he asked Antonio.

Antonio gestured with both hands. "I have pedal all way to floor. Truck is old and tired."

As the truck approached Volterra's Piazza Martini Della Liberta, Francesca jabbed him in the ribs and said, "This is where we get out."

"No." Antonio shook his head. "I take you to Albergo."

"Albergo?" Jake queried.

"Albergo is hotel or inn. Quaint and cozy, but in Volterra, always clean. Some fancy, some not so fancy." Antonio raised both hands and turned his eyes toward Jake. "Then I take you to momma's pizzeria. As you Americans say, pizza is on house."

"No," Francesca said. "After you've driven us all the way to town, we couldn't."

"She's right, Antonio. Paying for our meal is the least we can do for your hospitality."

"I have to come this way whether you ride with me or not. Is no problem. Please, I insist."

Jake nodded and Antonio seemed placated.

Antonio pulled his truck through a large archway. It was attached to the wall surrounding the village. The streets were narrow and cobbled. The buildings were faded and darkened by the setting sun. And medieval. He had never seen anything like it before.

"So, you like this little village, yes?"

"It is cool. Yes, Antonio, I like it a lot."

Antonio turned left Via Dei Marchesi then a quick right on Via Matteotti. He pointed and said, "Albergo is there."

The lobby wasn't much more than a check-in desk and room enough for one person to stand in front of the desk with one small piece of luggage. But he didn't mind, he stepped out onto the narrow street and stood next to the truck while Francesca checked in. Late October must be a heavy time for tourists as the small hilltop village was packed. Then again, as Halloween was rapidly approaching, so would the vampire and werewolf crazies. And what a perfect place to spend the last night of October.

After both Jake and Francesca checked in, Antonio drove them to his mother's pizzeria. A drive that took less than a minute. The engine backfired when Antonio shut it off. He raised his hands. "Truck is old, happens all time. Need repair, yes." He motioned to the pizzeria. "Go find table, I unload truck. Momma come take order." Antonio walked to the back of the truck.

Jake stepped onto the cobblestone road and blocked Francesca before she could step out of the cab. He pushed his GPS tracker in her face. "Check this out. The coordinates put Luzato roughly two hundred feet from here. Almost right across the street from that museum sign. There is a huge building in the background, what's that?"

"It's the Fortezza Medicea or the Medici Fortress. It's a maximum security prison now. Did you notice the porticato?"

"Is that the tunnel between the buildings that leads back to the fortress?" he asked.

"Yes, one of them."

"I also noticed there's a door to the left about fifteen feet inside that porticato."

She nodded.

"According to this tracker, Luzato is just on the other side. I'm thinking that's a good place to start," he said knowing exactly what she was thinking.

"I think you're right." She stood. "Let's gear up."

CHAPTER 47

Raleigh, North Carolina

After an exhaustive search of Daniel Luzato's code, he found nothing to indicate *The Jew* put any coding in Boris' hacking that could be traced back to him or anyone working on the Disruption project for Qasem Kasemi.

He removed his *tear down* checklist from his backpack, and began checking off items listed in order of importance. Timing and meeting all the deadlines were essential for success. He felt the pressure. A few hours, was all he had left to dismantle any evidence of Disruption that would connect him, destroy his computers and permanently erase all data on his hard drives. The countdown was under way with less than seventy-two hours until the time-bomb programs activated. By then, he would be in Europe at the casino, living high on the hog for the rest of his life. Even if the cards didn't fall his way, he had enough resources for many years to come. And there was always another option, he could return to hacking for extra money. Banking systems were easy money. And his specialty.

He did a systems check of each of the projects across the globe. All but one checked out within specifications as he expected. The other had never been put in place. That was the code stolen by Daniel Luzato. It was the most important piece of the entire project from Omar's standpoint; therefore, he was working on it personally. But, unexpectedly, Omar had gone silent and, as far as Boris was concerned, the Iranian general was on his own. Even if he did manage to defy the odds at the eleventh hour and acquire the flash drive, Boris had no intention of being located by anyone. Omar would have to figure a way to upload that virus by himself. And, even though he gave Omar detailed instructions on how to upload the files, he doubted the vile bastard could do it out without getting caught. Omar, like most of his project directors, was a disdainful prick.

As a matter of fact, there was only one project director out there he liked, and that was Ethan Wogahn. He was intelligent, cordial and polite. Wogahn followed instructions to the meticulous detail and had his project ready weeks before any of the others; some barely managed to get theirs up by yesterday's deadline. Two didn't even come online until this morning. He wondered how these morons managed to stay in business. If he ran his business like them he would not have customers.

At midnight in three days' time, he would find out whose projects worked and whose didn't. Who took shortcuts and who didn't. Who would die and who wouldn't.

He added one more item to his checklist—send a final message to Wogahn.

But first, time to dismantle.

He worked feverishly without any breaks for the next three hours. While he finished the last of the details on his main computer, he wiped the hard drive clean on his other computer. It was a preliminary wipe to start with, a simple reformat. In its present state, data could still be retrieved from the disk, but, before he left, he would send it and his main computer to a government-level data sanitation that met the DoD 5220.22-

M standards. Anything more than that was overkill. More importantly, he didn't have time to stick around while these wipes ran to completion. He had to start them and then leave. The time on his watch showed three hours until his flight left. An hour and a half before he had to be at the airport.

He continued down his list until he reached the last item, the one he'd added a few hours ago. He opened his email program and penned an email to Ethan Wogahn. After he finished, he reread it and made some slight editorial changes until he was satisfied. He hit send.

He put both machines into the data sanitation mode with special hardware he'd obtained for this very purpose, and then started the DoD 5220.22-M wipe. No turning back now.

He stuffed some clean clothes along with a few personal items in a small carry-on sized bag and placed it by the door. All his smaller electronic devices like his smart phones and tablets were destroyed. There could be no evidence to ever link him to his new life. He would get all new devices and computers after he set up his new life in Europe.

Several quick raps on the door broke his concentration, causing him to nervously swing around in his chair. *Who would be at my door?* He went over to the door and peered out the peephole—Ashley Madison. He unlocked and cracked open the door. "I thought you had classes all day?" She wore a sundress, way too short to bend down and pick anything up, and flip flops. Her hair was pulled back into a ponytail. Her long tan legs were a toned work of perfection.

"My afternoon lab was cancelled. Thought you might want to go out for lunch…," she licked her lips, "or stay in and pick up where we left off this morning."

Before he could answer, she pushed her way into his

apartment. She scanned the living room. She seemed befuddled after seeing all the computer equipment running on his kitchen counter, the dismantled and broken phones, tablets, and his luggage near the front door. "Going somewhere in a hurry?"

He clinched his jaw.

"Were you even going to say goodbye?" Her voice was pouty.

"Look, Ashley, I can explain." He stepped toward her knowing he had better come up with a good excuse. That was where he excelled. "I was going to leave a note—"

"Leave a note? After last night *and* this morning, all I rate is a note?" She put her hands on her hips.

"It's not like that at all," he explained as the lies came forward. "My sister was in a traffic accident in California. She's in intensive care. I'm going to see her, she needs me. We are very close. I only found out a couple of hours ago."

The anger in Ashley's face dissolved as quickly as it had risen and was replaced by the unmistakable look of compassion. "I'm so sorry. Is she going to be okay?"

"The doctors don't know yet. Said the first twenty-four hours were the most critical. I want to be there when she wakes up." He was good, she was buying it all. "I'll be back in a few days, I'm sure. I assumed you'd understand."

She gave him a big hug. "Of course I understand. Is there anything I can do?" She pushed back and pointed to his computers. "What's all that?"

"Nothing much, just computer diagnostic equipment. I've been having some issues lately."

He tried to block her, but she walked around him, over to the kitchen counter and looked down at the notepad. "What is disruption?" Next to the pad was his printed airline itinerary.

"I thought you said your sister was in California? This says Frankfurt, Germany."

Ashley was pushy and used to getting her way. He liked her aggressive nature in the sack, but not when it came to meddling in his personal life. If she had only left after he told her his perfect lie, it would have been okay. But, she couldn't leave it at that. Now she went too far. The nosy bitch still had her back to him, so he grabbed a stainless steel two-quart sauce pan from the sink, still dirty from breakfast, and smashed it against her skull. She wobbled back and forth for a second and then dropped to her knees. He held her upright with one hand by the ponytail and swung the pan at her head like a tennis racket. The second blow knocked her unconscious.

He dragged her into the bathroom by her feet and shoved her head over the tub. He smashed her head repeatedly with the pan until he noticed blood in her brown hair. He felt for a pulse on her wrist. Nothing. He rolled her lifeless body into the bathtub. He felt her neck for a pulse. Again, nothing.

He stood and looked at her. What a waste. Why did she have to be so nosy? Such a seductive young woman, and now, dead. He pulled the shower curtain closed and checked his clothes and hands for any traces of blood then went into the main living room. He doubled checked the equipment and made sure the data sanitation was well underway. It was unlucky for Ashley she had barged in like she did. He tried to get her to back off, but the end result was her own fault. He had a job to do and an identity to protect, so he ended Ashley Madison's life without remorse. Unfortunate, but necessary.

He had a resolve and stuck to it.

He could leave nothing that could ever link him to his new life.

CHAPTER 48

Eastern Colorado
5:00 P. M.

The cold wind hadn't quit blowing across the open plains for over forty-eight hours and it had severely hampered Ethan Wogahn's final preparations. Climbing the tower to adjust the arrays in lighter winds was one thing, but to climb several hundred feet when the wind was blowing nearly forty miles per hour was something totally different. The passing cold front two days ago whipped up the winds and dropped the temperature well below his comfort level. Hell, right now, everything was out of his comfort level and Omar was breathing down his neck for a final test result. One he didn't dare give to him until he could prove the arrays were in perfect alignment, which for some reason, all of the sudden, they weren't.

After Boris delivered the software with the decryption code that a white hat hacker had secretly installed on Boris' computer, Wogahn started running his final tests. The arrays had been aligned perfectly, but now he was getting a misalignment warning on the console inside the cinder block building that once belonged to a now defunct cable TV and internet provider. He didn't know if the wind blew it out of alignment or if it was the result of a bird strike, but something knocked it three degrees out of kilter and he had to reset it before he could run his last test.

D-Day was approaching fast and he wanted to be hell and far gone from Colorado by the time it arrived. In this case, *D-Day* was not June 6, 1944 nor did it have anything to do with Normandy, this D-Day was Omar's designation for *Disruption Day*. In reality though, Disruption had already begun. Omar's plan to start distracting the world from his true intentions by the timed distribution of small cyber-attacks across the globe, mostly in Europe, were currently in play. Although only nuisance attacks that could be easily reversed, the national news outlets were alarming the public as if it were the onset of Biblical Cyber-Armageddon. If those same outlets could transmit the news after Disruption, which they won't be capable of doing, they would certainly declare Armageddon had arrived.

His last contact with Boris was enlightening, but had also scared the shit out of him. Why would the young hacker put his neck on the line for him? Boris had created a new identity for him along with instructions on how to obtain his new identity documents and where to pick them up, a Post Office box in New Orleans, Louisiana, where the metropolitan area population was greater than five hundred thousand. A place where Ethan could easily get lost in the crowd. New Orleans was also a gateway city, meaning he could book an international flight out of the country to his new life on a Caribbean island. Boris also had deposited a respectable sum of money for him in a bank account, also in New Orleans.

It would be a long nineteen-hour drive, but he could do it in a day. A lot of energy drinks would be needed to keep him alert. He would set the timer on his countdown clock and leave, giving him ample time to escape the country before his time bomb went off delivering the virus Boris was exploiting through the chink in the United States military's armor. He needed two days minimum, three would be better, in case he encountered an unanticipated delay.

Murphy's Law.

The day the world crumbled from Disruption, he would be far away from the chaos.

He returned his concentration to the task at hand. It was time for him to climb. He layered his clothes and wore a down jacket, although it wasn't frigid, the wind could make it feel that way. Without the wind, he wouldn't have needed a base layer, now it was essential. After he was fully clothed, he slipped into a safety harness, strapped a tool bag to his waist and walked to the base of the tower ladder. He clipped his safety ring, much like a carabiner at the end of his fifteen-foot tether, to the safety guide line and started climbing. If truth be told, he had made this climb most times without the safety line, primarily because using it was such a pain in the ass and made the climb to the top of the aging nine-hundred-foot tower burdensome. With a safety changeover stop every twenty feet requiring him to unclip below the stop and re-clip above it, there was no fast climb to reach the top. It also meant if he slipped, the most he could fall was thirty-five feet. Sure, it would hurt and he would be banged up and bruised, maybe even a broken bone or two, but it wouldn't be fatal. And he was always careful.

The sky was bleak and the wind was brisk. The locals called it *fresh*, but all he felt was cold. With another arctic front expected to pass overnight, this one bringing freezing rain, he needed to re-align the arrays today before the tower iced over and he might not be able to climb back up for several days. Then it would be too late. It had come down to a now or never situation, and he hated those.

The higher he climbed the colder the rails became and the

colder his hands got, even through his insulated climbers gloves. Three quarters of the way to the top, he could see something was amiss with the dish. Something was there that shouldn't be, something large. A gust of wind buffeted his body against the ladder causing his foot to slip. He clung to the ladder in a desperate attempt to keep from losing his footing. He let go of the distraction from whatever was wrong with the dish and concentrated on climbing the remainder of the way to the top against the ever increasing wind speeds.

As he approached the top of the tower, it became clear what had caused the problem with the array alignment. Birds. Large birds to be more precise, had built a good sized nest on the south side of the platform using the dish as a wind block. He wasn't unfamiliar with the bird species of the area because he'd already had to remove several bird nests from the tower—but nothing this size. Although the nest was obviously still under construction, it had the makings of being a good six feet in diameter and three feet tall. Near the top of the tower, he was able to see a bowl burrowed inside the nest that was a good three feet wide and two feet deep. Not many birds make a nest this large and there was only one the illegal immigrants he'd hired had warned him about that built a nest at this altitude— the Golden Eagle.

Fortunately, the nest was empty, but for how long? Since the nest was relatively recent and still under construction, that could only mean one thing, the eagle would come back. There was no way he wanted to be around when the raptor with massive sharp talons returned. He knew he had to work fast. He climbed the remainder of the way to the top of the tower and out onto the small platform. He clipped his safety harness to the tower and prepared to crawl out to the nest

while battling the gusty winds and bone-chilling temperature.
Easing as far out as he dared, and keeping one hand tight on
the tower, he started kicking at the nest, knocking small pieces
off at a time. At this rate, it could take all night, he thought,
so he released his other hand and inched farther out onto the
platform.

Even with the nearly gale force winds, the smell of the nest
was horrid. Eagle crap covered half the platform. He spun
around and pushed hard with both feet against the weight of
the nest. It started breaking apart and falling off the tower in
small sections.

He heard the screech before he saw the source circling
above the tower and knew he had to hurry. He stretched out
prone on the platform and used his arms in an attempt to
push the remainder of the nest from the tower. He stretched
farther out, pushing harder, when something struck his arm
and swooped in front of his eyes with lightning speed. A gash
tore across his forearm ripping the fabric of his jacket. Down
filling blew away in the wind. He tried to locate the eagle, but
saw nothing of the bird.

Only a small portion of the nest remained, but it was on the
far edge of the platform and farther away from the rail than he
wanted to venture, but he had no choice. He couldn't realign
the array with the facility at Cheyenne Mountain with an eagle
nest blocking part of the line of sight. He inched out on his
belly using his hands and toes to slowly propel him toward the
edge. With one last heave, he pushed the last remnants of the
nest from the tower. As it plummeted toward the ground, he
heard the screech and the sounds of air passing through the
eagle's feathers and at the same time he felt the clawing to his
head. His orange Denver Broncos wool beanie ripped from

his head, he rolled toward the edge of the platform. He felt the flesh on his scalp rip under the power of the eagle's talons. Momentarily dazed, he knew he was rolling, but couldn't find a handhold. Blood gushed from his head, down his face covering his eyes and then he felt the edge of the platform disappear from beneath him.

He was falling, but only for a split second when his tether snapped tight, jerking him to a stop. He was dangling over the edge, swinging back and forth. He used the torn sleeve to wipe the blood from his eyes. Warm blood ran down the back of his neck while the pain from the cold wind slapped at his wound. He craned his neck upward, the platform was only five or six feet above him. Still, out of arms reach.

The raptor, flying full speed, dive-bombed striking him in the torso. His jacket ripped again. More down feathers fluttered into the wind like a kid blowing petals from a dandelion. The eagle landed a good blow, one right to the kidney. His body winced in pain.

He looked up again at the platform as he swung back and forth. He twisted around trying to see if the eagle was gone. He couldn't believe his eyes. The raptor was swooping in for another strike. As it approached with unbelievable speed, he kicked and thrashed and screamed in attempt to fend off the raptor. His gyrations worked. The eagle pulled away and flew out of sight to the east.

He allowed the swinging to stop before he attempted to pull himself to the platform, still not an easy task. He put one hand above the other and pulled himself upward along the tether. Then he repeated the same technique over and over. Reach with one hand, pull up. Reach with the other hand, pull up.

Still no sight of that damned psycho bird.

He was finally able to grasp the edge of the platform. With both hands gripping the edge, he pulled, struggling to lift his body. He swung one leg onto the platform and gingerly worked the rest of his body onto the platform. Once on the platform, he quickly rolled away from the edge and next to the dish, using it as a slight wind break while he caught his breath. The exertion overheated his body and now, he was sweating even with the cold gusts of wind rushing across him.

Eyes widened and body trembling, he kept a sharp lookout for the eagle while he removed his equipment from his bag. Thankfully, the bird was nowhere in sight, but with every shrill sound in the wind, he jumped. He checked the alignment and made the necessary adjustment. Then he tightened it in place with all the muscle he could muster. Convinced neither the bird nor the wind could knock the dish out of alignment, he packed up his equipment into the tool bag and secured it around his waist.

He made his way back to the ladder and gave one final check of the platform. In his peripheral vision he saw it. Circling high overhead was the eagle, but Ethan Wogahn had won this round.

He winced at the pain on his scalp. Not without a cost, though.

He continued staring at the mighty Golden Eagle, convinced the bird would return.

After Disruption, he was welcome to it.

CHAPTER 49

He had endured immense agony during the two torture sessions today, but Daniel Luzato was convinced Omar's plan would be stopped, which made his suffering a little more bearable. He'd given up most of the decryption codes the former general insisted on, thus allowing Omar's hacker to execute his black hat programs. Luzato knew they were ahead of time from his white hat hacking of Boris' computer. Some were DoS—denial of service—attacks to make computer networks temporarily unresponsive. Also Boris had planned several DDoS attacks. These distributed denial of service attacks were designed using a number of machines, seeding them with a Trojan virus and creating a botnet to overwhelm targeted servers. None of these were nearly as harmful as they first appeared on the surface, mostly inconveniences and nuisance hacks. Certainly things that could and would be remedied quickly by the intelligence community.

Some of the codes, however, when activated would allow Boris to gain remote access to sensitive military computer systems. Those attacks carried the potential for grave destruction on a global scale. These attacks would target the major powers, crippling their defenses. Omar's plan was to remove the targeted countries defense systems, leaving them vulnerable to attack and scrambling to regain control of their systems. Then he would launch an all-out assault against his sworn mortal enemy when no other country would be able to come to their aid.

To get the last group of codes, he had had to convince Omar the only way to get the codes was to get them from his laptop's hard drive where he had stored them in anticipation of today. A ruse that worked like a charm. If he had only one gift, it was that of keen foresight. It was the only reason he was still alive. But, that might not last much longer. Omar would surely return for the final time. This time Omar would come for the defense system commands Luzato had physically removed from Boris' computer and hidden someplace where neither he nor Omar nor Boris could get to them. It was *the* failsafe he needed to keep Omar from unleashing genocide of epic proportions rivaled only by the Holocaust. In a sense, for Omar, that was what it was—an ethnic cleansing. A massacre Luzato was prepared to die for in order to prevent.

Proud to die for.

That was when it happened. As if Omar had been waiting for him to finish his thoughts, the massive wooden door banged open and in walked Omar carrying a bag similar to a physician's medical bag. Walking close behind were two men, both dressed in black robes with black hoods and both carrying assault rifles. It had been months in the making, now, Daniel Luzato knew his time was up.

While one of Omar's henchmen held him at gunpoint, the other grabbed him, stripped his robe from his body and threw it on the floor, and wrestled him into the chair where his arms and legs were restrained with duct tape. Omar walked over and emptied the contents of the black bag onto the table in front of Luzato, an assortment of contraptions he had never seen before.

"As this dungeon rests beneath a medieval village," Omar said, "I think it only fitting you experience some of the inquisition tools from the same period." He reached down and picked the first one up and held it in front of Luzato's face. "This is a *thumbscrew*. Its purpose is... well, self-explanatory." He lifted another device, it had a pear shaped metal body divided in spoon shaped sections with a twist screw at one end. "This is called a *choke pear*." He pushed it closer to Luzato's face. "It was originally used as a gag to quiet victims while they were being tortured." He twisted the screw and the spoon shaped sections expanded. "I won't be using this in your mouth, if you understand what I mean." A sinister smile crept across his face. "It is effective. Just be happy I don't have a *Judas cradle*." Next, he held up a stick, much like the one he was beaten with earlier. "Of course, you remember the *batog*."

He flinched when Omar brandished it.

"As you can see, I have quite the assortment. There is a torture museum in this town I'm sure would love to add some of these to their collection." He waved his hand over his torture tools. "None of these are designed to kill, they are designed to make you suffer to the point where you beg to end the pain. Now the choice is yours. As you have witnessed with Germano and now know for yourself, I will stop at nothing to get what I want. Tell me where you've hidden the drive and I promise, death will be quick and painless."

He stared at Omar and said nothing.

"This is your last chance. If I proceed, I won't stop until you plead for death."

Nothing.

"Very well," the former Iranian Guard general said as he picked up a cat of nine tails from the table. "Gag him," he said to one of his men.

The man took a small rag and forced it in his mouth by applying pressure to his neck, which made him open his mouth involuntarily. With the rag still in his mouth, the man wrapped tape around his head several times covering his mouth.

When the man stepped away, the butchery began.

When he became aware of his surroundings again, he felt violated in every way. His eyes were swollen to the point where he could barely see through the slits. What he could see of himself was covered in blood. More blood than he'd ever seen before…except when Omar slashed Germano Caminiti's throat. He had no recollection of anything after Omar jammed the *choke pear* inside his rectum. He remembered the initial pain of the tearing of his anus. As it slowly subsided, it was replaced by an even greater pain as Omar twisted the turn-screw expanding the contraption inside his body. Everything after that was a blur. A painful, incoherent, blur.

Omar's voice.

It kept asking the same question over and over. "Where is your grandfather?"

What had he said? Did he break under pressure? Why can't he remember anything?

Then there was a different sound.

Sounds.

Voices yelling. Strange new voices.

Gunfire.

Total darkness.

And then…explosions.

CHAPTER 50

Jake and Francesca quietly entered the door inside the porticato. There was a small landing inside the door and then steps leading in one direction—down. The walls of stone were dark with age. A bare light at the bottom of the first flight of steps dangled from a wire wedged between two stones. Both emissaries quietly descended the steps, one at a time, with their silenced guns trained ahead.

The steps ended at a junction. To the left, another door, to the right, steps descended into darkness.

"The door or the steps?" whispered Francesca into her wireless voice-activated com system.

"Start here, work down." It was only logical, he thought. Going down first could open them both up to danger if, by chance, Daniel Luzato was being held captive below and someone was watching from this level. Of course, entering this room could expose them if the room was being monitored from above. That was a risk they would have to take.

"Agreed."

Francesca gently nudged the door open, allowing him to enter with his gun trained ahead. A short stone-sided hallway led to a single dimly-lit room, also stone-sided. In one corner of the room was a kitchen, equipped with all the modern necessities. In the opposite corner were four small beds and one slightly larger with a curtain that could be closed around it.

Next to the beds, a bathroom with an open door allowing light from the bathroom to cast a dust-filled beam across the beds. Half of the space in the room consisted of a small complex of computers and video screens obviously monitoring several closed circuit video feeds. In front of the video screens was a small man with black hair wearing a black robe cinched at the waist with a black belt of some kind. Fontaine's briefing suggested Islamic terrorists might be inside and this man fit that physical description. At least, he certainly appeared Middle Eastern from Jake's vantage point.

Francesca hand signaled him to come at the man from the opposite angles and quietly take him down. It was a good plan until a second man appeared in the bathroom door. Francesca fired a shot dead center to the forehead. The man fell hard banging against the door, dead before he hit the ground. The man sitting in front of the video screens whirled around, eyes full of terror as he stared at two weapons trained at his head. Jake held his finger to his lips. The man understood, he raised his hands and made no sound.

Francesca secured the man's hands and feet with zip ties and gagged his mouth. "Time for a nap," she said and then struck the man over the head with the butt of her gun.

In synchronized steps, he and Francesca moved closer to the monitors and watched the horror show on the screens.

"That has to be Luzato."

"Down the steps?"

She nodded. "I see two men…and him." She tapped on the screen.

"Qasem Kazemi," they said in unison.

Convinced the breathing man was no threat, he and Francesca returned to the steps and descended the dark stairwell.

Two ninety degree turns and four dozen steps later, they were standing in front of a massive wooden door. The temperature had dropped as they descended deeper underground. He reached out and touched the wall—cold to the touch.

"We are definitely at Etruscan level now, a good twenty-five hundred years old, maybe more."

He shrugged off the history lesson. His adrenaline was already pumping in anticipation of their next move. "We'll take out the goons in black first," he said. "Kill shots. I need Kazemi alive, though, so if you have to shoot him, don't go for anything vital. Capisce?"

"I hear you."

Two seconds later, they entered the room ready to fire.

As he came through the door he saw Kazemi hit the blood soaked Luzato with a stick and yell something about his grandfather and a USB drive. Both men in black spun around with assault rifles, which gave Francesca and him no time to do anything except shoot. To avoid confusion, and possible death, he and Francesca had a rule, never cross their fire, take out the target on their side first. It was an unwritten and unspoken rule. It hadn't failed them yet. Matter of fact, it made them an even more deadly combination. His style was the same as it was when his old friend Gregg Kaplan taught him a Delta Force mantra—*Two in the chest, one in the head works 100% of the time*—and that was how he took down hostiles. Francesca, on the other hand, was more like a surgeon, her shots almost always with dead accuracy. Depending on her threat assessment, it was one shot to the head or one shot to the heart. Rarely did she fire more than once. There was simply no need.

Both men in black fell to the hard floor. Blood puddles formed quickly beneath their lifeless bodies.

Kazemi turned in shocked surprise.

"Don't move," Jake shouted. He motioned with his gun. "Step away…now."

Kazemi side-stepped away from the blood-soaked hacker.

Francesca sprinted to Luzato while Jake kept his gun trained on Kazemi.

She leaned down. "It's over, Daniel, it's over. You are safe now."

Jake said to Kazemi, "On your stomach, hands behind your head, legs spread apart."

The Iranian did as he was told.

Francesca pulled on the collar and Luzato jumped. "No," he managed to say through a badly swollen face. "It will kill me."

Jake and Francesca both looked up at the sound coming from overhead. The lights went out and they were plunged into total darkness. There was a thud followed by the sound of objects rolling across the floor.

Before he could wrap his brain around what was happening, there were three explosions.

Concussion bombs. Flash bangs. And he was unprepared. One was bad enough, but three, in those tight closed quarters, he had no idea what was going on around him.

He couldn't hear and he couldn't see.

Seconds passed. A minute. Slowly his impaired vision could detect something moving around him. Shadowy figures. Someone lifted him and yelled something about him being alive. He vaguely recalled beams of light streaking through the smoky darkness of the dungeon. Someone familiar was barking orders, but his mind was still too clouded and his hearing too damaged to form any recognition. He heard something about the man in the chair. He tried to push himself to his feet, but he still couldn't move. Through the smoke two shadows picked up the chair with Luzato in it and carried it into the darkness.

"Get him some medical attention," the familiar voice said. "And someone get the lights back on."

Wait. It was coming back to him. Slowly.

The voice.

The lights flickered and came back on. His sight hadn't recovered from the blinding flashes of the concussion bombs and he struggled to see. And then he remembered who the voice belonged to—Marco Serreti.

He pushed himself to his hands and knees. "Francesca," he said. "Is Francesca—"

"I'm fine, Jake," she interrupted. "Where's Luzato?"

"I don't see him."

Serreti announced, "There is an ambulance on the way, he is being taken to the street."

Before he could speak there was a muffled explosion. The cellar shook. Dust fell through the cracks in the stone. Bare lights bulbs hanging from a wire shook and then swung back and forth.

"What was that?" Francesca asked.

Serreti's head nodded for one of his men to check it out. Jake stood and wobbled to steady himself. His eyes blinked several times while he tried to focus on the dingy cellar. Something was very wrong with what he saw.

Or didn't see.

"Shit." Francesca and Serreti looked at him. "Where the hell is Qasem Kazemi?"

CHAPTER 51

Marco Serreti shouted to his men in Italian, "Find the Iranian. Lock down the town if you have to, but don't let him escape."

"What the hell are you doing here, Marco?" barked Francesca.

"I am deputy director of AISE," he boasted. "It is my job to be here. But, I must ask you the same question, Francesca. What are you and this man," he pointed to Jake, "doing here?"

"This man, as you put it," she glanced at Jake and then to Marco, "is my partner, and you know damn well what we're doing here. The same thing we've been doing since we arrived in Italy, looking for Daniel Luzato."

"And now you have found him so you may leave Italy."

"Not until we have had a chance to talk to him."

"Will you two *please* speak English?" Jake interrupted.

Marco was about to speak when one of his men returned. The man was pale. He whispered something in Marco's ear. He turned his back to her and Jake and exchanged a quiet conversation with the man. Finally, Serreti turned around and said, "I'm afraid it will be impossible for either one of us to question Mr. Luzato."

"Marco, what have you done?"

"I did not know, Francesca, I am sorry."

"Did not know what?" asked Jake.

"The metal collar Daniel Luzato was wearing. It must have been wired, it…it exploded while my men were carrying him up the steps. All three men were killed instantly." He motioned to his man who returned. "I understand the stairway is rather gruesome."

She could not believe what she heard. Luzato dead? After she and Jake had been searching for him for days. To end like this, with nothing to show for it. *The Jew* was the key to stop Disruption. Luzato was the only one who could stop the impending cyber terrorism threat. And now he was gone, just like that. She hung her head low and closed her eyes. They were so close. After Jake retrieved their weapons from the floor where they fell when the concussion bombs exploded, he feverishly paced the floor and she wondered what was going through his mind. She could tell he was angry and then he proved her suspicions to be true.

Jake kicked the debris with his foot like he was attempting a field goal and then unexpectedly charged Marco, grabbed his shoulders firmly and pinned him against a stone wall.

"You couldn't wait," Jake yelled in Marco's face.

"Get your hands off me. Do you know who I am? I'll have you arrested for assaulting a government official."

"I don't give a shit who you are. I ought to kill you right now." Jake's forearm pressed tighter against Marco's neck smashing his face against the wall. "You couldn't stand it that someone found him first. You wanted to take the credit for saving him. You charged in here like the Cavalry and, without assessing the situation, snatched him up and hauled him off. And now he's dead. You pompous, egotistical, piece of shit. It's all your fault."

"I did not know," Marco pleaded. "He was injured. He

needed medical attention. I did not know the collar would explode."

Marco's man made a move to stop Jake from assaulting the deputy director. Francesca raised her weapon and pointed it at the man. He froze in his tracks.

She said, "Jake, let him go, I'll take it from here." She stuck her finger in Marco's face while Jake moved away. "You've done nothing but obstruct our investigation from the moment we arrived in Italy. You claim you want to help in the name of international cooperation, but in reality, you've done nothing but undermine our every step. Now I want to know something, did you have anything to do with Enzo Mantova's death?"

"Certainly not," his voice was shaky as he spoke. "How dare you accuse me of such a thing."

She jammed the barrel of her weapon against his temple. "I'll ask you one more time, did you have Enzo killed?"

"That's it," he declared without answering her question. "You and your partner get out. I will not stand to be questioned or threatened, not by you, and certainly not by your partner. You two get out of here. Get out of Italy. If I see either one of you again, I will have you arrested on sight. Leave Italy, Francesca, and never come back."

She had heard enough. She knew. Somehow, Marco *was* involved with Enzo's murder. He was too cautious to take the shot himself...or even be anywhere near when Enzo was shot. Marco was in Florence that morning looking for Enzo. And now Enzo was dead too. Just like Daniel Luzato. Too coincidental. "Jake, get your gear," she said without taking her eyes off of Serreti. "Marco, we will leave Italy and we will leave now. But know this, if our paths cross again, it will be very regretful for you." She pressed her weapon harder against his head. Serreti, face crimson red, was now panting. "Because I promise, on my father's grave, I will kill you."

Then she left.

†††

Jake liked seeing the AISE deputy director squirm with her gun pressed against his head. Francesca could certainly be a force to be reckoned with if you got on her bad side. And Marco Serreti just had. Before they left the dungeon he heard Serreti and his men speaking in Italian. More like arguing. He did not need Francesca to translate. He couldn't resist. He gave them the finger before exiting the heavy wooden door.

Three quarters of the way up the corridor, they came across the remains of the three men killed in the explosion. He didn't know what was in the metal collar, he never had time to even speak to the man. Francesca had tried to reassure the man he was safe when the lights went out and the AISE stormed the dungeon.

Serreti's men were intact although badly damaged. Blunt force trauma and shrapnel from the collar were their causes of death. They might have even been alive for a few seconds after the explosion. Daniel Luzato wasn't so lucky. Or perhaps he was the lucky one. His death truly was instantaneous. When the collar exploded, he was decapitated. His headless body lay next to the two other men, Serreti's men. It wasn't until they reached the landing where the control room door was that they found Luzato's head.

When they exited the building into the porticato and onto the street, several of Serreti's men were waiting. Not for them, though. The men had clearly been given instructions to let him and Francesca pass. The street was a beehive of activity. Polizia cars, with lights flashing, were blocking the streets. No onlookers allowed. Two ambulances dispatched to the crime scene were on standby to help victims. There wouldn't be any, not for the ambulances anyway.

The air was choked in silence as they headed to the hotel, both shell-shocked from losing *The Jew*—Daniel Luzato. Right now, their nonverbal communication to each other was understood—get their belongings from the hotel and get the hell out of Volterra. How they would get back to Florence, he would leave up to her resourcefulness. As soon as they had reached street level, both of their phones started dinging with incoming messages, but they both ignored them for the time being until they were out of harm's way. He knew who the messages were from anyway, at least he had a good idea who they were from, and Fontaine and Wiley would have to wait.

As with every mission, when the potential for danger existed, they didn't separate and stayed in the high alert mode, in case Marco Serreti changed his mind. He followed her to her room, she gathered up her belongings and followed him to his room where he did the same. Within three minutes they were back on the street, and Francesca was arranging for a very expensive taxi ride to the Florence airport.

The taxi showed up within ten minutes. A short time in reality, but it seemed like a long wait when constantly looking over your shoulder. And both of them were. The driver was not friendly, but then again, who would be when a fare called for service after 1:00 a.m. His tune would likely change after he received the extravagant tip they planned to give him after they arrived in Florence.

He and Francesca crawled in the back of the taxi. She

issued instructions in rapid-fire Italian and the man sped off in the direction Antonio's truck had come from just a few hours before. Francesca turned in her seat and watched the retreating town as they left the hilltop village behind.

He checked his messages, all but one from Fontaine, his were all tagged *Urgent*. They could wait. They would wait. The one that wasn't from Fontaine was the most important. To him, anyway. It was from Kyli and the fact she was able to send a message at all was great news.

He tapped on her message and read it while Francesca stared out the window.

> Jake,
> They told me I was out of it for a few days, even in a coma for a while. All I know is I felt worse than I have ever felt before, even Paris. :-) Remember that? My fever broke yesterday. I'm ready to leave, Jake. As soon as you can, come get me. I want to go home and I want you to take me, not my grandfather. Please be careful. I'm waiting for you.

He lowered his hand and let them rest in his lap. As if he didn't need any more motivation to make this his last mission, the message from Kyli cinched it. He could feel his partner's eyes boring into him.

"From Kyli?"

"Yeah. How'd you know?"

"That goofy look on your face every time you talk to her. Obviously she's doing better."

He nodded and then said, "Yes."

"She wants you to come get her when this is over?"

"Yes, but... how could you know?"

She put her hand on his shoulder. "Because I'm your partner...and a woman."

CHAPTER 52

Fontaine's messages were all the same: *Call ASAP.*

He would call Fontaine, but not until they were airborne when he could use the secure speakerphone. The taxi dropped Francesca and him at the designated hangar. With their bags in tow, they made their way to the aircraft.

The Citation was waiting and ready to go. The lone flight attendant, Jimi, met them at the bottom of the air stairs. "Sorry we had to cut your Florence adventure short," Jake said.

"I was still able to see a lot of cool things," she said with her never-ending smile. "I went to the Uffizi Gallery museum. I saw amazing works of art. And best of all I got to see Michelangelo's David."

"Tall naked man with big hands and feet?"

She laughed. "Something like that, yeah."

"Know our destination yet?" Francesca shifted her weight from one leg to the other.

Jimi nodded. "I heard the pilots talking about it. Since the Belgium office is out of commission, it is back to D. C. for the both of you."

"Figures. All the action is over here and Wiley wants us back at Commonwealth."

"We're all set," Jimi said as she climbed up the air stairs. "Come on, time to go."

He and Francesca followed Jimi into the aircraft and stored

their gear in the designated storage bins while Jimi closed the cabin door and locked it in place. They took the club seats so they could face each other while they talked.

"Hey Jimi," Jake called out. "Tell Mike we'll need the satellite phone connection to Commonwealth as soon as possible."

"I think he knows already. He said something about ten thousand feet."

"Sounds good."

Within seconds of the cabin door closing, he heard the whine of the jet engines being spooled. A few seconds later, the engines came to life with a thunderous roar and the aircraft started moving forward. Five minutes later, they were airborne and on their way for another Atlantic Ocean crossing.

"I don't know about you, but I'm ready for some shuteye," Jake commented. "It seems like a long time since I slept but it's only been a day."

"After we talk to Fontaine and Wiley, we should be able to sleep for a bit."

"Unless the old man gives us homework for the ride." Jake reflected on the events in Volterra. "Did we accomplish anything, or did we get a bunch of people needlessly killed?"

"You saw the monitors. You saw what was going down, Omar was going to kill Luzato whether we went in to rescue him or not. If Marco hadn't stormed the place, we would have captured Omar and Luzato would still be alive and hopefully help us thwart Disruption."

"How do you think Marco knew we were there? Do you think he figured it out on his own...or did we lead him to Luzato and Omar?"

"Take it from someone who knows first-hand, Marco is too stupid to have figured this out on his own," Francesca explained. "He was always taking credit for someone else's work and then throwing them under the bus."

"Do you think he put a tracker on one of us…or perhaps a bug?"

"Not a bug, maybe a tracker. Good question, though…and if one of us does, it's probably me. You just flew in from D. C. yesterday. How could it be you?"

"Seriously, though, would Marco stoop that low? Would he be so brazen?"

"I already told you, Jake. Marco is a snake. A callous, venomous snake."

"We should both be swept when we get to Commonwealth. Just in case."

She agreed.

Jimi interrupted, "Mike says Fontaine and Wiley are standing by." She pointed to the speakerphone on the table across the aisle from them."

"Thanks, Jimi." They both moved to the seats at the conference table, both still across from each other. He pressed the Connect button. "Jake and Francesca are on."

"Status report," Wiley ordered.

The next hour was spent recounting the past twenty-four hours, most of the time spent on the last few. He and Francesca exchanged speaking roles, helping the other fill in the facts.

"What about Air Malacca 910?" Jake asked, after discussion about the night's events had been thoroughly exhausted. "Did you find out where it went?"

"Before we talk about that, Jake," Fontaine said. "I want to confirm the technology we researched and discussed before you left does indeed exist."

"Can you be more specific?"

"Yesterday, in the Persian Gulf, one of our aircraft carriers, the USS Harry Truman, had an Iranian drone fly right over the top of it at no more than a hundred feet. Radar never picked it up. It was a visual spotting and when crosschecked with radar, there was nothing there."

"Are you sure, George?" asked Francesca.

"The Truman took quite a few pictures and videos. I've enhanced some of the better ones, definitely an Iranian drone. The drone was completely invisible to radar and caught our forces off guard. The Navy isn't commenting officially, but President Rudd insisted the commander of the U. S. Navy's 5th Fleet talk directly to Mr. Wiley. He spent over an hour on the phone with Rudd today about the ramifications."

"Now what?"

"This means Iran has experimental technology that is no longer experimental. It lends a tremendous amount of credence to our story about Air Malacca 910. None of this can go public. Not until it's over. Jake, when you and Francesca arrive, we will develop a new strategy. Your mission from POTUS is clear—seek and destroy."

CHAPTER 53

Commonwealth Consultants
Fairfax, Virginia

As it turned out, three tracking devices were found hidden in their belongings after they arrived at Commonwealth Consultants, two in Francesca's and one in Jake's. How someone managed to put a tracker in his pack was beyond him. The bigger issues were when and where he, or rather his backpack, had been comprised.

Francesca's position was that Marco had the devices planted while she was in Squillance attending her father's funeral. According to her, that was when Marco Serreti and AISE Director Lorenzo Barzetti first appeared and had likely planted the tracking devices. At least that was the premise she put forth in the conference room at Commonwealth, although it didn't seem logical to Jake, since the active RFID tracking device found in her backpack was in the exact location as the one found in his, both sewn into the padding on the left strap. In his mind, that meant they were planted at the same time by the same person. And the only time when both he and Francesca were not in possession of their backpacks was right after the Carabinieri arrested them in *The Jew's* flat in Rome. His first encounter with Serreti was then, in the interrogation room. He was not in possession of his backpack during that time and he doubted Francesca was either.

The presence of the tracking devices explained why Serreti kept showing up unannounced. In Vienna. In Florence. And again in Volterra. "What could possibly be Serreti's motivation for tracking us?" he asked while spreading his jacket over the back of his conference room chair. He sat down and returned his gaze to his partner. "I mean, what does he gain?"

"Like I told you before, Jake, AISE doesn't like outsiders getting credit for anything. It's an Italian pride thing, I guess."

"Well, that's stupid," he said and then he turned to Fontaine and Wiley. "So, George, tell us more about the drone."

"Like we discussed a few hours ago," Wiley started the conversation. "The USS Truman was caught totally off-guard. There was a low cloud cover and restricted visibility. A spotter in the control tower was the first to identify the bogey. It was less than a quarter of a mile from the ship when he first picked it up. It flew directly overhead. A cross check with radar showed nothing. Not a blip, not a primary target, nothing. If it were a hostile, we could have lost the carrier." He waited to see if anyone had questions. "This begins a new realm of warfare, one in which we are not on the leading edge. And this is a big problem as tensions with Iran have been slowly ramping up. Especially in light of who is involved with your portion of the investigation. If Omar went rogue, that's one thing, but imagine if he's doing the bidding of the Iranian government. This could also be a part of whatever he has planned. He, or they, could deliver WMDs undetected."

"It is our belief," Fontaine said as he tucked a yellow pencil behind his ear, "that the fly-by of the USS Truman was a test run for the Iranians using the stolen technology. If our Navy had spotted it and shot it down, then they would claim a drone malfunctioned and flew outside of their borders. They would offer their humble apologies and thank the Navy for eliminating a possible threat to innocent people. But that didn't happen. The drone flew over the carrier, turned north and returned into Iranian airspace before the USS Truman could get authorization to shoot it down. With the poor weather conditions, the whole incident was over almost as fast as it started. It was in visual contact for less than a minute in total duration. Not enough time to do anything about it."

"Have the Iranians commented?"

"They've been silent on the matter. The Secretary of State called Tehran directly. Of course, they denied any involvement and dismissed it as U. S. propaganda aimed at strengthening their argument to the United Nations in opposition of lifting economic sanctions against Iran."

"What about the pictures? How can they deny those?" Francesca's turn.

"They dismissed them as well. They didn't deny it was one of their drones, but instead claimed those photos could have been taken anytime in the past. They claim to have had no drones over the Persian Gulf at the time of the incident."

"What's our next play?" Jake questioned.

"Nothing," said Wiley. "We let the politicians work it out in their world. Our military bases abroad as well as all Navy and Coast Guards vessels are to remain in alert status until further advised. Rudd directed me to keep you two out of it. She wants you to remain focused on determining what Omar and his band of merry men are up to and stopping them before it's too late. She also wants us to locate, if at all possible, the 239 passengers who were onboard Air Malacca 910 when it landed in the Lut Desert."

"Has that been mentioned to the Iranians yet?" asked

Francesca. "And what did they have to say about that?"

"According to Rudd, addressing that issue with Iran at this time carries with it delicate diplomatic issues best handled at the Executive level. She wants to locate those passengers, dead or alive, before she takes the issue to the United Nations."

"We have proof," Jake said in a matter of fact tone. "George and I tracked Air Malacca 910 from where it disappeared and went silent, until it landed in the Lut Desert. Doesn't that count for something? How much more proof does she want?"

"She wants definitive visual evidence the heat signature belonged to Air Malacca 910 and not some other Boeing 777."

"How the hell are we going to get that without going into Iran?" Jake searched Fontaine's face.

"Rudd is authorizing a Seal team—"

Jake interrupted, "George, do you know where it is now?"

"I do."

Jake pressed both palms flat on the conference table and spread his fingers apart. "Are you going to share or keep us hanging?"

"Tell them," instructed Wiley.

Fontaine leaned back in his chair and locked his fingers behind his head. "When Air Malacca 910 left the Lut Desert, it flew and landed at Mehrabad International Airport in Tehran."

"That is surprising," Francesca said. "It's a public use airport, well, as public as any place in Iran can be."

"It landed at Mehrabad at three-thirty in the morning, so there was virtually no activity around the airport at all. It taxied over the Lashkari Expressway to the north side of the airport and disappeared inside a huge green hangar."

"So the Seal team knows right where to go, that's great," Jake said. "I'm sure we have plenty of capable Seals of Iranian descent."

"I wish it were that simple," Wiley interjected.

"What do you mean?"

Fontaine continued, "I set up an alert on the heat signature and continued running scans to present day. Air Malacca 910 remained in that hangar until two months ago. Plenty of time for the Iranians to reverse engineer the technology."

"Where did it go this time?"

"Chkalovsky Air Base," answered Fontaine.

"Russia?" Francesca raised her voice.

Jake couldn't believe it. Russian involvement put a completely different spin on their mission. He looked at Wiley. "Do you think the Russians have something to do with *The Jew* and *Disruption?*"

"I don't think so, Jake. I think Iran owed a debt to Russia and their payoff was delivering that technology to Moscow." The old man paused for a few long seconds and continued, "This technology in the hands of Russia is a very bad thing."

"Imagine the Russians outfitting all their long-range nukes with this technology," Fontaine added. "We would never see them coming."

"Or worse," Jake concluded. "Chkalovsky Air Base is the home of the Russian Federal Space Agency. Imagine if they put up a string of spy satellites that couldn't be detected. Or satellite-based weaponry. Russia would have the world by the balls." He glanced at Francesca. "So to speak." His eyes studied Fontaine and then Wiley. "Come on guys, surely the Seal team isn't going into Russia."

Wiley shook his head. "No, they're going into Iran to locate, identify, and hopefully rescue any hostages still alive. Rudd is talking to Director of Central Intelligence Scott Bentley as we speak. She wants the CIA to handle identifying the aircraft. The CIA already has operatives in Moscow."

Jake stood. "Right here. Right in front of you. Francesca and I both speak Russian."

"The CIA will handle this." Wiley wagged his finger at Francesca and him. "Which, under no circumstances will you have any part of…either of you." Wiley sat back in his chair. "Do I make myself clear?"

"Absolutely, boss." Jake said.

"No problem." chimed Francesca.

"Good."

Jake turned back to Fontaine. "Do you have any idea where the hostages were taken?"

"Only guesses right now, which is all the Seal team will have to go on." He explained how he tracked several buses that drove into the Lut Desert and then left a few hours later. The assumption was the passengers from Air Malacca 910 were taken to different locations where they were being held captive. "The only problem is that it is impossible to track every vehicle that went in and out of all those different locations over the past two and a half years, so they could have been relocated several times by now. Those buses started showing up within a few days after the airliner landed in the desert. Those people could be anywhere."

"Including dead."

"That's right, Jake," Wiley had a grave tone in his voice. "They all could be dead by now, and most likely are. Especially the ones who weren't with Hardwire Semiconductors."

"With Daniel Luzato dead," Jake said, "does this put us back to square one?"

Fontaine pulled the pencil from behind his ear and tapped it on the table. "Yes and no. But, mostly no. We have a lot more to go on than we did before this all started. Daniel Luzato is… was a master hacker. He has embedded so much information encrypted deep inside these programs that it might take me days to decipher them all. Days, I'm afraid, we might not have. I'm getting the sense Omar's *Disruption Day* is closing in fast. I haven't been able to determine exactly when yet and that is unsettling to say the least. It could be any day."

Francesca pushed her chair back and stood. It was something she did frequently in these meetings. "What will happen when that day comes? Do you have any idea?"

"I shudder to think of all the possibilities."

"So with Luzato dead and Omar missing…" Jake rolled through all the feasible options to get them back on track and came up with only one. "I think I should go back to the beginning. Boris."

"Speaking of Boris," Fontaine said. His legs started bouncing which was typical when he got excited or nervous. "I got a ping on Boris' computer. It took some doing, but I finally tracked him to a public server at the Frankfurt, Germany airport. I scanned all the outgoing passport names, but nothing strange stuck out."

"You know," Francesca said. "While I was talking to Enzo Mantova in Florence, I showed him the photos we'd taken from the dead guy's apartment in Vienna. He recognized Boris. Said he would never forget him. Something about losing ten thousand Euro to him last year at a gambling casino."

"Did he say where?" asked Jake.

"No, he didn't get a chance. I asked him where and then his head blew off."

"Did he say anything else? Anything at all?"

"Some place that starts with a B, I think."

"Well, that doesn't narrow it down mu—"

"Wait," she interrupted. "He said something about a party…a secret agent party. Said Boris goes every year."

Before she could finish her sentence, Fontaine was already punching keys on his keyboard. "Here it is," he said, his voice almost shouting. "The Secret Agent Party at Casino Baden-Baden. And guess what?"

Jake shrugged his shoulders. "I give up."

"This year's party is tomorrow night."

CHAPTER 54

Eastern Colorado

Boris' email was unexpected. Not so much the email itself, as his words of encouragement and instructions. Boris had seemed to look out for Ethan Wogahn's best interests from the beginning. Always his champion. Always giving him extra personalized attention and running interference from Omar whenever necessary.

Wogahn read over the checklist Boris sent in the email, some of it redundant from an earlier email and then again from their video chat. Now, though, there seemed be an urgency in his email as opposed to reinforcement of previous messages. He got the feeling Boris wanted him to drop everything and leave Colorado immediately. Maybe Boris knew something he didn't want to share, something about Disruption. Omar had gone silent, which wouldn't necessarily be out of the norm except that his project was less than forty-eight hours from initiation. Could something have happened to Omar? Arrested, perhaps? Dead?

The more he thought about it, the more uncomfortable he felt staying put any longer. Boris was right about one thing in his email, there was no need for Wogahn to remain at his station. Everything had been put in motion. The software was uploaded, the arrays aligned and ready to deliver the malicious computer code. Yes, Boris was right; time for him to leave.

He checked off every item on the checklist and then triple-checked them again and again. Everything was set and on autopilot, so to speak. He went to his living quarters inside the tower building and examined the gash on his head, the one made by the eagle's talon while he was on top of the tower removing the bird's nest from the dish. The skin around the wound was bright red and, even though he'd soaked his wound in alcohol from his first aid kit, it appeared the gash might be developing an infection. No telling what bacteria was on the bird's claws.

He doused more alcohol on the wound and threw the bottle in his bag. He towel-dried his hair and finished packing his bag. He needed to make the sixteen-and-a-half-hour drive to New Orleans today in order to could catch his flight tomorrow. Boris had made those arrangements, including backstopping his new identity on the island of Cayman Brac where hopefully, he could live out his days in peace and quiet in the tropical sun drinking rum drinks and living the carefree life in the Caribbean. And perhaps one day, in the distant future if the fervor from Disruption died down, he could return to the States as a visitor under his new identity.

He collected his bag and headed to his pickup truck parked outside the concrete block building. His eyes darted about the area making sure nobody was watching. The tower was covered with ice from last night's storm. It was a good thing he had removed the bird's nest yesterday. He studied the cloudy Colorado sky in search of any sign of the creature that left the scar on his head, but saw nothing. When he opened the truck door, ice cracked from around the edges of the door frame. He hated freezing rain, he'd had plenty of it when he lived back east. What was he saying? He hated the cold.

He started his truck and turned the heater on high. Reaching behind the seat he pulled out an ice scraper and went to work on the windshield. Next he scraped the side windows and rear window of the standard cab truck. When that task was complete, he crawled in the truck. A blast of heat hit him in the face. He made the necessary adjustments and slipped his phone into a holder attached in the CD player. He had already mapped his route and plugged it into the Google maps app on his phone. US 287, the highway the tower was on, took him all the way to Fort Worth where he would turn eastbound on I-20. He would stay on I-20 until turning on I-49 southbound until some unpronounceable town in Louisiana called Opelousas. From there he turned eastbound on US 190 until I-10, which would take him into New Orleans. It seemed easy enough, it was just a long ass drive. One he wasn't looking forward to, but the thought of being in the Cayman Islands by tomorrow night was all the motivation he needed. If he combined his stops for gas, food, and bathroom breaks, he should be able to pull into the hotel next to the Louis B. Armstrong Airport by 11:00 p.m. Central time. That would give him plenty of time to pick up his documents from the Post Office box and rest before his 10:50 a.m. flight tomorrow morning. New Orleans to Grand Cayman with a 40-minute plane change delay in Houston and arrival at Grand Cayman before five in the afternoon.

He filled up his truck twenty minutes down the road in Lamar, Colorado. His next planned stop wasn't until Wichita Falls, Texas…provided his bladder cooperated.

Somewhere around Dallas along I-20, he developed a headache that progressively worsened the longer he drove. In Shreveport, the pain became almost unbearable and radiated from the gash on his head. He stopped for gas and a bathroom break, taking his first aid kit with him to the bathroom where he looked at his head and noticed the red inflammation had spread outward in streaks from the wound. He knew the signs; infection had happened despite his best efforts to prevent it with the use of alcohol. He debated visiting one of the many urgent care facilities he saw in town, but opted to gut it out as long as he could. If it didn't get better by New Orleans, he'd find an urgent care facility there…or a hospital.

By the time he reached New Orleans, the pain was so severe, he could barely see due to blurred vision. Some of that might be contributed to seventeen hours of basically nonstop driving, but most, he knew, was from the wound. Pain pills hadn't helped. He had been pounding ibuprofen for the past six hours. At least prescription strength milligrams, if not more. His head felt hot to the touch.

He retrieved his documents from the Post Office box before going to the hotel. As Boris had promised, the exterior doors of the Post Office were unlocked, thus allowing Wogahn 24-hour access to the box. Inside the box he found a single envelope. He opened it and realized Boris had gone the extra mile to help him out. Inside were a Louisiana driver's license, a matching passport, several credit cards and a surprise—cash. Five thousand dollars in a variety of denominations. He tucked the envelope under his arm and returned to his truck.

When he reached the hotel, he put on his ball cap and went inside to check in. He used his old identification as Boris had instructed. "Don't use your new identity until you check in for your flight at the airport," he had said. "Nothing to trace your moves before catching the flight." After getting his room number, he asked the desk clerk for the location of the closest hospital or urgent care facility.

He never got an answer.

A wave of pain washed over him. The lights dimmed. His ears rang. He heard muted voices in the background. Blurry figures moved toward him.

And then the lights went out.

CHAPTER 55

Casino Baden-Baden
Germany

It was the first time Jake had worn a tuxedo in over two years, and even then it wasn't during a mission. Most of his assignments involved tactical clothing, but not tonight. Tonight involved mingling with a crowd he rarely rubbed elbows with—the very rich and egotistical. He'd had a few run-ins with some pretty big egos in the past, but nothing near this level of pomposity. That was his expectation, anyway.

It became obvious to him when they landed at Baden Airpark and he saw the tarmac lined with rows of multi-million-dollar business jets. *Lifestyles of the rich and famous. Or rich and wannabes.*

Baden-Baden was located at the north end of Germany's famous Black Forest along the banks of the Oosbach River. An area long steeped in tradition, Baden-Baden was known for many things, most notably the love of the arts, hot springs spa baths, and gambling. A cultural mecca tucked in a quiet valley where tourists traveled from the far reaches of the globe to enjoy what this small town had to offer—the finest of everything. From fine wine to fine food to shopping, horse racing, and much more, Baden-Baden was where the rich, and almost rich, came to spend their money and be pampered in style.

Before they left Fairfax for Germany, Wiley had ordered a tailor to fit and customize his tuxedo as well as Francesca's evening gown. His tux was made up of a black coat with lapels, black pants, black bow tie, black cummerbund and a white shirt. The bow tie was not the clip-on kind but one that required tying, something he had extreme difficulty with despite the tutoring from the tailor. Finally, though, he got it right. On the fourth attempt.

He hadn't seen Francesca's gown until she came out of the bedroom on the Citation, she was dressed to kill. With her gun strapped to her thigh beneath her evening gown, he meant it literally. He had never seen her in formal attire and was amazed how beautiful she looked as she sashayed toward him. "Wow," he said. "You look…well, stunning." She wore a red sequined evening gown, although she called it lacquer instead of red, form fitted to her curvaceous figure with a ruched bodice. It was strapless with a fold-over neckline. She wore a triple-band of tiny white pearls around her neck that dropped to just above her neckline.

"You clean up pretty good yourself, Jake."

He reached into his traveling bag and pulled out a small box. Inside were two custom molded earpieces and two miniaturized microphones. They each turned on their com units, inserted their earpieces, and attached the microphones inside their clothing, his behind his lapel and hers inside the neckline of her dress. After testing their units, they descended the air stairs of the Citation and walked to the transportation area.

He thought it odd that he and Francesca were going to have to ride the bus from the airport into town, until he saw the bus was full of other formally attired people just like them. They blended in with all the tuxedos and evening gowns, playing the part of the young rich couple who adored each other, roles Wiley had scripted for them. At the airport they loaded onto bus # 205, which took them to the Baden-Baden train station where they joined the crowd shuffling from one bus to bus # 201, which dropped them off in town right in front of the casino.

Casino Baden-Baden was located in the Kurhaus, which was built in the 1850s in a style inspired by the Palace of Versailles and was filled with rooms honoring French royalty who never set foot in the Kurhaus. The large building frontage sported eight white columns with a grand entrance centered in the middle. Unlike past years, this year's Secret Agent Party was a closed venue. After they arrived at the airport, a courier delivered their invitations, which without, entrance would be denied. It was delivered under their assumed identities for the evening, James and Elizabeth Murray.

As they approached Casino Baden-Baden, Francesca slipped her arm through Jake's as she scaled the steps with him to the door. They waited in line while those ahead presented their invitations and were allowed to enter. As their turn arrived, he reached into his tuxedo jacket and produced their invitation. The woman working the door said something in German, smiled and said with a thick, but understandable accent, "Mr. and Mrs. Murray, enjoy your evening…and good luck tonight at the tables."

As they entered the grand foyer with its red walls and red carpet all adorned in gold trimmings and crystal chandeliers, they were greeted by a large sign with a picture of Daniel Craig as James Bond pointing a gun directly at them. The sign simply read:

SECRET AGENT PARTY,
CASINO BADEN-BADEN

Below that, the date. To the right of the sign and inside a roped off area was a silver Aston Martin DB5.

"Wow, look at this car. Just like the ones in the James Bond movies," said Jake with the enthusiasm of a little boy getting his first BB gun at Christmas.

"Actually," a man's voice commented from behind them, "this is *the* Aston Martin used in the movie *Skyfall*. Not the one they shot up, of course."

Jake and Francesca spun around to face the man.

"It's on loan to us for this event," the man said. "We acquire one every year. Last year it was the Alfa Romeo driven by the villain in *Quantum of Solace*. We try to get a different car every year, but mostly they give us Bond cars...and mostly Aston Martins."

"Impressive," Jake said.

The man put out his hand. "My name is Adlar. I am one of the croupiers at Casino Baden-Baden. I hope you'll find your way to my table tonight. It is the *Casino Royale* American roulette table. The casino is over there." He motioned to his left. "The casino has flown in quite a few look-alike characters from several of the Bond movies as well as quite a few stunning Bond girls. At the Belvedere bar, be sure to order the *Belvedere Vodka Limited Edition*. Shaken not stirred, of course. If you get hungry you can make your way to our exclusive *Live and Let Dine* restaurant." He gave Francesca a subtle wink and scooped her hand in his. "For you, ma'am, take your man to the perfumery table and get him the newest fragrance that makes every Secret Agent irresistible, a bottle of the *James*

Bond 007. Festivities don't officially kick off for another thirty minutes. Please feel free to learn your way around the casino." He kissed the back of her hand and let it go.

"Thank you, Adler," Francesca said. "We'll make a point to come to your table tonight, won't we, dear?" She leaned over and kissed Jake on the cheek, leaving a small trace of lipstick, which she used her finger to remove.

"Count on it, Adler. *Casino Royale* table, we'll be there." Jake gave him a thumbs up, locked his arm around Francesca's arm. "Shall we?" He tipped his head to Adler and led Francesca toward the casino.

"Good thing George was able to hack the casino's computer and get tonight's floor plan," he said. "Otherwise we would be scrambling to find our way around. We need to find a nice hidden spot so we can keep an eye out for Boris."

She nodded "Someplace where we can see him come in and he can't see us."

He looked around the room. "It's going to be tough as the crowd gets bigger."

They wandered around for quite a while and finally wound up at the bar where he ordered the *Belvedere Vodka Limited Edition*. "Shaken, not stirred," he said to the bartender as Adler had suggested.

"The bartender replied, "Excellent choice, Mr. Bond."

"Man, these people get into this," said Jake.

He sipped the extraordinary drink and checked out the casino gambling floor with its card tables, roulette wheels, and craps tables. He felt like he'd been dropped into a real Bond movie.

Francesca jabbed her elbow into his ribs. "Having fun?"

He continued staring straight ahead. "Yeah, I am. I think

this is cool."

"Stay focused, Jake. We have a job to do. We need to be on the lookout for Boris."

"No, we don't."

"Dammit Jake—"

"Boris is already here. He just walked through the front door."

CHAPTER 56

"Francesca, time for you to start working the room," Jake said. There was still a possibility Boris might recognize him from the subway chase in Washington, D.C., therefore he needed to keep his distance. At least for now, until the moment was right for a confrontation.

Boris had never laid eyes on Francesca before, so she was tasked with first contact, which actually wasn't going to be for a while. Several things needed to happen first before either one of them made a move toward their target. He and Francesca spread out to ensure their target was always within sight.

Jake did not want to risk being discovered by Boris. However, he did not want to chance losing him in the crowd either. As start time for the event ticked closer, the swarm of gamblers inside the casino got bigger and bigger, to the point where Jake decided he needed to move around. As a precaution, he kept to Boris' back most of the time or gave him a wide berth if he was forced to walk in front of him. Fortunately, Boris was wearing a white on black tuxedo—white jacket, black pants, so he was easy enough to spot in the crowd since he was one of the few wearing a white jacket. He knew by Boris' body language the guy was not surveillance-conscious. He was young and cocky...and oblivious.

"Is he ever going to find a table?" Jake whispered into his microphone.

"He's doing what most of the gamblers are doing," she replied. "Scoping out the competition at each table. I think he's taken an interest in the pot-limit Texas hold 'em table near the back wall right in front of the smokers' casino."

Casino Baden-Baden was a non-smoking casino, however, to accommodate the smokers, there was a smaller casino attached to the rear of the main casino gambling floor.

"Excuse me," a deep gruff voice said when he bumped Jake.

Jake had to strain his neck upward to see the man's face. "My fault entirely," Jake said to the man now grinning. His mouth was full of metal. *Jaws*. Behind him was a short blonde with horn-rimmed glasses and pig tails. A couple right out of the movie *Moonraker*, he thought. *This place is like being on a movie set.*

He glanced back to the spot he last saw Boris. Boris was not there.

"Francesca, do you have eyes on target?"

"He is sitting down at the Texas hold 'em table."

Jake's eyes swept across the room in the direction of the Texas hold 'em table. Every gambling table in his sight had two or three Bond girls. Some of the Bond girls were taking drink orders. Some standing next to gamblers with their arms around them. Strolling through the middle of the casino was a short Asian man wearing a metal top hat—Oddjob, the henchman from *Goldfinger*.

It's like a Halloween Bond party for gamblers.

Through the crowd of the Bond look-alike characters, he located Boris. And Francesca.

Francesca sauntered around the Texas hold 'em table where Boris was sitting and Jake knew she was sizing him up. Not just as the notorious hacker, but as competition for the other gamblers at the table as well. He had taken €10,000 from the late Enzo Mantova, Francesca's confidential informant, at last year's Secret Agent Party, so he had to possess some level of competency at the table. A lot could be learned about an opponent by watching him gamble, especially if he didn't know he was being watched. And that was Francesca's job for the moment. She was good at reading people, especially body language. Her alarm bells always rang well before his did. And that had saved his ass a few times.

†††

She knew Jake needed to keep a low profile until Boris let his guard down. And that wouldn't happen until long after the card games had begun. When he settled into the game, he would become more relaxed and the fact he had already ordered another drink would help.

The dealer was a stunning Bond girl dressed in a low cut evening gown who bore a remarkable resemblance to the *Vesper Lynd* character in *Casino Royale,* one of Francesca's favorite Bond movies. The players at the card table ranged from seasoned players to the lucky rookie who did not understand the dynamics of the game.

She believed Boris was probably somewhere in the middle. This was a game of which a knowledge of probabilities was one of the most important factors. That was what allowed a gambler to win even with bad cards through the *bluff.* Right now, Boris was sizing up the other players at the table.

He was at the pot limit table, a confidence builder she figured. She was certain later he would want to try his hand at the no-limit Texas hold 'em table, because he kept glancing in the direction of the table. He folded his cards on the first two rounds, one time without even calling the blind after looking at his hole cards. He wouldn't do that again, she knew, after he pounded his fist on the table when the dealer laid the flop on the table. Maybe it was for show, although she doubted it. She had seen his hole cards, a two and an eight, the worst hole cards to have, but the flop produced a two and an eight, which would have given him two pair as starters…if he hadn't folded. The third hand he folded after the turn and then his luck changed. He won the fourth and fifth hands. After he raked in his chips, he leaned back in his chair, arms folded. She was standing across the table from him on the sixth hand and detected a slight twitch of his left eye when he peeked at his hole cards. He called the blind as did all the players at the table. The flop produced an ace, a king, and a seven. The bet was raised twice before it reached him. His brow creased ever so slightly and he called. A three fell on the turn card. Again, the bet was raised twice before reaching him. This time he raised. Everyone called.

The river card was an ace and Boris' face and body were stone cold. Not a twitch, not a fidget, nothing. The dealer called for final bets. The first player raised. The second, third, and fourth players folded. The fifth player bet the limit. The sixth and seventh players folded. It was Boris' turn to play. He took a few shallow breaths and called. She was standing behind the man who bet the limit and knew his hole cards were a pair of kings. This would be interesting, she thought, to see Boris' reaction regardless of the outcome. Everyone else at the table folded leaving only Boris and the man she was standing behind. The dealer called for the man to show his cards.

"Full house," the dealer said. "Kings over aces."

She noticed a slight, almost imperceptible, curl in the corner of his lip. The dealer motioned for Boris to show his cards. He showed no emotion as he turned over one card at a time, starting with the king. Boris paused and Francesca had already figured out the outcome. *Nice deception.* Boris was smooth, she had to give him praise, but he did have tells. He turned over his last card and the gallery around the table gasped and then cheered.

"Full house," the dealer said to Boris. "Aces over kings. You are the winner."

Boris raked in his winnings, threw a chip tip to the dealer, and got up from the table without saying a word.

He headed straight for the bar and she saw Jake duck around the corner and out of eye shot of Boris.

"He's a slick player," she whispered into her microphone. "I'll give him credit for that. But his eyes betrayed him."

"Tells?" asked Jake.

"Yep. And that might be the death of him."

CHAPTER 57

The bartender, with many-colored bottles adorning glass shelves behind him, was refilling a drink for Boris.

When Jake saw Boris heading in his direction, he lowered his head and walked in a perpendicular direction and out into the main gambling floor. Now, he was at least forty-five feet away leaning against a column across the casino from the Belvedere bar.

"That's his third martini," he said to Francesca as Boris downed the drink and ate the olive. "What's going on?"

"Although, he disguised it well," her voice in his earpiece, "he was nervous as hell. He's letting it all out now. He's overwhelmed with mixed emotions. Ecstatic over winning and scared shitless at the same time. He's building his confidence. Earlier he was eyeing the no-limit Texas hold 'em table. I'm pretty sure that's his goal for the night. It's where he won big over Enzo last year, so my guess is he's trying to psych himself first."

"By getting drunk?"

"He won't get drunk. Just enough liquid courage to take a chance at the big boy table. It might also make him careless. I studied the no-limit table, a much different caliber of player there than the pot-limit table where Boris just won. No rookies at this table, only professionals. I imagine he'll wait a bit before buying in at that table, probably play a few games of chance first where he isn't going head to head with the competition."

Francesca was right. Boris stopped drinking after the third martini and went to the bathroom. When he returned a few minutes later, he headed to the roulette table.

The *Casino Royale* table.

Adlar's table.

By his own admission, Jake knew nothing about roulette, except a ball spun around in a wheel and eventually landed on a number. He didn't know how to bet, what the odds were, or what strategy, if any, might exist. In reality, he didn't care. In his college and Navy days, he was good at Texas hold 'em and blackjack. And it was fun. But, most of the time, he was playing against a bunch of drunks who were out to have a good time and drink. That was the appeal for him as well.

Boris placed several chips on different parts of the board. Jake was mystified at his logic. "What the hell is he doing?" he whispered to Francesca.

"It isn't random, Jake. He's using a system to maximize his chances. But it's still a game of chance and all systems ultimately have a negative result. If you hit, take your money and run, otherwise you're almost guaranteed to lose money."

Which was exactly what happened on the first spin. Boris hit and hit big. The crowd around the table started yelling. Cheering, actually. He took the house for €3700. His system, as Francesca indicated, must have worked. He gathered his winnings and left Adlar's table.

Boris went to the craps table next, as Francesca had predicted, another game of chance and another game Jake didn't give a damn about. He liked card games, blackjack and Texas hold 'em. They were more interactive with other players, which was the appeal. He also wasn't a serious gambler, small time all the way. On a couple of trips to Vegas, he had limited the amount he would spend on gambling to $500. The first time he lost the full $500. The next time he won $500. It was a wash. He preferred poker night with his beer buddies as opposed to serious gambling.

From their briefing and from the words of Enzo Mantova, Boris was a serious gambler, so much so the hacker had acclaimed notoriety in Baden-Baden after last year when he left Germany with over €300,000 in his pocket. A repeat performance he no doubt had planned for tonight.

Jake moved as close to the craps table as he dared to see how Boris was betting. It didn't work, he couldn't get close enough to see the inside of the table, because Boris' new fan club had followed him from the roulette wheel. "How's he betting?" he asked Francesca.

"Another system, much like before, but he's laying down a lot less in chips."

"Saving it for the no-limit hold 'em table."

"You think?"

A woman threw the dice.

"He lost," she said.

"Is he betting again?"

"Yep. Not as much, though." Francesca edged next to Boris at the table. He locked on her eyes, and she returned his gaze with a flirty wink. Even though she wasn't wearing heels, Boris was a good two inches shorter than her. He actually had to lift his chin to look at her eyes. "Good luck," she said to him.

He said nothing. The stickman passed him the dice and he rolled. And won.

His winnings payout was small since he bet small. "You brought me luck," he touched Francesca's bare arm with the back of his index finger. She smiled. He placed substantially larger bets for the next roll. The stickman pushed the dice to him. Boris picked them up and held them out to Francesca. "My lucky charm. Roll for me."

"I couldn't," she protested. "What if you lose all your money? I don't want that on my conscience."

"Please, Miss…?" Boris said.

She answered with her false identity for the night, "Beth. Beth Murray."

"I'm Alex. If I lose, I lose. It is, what it is. Beth, please, I insist."

She took the dice and rolled.

The crowd yelled and cheered.

One of the base dealers handed him a stack of chips. "Your winnings, sir. €12,000."

Boris took the chips and kissed Francesca on the cheek. "See, you are my lucky charm after all." He stepped back and Jake saw him check her from head to toe. "I am headed to the no-limit hold 'em table next, I would consider it an honor if you would accompany me."

She hesitated.

"Do it," Jake said into his microphone.

She hooked her arm through Boris' and said, "Sounds like fun."

As they walked arm and arm away from the craps table, she ran her free hand through her hair, giving Jake the finger.

CHAPTER 58

As Francesca and Boris approached the no-limit Texas hold 'em table, an angry elderly gentleman was leaving the table. He headed for the exit in a huff. He had lost an all-in heads-up hand to the woman sitting to the left of him. She was younger, mid-thirties maybe, and very petite. From his vantage point, Jake could see her outfit, a low v-cut blue and gold dress that stopped below the knees and red boots. Western boots. Around her neck she wore a gold necklace with a turquoise gem dropping into her cleavage. Her motive seemed obvious to Jake, distract her opponents and take their money. Seemed like it worked on the man who just lost all his chips.

Boris bought the seat and placed his chips on the table in front of him. "You'll stay by my side until I have won everybody's money, right?" His statement was heard by many of the players at the table. They did not seem amused.

"Yes, but I must run to the restroom first. I promise, I'll come right back."

Boris let her hand slip from his. "Do hurry."

"I will. This is not something I want to miss."

Jake watched Boris from behind him and to the left where he was leaning against a column.

Francesca hurried toward the restroom and glanced in his direction. "Stay put and keep an eye on Boris. I'll talk while I walk." She explained what she had analyzed from Boris' demeanor and unfolded her plan for the evening. Her strategy sounded good to him although he did have a few minor concerns.

"Do you think I can pull it off?" he asked.

"Jeez, Jake, you don't have to win. Just do what I said and I'm certain how he will react."

She disappeared into the Ladies room and reappeared after several minutes. She went back to the table where Boris was sitting and put her hand on his shoulder. "See, that didn't take long. What happened while I was gone?" she asked Boris.

"Crappy hole cards. I folded the first two hands."

Jake couldn't see Boris' hole cards, he was too far away, but Francesca signaled that on the third hand, the hand after her return to Boris' side, he indeed had a remarkable improvement.

She whispered in Boris' ear, "Would you like a drink?"

"Not now."

"I'm ordering one."

"Hail one of the Bond girls to get you a drink. I don't want you to leave again."

"How could I leave?" she said with a seductive smile. "I'm your good luck charm."

"That you are."

Time clicked by slowly while he was leaning against the column and his legs cramped from standing for so long, so Jake paced back and forth, always staying behind Boris' back and out of the hacker's peripheral vision. He would continue to do so until she signaled him to make his move, which happened after an hour and a half.

Boris had won most of the hands since Francesca returned to his side. His superstition seemed to have convinced him she was indeed his reason for winning, and he made sure she stayed close by his side. On the previous hand, Boris, or Alexei Nikahd, or Alex Skylar as he now called himself, won his biggest pot of the night in a heads up dual against an African man sitting across the table and to the immediate right of the dealer.

"Now is a good time," Francesca spoke softly.

Jake took her signal and quickly walked to where the man who folded was vacating his seat.

"What did you say?" Boris asked Francesca.

"I'm having a good time," she lied to Boris. He was so distracted with the game; he did not question her again.

As Jake approached the seat, another man stepped out of the crowd. "I was going to sit there," a tall thin man with blue eyes said in a German accent.

Jake blocked the man with his arm. "I've been waiting over an hour for a seat. Better luck next time."

"Prick." He knocked Jake's arm out of the way.

At the far end of the table, an oriental man with long gray hair pulled back into a ponytail stood. "You may have my seat. This table is too rich for my blood."

"There you go," Jake remarked to the man. "No need to be upset, we both got a seat at the table." Jake sat down and placed his chips in front of him on the felt table. He stared directly at Boris, who was showing no indications of recognizing him, and said, "Sorry for the...disruption." He added emphasis to the word. Still no reaction from Boris. At the dealer's request, the two new players bought into the game.

The dealer directed Jake. "Sir, you are small blind. That will be two thousand five hundred euro."

Jake counted his chips and pushed his blind forward. The woman to the left of the dealer pushed her big blind in front of her as well. The dealer dealt the hole cards. Ten players at the table of various ages and nationalities all with the same purpose—win as much money as they could by trying to bankrupt their opponents.

The first ten hands went by and Jake folded more hands than he played. Then again, his true purpose was Boris and the only player he was studying was Boris. So he stared. The whole time he kept a hawkish gaze on Boris. The hacker shot him an angry glance, put his hand on Francesca's thigh, and stroked it. He obviously wanted to distract Jake. Good play. It took him a few seconds of self-restraint to keep from leaping across the table and knocking the asshole out. He saw the glare in Francesca's eyes tell the hacker to let go.

Playing Texas hold 'em with his old Navy buddies had never held this level of intensity, not even when the pot grew to a mountain of chips. Those pots never reached more than two or three hundred dollars. Tonight, the stakes were much higher. And not just the card game.

The dealer dealt the hole cards. It was barely perceptible, but Jake saw Francesca's signal. Time to make his move, he just hoped the cards fell his way. He took a covert peek at his hole cards, much the same as everyone at the table did. He had good cards—a pair, both high cards—at least he hoped high enough. His hole cards were a pair of tens. When it was his turn to bet, he quickly raised and returned his stare. Francesca's plan was working. Boris sat rigid, his lips pressed tightly together as he rechecked his hole cards. Then he glanced at Jake. Bingo.

Before Boris could turn away, Jake pronounced, "You look quite familiar. Do I know you?"

"I don't think so," the hacker replied.

"No, I'm sure we've crossed paths before." He paused and

then continued, "Ever been to Washington D. C.?"

Boris fidgeted in his seat. "Never have, no."

"Yeah," he dragged out the word. "I'm pretty sure you have. Perhaps on the Metro?"

Boris froze. He studied Jake with piercing scrutiny. At that moment, Jake knew Boris had finally put together the puzzle.

"Sir," the dealer announced while addressing Boris, "it is your bet."

"Call." He counted the chips and pushed them forward.

After all bets and folds were in, the dealer laid down the flop to the remaining seven players. A ten, a five, and a three. He kept an unrelenting stare on Boris. Francesca signaled him to bet. Which he did by doubling the pot.

Two more players folded and the field was reduced to five.

The turn card was another ten.

Jake bet the same as the previous bet, double the pot. Three more players folded leaving only Boris and Jake.

Sweat had begun to form above Boris' brow. The hacker called the bet.

The river card was a five.

It was Jake's bet first, he matched the pot. Boris quickly raised, tripling the pot. Jake hesitated. This time he was on his own. He didn't know what Boris' hole cards were and Francesca didn't know his. The odds were overwhelmingly in his favor. Only two types of hands beat his four of a kind, a higher four of a kind or a straight flush. Those odds, with the cards on the table, were a long shot for Boris. Jake's and Boris' eyes lingered on each other. Like when you were a kid. Who could hold their breath the longest? Only this time it was who would be the first to blink.

Boris blinked.

Jake went all in.

Boris called.

Even if Boris lost, which was almost a guarantee, Jake knew the hacker wouldn't be close to wiped out. He would still have more chips than three other players at the table.

"Gentlemen, show your cards," the dealer said. He looked at Jake. "You are first."

Jake turned over one card at a time, as Boris had done earlier in the night. The first card he turned over was a ten. The crowd that had gathered around the most observed table in the casino, buzzed with excitement. He turned over his other hole card—another ten. The galley broke into a combination of gasps and cheers.

"Four tens," the dealer proclaimed. He looked at Boris. "Your play."

"Son of a bitch," Boris cocked a brow in surprise and then mucked his cards.

"Four tens," the dealer declared to Jake. "You are the winner."

Jake wondered what the two cards lying face down on the table were. It was the player's choice to show his cards or *muck* and concede the pot.

The hacker picked up his chips. "I'm not playing against him. He creeps me out. Always staring."

Francesca rubbed her hand up and down his arm. "Let's get some fresh air."

"I think I'll call it a night," Jake heard Boris say to Francesca. Even with the ambient noise of the casino, which was loud, he could still hear remarkably well with his earpiece.

"You've lost one big hand," she reasoned. "Get some fresh air, shake it off, and go get back on the horse again."

"Maybe you're right," he relinquished. "But, I'm not going back until that guy leaves the table."

Jake watched Francesca and Boris retreat out the back door toward the garden. He gathered his winnings, tipped the waiter, and called to be cashed out. A casino employee counted his chips and wrote him a voucher.

So far, Francesca's plan had worked flawlessly. Until he heard her grunt, followed by thud. In a weak voice he heard her say, "Jake. Help."

CHAPTER 59

He wasn't sure if he was dreaming or in a dreamless nap where he couldn't remember anything at all. He had no idea where he was or what had happened to him.

When he opened his eyes he saw nothing, but a white blur. His ears ringing full of sounds. Thumping. Swishing. All foreign, except the steady ringing in his ears, which was more like a high-pitched buzzing. That felt as if it was inside his head, the other sounds were external. They had a steady beat, like music, but bad loud music, instruments and beats that didn't go together, but each with its own distinct sound.

With each beat of the sound, a throb drummed in his skull. Or was it on his skull. He tried piecing together the last things he remembered but it was still in a fog. He breathed deeply and let his groggy mind run a diagnostic of his body. Fingers and toes working, check. He ruled out paralysis. One step in the right direction. He opened his eyes again, still a white blur. He narrowed his eyes and focused on the blur. Slowly a pattern developed. Tiny squares, like a mesh, obscured his vision. He wasn't blind, good. He lifted his right arm. It moved and abruptly stopped. He lowered it and tried again, same result. He tried his left arm and the same thing happened. He jerked his arms violently and felt the restraints dig into his skin. The same with his legs. Where was he and why was he restrained?

He concentrated on the sounds, they had changed. The

thumping noise sped up but the swishing noise kept its steady pace. He felt something clamp down on his arm. Tighter. Tighter. It held pressure for what seemed an eternity then slowly released its grip with a hiss. What the hell? Then the thumping slowed. The sounds. They were mechanical.

He lifted his head. A sharp pain radiated across his scalp with such intensity he thought he was going to vomit.

And suddenly, he remembered.

It was the last memory he had—nausea. Prior to waking up in here, wherever here was, he was checking into a hotel when nausea overwhelmed him. Now, Ethan Wogahn could only assume he was in a hospital somewhere in New Orleans.

How long had he been unconscious? Had he missed his flight? Why was he shackled to the bed?

He heard the door open and two voices arguing as they entered the room, a doctor protesting the intrusion and someone who claimed to be with Homeland Security. His only thought, they had traced him back to the tower in Colorado. As unlikely as it seemed, that could be the only explanation.

A hand gently touched his shoulder. "Mr. Wogahn, I am Dr. Tara Singh, how are you feeling?"

"My head hurts and I want to vomit," he replied. "Why am I restrained?"

"You are in a high security hospital room at Tulane Medical Center. Do you remember what happened?"

"I can't see through this stupid bandage. Can you take it off?"

"I cannot remove it," Dr. Singh said, "but I can pull it away from your eyes."

He felt her warm soft hands pull the gauze from his eyes and the room sluggishly came into view with Dr. Tara Singh's face right above his. She had dark skin, brown eyes and black hair draped over one shoulder. "Is that better?"

He didn't answer.

"There is a man here from Washington D. C. to see you. He wants to ask you some questions. Do you feel up to it?"

"And if I say no?"

Before the doctor could answer, a big man with a bald head stepped forward holding a badge. "That's a privilege you don't have, Mr. Wogahn…or whatever your real name is?" He twisted his head and spoke to the doctor. "Leave us," he demanded.

"But—" The doctor started to protest, but the big man raised his hand.

"This is a matter of national security. Leave now or I'll have you escorted out."

"I'm calling the administrator." Dr. Singh stormed out of the room.

"Why am I handcuffed to the bed?"

"That tends to happen when we encounter someone with as many identities as you. You checked in the hotel as Ethan Wogahn and subsequently passed out. When the EMT's searched for ID, they found another full set under a different identity. By law, they reported this to NOPD. The local LEOs took your prints and, lo and behold, they showed up on the terrorist watch list under a completely different name. Starting to get the picture? I want to know everything. Right now. If you refuse to cooperate, I'll make sure you're on the next transport to Gitmo before that jackass in the White House closes it down."

"You're bluffing."

The man pressed his cupped hand on Wogahn's head. Blinding pain ripped across his skull. His pulse quickened.

Every sinew in his body tightened until his body was as rigid as a board.

"Try me."

††††

Jake found Francesca next to the water fountain in the garden, the side of her head bleeding.

"I'll be okay," she yelled as he ran onto the back veranda. "He went that way, Jake. Don't let him get away this time." She made reference to Boris eluding him in the Metro station when the hacker threw the old woman on the tracks in front of an approaching train.

Jake took off running in the direction Francesca indicated. He reached a paved roadway where the footsteps grew louder and were moving uphill. The road was curvy and steep.

As his vision adjusted to the darkness, he could see a silhouette sprinting uphill, a hundred feet in front of him, but with the brightness of the moon Boris' white tuxedo jacket stood out like a beacon.

While he ran, he reached inside his jacket and pulled out his pistol. This time, Boris wasn't getting away. He fished around in the left jacket pocket and pulled out his silencer, screwing it on while he ran. He was closing the gap. Over his own heavy breathing, he could hear Boris' breathing coming in hard short spurts.

Boris took a hard left at a streetlamp and disappeared out of his line of sight.

When Jake reached the lamp, the paved road split. The road he was on, Solmsstraße, went straight ahead. Boris turned up the steeper pathway, Stourdzastraße. The path narrowed substantially and now it wasn't paved like before. His lungs and heart were pumping as he pushed harder. He was gaining on Boris.

Then it happened.

The bastard disappeared.

Jake reached the spot where he had lost the hacker and spun in a circle. *Shit.* Boris was getting away again. Straight ahead and up the hill, he could make out the faint outline of a church. A chapel really, gauging by its size. He raised his weapon and kept it trained ahead while he pulled his penlight from his pants pocket. Jake stood still, silenced his heavy breathing and heard the crispy crunch of brittle leaves. He shined his light in the direction of the sound, and caught the glimpse of a figure of a man vanish behind the far side of the chapel.

As he approached, he ran across a metal marker that identified the chapel as the Rumänisch Orthodox Stourdza-Kapelle. He remembered reading about it with Francesca as they were studying the layout of the area surrounding the casino. The Stourdza Chapel, a Romanian Orthodox Chapel, named after Prince Mihail Sturdza.

Holding his tactical flashlight over his pistol, he warily rounded the corner of the chapel. There were no streetlights at the top of the hill or lights of any kind at all around the chapel. Looking downhill, he could see the city lights of Baden-Baden. At the top of the hill, only darkness. This side of the chapel was darker as the light from the moon was blocked by the shadow of the building.

He stepped a few feet away from the wall. "You're not getting away this time Boris," he called out. "Or should I call you Alexei Nikahd? We're on to you and Kazemi. Your plan for Disruption is over."

No reply and no sound. He kept moving, searching for his target.

He heard a sharp noise to his left. He turned with his weapon and light. Nothing. Before he could turn back, he caught something moving in his peripheral vision, but it was too late. The tall wooden beam that was leaning against the building crashed into him, knocking him to the ground. His gun and light scattered from his hands across the ground.

A shadow lunged at him from the cover of darkness. He rolled and kicked at the man's legs causing him to stumble. Jake jumped to his feet, but Boris was faster.

Boris charged, knocking him off balance while smashing his ribs with a brick. Jake grimaced at the pain shooting through his chest. He rolled to the hard ground and saw Boris rushing toward him with the brick held above his head.

Boris reared his arms back, aimed for Jake's head and slung it. Jake rolled sideways as the heavy brick struck and grazed his shoulder. He heard his tuxedo jacket rip and felt his flesh beneath tear apart. Boris pounced, pinning him to the ground, and began swinging his fists wildly like a girl trying to fight. Jake blocked a right and countered with a hard jab to Boris' nose. The loud crack meant it was probably broken as blood gushed down the hacker's face. Jake twisted and raised his hips, shoving Boris off of him. The hacker fell to his side curled in a fetal position, holding his nose. Jake grabbed him by his long black hair, raised his head, and smashed his fist into Boris' jaw. The man fell backward hitting the ground with a thud. "Give it up, Boris."

Boris rolled to his hands and knees and crab-crawled away. Jake took two steps forward and drop-kicked him in the gut. The force of the kick arched Boris' back and then the hacker's body collapsed flat on the ground. Gasping and groaning in pain, he lifted his head and retched.

"Had enough?" Jake asked.

The hacker raised his hand from the ground. "Enough," he cried. "Enough."

Jake stepped back and waited for Boris to gather himself.

"What are Omar's plans? What are his targets?"

Boris struggled to his feet. Hunched over, wiping the vomit from his face, he exploded in laughter. "Idiot. You can't stop it. Disruption is going to happen...whether you kill me or not."

Jake stepped forward and bunched two fistfuls of the young hacker's jacket in his hands. "You miserable son of a bitch. What are the targets?" He shoved him against the white and pink striped exterior wall of the chapel. "Can you stop it?"

"I can stop it, but *only* I can stop it."

"You stop it and I'll let you walk back down the hill with your legs still intact. Otherwise, the interrogation starts now."

Boris twisted his lips in a half smile. "Fuck you."

Jake smashed Boris' head against the wall and held him with one hand while he pounded him in the chest. Boris tried to slide down the wall, but Jake was relentless. He held him up with one hand and smashed his fist into Boris' face over and over so hard his fists were covered in blood. Jake loosened his grip and let Boris slide down the wall to the ground.

Jake was heaving hard and staggered backward from exhaustion. His hands were numb and sticky. Across the ground, his penlight's beam was shining across the barren earth. He picked it up and started searching for his gun. He finally spotted it in the edge of the grass. He walked over and leaned down to pick it up.

Before he could reach it, he heard running footsteps and the unmistakable sound of a switchblade. He turned. The shadow was nearly on top of him, the blade glinted in the moonlight. Then at once, a flash, a pop, and Boris dropped to the ground.

"How do you like your good luck charm, now?"

Francesca.

CHAPTER 60

It was after two in the morning before Jake and Francesca were allowed to leave the hilltop and the Stourdza Chapel. Elmore Wiley intervened and dealt with the local police. In reality, he made a few phone calls and whoever he called were the ones who handled the police on their behalf. Francesca's injuries were superficial, a large goose egg and a few minor cuts on her head caused by Boris hitting her over the head with a bottle. He and Francesca were released and informed they could leave the country whenever they desired.

Not before he cashed in his winnings was that going to happen. Wiley had wired the money to a Baden-Baden bank that, in return, issued a €150,000 credit redeemable at the casino. He cashed in €312,000. Not a bad night's take. Thanks to Francesca. It was her plan, she figured out how to get into Boris' head, Jake just executed her plan.

The casino provided a driver to take them to the airport. Jake was given a *comp* voucher and an invitation to return to next year's Secret Agent Party. Something he intended on using. Only this time, he would bring Kyli.

By the time they arrived back at the airport it was almost 4:00 a.m. local time. He and Francesca were greeted by a sleepy-eyed Jimi who relayed their instructions from Wiley, take an hour to freshen up, eat, then they were to call Commonwealth Consultants for a briefing about Disruption.

"Did you get into town at all?" Francesca asked Jimi.

"Yes, the three of us," she made reference to herself and the two pilots, "went to one of the spas and got the royal treatment." She laughed. "There isn't a spot on my body that didn't get scrubbed."

"How was it? Enjoyable?"

"It was fantastic. I had to lower my inhibitions a little, though, to be in a spa full of naked people, including those two." She flashed her eyes toward the cockpit. "After a few minutes I acclimated, though, and it got to be a lot of fun. The spa treatment part was awesome. If you've never done it, then I highly recommend you do."

"Not this trip, I'm afraid," Jake interrupted the women's discussion. "We won't be going back into town. I'm sure Wiley will have new assignments when we call in."

"He always does," added Francesca.

Jake and Francesca showered and changed inside an aviation operation at the southwest end of the airport. As cool as it was wearing the tuxedo for the Secret Agent Party, it felt good to put on comfortable clothes again. Although only a bruised abrasion, Jake cleaned up the wound and put a small butterfly bandage on his shoulder. When they returned to the aircraft, Jimi had heated up a large breakfast and was setting it on their respective tables.

"Eat up," she said. "Your call is in thirty minutes."

They stashed their belongings and sat in the comfortable leather seats. With their bellies full, the events of last night were taking their toll and making Jake feel tired and sleepy, not just him, but Francesca as well. He saw her eyes get heavy while they sat back and rested in their seats waiting for Wiley and Fontaine to call.

As was the norm with both Fontaine and Wiley, the encrypted conference call came through when they were told it would—to the exact minute. There was a lot to be said about reliability, which was one of the cornerstones of Wiley's work ethic. One he demanded from all his employees.

"So, Boris is dead." Wiley's tone was matter of fact. "Did he tell you anything about Disruption?"

"No, sir," Jake replied.

"Did you give him a choice?"

"Yes, sir. I did. I told him that if he gave up Disruption, we would make sure he didn't get the death penalty." Jake decided to not tell the old man what he actually said.

"You didn't have to kill him, though. You could have brought him in. I'm sure we could've broken him."

"I didn't kill him."

"I did," Francesca intervened. "It was either shoot Boris or let him kill Jake."

"And you always shoot to kill?" Jake could hear a touch of sarcasm in Wiley's voice, something extremely rare for the old man.

"Yes, sir… And I never miss."

There was an uncomfortable pause, long enough that Jake was wondering if the connection had been terminated and then Wiley spoke. "George has uncovered something from the encrypted messages in Daniel Luzato's code, including the *time bomb* date for Disruption. Halloween night at midnight Greenwich Mean Time. That's today in case you haven't looked at a calendar lately."

"Nineteen hours," Fontaine chimed in.

"Are we any closer to knowing the targets?"

"I know a few, Jake, but between Mr. Wiley and myself, I

think we have figured out who the main target is."

"Israel," Wiley said. "One of the main points of attack for Disruption is the Iron Dome. The Iron Dome is a missile defense system approved in 2007 by Israel's Minister of Defense and has been in operation since 2011. Simply put, it is designed to intercept short and medium range rockets and mortar shells, typically fired from the Gaza Strip. Using cameras and radar to track incoming rockets, it is designed to shoot them down within seconds of their launch. The Iron Dome defense system is effective for rockets fired up to 70 kilometers away. It determines where the rocket will land and does not target rockets or missiles directed at uninhabited areas. The Iron Dome is jointly funded by the United States, so this country has a serious stake in preventing Disruption... and the potential destruction of Israel."

"If Israel has the Iron Dome," Francesca said. "Then what's the threat?"

"This falls back on those Hardwire Semiconductor engineers on Air Malacca 910. HSI is at the forefront of point of sale technology, the kind of technology that protects credit card processing, banking transactions, encrypted data transfer, to name a few. Their technology provides the type of encryption used to keep the bad guys from stealing every country's secrets. It's in your computers, it's in your phones. In today's 21st century world, it's in almost everything. Without it, there isn't a civilized country in the world that wouldn't be vulnerable to malicious hackers and cyber warfare."

"Who's behind it all?" Jake asked. "Iran or Russia?"

"Russia isn't in this fight. Iran owed them big time. While the whole world was imposing economic sanctions on Iran, Russia was slipping them supplies left and right. Our government knew it, the United Nations knew it, but in reality, what was anyone going to do about it?"

Wiley didn't give him a chance to answer. "This is Iran all the way."

"What's their motive?" asked Francesca.

"The United Islamic Alliance."

"I thought that was a joint Islamic effort to unite the Shiites and the Sunnis," Jake said.

"As far as the public's perception, yes it is. But, that isn't its true purpose. The truth is, it's still under everyone's radar except for the most sophisticated of the intelligence communities. With Iran, it is fairly complex. Iran is basically a theocracy since the ultimate decisions are made by their religious leader. If they topple Israel, that would strengthen their relationship with the Arab countries in the region and elsewhere in the world where Islam is the predominant religion. The one thing that all of Islam is united on is that Israel is the enemy. Syria, Egypt, Iraq, Saudi Arabia and other neighboring countries would certainly fall in line and form an alliance with Iran at its lead, much like the axis power during World War II. Thus, thrusting them as the head and sole leader of the United Islamic Alliance. These UIA countries still basically control the world's oil supply and collectively a big chunk of the world's wealth. They would also control the Persian Gulf. Other Islamic countries like Indonesia and some Northern African countries would also follow suit and join UIA. With Iran as the leader of UIA, the Middle East would quickly fall under Iranian control. Iran would be the world power they have always wanted to be."

"I still don't get it," Francesca stood over the conference phone. "How does this tie into the Iron Dome?"

"I'll tell you." Jake thought he could detect irritation in

Wiley's voice. "Hardwire makes chips used for encryption for point of sale applications and they also make most of the encryption chips used in maintaining cell phone towers. Almost all of the telephone communications in Israel is wireless or cellular. The encryption chips Hardwire makes are used for maintaining Israel's cell towers. The Iron Dome relies one hundred percent on wireless technology. Those HSI engineers possess the knowledge and capability to effectively shut down the Iron Dome."

The realization of Wiley's words must have flabbergasted Francesca. She sank into her seat and looked defeated.

Jake pulled the conference phone closer to him. "What's our next move?"

"I am busy with Daniel Luzato's code, trying to decipher more messages," Fontaine said. "He was good. Better than I could ever be, but I'm slowly getting there. I have found one message repeated over and over, but I don't know what it means. It must be significant. Why else would he embed the same message in his code over and over?"

"What's the message, George?"

He heard Fontaine rustling papers and then the analyst said, "Israel's fate rests with the Star of David."

"That's it?" Francesca straightened up in her seat. "Who could possibly figure that out?"

Jake replayed the events of the past few days and announced, "I can."

CHAPTER 61

"Are you sure?" Wiley said to Jake. "We're running out of time and can't afford a wild goose chase."

He explained to the team what he knew and how he knew it.

"All right, Jake. You and Francesca handle it. And watch your back."

He disconnected the conference call after a few more minutes and relayed their new destination to the pilots.

Francesca sat quiet for several minutes. He could tell something was on her mind. "What?" he finally asked.

"Why didn't you tell me before now?"

"Mainly, because Marco was around and regardless of whether you think otherwise, I don't trust him. And honestly, I forgot about it until George relayed the coded message. Then, it all started making sense."

"For what it's worth, Jake, I don't trust him. Now, more than ever. If it's any consolation, he's going to pay for putting those RFID trackers on us. No telling what else he's done."

The aircraft began to taxi and within a few minutes was airborne—destination Salzburg, Austria.

They discussed many things on the short flight from Baden-Baden to Salzburg. In particular, the fact neither of them had ever flown in an aircraft on floats. Or landed on the water.

Wiley, although born in the United States, was of German

heritage and had family in the region surrounding Salzburg, a cousin who flew for a flying service based at a nearby airport. And one of those aircraft was a turbine powered, single-engine de Havilland Otter—on floats. Most of his trips involved flying fishermen, mostly tourists, to remote mountain lakes for a day of fishing. Weather permitting, he'd drop them off in the morning and pick them up in the late afternoon. Unless they were also campers, in which case he would return to pick them up at a designated place and time.

It was only 385 kilometers and took less than an hour, including taxi time. As the Citation taxied to the ramp, Jake looked out the window and recognized what had to be their connecting flight. It was white with a yellow stripe running from the propeller to the tail cone. The leading edge of the wings were equipped with de-icing boots. It was mounted on floats with retractable wheels for landings on water and extendable wheels for landing on terra firma. Standing beside the aircraft was an elderly man who, from a distance, could have passed as Elmore Wiley himself with slightly darker hair. He wore aviator style sunglasses and a jumpsuit bearing the same logo as the one painted on the tail of the aircraft.

Jake snatched up his backpack and gestured to Francesca, who was still sitting with her seatbelt fastened. "Grab your gear and let's go."

She didn't move.

"Francesca," he raised his voice. "Move it."

"I'm not going with you, Jake."

He thought it was a joke. "Quit kidding around. We have our instructions from Wiley."

"I have a different mission."

"No, you don't. Wiley expects us to handle this together…

as a team."

"I know. But, this time, you'll have to deal with it on your own. I have something else I must take care of. After that, if there's time, I'll join you."

He studied her face and knew it was a lie. "Francesca, you mean if you're still alive you'll join me?"

She said nothing.

"The old man is not going to like this."

"Jake, this is something I have to do. Something occurred to me last night in Baden-Baden and if I'm right, Wiley will understand."

"And if you're wrong?"

"If I'm wrong…" she paused for an awkward length of time, "it won't be his problem to deal with anymore. And neither will I." Her tone had a note of finality to it.

"Can't we do this together? We can take care of this first and then we can take care of your issue…together. Like partners are supposed to do."

She held his gaze for several seconds yet said nothing, but he knew what his partner was thinking. She might be the one who could read a person, but they had been on too many missions together, and spent more time together than most married people for him not to know what was on her mind.

As the aircraft came to a stop next to the floatplane and Jimi opened and lowered the air stairs, he waited, as they exchanged unspoken words. He knew they might never see each other again.

"We've come a long way together, partner," he said.

He thought he could detect moisture building in her eyes. Something he'd never seen before.

He slung his backpack over his shoulder.

"Take care of yourself, Francesca. I hope you find what you're looking for."

She did not have to respond. Her eyes told him.

Jake walked out of the aircraft.

†††

Hallstatt, Austria

Wiley's cousin, Klaus Unger, had similar facial features and stature, but when he got close to the old man's cousin, he could see that was where the resemblance ended. At a distance, it seemed an uncanny resemblance. Not so much up close.

The descent onto Hallstätter See, or Hallstatt Lake, was long and gradual. They entered from the valley to the north over the town of Bad Goisern and flew south between the mountains surrounding the lake toward the small lakeside village of Hallstatt. A picture perfect moment captured from a travel brochure. The midday sun highlighted the fall colors in the trees on both sides of the lake. Yellows and reds and greens blended together to create a kaleidoscope of color. Boats, large and small, were out in force and Klaus maneuvered the aircraft to set up for a landing near the eastern shore.

He had been forewarned it would be a quick drop-off at the dock. Klaus wanted to get out of Hallstätter See and enroute to his afternoon pick up at a lake nearly two hours away. After the long taxi across the lake to the western shore, Klaus aimed the de Havilland Otter straight toward the dock and at the last moment kicked the rudder and the aircraft rotated ninety degrees to the left and gently bumped the side of the dock. Two young men grabbed the starboard float and held the aircraft in place while Jake deplaned onto the dock. With a quick push off by the two young men, Klaus Unger powered the aircraft to the middle of the lake, turned north, and took off in the direction from which they just came.

Wiley had Fontaine reserve and pay for two rooms at the Seehotel Grüner Baum overlooking Market Square and the salt-filled mountain to the west. Jake decided to check in first and ask for directions from the front desk clerk. He had plenty of time to retrieve the item later, so he didn't see a reason to rush. Besides, some things were best handled under the cover of darkness. Breaking and entering was certainly one of them.

Of the two rooms, he chose the room with a balcony overlooking Marktplatz, or Market Square. He ordered a glass of wine from the bar downstairs and took it to his room where he sat on the balcony and watched the people as they milled about, going in storefronts or sitting at tables in front of the cafes facing Market Square. From his balcony he could see the square wasn't actually square so much as shaped like an arrowhead, wide at his hotel and tapered toward the western end where it ended and a narrow street meandered out of sight. Directly in front of the hotel was a statue featuring the Holy Trinity and beyond that a fountain where two young kids took turns dipping their hands in the water and splashing each other.

After he finished his glass of wine, he retrieved his weapon from his backpack and tucked it in his belt holster behind his back. He slipped on his jacket and left the hotel in search of the resting place of the Star of David.

CHAPTER 62

Despite Marco Serreti's warning, Francesca did return to Italy, this time under one of her more obscure false identities, one she had never used in the past. She was sure the AISE deputy director would have issued an alert at all airports to detain her. He had to know she would come after him. He would have given authorities her true identity and any aliases she might have used over the course of the last three or four years. Identities he might have become aware of, anyway. The man she found so hard to resist, she now regarded as contemptible in every way. The clock was ticking down and time was not on her side. According to Fontaine's most recent communiqué, Disruption was scheduled for midnight.

Tonight.

She had less than nine hours left before, according to Wiley and Fontaine, the world would be plunged into pandemonium. This time tomorrow, the world would likely be a different place altogether.

Betrayal was not uncommon in her line of work, yet Marco's betrayal was worse. He used her vulnerability against her, to track her, to get to Enzo, and no telling what else. She had to mitigate the damage he had done. And the only way was by confronting him. Face to face. She planned on calling him out. His answer determined his fate.

Guilt swept over her about the decision not to accompany

her partner, but she convinced herself Jake could handle Omar by himself. She needed retribution against the man who had once been her lover.

She waited inside the Citation while Jake boarded Wiley's cousin's seaplane. As soon as the seaplane's wheels were up and the plane was enroute to Hallstatt, she debarked Wiley's airplane with her go bag.

Covertly, she had already made arrangements for a small aircraft charter to take her from Salzburg to Rome's Urbe Airport where she would be a short four kilometers from her destination. She hated lying to Jake, or rather, not telling him where she was going and what her personal mission was, but he would have only tried to talk her out of it and this was one of those moments where his ignorance was in his best interest. And hers, too.

The taxi ride took ten minutes to her drop off point, which was still about a half a mile from her destination. This was a clandestine mission and being dropped off at the door was simply too risky. She needed to make a calculated approach to the residence, because breaking into someone's home in broad daylight without a plan was not only brazen, but stupid. She was in the Trieste section of Northeast Rome, a more affluent area of town, yet one that still held much of the charm of Italy. Her taxi drop-off was the traffic circle at Piazza Annibaliano. After a quick stop at a coffee shop on the corner, she walked up the shady side of Via Asmara following the bend in the road and past ambassador row, a short stretch of the street where more than one foreign country housed their ambassadors. Guards dressed in camo fatigues bearing assault rifles patrolled the exterior walls of the residences.

She crossed Via Asmara and turned left and continued

down Via Makallé until she reached a line of park benches on her left. From this vantage point, she could see the penthouse atop the six level building. She sat down, dug around in her pack, and retrieved a burn phone she had purchased the day before in Baden-Baden. She placed a call to AISE headquarters and asked to speak to Marco Serreti. As soon as he picked up, she ended the call and disabled the burn phone. She tossed the pieces in a garbage receptacle on the side of the road.

Now, she knew Marco was not in his penthouse and, having done so many times over the span of several years, she knew exactly how to get in without ever being seen. It was a routine she had rehearsed and executed many times when she worked for AISE and was secretly seeing Marco, a practice forbidden by AISE Director Lorenzo Barzetti. To see each other, they had to be sneaky, avoiding all cameras as well as security at the main entrance to the building. And she still had the key to the rear gate and, unless the lock had been changed, she was as good as inside Marco's penthouse suite. Even then, she could pick it within seconds. It was a simple lock with the most basic of tumblers.

Typical of Italy, her key still worked. Security had never been a strong point. She slithered through the gate, weaved her way through the garden to the freight entrance, where she took the freight elevator to the fifth level. She pulled on a pair of gloves before continuing to the stairway door. A special access key card was required to take the elevator to the penthouse floor, one she did not have. In the past, Marco usually met her at this level. The stairway door leading to the penthouse was always locked, but she had picked the lock several times before and intended to do the same again now.

Not much had changed inside his penthouse suite. The

furnishings were still the same as she remembered. Nothing rearranged or new. His Italian leather living room furniture was still in the same place facing the plate glass window overlooking much of Rome's northeastern part of town. She skulked throughout the suite, checking rooms and doors and drawers. There was a déjà vu sensation seeing the place again after so many years. With the exception of one locked door and the picture of a strange woman in a frame on his wine cabinet, everything seemed the same. She went into his bedroom and opened drawers in his dresser. His handguns were hidden in their usual places. He always took precautions by hiding guns in different places in the penthouse, a necessity, in his eyes, for someone in his position.

The locked door proved no match for her lock picking skills, but there was no way she could have prepared herself for what she found inside. She stood motionless in the doorway of the small room, her eyes and mouth frozen wide open. It was a shrine of sorts. Not a holy sanctuary. A shrine to a woman. There were pictures of Marco and the woman tacked to the walls of the shrine. A pictorial history covering one full wall and most of another. The room was not much larger than the size of a utility closet. On a small table against a wall were several candles and a photo album. There were handwritten letters, love notes on napkins, even news clippings with the woman's picture and name. She thumbed through a ledger. What she saw was a recording of every movement the woman had made over the past few years. Marco was a stalker and had been for years.

On the back wall were photos of other subjects, all of them she recognized. There were photos of Elmore Wiley and Jake. Another, in particular, that drew her attention was a photo with a red X marked across the photo. The face behind the red X was a familiar one. And now a dead one. It belonged to Enzo Mantova.

I knew that son of a bitch had him killed.

There was a photo of Wiley's lab, MEtech, in Belgium and above it a photo of a small building she recognized as Wiley's electronics factory in El Paso. Each was crossed out with a red X. She studied the photos and understood what she was looking at—targets.

It was all making sense, now. The engulfing fear made her feel like she had a knife stabbed in her gut. This small room was a revelation of answers. Her trepidation now turned to outrage.

She stared at the woman in the picture. She reached out at the picture and ran her finger along the scar on the woman's left cheek.

And saw herself staring back.

CHAPTER 63

Hallstatt Charnel House had existed since the 12th century. It came from the Latin word *carnarium* or *carnis*, meaning flesh. He paid a €1.50 fee to enter the small building and was handed a laminated sheet of paper explaining the Charnel House, or Bone Chapel, and its purpose. In all caps at the bottom of the sheet was a reminder to return the sheet before leaving.

The building itself, Chapel of St. Michael, was small and sat in the rear corner of a terraced lot behind the Catholic church next to a well-tended graveyard. His recollection of the photo Marie Rizzo had shown him in Venice from the belongings of Ricardo Manzone was a good precursor of what to expect when he walked inside the Bone Chapel. Otherwise, the thousands of bones and hundreds of painted skulls would have been a shock. He studied the layout of the Bone Chapel, skulls lined up in rows and tiers on tables fifteen or twenty skulls deep with the bones stacked neatly beneath. Somehow, it didn't seem as morbid in person as the picture made it seem.

He read the information on the laminated sheet.

The graveyard was cramped with limited land in this small hillside village next to the lake which bore the town's name. Ten to twenty years after burial, bodies were exhumed. The skull and large bones removed, cleaned and bleached by the sun until there were no visible signs of decay, then they were placed inside the Bone Chapel as their final resting place and left on display. Jake pulled out his iPhone and snapped a picture of the laminated sheet and several more of the Bone Chapel itself.

According to Marie Rizzo at the Casa Israelitica Di Riposa, centuries ago Manzone's ancestors made a benefaction of land, the land on which the Hallstatt Charnel House now rested, in exchange for permanent family burial rights inside the Bone Chapel to any heirs who so desired. Manzone's parents were the first to exercise that right since the mid 1800s. And now Ricardo Manzone had exercised that right as well. The oddest thing of all, it seemed to him, was that a Jewish family had permanent rights to a Catholic chapel.

Jake leaned over the chain separating the bones and skulls from the viewing area, and lit a candle in front of the skulls of Ricardo Manzone's parents. "Now to find your son," he whispered to the skulls.

He returned the laminated sheet to the man collecting the admission fee and walked into the graveyard in search of a grave. There were three fresh graves and one empty hole cordoned off from visitors and spectators. None of the fresh graves belonged to Ricardo Manzone leaving him to rationalize the empty grave must be in the process of being prepared for Manzone. But where was the body now?

He walked back to the man taking admissions to the Bone Chapel and asked, "English?"

The man held his thumb and forefinger close together, "Wee bit."

Jake pointed to the empty hole. "Where is the casket that will go in there?"

"Cas? Ket?"

"Body," Jake said.

The man smiled. "Ya, ya. Body in church." He pointed to the back of the Catholic church. "Ceremony in two days."

Jake nodded in appreciation. "Danke."

"Bitte."

It was the middle of the afternoon and all the doors to the church were locked. There was no way in without breaking in and that was not something he could easily do in broad daylight. He should wait until dark, or dusk at the earliest. Even then, there might be tourists milling about. He looked at his watch, 3:00, nine hours until Disruption. Not good. Right now, he needed his partner and her lock picking skills.

He covertly checked the church's doors again, not to see if they were locked, he'd already done that, but to check the sturdiness of the doors themselves. If they were locked now, they would certainly be locked later. He needed to find the weakest link. The door he could smash through or kick in with the least amount of resistance. He found that door on the back side of the church, but with the continuous flow of people around the church and the Bone Chapel, if he tried to break in now, he would easily be spotted. What he needed was a diversion. Something else to divert everyone's attention while he entered the church.

A sidewalk wrapped around the front entrance with a small stone wall and chain rail to protect tourists, or perhaps parishioners, from falling the thirty feet or so to the cobblestone road below. Then he saw a potential target, a possible diversion, and not just a visual diversion but an audible one as well. But, it was a long shot.

Literally.

He scanned the area behind and on the terrace above the church for a suitable concealed location. He circled behind the graveyard and down a narrow lane to a set of stone steps leading to the terrace above the church. He took the steps two at a time until he reached a stone pathway which led him to a small wooded area right above the Bone Chapel. This vantage point gave him a downward view of the village and the lake. One he needed to determine if this was a suitable position.

It was.

At a dock by the lake was a small fuel depot with three small fuel tanks mounted side by side on stilts at the water's edge. Inside his jacket he pulled out his silencer and his .45 caliber Glock 21 and screwed the silencer in place. He used a low fork in the tree trunk to steady his shot. The fact it also concealed him from view was an added benefit. He knew if he could get one of the tanks to blow, the others would follow in short order. Even though he was using a silencer, that didn't mean his shots were without sound. On the contrary, the sound suppressor only muted the sound to a certain degree. Anything more than two quick shots would certainly draw attention to his position.

He took careful aim and gently applied enough pressure to disengage the trigger lock. With a gentle squeeze he fired one round at the tanks.

Nothing.

His shot went slightly high and the bullet sailed over the tanks and into the water. He readjusted and squeezed the trigger again. This time his round hit pay dirt and the tank closest to the water's edge exploded in a billowing ball of fire.

He quickly abandoned his perch and hustled down the stone pathway reversing his course. Down the steps and up the narrow lane to the back of the church. The crowds had already reacted to the fireball in the sky. Not a soul paid any attention to what was going on behind them.

He sat tight until the next tank blew then he used a front kick, driving the heel of his foot into the back door. The door was solid and proved to be resistant. Several more rapid kicks and the door finally broke loose from the lock. *I need Francesca to teach me her lock picking skills.*

Once inside, he slammed the door shut and angled a chair beneath the door knob to keep it closed.

What little light there was inside the back of the church came from small beams of sunshine filtered through tiny dirt-caked windows. He remained still while his eyes adjusted to the dimly lit room.

Soon he realized, he was not alone.

CHAPTER 64

Francesca didn't understand this obsession Marco had for her, but he clearly had one. Way past infatuation, this was downright sick. She knew he was hung up on her, his jealousy and controlling personality were the two big reasons she broke it off with him and left Italy for Commonwealth Consultants. At first, he kept calling and begging her to come back, but like most things in life, given time, they went away. And now seeing it face to face, she realized Marco's crush on her went way past the realm of normalcy. She thought he was just a jerk, but now, it seemed he was a much more dangerous and troubled man than she could have ever imagined.

Her attention returned to the photo album. Something else was troubling her about it. She opened it and studied it page by page. Newspaper articles with dates ranging from as recent as her father's obituary and funeral announcement to her public accommodation for outstanding service in AISE many years ago, shortly after she had started with the secret Italian intelligence agency.

Then came the handwritten notes from the period when they were secret lovers. He'd saved them all. For some that might seem romantic, but put in perspective with the rest of the room, it was disturbing.

Pages ripped from a ledger were stuffed in the back of the album. These were the most telling and upsetting of all.

Marco Serreti had been tracking her every movement since the day she left AISE. One of the first entries was Elmore Wiley's electronics factory in El Paso, Texas, her first day of employment as the first of Wiley's emissaries. Six months later, there was the entry about her meeting in San Sebastian, Spain. That was the first day she met Jake Pendleton. She had passed him an envelope for his first mission as an emissary for Wiley. And there were many, many more. Hundreds of entries. The only way he could have tracked her was with the RFID tracking dots they found inside her backpack. Hers and Jake's…but there was no mention of Jake on these pages. The most recent entries were in Europe. Squillace, Rome, Venice, Vienna, Florence, and the last two entries were Volterra, where he was responsible for the death of Daniel Luzato, and finally Fairfax, Virgina. And that was when they discovered the tracking dots. The bastard knew almost as much about her life as she did.

Of all the entries, it was the recent Florence entry that infuriated her the most. It turned out Enzo Mantova was not Marco's target after all—she was. The AISE sniper had missed her head by inches—and killed Enzo by mistake.

She closed the book and continued rifling through everything in the room. Then she checked the drawers beneath the table where he'd built this sicko shrine. Inside was a pen and a single book—a journal. She picked up the book and opened it to the first page. The entries were all dated and written by hand. Marco's handwriting.

She flipped through the pages. Instinctively, his words caused her to cover her mouth in horror. The more she read, the darker his entries became. Captured in the journal were his deranged thoughts and desires, not only toward her, but toward everyone he'd met. His aggressive obsessions all written down.

And actions he'd already taken against his perceived enemies, as well as planned actions for his newer ones.

Marco Serreti was a troubled soul.

She didn't know a lot about psychiatry, but she did know a little, and from what she could recall from her training, Marco Serreti exhibited many traits of a narcissistic personality disorder mixed with additional paranoid symptomology. It appeared he had paranoid delusions, which he not only acted on, but in so doing, had no regard for loss of human life. He was one messed up bastard with sociopathic tendencies. Meaning he would stop at nothing to obtain his goals. A very dangerous man.

Marco Serreti had surreptitiously hired someone to not only break into Elmore Wiley's factory in El Paso, Texas, but also to plant explosives at the MEtech lab in Belgium. And that explosion almost killed Kyli Wullenweber, Wiley's granddaughter and Jake's love interest. It appeared there was a deeper motive. Marco wanted to destroy Elmore Wiley and everybody close to the old man. Thus, the picture of Wiley on the wall. The one right next to Jake Pendleton.

She raised her head at the sound and took a sharp intake of breath. The elevator doors clunked open at the penthouse level. She hurried from the secret room and closed the door behind her. Perhaps it was the owner of one of the other penthouses on the top floor, there were four of them occupying each corner of the building and all four shared the same elevator. That thought evaporated when she heard a key fumbling in the lock.

She ducked behind the wine cabinet. Surprise, speed and aggression was necessary to take down Marco. She pulled out her silenced weapon and waited.

The door opened and she heard Marco walk into the room, dropping his keys on the kitchen counter. He was rustling paper and then she heard the clunk of something heavy being placed on the counter top.

Now was the time.

She jumped up with her gun aimed in the direction of the sound. Two startled eyes stared back at her. It wasn't Marco. The shocked woman fainted and fell to the floor.

Francesca rummaged through the woman's Italian leather purse while Gabriella Roselli sat on the edge of the sofa with her face buried in her hands weeping. She had threatened the woman that she would shoot her if she moved. Gabriella, it seemed, had been seeing Marco Serreti for almost a month. She was the woman in the picture on top of the wine cabinet. Gabriella thought Marco was in love with her. She was unaware that just a few days ago, he had made love to Francesca in Vienna, something she regretted now more than anything she'd done in her life. Knowing what she knew now about Marco Serreti, she would rather suffer the fate of Daniel Luzato than be involved in a relationship with her former partner again. He was an insidious virus to women who needed to be eradicated.

"I know who you are," the woman said. Her voice broken and mixed with a whimper.

"And who might that be?"

"You are Marco's old partner."

"That's right."

"He said you were crazy. Told me you were obsessed with him. He said the director fired you for stalking Marco."

Francesca laughed. "Is that so?"

"He was right. You are a crazy bitch."

"You know something, Gabriella? I've known Marco Serreti for a long time. I know more about the man than you ever will."

"That's not true. Marco and I are in love."

"Oh? Do you think Marco knows you're here?"

"No."

She dumped the contents of Gabriella's purse on the marble counter top and pushed them all to one side. She patted every square inch until she found what she was looking for. "You say Marco doesn't know you're here?"

"I told you that already." Gabriella had stopped crying. "I came over to surprise him. I was going to make him his favorite meal."

She pulled out her knife and popped it open with a click. Gabriella's eyes filled with fear. "Relax, I'm not going to hurt you. I am going to prove your boyfriend knows exactly where you are every minute of every day." She started to slice the stitching on the purse strap.

"Don't," Gabriella shouted. "That was a present from Marco."

She sliced open the strap at the seam and dug the blade inside and fished out something the size of a small button. "Then that's how long Marco has been tracking you." She held up the item for Gabriella to see.

"What is it?"

"It's a tracking dot. AISE has been using them for years. Got the technology from the French…who I'm sure got it from some other country."

"I don't understand," Gabriella said as the tears started flowing again. "Why would he want to track me?"

Francesca still holding her pistol, walked over to Gabriella and held out her hand. "Because he's a controlling sick bastard." She placed the tracking dot on the table in front of Gabriella. "Take my advice and run as far away from Marco Serreti as you can."

Gabriella picked up the dot and held it in front of her face. "Why would...? I don't believe this. This is one of your tricks. Marco would never..."

She waved her pistol at Gabriella. "Get up," she said. "There's something I want to show you."

CHAPTER 65

The door didn't open into the main sanctuary of the church, but rather into a back room behind the altar. Mostly it resembled a small storage room for items used during church services. Along the rear wall of the building was a stairwell leading down. Next to it, an elevator, or rather a dumbwaiter of sorts operated by a pull rope. It was large, probably two meters by three meters, large enough to shuttle a casket up and down. Since he saw no sign of a casket in this room, it stood to reason the body of Ricardo Manzone must be below the church. Then he heard it again. The same sound as when he burst through the door.

Actually, it was a combination of scurrying and shuffling. Sounds, plural, more than one, and they were not being made by the same source. He recognized both sounds. One, tiny nails or claws scurrying across the wooden floor. Probably a mouse or a rat; God knows he'd heard—and seen—his fair share on many of his missions over the past few years from underground tunnels beneath ancient ruins in Ireland to the basement of the American Museum of Natural History in New York. Harmless, but unsettling, especially when his senses were on high alert from the perceived presence of danger. Which brought him to the second sound, shuffling of footsteps. Definitely human, and the source of the alarm bells ringing in his head. He wasn't alone, and whoever was in this dark room with him, was probably a threat. And, as unlikely as it seemed, he could only think of one person who could pose such a threat.

He was wrong.

Not about the rat, that creature he spotted as soon as the second source moved again. It was that second source he was wrong about. The sound was made by a frightened priest. He had heard the explosions and when the back door burst open, he assumed the person responsible was coming for him. Partially correct. Not the coming for him part, the person responsible part, but he wasn't going to tell that to the priest. Although, he could understand the priest's confusion as the holy man was staring down the business end of Jake's weapon. The man's hands trembled while he held a book clutched against his chest.

He lowered his gun. "English?" he said to the priest hoping he could talk his way out of this predicament.

The priest nodded.

"Good. I mean you no harm. I hope you will believe me, but there is a matter I must attend to…and I could use your help." He hoped this tact would work on the priest. It was human nature to trust, especially when you've been asked to help. It might be flawed human nature, but no less true. He used to be that way—trusting—but not anymore. Tragedy and trauma does that to a person. He could count the people he trusted on one hand, literally, there were only five, and one of those was his estranged ex-partner, Gregg Kaplan, who he hadn't seen in years and had no idea where the man was or if he was even still alive. "I must see the body of Ricardo Manzone. This is a matter of international security."

"I'm afraid what you request is impossible. Mr. Manzone has

been prepared for burial, his body must remain undisturbed. It is a strict ritual of death that cannot be broken."

"You don't understand," he explained. "The world is on the brink of a disaster." He glanced at his watch. "We have less than seven hours before the world falls into chaos. Many people could die if I don't get into the casket."

"I am sorry," the priest said, "but, I cannot allow it. I am a holy man, if this is the end, then I accept it as God's will."

"This is not God's will," he said riled. "This is the work of a mad man." Just as he was about to speak, his phone vibrated in his pocket. It was Fontaine. He raised his weapon and gestured with the barrel toward a chair. "Sit. And don't move until I tell you to." The priest did as instructed; holding the book in one hand and fingering the cross hanging from his neck with the other.

Jake routed the call to his earpiece.

"Go."

"Jake, have you located the item yet?"

"Not yet, but I'm close." The priest was listening so he was guarded over how much he said.

"I have some news for you."

"Go ahead."

There was a pause on Fontaine's end. "Jake, is everything okay? Are you alone?"

"I'm good. Not alone, but I can listen while you talk."

"Understood," Fontaine replied. "I gleaned some more information from Daniel Luzato's code, I found a list of targets, most are relatively benign in the sense they cause nothing more than inconveniences until they are rectified. Some are not so benign. Downright harmful and could endanger many lives. Not just thousands of lives, but hundreds of thousands, perhaps millions. It seems there are ten critical sites set to activate at midnight your time. We don't have exact locations yet, just general areas. I'm trying to pinpoint the locations now, but the process is slow. President Rudd knows and has started advising foreign leaders. CIA and NSA are pitching in their resources to help locate them as well. This is a well-orchestrated and choreographed cyber-terrorism attack against the world. Actually most of the world. There don't appear to be any attacks aimed at Muslim countries. I'm willing to bet this has been years in the making. Our Department of Defense has started mobilizing assault teams around the globe in concert with foreign governments. As the exact locations become known, the assault teams will attack and neutralize the sites."

"If it's not too late," Jake interrupted.

"Correct. Let's hope that's not the case. We still don't know the potential severity of these strikes. Jake, this could be a non-event or it could be a global breakdown. It's possible these attacks could incapacitate the modern world for weeks or months. Maybe even years for some countries. I'm talking horse and buggy days. The potential is there to render all modernization and mechanization useless. No computers, no internet, no motorized transportation, no electricity…nothing. Everything gained from the industrial revolution could be immobilized at once. Power plants and grids would be shut down and the operators locked out. Generators would provide some relief…but with all communication systems shut down, what good is it?"

"Western countries could recover pretty fast though, right?"

"The United States infrastructure would recover rather quickly, but we'd still be isolated from the rest of the world. Some countries would certainly recover faster than others.

What troubles me is it would put the primitive militaries on a level playing field with the rest of the world."

"Actually, that isn't true. We rely on technology-based warfare. It would give them the advantage. And a big one at that."

He noticed a change in the priest's expression. Fontaine kept droning in the background, but he was more concerned with the priest. He watched as the man's eyes opened wide, like when he stuck his gun in the man's face. But, this time that was not the case. Then he felt a draft of air. He whirled around with his gun steady, but never got the chance to fire. Something crashed into his arm knocking his weapon free. It tumbled across the room and slid underneath an old broken pew. He craned his head to see his assailant.

Qasem Kazemi.

Omar.

And the man was pointing a gun in Jake's face.

CHAPTER 66

Francesca wasn't prepared for Gabriella's reaction to Marco Serreti's secret room. She thought the woman would get a glimpse for who he really was, a mentally ill man drenched in evil obsessions. Instead, Gabriella accused her of staging the room because she was still in love with Marco. Her attempt to get Gabriella out of the picture and out of Marco's life. Until she showed Gabriella the entries in Marco's journal, penned in his handwriting that she obviously recognized, which started the day Marco and Gabriella first met.

The first entry started out flattering and spiraled downward. He penned his physical attraction to her because of curvaceous and buxom figure and how he found her sexually irresistible. The flattery stopped there. Then, he referred to her as *donna stupida*—stupid woman. From there he chronicled their sexual escapades in illicit detail, holding back nothing. Comprehension finally hit when she read his words about when Marco and she were together, he fantasized Gabriella was Francesca.

Hers tears flowed freely.

Francesca put her arm around Gabriella's shoulder. "Marco needs help," she said in an attempt to comfort the distraught woman.

"Oh, shut up," Gabriella shouted as her mascara ran down her cheeks. She pushed Francesca's arm away. "You're the one he's in love with. All he did is use me. I feel...I feel sick."

"You're right about one thing," Francesca replied. "Marco did use you and you have every right to be angry as hell. But, look at this room. This is where he keeps all his dark, warped secrets. This is not love. This is the work of a madman."

"Manipulating," she uttered.

"I beg your pardon."

"Psychotic manipulation." She put the AISE tracking dot on the table and slid it across toward Francesca. "He's a lying bastard…and I fell for it. I fell for it all. I thought he was the one. I thought he loved me." She broke down into a weeping fit. "I have to leave." She headed out of the small room toward the front door.

Gabriella was still in her line of sight when Francesca heard the door to Marco's penthouse open. The woman froze.

She heard Marco jingling his keys and then he said, "Gabriella, what a nice surp—" He stopped mid-sentence. "Gabriella, you've been crying. What's wrong?"

The woman said nothing. She pointed to his secret room and, in a barely audible voice said, "You're a sick bastard."

Francesca heard Marco's tone. "Stupid bitch," he barked. "You had no right to invade my privacy."

She heard Marco stomp across the room and heard Gabriella shriek. *Time for a little interference.* She stepped out of the room with her weapon aimed directly at Marco's head. He stopped.

He let out a sudden gasp. "Francesca? "What are…?"

His expression was that of someone who had experienced an epiphany. In fact, that was exactly what had happened. She could see the pieces falling into place in Marco's mind. His expression spoke volumes.

"Sit down." She motioned with the barrel of her gun.

He didn't move.

She fired a silenced round into his sofa. "Sit. Down."

He sat on the white sofa. The same spot where Gabriella sat crying a few moments earlier.

She raised her weapon. "Your pistol," she said. "Put it on the table."

He hesitated.

"Now," she commanded. "And do it slow and easy."

He reached into his jacket and removed his firearm, placed it on the table, and gave it a little push. The gun slid across the coffee table.

"The Walther, too."

He reached down raised his pant leg and removed the small handgun from an ankle holster. He placed it on the table and gave it a push.

"Come on, Marco," she said, "and the knife."

He reached his hand behind his back and unclipped his spring-action knife from his belt and placed in on the table.

"Oh, my God," Gabriella muttered between the tears.

"You see now how dangerous Marco can be?"

Gabriella nodded. The woman was trembling.

Francesca kept her distance. The man was deadly in close quarter combat. Too good to let her guard down now. She held her gun trained on Marco and said to Gabriella, "Get the weapons and bring them to me." The woman started to move. "And be careful. He's a tricky bastard."

Gabriella went over to the table and picked up the two handguns and slid them across the floor toward Francesca. She leaned across the table and reached for his knife. "No," Francesca shouted.

Several things happened at once. Marco clasped Gabriella's

wrist and yanked her across the table and in front of him. At the same time, he lifted her, using her body as a shield. Francesca fired, the bullet missed the moving target and struck the wall behind him. With his free hand, he grabbed the knife, popped open the blade, and pressed it against Gabriella's neck. He stood, holding her in front of him, and pressed the blade hard enough against the woman's neck to draw a trickle of blood.

"Let her go, Marco," Francesca commanded. "This is between you and me."

"Not a chance. I know you, Francesca. If I let her go, I'm as good as dead."

"Do something," Gabriella screamed. Tears started flowing again down her smudged face.

Francesca side-stepped toward the door in an attempt to cut off any attempt Marco might make to escape. She kept her gun aimed at him. "I read your journal, Marco. I know everything. All the things you are responsible for. I don't know whether to call the director, or kill you myself. One thing is certain, if you kill Gabriella, I'll put a round in your head."

✝✝✝

Omar's eyes were more evil than the pictures. Jake didn't really get a good look at Omar in Volterra before the lights went out and Marco Serreti and his men stormed the underground dungeon with flash bangs. By the time he had recovered, Omar was gone. Now he was staring at the former general of the Iranian Revolutionary Guard in the dimly lit back room of the Catholic church in Hallstatt, Austria. He truly was the epitome of evil. If Jake could equalize the advantage, tonight would end in a classic showdown of good versus evil. But, leveling the playing field was a big *if*.

"You, priest," Omar turned to the trembling holy man. "Where is Ricardo Manzone?"

The priest lowered his head and shook it.

Omar fired a round at the wall of stone.

The holy man jumped. "In the preparation room," the priest answered with a shaky voice. "Directly below us."

"Much better. Now get up and lead the way." He stared at Jake. "Try anything and you're as good as dead."

But, Jake knew the odds. And they were stacked against him at the moment. His life was ensured only until Omar got his hands on the Star of David. And even that might not be a guarantee.

The priest led them to the dark stone stairwell that led to the preparation room. Omar made Jake put his hands on top of his head, interlock his fingers, and follow the priest down the stairwell into the room below.

"Is there a light?" Omar called down to the priest.

Without saying a word, the priest flipped a light switch mounted on the side of the wall. It was a metal box. A shielded cable ran upward from the box and disappeared into a hole in the ceiling of the preparation room. When he reached the bottom step, Omar shoved Jake into the middle of the basement. The cellar itself was cavernous and served as a preparation room for bodies to be buried in the cemetery, which, in this particular case, Manzone's body would be exhumed in twelve years and his bones placed in the Charnel House.

"Why do you wish to defile the dead?" the priest asked.

"Strange that a Catholic priest would ask such a question," Omar ridiculed.

"Are you referring to the massacres of the Reformation period?" Without waiting for an answer the priest continued, "It is true, the Roman Catholic church massacred miners in Hallstatt, many of them Jews. Roman Catholics removed skulls from the grave, exposed them to the moon and light and then decorated them. It is the foundation behind the Hallstatt Charnel House. It is also true the Roman Catholic bishop of the time used Papal troops to slaughter evangelical Christians. With the exception of early to mid-1900s, Jewish families have lived here in peace. Although our religious beliefs are radically different, Ricardo Manzone has a legacy to the Charnel House. One I will defend to the death to protect."

"You may very well get your wish, holy man."

There were two boxes sitting next to each other against the rear wall of the preparation room, each one distinctly different from the other, and both resting atop catafalques. One was a modern casket and the other an aron, a simple wooden casket used in Jewish burials and believed to equalize people in death to enable the return to dust. Both were locked closed with chains and padlocks. Jewish burial required a wooden casket in keeping with the biblical teaching of Genesis 3:19—*For dust art thou and to the dust thou shalt return.* He knew which casket held Ricardo Manzone and the priest knew, but would the Shiite Iranian general know which was which?

Omar looked at the priest and said, "Which one is Manzone?"

Question answered.

The priest stalled.

"Give me the keys, I will find out myself," the general ordered.

"I will not help you," the priest shouted. He backpedaled

from Omar with one hand clutching his cross.

Jake could see what was happening before it unfolded. "Stop," he yelled.

The priest ignored him and bolted for the stairwell. Omar aimed his gun at the priest and fired. The holy man fell to the cold stone floor with an expanding circle of blood staining the back of his religious garment.

In a way, Jake owed the priest a debt of gratitude. He had distracted Omar long enough for Jake to reach to his side, remove and open his knife. Before Omar could turn his attention away from the fallen priest, Jake sprung.

He dove at the man wielding the gun, tackling him to the floor. The elderly general was stronger than Jake gave him credit for. He soon realized how much stronger when Omar slammed his elbow into the side of Jake's head. The blow rolled him past the general. They both stormed at each other with the same close quarter defense. Jake's knife wasn't in position and neither was Omar's gun.

When the two collided, the gun fired.

CHAPTER 67

The bullet ricocheted against the stone wall and struck a garment closet at the far end of the basement. Omar and Jake landed on the ground after colliding with each other. Jake rolled in the direction of the general and mounted him in an attempt to pin his gun hand to the ground. Now it was a street fight. The men wrestled back and forth with Jake's hands wrapped around Omar's wrists, the gun still in one of the general's hands. He managed to swing the old man onto his stomach and repeatedly slammed his hand into the ground. The man's fingers opened up and the gun broke loose. Jake scrambled for the gun, but the general managed to knock it out of reach of both of them. Jake raised up and readied himself to throw a right punch when the general walloped him with a left hook. Jake fell back and his head collided with the hard floor. Stunned, he remembered the man's dossier, Omar was a boxer as a young man with the Iranian Revolutionary Guard.

Both men jumped to their feet and squared off at each other.

Jake felt a trickle of blood roll from his lip to his chin. "Not bad for an old man," he taunted.

"Not only is this old man going to kick your ass, he's going to kill you with his bare hands when he's through."

"Big talk, old man."

Jake raised his fists. Omar parroted the move, then he

advanced. Jake sidestepped. Omar matched his move and advanced another step. It was obvious the old general had remained proficient, he still looked like a boxer. He had the stance, he had the moves, he even had the strength, as Jake's jaw could attest, although he didn't have the youth. Omar did have one expectation that would give Jake the upper hand. The old school boxer's goal would be to throw punches, weaken his opponent and knock him down. He would expect Jake to fight in the same manner.

He would be wrong.

Jake's goal was to proceed with punishing violence. Win at any cost. Taking whatever extreme measure was needed to get the job done. And if that meant fighting dirty, so be it.

He waited for Omar to advance again, putting him close enough for Jake to use a technique he learned at *The Farm,* the CIA tradecraft skills facility in no man's land, Virginia. He didn't have to wait long. The general advanced.

With lightning speed, Jake dropped and made a powerful leg sweep to the side of Omar's knee. A loud crack and the old man's knee buckled.

Omar shrieked in pain and collapsed to the floor. He rolled on his back and grabbed his knee with both hands. Jake sprang to his feet, walked over to the Iranian general, and without a single hesitation, kicked him in the head as hard as he could. Blood sprayed from the man's face, and then his body went limp.

Omar didn't move.

Jake picked up Omar's gun and slipped it between his belt and back. He found his knife, closed the blade, and slipped it back in his pocket. He hurried over and checked on the priest. He rolled the man on his back, he was still alive, but in a lot of pain. The wound wasn't as bad as it first appeared. The holy man would live.

"Father, time is of the essence. There is an item in Ricardo Manzone's aron I need in order to stop a major catastrophe. After I retrieve the item, I will take you to the local clinic."

"That is impossible, my son," said the priest with pain in his voice. "Although I'm Catholic, I am in charge of Shmira until Mr. Manzone is interred. The only reason I was upstairs when you burst through the door was to see what the loud noise was. Unless you can find a replacement Schomer to watch his remains, I must stay here with his body. It is his tradition and as a man of God, I will honor that tradition. The Taharah was performed yesterday by the Chevra Kadisha."

He understood what the priest was explaining. The Taharah was the traditional washing and dressing of the deceased with dignity by trained members, the Chevra Kadisha. The Shmira was the traditional watching of the remains until burial. Done by a Schomer or watcher.

It was honorable the Catholic priest had gone to so much trouble to recognize, and even participate in, the Jewish burial traditions since the beliefs of the two religions were worlds apart in so many ways. Jake, face rigid with tension, said, "Father, I will find another watcher, I promise, but first I must get into the aron. Right now."

The priest, seemingly unsure of a decision, relented. He reached into his garment and pulled out a key handed it to Jake. "Thank you, Father."

Jake inserted the key in the padlock. The key was not turning the lock. Breathing in short rapid breaths, he tried again. It worked. He inhaled sharply and slowed his breathing. Next he slipped off the chains holding the aron shut and let them slide to the stone floor. He slowly opened the lid to the aron.

Ricardo Manzone had a peaceful expression in his aron. The Chevra Kadisha had dressed him with his tachrichim, or traditional burial shroud. The garment symbolized equality and purity. His hair was long as was his beard, and both were as white as chalk. He marveled at how much Daniel Luzato resembled his grandfather. Manzone's hands were placed one on top of the other and rested on his chest with the necklace clutched inside the lower hand.

Israel's fate rests with the Star of David.

Now was the time to find out what that ominous statement actually meant. His stomach in knots, he slowly lifted the dead man's hand and removed the necklace from its grip. Indeed, it was a Star of David, and as Marie Rizzo had described, sterling silver and gold, and clunky. He lifted it. And it was heavy. He reached behind Manzone's neck and unclasped the necklace then removed it from the aron.

He inspected the necklace carefully. The silver chain was threaded through the eye of a bulky pendant replica of the Star of David. He pulled the chain through and placed it on Manzone's chest. He had hoped it was more like a large locket that opened, but that was not the case. It was more like a medallion. He turned it over. It appeared the Star of David was secured to the eye that the chain slipped through by a tiny screw.

He pulled out his knife and stuck the tip of the blade inside the grooves of the screw. He turned counterclockwise, carefully, trying not to strip the head of the screw. It turned a small bit at a time and then the knife blade slipped. He repeated this process until it had turned about a quarter of a turn, at which point it unscrewed freely the remainder of the way using only his fingers. He flipped the medallion over and the tiny screw landed in his palm. The cap seemed like it would come off with ease, so he gave it a light tug. The cap slid off.

He finally understood.

Israel's fate rests with the Star of David

Inside a compartment was a tiny USB drive. Whatever was on this drive must be the key to *Disruption*. He glanced at his watch. Only two hours left until midnight. The contents of the drive needed to be sent to Fontaine immediately. He pocketed the thumb drive and put the necklace back together. He placed it back in the hands of Ricardo Manzone and closed the lid to the aron.

Omar was in front of him, staring, and holding a long metal rod in his hand poised in a striking position.

"I'll take that," he said extending his open palm in Jake's direction.

In his peripheral vision, Jake saw him behind Omar's left shoulder. The priest. He was moving fast toward Omar with a thurible raised in the air. He held the metal censer used to burn incense during worship services by the chain.

A creak beneath the priest's feet caused Omar to swing around.

Jake reached behind his back and pulled out Omar's gun and aimed it at the man's head.

"Father, stop," Jake yelled.

He fired.

Omar's head caught the bullet in the temple.

A pink mist flew from his head and Omar dropped to the floor.

Qasem Kazemi was dead.

CHAPTER 68

The deadline loomed.

After retrieving this gun from beneath the pew upstairs, he exited the back of the church. It was dark outside and the quaint little village was lit up in full splendor. A small group of people were still buzzing around the waterfront where the fuel tanks exploded, including someone dressed like some sort of local constable.

He tried to act casual as he speed-walked through the narrow streets on his way back to the Seehotel Grüner Baum. He entered the tiny foyer and found his way to the stairs and quickly bolted the two flights to his room. After locking his door behind him, he opened his laptop and ensured he was connected to the hotel's wifi. He inserted the USB drive and studied the contents. Rubbish as far as he was concerned. He speed-dialed Fontaine on his phone who walked him through the upload to a sequestered folder on Commonwealth Consultant's server.

"You cut it close," Fontaine said to Jake with an air of sarcasm in his voice.

"By the way, you're welcome. I almost died, but, hey, no big deal, right?"

"Let me take a gander inside the folder."

"Make it fast."

"You got somewhere to be, Jake?"

"In a sense. I made a promise to a priest and I have every intention of fulfilling it."

"Didn't know you were a religious man, Jake." Fontaine who could be heard clicking away.

"I'm not, but I am a man of my word. Besides, if it weren't for him, what you're looking at might be in the hands of Omar."

Nothing.

"George?"

Nothing.

He pulled his phone out of the case and looked at the screen, the call was still connected. "George, are you still there?" He could hear papers rustling in the background.

"Jake," Fontaine finally said. "I have to go…right now."

"What's wrong?"

"I'll explain it to you later. I have to call the Israelis right now…and this is a matter of life and death."

†††

It had been a stalemate for well over an hour and Francesca was growing tired of Marco holding the knife blade against Gabriella's throat. She had successfully thwarted every attempt the AISE deputy director had made to escape or communicate with the outside world. Like a chess match, with every move Marco made, she countered with an offensive of her own. When he moved toward a door or window, she cut him off. This time, Marco would not win.

Ultimately, she had him pinned inside a bathroom. No windows. And best of all, she was blocking the door. No way out except through her. Something he had already tried and failed as she refused to relinquish her advantage.

"Marco," she said. "I can do this all night."

Gabriella had not fared well. Her breathing came in gasps. The crying was replaced with fear. Her bloodshot eyes were swollen and the tears left dark streaks down her face. Her quivering lips could not be still. But, most humiliating of all, she peed on herself an hour ago and her pants were starting to reek. "Accept reality, Marco. It's over. Over in many ways. You and I, what never should have been, will never be again. Your career. Your dreams of one day becoming director. All evaporated. Let her go, and you get to live. That's the only way out of this mess you've created for yourself."

"Is that so? What if I kill you both?"

"I don't know how you'll pull that off because you're not getting past me alive and if you kill Gabriella, you will have drawn your last breath. The way I see it, you have two choices. Either give up and go to jail or die. You decide."

"Please, Marco," Gabriella pleaded. "Let me go and I promise you'll never see or hear from me again. I'll never say a word, I promise. That woman is trying to frame you. I told her I did not believe all her lies. Just let me go. I'll testify to it. This woman broke into your apartment. She staged the room to make you look bad. When I talk to the director, I'll explain it to him. Then you and I can be together." She spat in Francesca's direction. "That woman will be put in prison for the rest of her life."

Francesca noticed Marco release tension on the blade. She could tell Gabriella felt it as well by the glint in her eyes. He removed the blade from her neck and lowered his knife arm to his side while he still held Gabriella tight around the waist with his other arm.

"You're right about one thing, Francesca, You and I never should have been."

He stabbed the sharp blade into Gabriella side and then, in one smooth motion, removed the blade and threw it side armed at Francesca. She lunged to her right, but not before the blade plunged into her left shoulder. She grunted at the searing pain, but managed to notice Gabriella had slumped away from Marco. Her finger on the trigger didn't hesitate.

Hesitation had never been a part of her repertoire. As a matter of fact, she was known for the opposite at Commonwealth Consultants. Jake analyzed a situation and acted in the way he thought most appropriate. She, on the other hand, acted fast, without hesitation, and with deadly force. As she did now. Her first shot struck Marco in his right shoulder. Her aim was dead on and she knew his rotator cuff just shattered. He let out a wail and stumbled backward, wobbly on his feet. He released his grip on Gabriella and she fell to the tiled bathroom floor. She pumped another round in his gut and another in his knee. All with pinpoint accuracy with the sole intention of inflicting as much non-lethal pain as possible. He fell to the floor, screaming.

"How does it feel now, you sick bastard?"

He squirmed and pushed himself away from her using his good arm and good leg, leaving a trail of smeared blood on the floor, until he could go no further. He had backed next to the bathtub and pulled himself into a sitting position.

"Francesca, please," he begged. "Give me time to explain."

She stared down at him. The monster was gone. On the floor was a sniveling coward. "I'm sorry, Marco. Your time has now expired."

She fired another round. This one to his forehead. His head

snapped forward and back. Bone, blood, and brain splattered against the tiled wall.

His head fell forward.

Marco had half a skull.

Her weapon fell from her hand and landed on the floor. She rushed to Gabriella's side. Her injury was serious, and blood poured from the wound. Francesca grabbed a towel and pressed it against the woman's side. "Hang on Gabriella, you will make it." The color was draining from her face and her eyes had a hollow stare. "Gabriella, look at me. Look. At. Me. You will make it. Just stay with me, okay? Okay?" Francesca knew the woman was going into shock. She gently slapped the woman's face, and Gabriella let out a sudden sigh. "Speak to me Gabriella, tell me you understand."

Gabriella gulped. "Okay," She said in a barely audible voice.

She half carried, half walked Gabriella into the living room when she realized the better option was to call for help.

She had Gabriella hold pressure on the towel while she placed the emergency call. She picked up the phone and scanned out the large plate glass window overlooking much of the skyline of Rome. Lights twinkled in the distance, first individually, followed by large sections. The power in the penthouse blinked off and then back on. The phone line disconnected. Power to the penthouse went out plunging her and Gabriella into darkness. She surveyed the city of Rome and watched the entire skyline go dark.

†††

A promise was a promise.

He had been in the bowels of the Catholic church less

than an hour watching the body of Ricardo Manzone when the lights went out. He pulled out his iPhone—midnight. No Service. It was his turn to be Schomer. He couldn't recite psalms but he could be a watcher. It had happened exactly as Fontaine had predicted.

Disruption.

The priest, despite his gunshot wound to the back, was a man of great fortitude, strength, and willpower. Jake knew the holy man must have been in excruciating pain, but he never left Manzone's side. And neither would Jake. Not until someone came to relieve him or arrest him.

When he returned to the preparation room, the priest had moved Omar's body away from the aron and placed it next to the wall and covered him with a sheet. Jake found a medic who followed him to the church and hauled the injured priest to get medical attention. Explanations would eventually be demanded of him, but right now, the authorities everywhere in the world had their hands full.

It was difficult for him to imagine what the future might hold in the light of day. How much damage had Disruption caused? Could it be repaired? And if it could, at what cost?

Fontaine's last words confirmed what he'd believed, there was a threat to Israel and it probably had something to do with the Iron Dome. Jake was thousands of miles away in a secluded little mountain village in Austria. In many ways, perhaps he was better off. On second thought, in all ways he was better off. Small town confusion versus worldwide chaos. One thing was certain, the world would be a different place in the light of day. How different remained to be seen.

He thought of Francesca, was she alive or dead? Whatever it was she had to do must have been very important to her to defy Elmore Wiley's instructions. He assumed it had something to do with Marco Serreti. It was the only possible explanation he could fathom to warrant her insubordination.

His thoughts turned to Kyli. He couldn't wait to see her again. No telling when that would be. His thoughts were interrupted when he heard a noise. Someone had entered the church. He followed the sound of footsteps and then he saw the beam of a lantern pierce the darkness of the basement. An elderly man in full traditional Jewish attire emerged from the room engulfed in darkness.

"Mr. Pendleton," he said. "I am Rabbi Joseph Kantor, the Schomer. You are hereby relieved." The old man held out a small flashlight. "You will need this to find your way to your hotel. It is darker than I've ever seen before. The only light is the moon and stars."

"How is the priest?"

"Father Dominic is resting comfortably. The doctor said he will be fine. The bullet struck nothing vital."

"He is a strong man," Jake said.

"Indeed." Without another word, the rabbi pulled a small book from his garment and started reading next to the aron of Ricardo Manzone.

Jake clicked on the flashlight and found his way to the street. He walked to the front of the church and gazed into the eerie darkness. Twinkling starlight danced upon the black waters of Hallstätter See.

The rabbi was right.

It was the darkest of darkness.

And all of the sudden, the lights came back on.

EPILOGUE

One month later
Fairfax, Virginia

In a sense, *Disruption* was the best thing that could have happened to the West. It awakened all the naysayers who had turned a blind eye from the real threat—cyber security. Oh, some contended it was a big issue and now the media was flooded with politicians jumping on the band wagon saying *I told you so.* The same politicians who had voted down bills with constructive measures to address the growing cyber threat to, not only the country, but the entire world.

Now, they saw it for what it really was, a global issue.

In the days and weeks following *Disruption*, the world had learned a lot. Iran and its hacking squad, Tarh Andishan, had been given the brunt of the blame. Not willingly, of course. The world, including the Arab Muslim countries, pointed fingers and placed blame on Iran's actions all the while disavowing any advance knowledge.

After all, that was what *Disruption* boiled down to—Iran's planned destruction of Israel. The rest, although intended to do damage and create mass chaos, was nothing more than a smokescreen for their true intention.

The man who allowed it all to happen was ultimately the

man who saved Israel and the world—Daniel Luzato—*The Jew*. And he paid for it with his life.

President Rebecca Rudd sent teams into Iran to locate the passengers of Air Malacca 910, but none could be found. Nor was there any sign of the HSI engineers, although their code signatures were found in some of the hacking software used during *Disruption*.

She also covertly sent CIA operatives into Chkalovsky Air Base in Russia in search of the actual Air Malacca 910 B-777 aircraft with specific instructions to destroy the aircraft, but when they arrived at the hangar where Fontaine had tracked the aircraft using thermal imagery technology, the hangar was empty. After exhaustive reviewing of the satellite scans, it was deduced the only possible scenario was the aircraft had been disassembled and the parts trucked away to another location.

All in all, *Disruption* lasted a grand total of nineteen minutes and forty-one seconds. 1,181 seconds. A number representing the year the Roman Catholic Parish church of Hallstatt, Austria was founded. The same year Daniel Luzato's Jewish ancestors donated the hillside land to the church where the Hallstatt Charnel House now resided.

Daniel Luzato had installed self-destruct coding in the software he stole from Boris, so when Omar retrieved the altered code and had Boris upload it, the new code contained the kill switch. As fast as *Disruption* happened, it ended.

Power grids shut down...all of them, temporarily plunging the world into a brief moment of the dark ages. But not all at once. Luzato programmed a complex rolling shut down and a rolling restoration. Transportation systems briefly shut down world-wide. As a precaution, and at the behest of Elmore Wiley, President Rudd coordinated a banking and stock market holiday in a successful attempt to thwart a global financial catastrophe.

Seal teams were able to disable seven of the ten tower sites prior to *Disruption*. Two of the remaining ten were in hostile countries and one was in the United States. The tower in Colorado activated as planned, uploading the virus to America's satellites, and crippling NORAD. But, only for nineteen minutes and forty-one seconds. The end result was exposing serious flaws in the system the United Stated government didn't realize existed. Those flaws have since been rectified.

How many more flaws existed, though? Next time, there might not be a Daniel Luzato out there to save the day...or the world. Next time, the world might be cast back into the technological dark ages. Next time, the cyber terrorists might win.

As for the Iron Dome, when Fontaine hung up after Jake had transmitted the data from his Hallstatt hotel, the analyst aborted all protocol and took the issue directly to the Director of Mossad. Even though the director had serious doubts that the Israeli defense system could be compromised, Fontaine convinced him to take a blind leap of faith in the intelligence of his country's greatest ally and a dead Jew named Daniel Luzato. Mossad director Eli Levine allowed Fontaine access to their defense system mainframe where he uploaded the software of Daniel Luzato. The software changed the cell tower encryption and prevented the collapse of the Iron Dome. When a barrage of missiles were subsequently fired at Israel, their defense system was in perfect working order and missiles were shot down before they could reach their intended targets. The attempted barrage lasted less than five minutes before Iran realized something terrible had gone wrong with *Disruption*. By then, they had tipped their hand and revealed their true intentions.

Jake had to spend an extra day in Hallstatt due to the lack of transportation to its remote location, but he didn't mind. He was able to finally see it for the beautiful lakeside mountain village it truly was. Father Dominic told the authorities his version of what happened in the church and how Jake prevented the former Iranian Revolutionary Guard general from causing irreparable harm to the world. Interpol showed up and took Qasem Kazemi's body. Their testimonies were taken and the United Nations was in the process of imposing the most detrimental economic sanctions against Iran ever imposed on any nation.

When he finally arrived in Salzburg, Wiley's Citation was waiting for him at the airport. Francesca was onboard. She briefed him on what had happened in Rome. Instead of calling the police, she called AISE Director Lorenzo Barzetti and explained what had happened. The officially released story to the Italian media outlets was that Serreti's penthouse was broken into while Marco Serreti and his girlfriend were inside. He was now considered a homicide victim of a home invasion robbery. After a comprehensive debriefing, Gabriella Roselli was treated and released. She was also considered a stabbing victim left for dead during the home invasion at Serreti's penthouse. Barzetti offered Francesca a job with AISE, not her old job, but Serreti's job as deputy director. She neither accepted nor declined his offer. He gave her two months to make up her mind.

Jake and Francesca flew from Salzburg to Brussels where they picked up Kyli who had fully recovered after the explosion at the lab. The decontamination at the lab was complete, but the inspectors found structural issues on three floors of the MEtech building caused by the explosion. So, Elmore Wiley decided to raze the building and start over from scratch.

Maybe.

He was still on the fence about replacing the lab since Kyli wasn't sure she wanted to return to Europe anytime soon—if at all.

Which brought Jake to the present.

The conference room at Commonwealth Consultants was a full house for the briefing. In reality, it was a SCIF, a sensitive compartmented information facility. President Rebecca Rudd summoned all her minions for this meeting. Of course, Wiley's employees were also in attendance, George Fontaine, Francesca Catanzaro, Wiley, and himself, but also sitting at the large mahogany table were outgoing Director of Central Intelligence Scott Bentley, his soon to be replacement, President Rebecca Rudd, as well as the heads of the FBI and Homeland Security along with the Chairman of the Joint Chiefs of Staff. The heavy hitters. The movers and shakers. *The* decision makers. And as one might expect, they were tucked inside the most heavily guarded building for miles around.

Jake, though, had something else on his mind. Or rather someone. And she was standing on the other side of the privacy glass looking at him. He had wrestled with this decision for a long time, or perhaps the better word was avoiding it for a long time. Now, he was sure of his feelings.

Without saying a word, he stood, never taking his eyes off Kyli. President Rudd was speaking and stopped mid-sentence.

"Mr. Pendleton, do you have a question?" she asked.

With his eyes still locked on Kyli he said, "Madam President, gentlemen, forgive me, but there is something I must do."

"Can't it wait until after the briefing?" Rudd asked.

"No ma'am. This can't wait another moment."

Jake Pendleton walked out of the room.

AUTHOR'S NOTES

First things first—acknowledgements: To Debi, who still gets first read…and for good reason, she keeps me from seriously embarrassing myself. Once again, she claimed DISRUPTION would be her last book to edit. We'll see about that! Yes, I had to beg and grovel, but she eventually came around. And for that, I am truly grateful. Her input is an integral part of my writing & editing process. She gives me great ideas and suggestions along the editing path. Those ideas make my stories much better. She also punches up an element where I find myself lacking at times…emotion. Debi, thank you for giving in and editing yet another book. For that, I'm eternally appreciative. And so are my readers.

With each new book I write, the list of acknowledgements typically grows. I am indebted to those who have graciously volunteered their time and energy to steer this author in the right direction. Perhaps it's their occupational expertise or past experiences that have provided me, through interviews and discussions, a rudimentary foundation to write of things about which I know nothing. To each of those, you have my sincerest gratitude.

Every author understands the true value of beta-readers. Not only are they extra eyes on your manuscript, they are readers who donate their time to provide honest, unbiased, and unabashed input. These are volunteers whose motivation is simply to help me make this the best book possible. This time around, however, the list got smaller instead of larger, but not by much, and my hope is that those who couldn't participate this round will on the next book. Thanks again to Debi Barrett, Tim Eyerman, Cheryl Duttweiler, Terrence Traut, & Early McCall.

Special thanks to Mary Fisher of Mary Fisher Design, LLC who always creates awesome covers; again with the special artistic touch of Kelly Young. She took my ideas and used her talents to take this cover well beyond my expectations.

As you might have deduced, this has been my most location-intensive researched book to date. I found several locales not suitable for this storyline, however quite a few were. And yes, they were awesome places to visit. I hope you enjoyed the extra touch.

Lastly I want to thank you, the reader, for buying this book. It is my genuine hope that you found this story entertaining and that those unexpected twists and turns left you smiling…or perhaps cursing…either way, it works for me.

Is it fact or fiction? — This is something I've tried to include in the back of every novel for those of you who like to differentiate reality from this author's … for lack of better words, exaggeration or make-believe world.

Rome, Vienna, Venice, Florence, Baden-Baden, Volterra, and Hallstatt are as depicted in this book. The history surrounding each is also factual.

There is a Secret Agent Party held at Casino Baden-Baden, however, it is open to the public. The depiction of the party in this book is a fabrication...to some extent. Much of its basis is accurate, though.

What about all that hacker stuff? Tarh Andishan is a real Iranian hacking group. The terms used are straight out of the hacker's glossary. Many of the hacking instances mentioned in the fictional storyline parallel real-life occurrences, such as attacks on the power grids, transportation systems, hospitals, governments, corporations, just to list a few.

Air Malacca 910 sounds very similar to the real-life questionable fate of Malaysia Airline Flight 370 that went missing on March 8, 2014. Strange how that happens sometimes. Google "MH 370 conspiracy theories" and see what other similarities might pop up!

The Hallstatt Charnel House is exactly as depicted in this book. Everything that occurred inside and underneath the Catholic Church (which is real) is all fiction.

Lastly, the Iron Dome that protects the land of Israel. What I wrote about the Iron Dome is accurate although vague. The complexities of the system are too overwhelming to go into with much detail.

CHUCK BARRETT